OFF THE GRID

NEW YORK TIMES BESTSELLING AUTHOR

K. BROMBERG

PRAISE FOR K. BROMBERG

"K. Bromberg always delivers intelligently written, emotionally intense, sensual romance . . ."

—*USA Today*

"K. Bromberg makes you believe in the power of true love."

—#1 *New York Times* bestselling author Audrey Carlan

"Always an absolute must-read."

—*New York Times* bestselling author Helena Hunting

"An irresistibly hot romance that stays with you long after you finish the book."

—#1 *New York Times* bestselling author Jennifer L. Armentrout

"Bromberg is a master at turning up the heat!"

—*New York Times* bestselling author Katy Evans

"Supercharged heat and full of heart. Bromberg aces it from the first page to the last."

—*New York Times* bestselling author Kylie Scott

ALSO WRITTEN BY K. BROMBERG

Driven Series
Driven
Fueled
Crashed
Raced
Aced

Driven Novels
Slow Burn
Sweet Ache
Hard Beat
Down Shift

The Player Duet
The Player
The Catch

Everyday Heroes
Cuffed
Combust
Cockpit
Control (Novella)

Wicked Ways
Resist
Reveal

Standalone

Faking It
Then You Happened
Flirting with 40
UnRaveled (Novella)
Sweet Cheeks
Sweet Rivalry (Novella)
Sweet Regret

The Play Hard Series

Hard to Handle
Hard to Hold
Hard to Score
Hard to Lose
Hard to Love

The S.I.N. Series

Last Resort
On One Condition
Final Proposal

The Redemption Series

Until You

Holiday Novellas

The Package
The Detour

This is a work of fiction. Names, characters, organizations, places, events, and incidents are either products of the author's imagination or are used fictitiously.

Copyright © 2023 by K. Bromberg
All rights reserved.

No part of this book may be reproduced, or stored in a retrieval system, or transmitted in any form or by any means, electronic, mechanical, photocopying, recording, or otherwise, without express written permission of the publisher.

Published by JKB Publishing, LLC

ISBN: 978-1-942832-73-7

Editing by Marion Making Manuscripts
Formatting by Champagne Book Design
Printed in the United States of America

OFF THE GRID

PROLOGUE

SUGAR.

Little popping sensations burst and snap as I close my mouth around the fluffy, cottony substance. It soon dissolves on my tongue.

I eat the pink cloud first.

A small pinch of it for every lap.

Another bite for every time my dad's car flies through the narrow back straight making my chest rumble and my ears vibrate beneath my headset.

I try to time it so it lasts until the halfway point of the race. I know it's halfway when my mum moves to the front of the box we sit in. That's her thing. Her good luck position. The place she stood when my dad last won a race.

The blue cloud of sugar is next.

I play the game again. One piece for each lap.

Until one piece is left.

I save it for him.

I don't eat it so that when he gets out of the car and rushes over to hug me, he can put it on his tongue, make an exaggerated smacking sound, and say, "Mm-mmm-mmm, victory is sweet."

I'll giggle because he sounds silly saying it with his hair all sweaty and helmet marks creased into his cheeks.

Then he lifts me up on his shoulders so I can see all the people patting him on the back, congratulating him.

So many people love you when you're a driver—especially when you finish on the podium.

But not like I love him. Or like Mum does.

My body vibrates as another pack of cars zoom through the final straight at the grandstands. But I don't look up this time. I'm too busy staring at what's left of my blue cloud of sugar. Too busy wondering if I take another small bite, if that'll leave enough for my dad.

There's no way it's going to last—I look up to the television in the booth to see the number on the screen—ten more laps.

No way at all.

I lick my lips—the sugar sticky there. Maybe if I skip a few laps. Maybe that'll be okay, and he'll never know I messed up.

"Goddammit."

I hear the curse even with the headphones on and glance up. Mum has stepped back from her lucky spot. Gunther, the guy who tells Dad what to do, is mad.

Again.

He likes to yell at Dad and throw his headset sometimes.

He takes too many risks.

He's going to get somebody killed.

Why do we keep rewarding his daredevil ways?

It paid off this time. What about the next though?

I memorize what Gunther says in the booth. Then later, when Dad's tucking me in, I tell him what he says. We giggle at how silly his threats sound.

I won though, right?

I took a podium though, right, Spencer?

I finished high in the points though, right?

That's what he says with a smile, a wink, and then a ruffle of my hair before turning out the lights. "Victory is sweet" is then repeated before he clicks the door closed so I can fall asleep and dream one day of being just like him.

"Goddammit, Riggs," Gunther mutters again.

I take another bite of candy floss and grin from ear to ear. I'll get to use the *GD* word tonight when I tell Dad what Gunther said. He never makes me pretend.

Mum gets mad at that.

Dad will hold his finger to his lips to tell me to say it quieter so she can't hear.

Gunther says something else. *Loudly.* But between the whoosh of the crowd and another person's shout, I can't make out what it is.

There's a scream. Then gasps.

I look up at the wall of people in front of me.

Then I look where they're looking—the big television overhead.

Smoke and parts are flying everywhere.

Tires.

Gravel.

Blue parts.

Dad's car parts.

It's quiet in the booth. I rip my headphones off but it's still silent.

"No. No. No. No." My mum repeats the word softly. Over and over as she shakes her head back and forth, her hand to her chest.

If I'm ever in an accident, watch my hands, son. If they're moving, that means I'm okay.

They're not moving.

I stare at them. Waiting for them to move.

Then the fire erupts.

Then my world changes forever.

CHAPTER ONE

MY SHOES SQUEAK ON THE SLICK FLOORS OF MORETTI Motorsports headquarters. The hall from the reception to my dad's office is like a timeline of our F1 history from the 1960s through to the present. Pictures line the walls. The livery for each year. The drivers under contract. The victories had.

I move slowly through the walking museum, taking in the pictures around me while reliving some of them in my mind too. The moments only a young girl would remember. Being on my nonno's shoulders as he walked through the paddock. Hiding behind my father's legs as he listened in on drivers' meetings. Looking up at podium after podium with a Moretti driver on it and worrying if the spray of champagne touched my skin in any way, that I'd get drunk and be in trouble.

I can feel him here with me in these halls. My nonno. His broad smile and rumbling laugh. The sour sting of the lemon drops he'd let me sneak out of the container he always carried with him. The way he'd lean over and explain something in my ear so I'd understand. How my little hand disappeared inside his. His curse-filled verbal tirades when the car went into a wall or spun across a chicane. The way he'd lift a glass after a race and toast his drivers.

My smile is automatic thinking about him. The man who started this empire for our family. I bet he never would have thought his father, my great-grand nonno, making a fortune selling off his olive oil businesses would result in starting and owning an F1 race team that has stood the test of time.

Just barely.

So many years. So many memories.

And then I approach the pictures of the year that I stopped caring about racing. The summer that made me never want to be around F1 again.

My feet falter as I stare at the pictures. I fight the memories from coming. Memories I've buried but that still exist under all the hardened scar tissue.

"That was such a great summer, wasn't it?" My father's voice booms down the hallway as he slowly makes his way toward me. The cane in his hand is new and something I try not to focus on too long despite how hard it is for me to see.

I glance back to the photo he's looking and smiling at as he approaches. "It was your last summer before leaving me for university in the States. We took eight podiums that year. Had a run at the championship. I remember it like it was yesterday."

So do I. And so wish I could forget.

"I don't remember all of it," I say truthfully but lie about the reasons why. "I was overwhelmed, settling into university life, fighting being homesick, adjusting to the American way of doing things"—dealing with everything *else* that happened—"that I have to be honest, following the team that year wasn't a top priority."

"Or any year after that for that matter," he says, the comment made without malice, before finally stepping up beside me, placing his free arm over my shoulder, and pulling me against him. He presses a kiss to the crown of my head like he used to when I was little. I focus on that, on the feeling of him being there—*my hero*—and not the fact that he needs a cane now. Not the fact that his physical body feels weaker than I remember the last time he hugged me.

"Isn't that what kids are supposed to do?" I ask.

He nods. "Yep. Going off to conquer the world is the natural evolution of things, but that doesn't make it any easier on a parent when you do. I could tell you a thousand times how proud I am of you, but it will never quantify just how much."

I let his words resonate but then shake off the melancholy that comes with them. I smile and sink into the feel of him, so happy that I can. "Hell, I know where to come when I need an ego boost."

"Always." He steps aside and winks. "Now, come on. I want to talk to you about a few things."

"Should I worry about what these things are?" I tease.

"Nope," he says with a hint of a smile in his voice as we head toward his office.

"Nope? That definitive, huh?"

"That definitive."

We enter his office and its glass wall of windows that overlooks the depths of Moretti Motorsports. The center area of the building is open with each floor visible. Engineering. Marketing. Training. Publicity. Logistics. The dozens of things that must be done daily to make this team work at the top of its game.

"Things look . . . *busy,*" I say as I turn my back on the whole army of people working beyond and take a seat on the opposite side of his desk as he does. I notice the slight tremor to his hand again but don't comment on it.

"Things are busy. Very, in fact. It's looking to be a promising year if the first few races are any indication." He smiles. "Then again, every season starts out that way, huh?"

"What did Nonno used to say? Fresh tires, untouched walls, and skilled drivers are all we need."

"True. Very true." He smiles softly as we both think of my grandfather. The giant in our lives and in the sport. "Let's hope to the *race gods* that we can have luck with all three of those for the entire circuit this year."

"*So . . .*" I prompt. I wasn't nervous when he asked me to come see him. He's an extremely busy man so I didn't think twice of his invite. It's just a dad asking to see his daughter while she's in town. But now that I'm here, to say I'm cautiously curious is an understatement. "You wanted to see me?"

"Always all business. Always keen to get the hell out of here as quickly as possible." He smiles. "I'm hoping to change that."

"Meaning?"

He stares at me for a beat and then drops the bombshell. "I want you to come home. Here. To work at Moretti."

"Oh." *That* was not what I was expecting him to say. "But I do work at home. In Italy," I say reflexively, talking about my position at the original family company—Moretti Olive Oil.

But before I can properly process the magnitude of what he's just asked me, he disregards my comment and drops an even bigger bomb.

"More specifically, I want to start teaching you the ropes so you can take the helm from me . . . and run Moretti Motorsports yourself in the near future."

I stare at him, frozen in place and blinking rapidly as if that will make his words digest any faster. "Dad. I . . ."

"I know. I know." He raises his hands up, the tremor barely noticeable, and his smile bursting with pride. My chest constricts from competing emotions. "It's a huge thing and I'm springing this on you out of the blue. I know you're not good with surprises, and I should have led into it more . . . but is it such a bad thing that I want you here? With me? With us? Being a part of what you used to love? To carry on the legacy?"

I've learned to block emotions, and right now it's coming in handy. Otherwise, the emotion thick in his voice would have had me already agreeing.

"Dad." His name is a sigh. A question. A *holy shit.* "I don't understand. What about Uncle Luca? Isn't he—wasn't he supposed to be the one?" I'm at a loss for words, and I'm not sure if that's good or bad. My uncle Luca is second-in-command here. Always has been. It's understandable to think he'd be the natural successor when my dad stepped down.

Or when his illness prevented him from performing his daily duties adequately.

"Yes. That is the presumption everyone has. But Luca and I have discussed this at length. In fact, he wanted to be here to be a part of this discussion so you'd know you have his blessing, but he has meetings he couldn't cancel. He's a shrewd businessman who understands the *why* to this change in direction. He'll remain the steadying hand behind the scenes while you're the charismatic one to the public. You'd be a team, but it would be one hundred percent you, kiddo, if that's what you wanted."

I fight the urge to shove up out of my chair and move. To abate the sudden restlessness in me that his request has just caused. "This is a lot. Like . . . wow."

He gives a measured nod. "It is. I know. But then again, this"—he points to his own body, which will eventually ravish itself until it can't survive anymore—"was never supposed to happen like this."

"Dad," I repeat. The lone syllable is a mix of emotions. Resignation. Sadness. Despair. It's easier for me to pretend it's not real. That his diagnosis will end differently or that a medical breakthrough will prevent the unmitigable result of this disease.

"I know." His smile is soft. Bittersweet. More sad than anything because, as he's explained to me before, he doesn't want me to have to watch him decline—which will inevitably happen. "But it is what it is. We have time—hopefully lots of it, right?"

I nod, hearing the hope in his voice and wanting to cling to it. "Yes. We have all the time in the world because you're a stubborn man." I shoot for a pie in the sky comment that we both know is a lie but that we cling to anyway. "So it's a moot point that you're asking me to step in."

"Let's just say I'm doing the whole preparing for the worst, hoping for the best scenario, Cami." He rises from his seat and makes his way slowly to the windows and his company beyond.

I used to ride on those broad shoulders. I used to grab on to his hair with my little hands and sing silly songs with him while he walked through these halls shadowing his own father.

The memories come out of nowhere. So many. So unique. So damn pure. I hold tight to them as he gathers his thoughts.

"We've taken only five podiums in two years, Camilla. We haven't won a race in four." Both of those things weigh heavily on him as they should any team owner. But my dad isn't any team owner. He's the one running an iconic brand that has been known and respected worldwide since its insanely successful inception. "We're underperforming. The chances we do have get blown for one reason or another. We've become the team people see but don't notice. The team that's beginning to be forgotten about or even worse, looked at with pity. We're just *there*."

"It's been a bad couple of years. Every team has those. But I don't understand what the team's success has to do with me. You know this business inside and out. Wouldn't that make you and Uncle Luca the right men for the job to turn things around?"

Not to mention the fact that I'm grossly unqualified to run this behemoth. Do I know a lot about the business due to years of exposure? Sure. Hell, it's the only thing we talk about at most family functions. It's what we take family trips around.

Do I have an invested interest in the company to succeed? Absolutely.

But neither of those things give me the skill set required to be able to run this place. They can help, sure, but they definitely aren't what is needed to step in and lead.

The last thing I want to do is to step into a role and fail the legacy left to me.

"Dad, being a Moretti by name doesn't mean I know what to do or that it'll guarantee I'll be good at it."

He gives a slow nod and then turns to face me, his hands now in his pants pockets. I'm not certain if that's to control his shaking for my sake. He's gotten rather good at hiding it as best he can. "You're right. You could look at it that way. That Luca would be the natural choice or that there is a high probability of failure with nepotism. Or you could say that clearly what we've been doing—what Luca and I have been doing at the helm—isn't working. Some might even say that we're dinosaurs who are stuck in our ways."

"Then they'd be wrong."

He holds a finger up to make a point. "Or, you could look at it and think that we need a fresh pair of eyes. A new perspective. Someone who can come in here and not only learn the ropes but who can build a team while putting her master's degree in marketing to good use."

"I'm twenty-five. Do you realize how ridiculous this sounds? Putting someone my age in control of all of this?" I hold my hands out to motion to everything beyond the glass.

"That's why we'd start the process now. I'm not naïve in thinking you could just step in on day one and be ready to go. It'll take a few years for you to grow into this position. To learn the ins and outs. I want to be able to teach you while I'm still able to."

"I thought we weren't going to talk about that," I warn, because if we don't acknowledge his illness, then it can't be happening, right?

"I must look toward the future, kiddo, and doing that means I know this place will be taken care of. Protected. Have a future."

My tongue feels thick in my mouth as I struggle with what to say to that.

There's absolutely nothing I can say, so I focus back on me. On dispelling this idea of his that equally terrifies and intrigues me, even though I'd never admit to either because both are polarizing.

"Who in their right mind would take direction from me when they know more than I do?"

"Since when do you care what people think?"

"This is a little different than caring what people think. You can't lead without being respected. You can't—"

"That's exactly why we'd hire you as a special consultant to create an aggressive media overhaul campaign for Moretti. Branding. Social media. Stepping Moretti into the twenty-first century. Everyone knows you know marketing. Look what you did with the recent rebranding campaign you spearheaded."

"Yeah, but that has to do with olive oil. With the company product," I say mentioning our family company, Moretti Olive Oil. "That doesn't translate to racing."

"It doesn't have to. I want you to rebrand us. You know us and our product and what we believe in better than any outside hire could. And while you're doing that publicly, you'll be learning the ropes of everything else behind the scenes. You'll shadow me and become a utility player of sorts. A person who can step in at any position when it's needed. That way the employees will see you learning, will see you in each role, and learn to trust that you understand the business and how to run it."

"I hear what you're saying, but don't think anyone's going to buy it."

"They will."

"How, Dad? What will I bring to the table that your huge marketing department hasn't already?"

"Youth. A different perspective. An outside viewpoint."

"You can hire anyone to do that."

"I don't want anybody. I want you." He shrugs unapologetically. "We're old school here. We've been doing the same thing year in and year out. I can bring new people in all I want but it seems like they keep getting bogged down in the confinements of what we used to be. We need a reinvention. The race team is seen but not known. We exist but there is no excitement, no spark. I need a buzz created so even if we aren't winning, people are still watching. That will bring in bigger sponsorships, more money so that we can make a leap in the constructors standings."

"That's a huge supposition."

"No, it's not. It's just what this company needs. *You're* just what it needs."

"A fresh perspective and a marketing campaign doesn't guarantee success."

"It doesn't. But it puts you before the employees. It makes your work ethic known and proven. That way, by the time this gets noticeable," he says, motioning to his body and the Parkinson's slowly trying to take over, "you'll already be known, and people won't be as concerned about you taking on a leadership position."

I stare at him and shake my head, knowing this point is moot but reiterating it anyway. It won't be the first time I've brought it up. "I still don't understand why you feel the need to keep the diagnosis a secret. It must be exhausting."

"It is, but let me keep my pride a little longer, Cami." His voice is soft. His smile is reticent. "I don't want to feel like a monkey in a zoo with everyone watching me in a cage and waiting for my body to show a sign of it. I don't want to be coddled. I don't want exceptions made. I don't want to be the topic of articles so someone can use this as a way to say F1 is inclusive or the like. I just want to be me for as long as I can."

Tears burn the back of my throat, but I fight them off. It's the first time he's given me a reason for his secrecy.

The first time I understand the why behind it.

"Okay," I say softly. "But how are you explaining the cane?"

"Hip issues. Doctor's orders." He shrugs with an unapologetic grin. "I rarely need it so the excuse passes. Mostly only when I'm stressed, because stress exacerbates the symptoms. Another reason I need you on board. Knowing you're here and will run this place with integrity and determination like our family has for generations will help with that."

"But what about *my* job? I can't just up and leave."

"Sure you can. That's the beauty of working for the family company," he says and lifts his eyebrows in challenge.

"You raised me to finish what I started. I'm as much of Moretti Olive Oil—probably more so—than I am this company."

"But I also told you that when opportunities arise, to not let them pass you by."

Jesus. He has an answer for everything.

"Besides," he says, "if I recall correctly, a few weeks ago, you were the one who said you felt stagnant. I'm offering you something different. Something new and challenging. There are only ten F1 teams in the world. We're one of them. I'd think learning how to oversee one would intrigue you since glass ceilings are something you seem keen on smashing."

"It's just . . . *a lot.*" I chuckle out the last word. Because it is. All of it. The ask. The abruptness of it. The possible upheaval of my life. *Your diagnosis.*

The Moretti family started its empire in the late 1800s first growing olives and then learning to process them into olive oil. That's been where my place has always been expected to be, at Moretti Olive Oil. Helping run *that* giant. *Not this one.*

"It is. I know it is." He twists his lips as our gazes hold, before a soft smile turns the corners of his lips up. "Part of this is me wanting to leave this sport better than I was born into it. We need more women in it. And not just so we can say you're here but because you come at things differently. See other angles. Look at problems from a different viewpoint. Have opinions that are no doubt different than the owners—who are all men."

"And the other part?"

His smile reaches his eyes. "Maybe I want that connection with you like we used to have. When you were little, then when you were a teenager and we'd sit in the paddock with our chests rumbling, our ears buzzing, and our hearts pounding during a race. Call me nostalgic, tell me I'm growing old, but I miss those days with you."

Jesus. Talk about grabbing hold of my heart and squeezing it. I'd *run* from the sport. My only focus had been on getting away. For my own sake. But selfishly, I never stopped to consider what he'd lost. How my abrupt absence, and the years that have followed, affected him. I'd been too busy reeling from . . . and well, running.

Coping.

Healing.

"I miss that too." And I do. They are some of the best memories. "It's just . . . I don't know, Dad."

He angles his head to the side and studies me. I feel nothing but love from him despite his scrutiny. "There hasn't been a single moment where you said you think it's a good idea or that you're excited. Not even a smile over it. You want to tell me what's really going on, Camilla? Why you don't want this opportunity?" He stares at me with a look in his eyes that hints that he knows his words to be true. That there is so much more to the story about why I walked away.

I open my mouth and close it. All those times I'd sit on his or Nonno's shoulders and tell them I wanted to run this place rush back. This was my dream. My biggest hope.

My eyes are drawn to the picture of my great grandfather on his credenza, my nonno, my uncle Luca, my dad, and me—four generations of Morettis. The past. The present. And what was supposed to be the future.

Anyone could look at it and see we're related. The dark hair. The olive skin. The light brown eyes. Our mannerisms.

I'm proud to be part of this family, this legacy. I hate that I'm hesitating on his request.

"Cami?" he prompts.

"No reason," I lie. "I found my thing with marketing. I'm good at it, that's all."

He doesn't respond and when I finally look over to him, he's studying me. That's never a good thing. The man can read me like a book.

There's a reason I had to put space between us—a whole ocean—until I could deal with the new reality the chain of events left me accepting.

"You *are* good. That's my point. The team needs you. The company needs you. *I need you.*"

And the dagger twists with those last words.

I pinch the bridge of my nose, my own internal war being waged that he has no idea about.

"I tell you what, kiddo. Give me a year. The rest of this season, actually. Come work with me and if after that time, I haven't won you over and you still don't want this, I'll never ask again. You can go back to MOO and be done with racing," he says, the name we fondly call Moretti Olive Oil.

"You're trying to reel me in because you know I won't want to leave you, aren't you?" I tease.

"Can you blame me?" He laughs and his smile lights up his eyes.

"Can I have some time to think about it?"

"Of course. But, Cami, I need you on this. I really do."

"I know. I just need to think things through."

He turns back to the Moretti world beyond.

"I'm here if you need to bounce things around. Just like always."

"Thanks, Dad."

But that isn't true. He's sick and, one day, sooner than we ever expected, he won't be here.

And that's the day I'm dreading more than any other in the world.

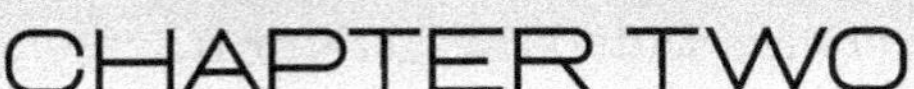

CHAPTER TWO

Riggs

A BLUR OF COLOR IN MY PERIPHERY.

Not individual fans. Not sponsor banners. Not the gray of the speedway walls.

Just a moving wall of color as I fly over the starting grid and out to turn one.

"Garcia is two point one behind," Pierre says in my ear as I take the car to the limit, waiting to be told I'm pushing too hard.

But it doesn't come.

Not a word over the radio.

They know we need this win.

Have to have it.

I let up slightly on speed as I hit the apex of the turn—can practically feel Garcia bearing down on me as I slow—before hammering it back down again, my thumbs flying over the buttons on the steering wheel.

Four laps to go.

Four laps to hold this motherfucker off.

"The tires," I say as I fight the car out of the turn. I've been fighting it all fucking day to stay in the lead. "I think we—"

"It can't be undone."

I grimace as I hit the straight out of the turn—my hands tired and neck aching—trying to put as much distance between Garcia and me as possible.

We should've changed the tires.

I told Pierre before we boxed. He didn't think it was necessary. He can look at all his fucking metrics—have the crew advise him—but I'm the one in this car. I feel them vibrate. Slip. Not command them how I should be able to.

And right now my body is paying the damn price for the fuck up.

Let's just hope it doesn't cost us the race too.

We need a win.

Hell, we need a fucking podium.

Anything to gain some points. To earn some sponsorship bonuses.

This circuit runs solely on money. And when you don't have it, it's nearly impossible to win.

We might all have the same cars, but money makes the entire world around the cars go round.

"Good job," Pierre praises in his clipped but soothing tone. "Two point eight now. We need to push on this lap. Try to gain more space this sector."

"Understood," I say, my voice a vibrated mess as the Gs hit me harder with each kilometer per hour I pick up.

I've been around this loop thirteen times already, but I still replay what's coming next in my head. I still map out what I need to do.

Let up for the chicane coming soon. Then a sharp left. Then a sweeping left followed by a subtle S curve. Then the wall that calls to every car here to rub against it before heading into a narrow passage where it's single file.

If I can hit that with Garcia still behind me then I'll be sitting pretty.

"Push. Push. Push," Pierre encourages, and I respond accordingly.

He's watching the car's gauges. He knows what's running hot and my split for each sector. He's my eyes, my ears, my instructor.

The conscience on the track that I don't want but that I need.

I grip the wheel and fight the turn, my tires hitting the rumble strip as I hit the S curve and come out of it.

"He's on your right. Closing in."

Fuck.

C'mon, Riggs. C'mon. C'mon. C'mon.

I focus on the tasks that are second nature. On the skills I've honed on the sim and with reaction drills. On the hours I've spent studying and feeling every fucking curve of this track.

Another turn comes, a sharp right. My brakes lock up momentarily. The screech. The smoke. The shudder of the wheel.

Shit. I fight through it as I slide off my line but gain control.

"Point eight seconds."

"Got it." I recover my control, my pulse racing and adrenaline pumping.

I push the car into the next straight, needing to get more than a second ahead of Garcia to prevent him from using DRS. No way I'm going to let that fucker have a chance to slingshot past and overtake me.

We go into the next turn and when I slow for it, he tries to take the outside. I fight him off and hold on, accelerating rapidly to put distance between us.

"Push, Riggs."

Fuck off, Pierre, I'm busy.

Thoughts I shouldn't have but do as I force the car to its brink.

"One point one."

I breathe a sigh of relief. I'm going to be able to hold on. I'm going to win this fucking race. I'm going to—

The car shimmies and suddenly, the force on my body lets up. The lights on my steering wheel flash. The car slows.

Garcia flies past me.

Then Montpier.

"Pierre," I shout into my helmet but know there's nothing he can do.

The engine just blew. It's fucking toast.

The race is lost.

Fuck.

The word is on constant repeat as the caution flag goes up.

As I climb out of my car.

As the race marshals clear my car.

As I stalk into the paddock, slam the door behind me to my space, and pace the small area, trying to abate the misplaced energy that's eating me alive.

I'm so close. So fucking close I can taste it. To the win. To making the jump to F1 and hanging on this time. To making some fucking money that I can keep instead of having to pour it back into this sport I love and hate. Love because, how can I fucking not? Hate because, I can have all the talent in the goddamn world, but it's hard to be seen when you have subpar shit—cars, engines, support.

So many of my friends, the ones I grew up karting against are there, living the dream at the pinnacle of our sport. And I've yet to join them permanently.

I had one chance. One chance that came and went and has forever put an asterisk next to my name.

I pinch the bridge of my nose and squeeze my eyes shut, ignoring the twenty texts lighting up my phone in the corner of the room.

From my agent.

From my mum.

From my friends.

It's okay. You did great regardless.

Great race.

Too bad about the engine.

You'll get them next time.

I don't have to read them to know what they'll say. To know they're positive and supportive and everything in between.

It's the last thing I want when I'm busy beating myself up over what just happened. Over the shit I'm more than certain I'm about to get in the coming minutes.

There's a knock on the door. Then it cracks open and Fontina peeks her head in. "Presser time."

"How bad is it?" I ask.

"Which part? The part where you rubbed tires with Bickman and he went into the wall?"

"We were wheel to wheel. It's not my fault he has issues with spatial awareness. Hell, I followed protocol. I had the edge. I had the right of way."

She lifts her eyebrows and just murmurs, "Hmm."

Great. Just what I want to hear.

"He wasn't hurt, right? That hasn't changed?" I ask and she shakes her head. "Good. It's racing. That's all it is. You know damn well he would have done the exact same to me if the tables were turned."

She rolls her eyes, but her eyes are somber. "Talking points for the presser. It was a great team effort. The ongoing issue with the engine has now been diagnosed and will be fixed. Reiterate that you have never intentionally hit anyone and that you'll be reviewing the tapes to learn from today and improve."

"Wait a minute," I say and put a team hat on as her last bit registers. "Is that what's being said? That I purposely put him in the wall?"

Fucking hell.

She shrugs. "You don't exactly hide the fact that there is no love lost between the two of you."

"I'd never take that on the track."

"I know that. You know that. The public thinks what it will."

"Fucking great," I mutter.

"Rainbows and unicorns, Riggs. That's all you have to think, and you'll smile."

"More like heels and lingerie." I snort.

"Whatever floats your boat, but I'm not providing that visual for you."

"Oh. I wasn't aware you had visuals of unicorns to provide."

"Smart-ass." She waves her hand. "Let's go."

I groan but make my way to the post-race press conference. It's the last place I want to be—it's no one's when you DNF a race—and hell if it's not the bane of my existence lately.

"First chair to the right." Fontina directs me and then whispers, "Unicorns and rainbows."

I take a swig from my water bottle and head to the hot seat. Mundane questions ensue and mostly being asked of my counterparts. Thoughts on their race. Things they hope to accomplish. Then it's my turn.

"Riggs, there has been a little talk about your inconsistency and reliability and a lot about your recklessness on the track. Do you care to make a comment on that?" a reporter asks.

"I'd say they should climb behind the wheel where you're directed to drive as fast as you can to win a race, all while riding that fine line on not pushing the engine too far or knowing that your opponent's tire is an inch from yours. Engines blow. Cars connect. Things happen. There's a reason few make it this far, and it's not because it's easy."

"So are you saying you're at fault for the engine blowing today?"

"I'm saying that we're a team and we're all at fault when things go bad and all to be praised when things go great." I toe the company line when I'm damn well pissed that the same goddamn issue we've had with the engine the last four out of six races presented itself yet again this race.

"There was talk on the radio about a decision with tires," another reporter jumps in.

"And?" I prompt, treading lightly. I can't remember the exchange I had with Pierre. The exchange that is public. All I can hope is that whatever I did say, it's not about to be used against me or used to put me on the spot.

"It seemed you were upset by the decision not to box," the reporter says.

I give a half chuckle and a shake of my head. *Play the game, Riggs.* The desired ending is to move past Formula 2 and onto Formula 1. Voicing the smart-ass remark like you'd love to isn't an option.

"I can have any opinion I want, but my crew is reading my car for me. They know what's best and whatever they say is what goes. Teamwork is the only way any success can be had in this sport." I clear my throat and raise my eyebrows as if to say *are we done yet?* I'm known for not particularly loving these pressers.

"That's not exactly what you said on the radio though," he presses on.

"It was in the heat of the moment. Adrenaline was running high. It happens. My crew knows I respect them and their opinions. At the end of the day, that's all that matters," I say.

"And Bickman?" a voice calls out from the back.

"I'm glad he's okay. No one ever wants to crash or be the reason someone else crashes. Just like things are said on the radio that you regret, things happen on the track that you do too. We touched tires. It could have just as easily been me in the wall and you asking him why he put me in the catch fence. Sometimes it just happens." I smile and rise from my seat, pretty much done with this.

"Riggs is short on time today," Fontina says, taking my lead.

"One more question, Riggs," a voice shouts out that I know all too well. Harlan Flanders. *Fuck.* "Do you think your last night's late-night antics contributed to today's results?"

What the fuck is he talking about?

I stop in my tracks and level a glare at the reporter. "You mean the sponsorship dinner the team had *two* nights ago?"

"No. I'm talking about the club, the booze, and the dancing on the stage."

I chuckle. The fucking prick. Trying to paint a picture to the public, to F1 teams, to my own goddamn team, that I don't take this seriously.

Trying to sabotage me with rumors.

"Unless the club was in my bedroom, I assure you I wasn't there. But hypothetically if I were there, how would that correlate to a blown engine today?"

"You tell me," he challenges in a way reporters often don't. But then again, this one will, considering I unknowingly stole his girl a few months back. Well, not so much stole—perhaps, *borrowed* is a better term. I'm not one to keep anyone around long—and long means for a night or two.

If I had known I was playing with fire, I never would have slept with *her.*

And how was I to know they were together? I took her at her word that she was single.

She pursued.

I reacted.

We had fun. The fun ended. I moved on.

Apparently, he hasn't, because it's the same shit, different presser.

I chuckle and the smirk on my face is pure *fuck you* back at him. "Did you have a real question, Flanders?"

"You pushed the car too hard," he says. "You take too many risks."

And your girlfriend gives great blow jobs. Especially how she does that little twist of her hand and flick of her tongue.

I raise my eyebrows in response as several people in the room shift uncomfortably, clearly sensing there's more going on here than just a simple question and answer exchange.

And how can they not think differently when the fucker's been on my arse for the past few pressers with bullshit like this?

"I'd think that not having a clear head and being focused on things other than racing might do that to you," he continues.

My smile returns and it's fucking arctic. "I take my job and those who have invested time and money in me very seriously. The only opinions that matter to me are the owners, my team, and the fans. Yours is irrelevant. If you're trying to make a name for yourself, do it on someone else's back."

I stand from my seat next to my fellow drivers, stare into the darkness at wherever the fucker is sitting, and grin. Then I walk out of the room, only catching a glimpse of Fontina giving me *the look*. The one every racer knows that means their PR minder will have to do some clean-up for them.

"What?" I ask as we walk down the hall, her short legs struggling to keep up with mine.

"If you have to ask me, *what*, then you already know," she says.

"The guy's a prat. He has it out for me. You know it. I know it. And I'm pretty sure the whole goddamn fan base knows by how he keeps coming after me."

"It appears that way, but the press is still our friend," she says and pats me on the shoulder.

Fuck, do I know it. They can make or break you. And while I've fucked up plenty during my tenure, I know who butters my bread.

The team. The press. The fans. Social media.

"He was pushing for a reaction. I didn't give one. You should be impressed by my restraint."

"That depends if you're going to say anything other than *no comment* to the reporters milling around outside of the turnstiles when you head to the parking lot."

"Depends on who's still around," I tease.

"This is the only time I'm going to say I'm hoping it's lingerie and heels so you're preoccupied."

"No complaints there."

Fontina rolls her eyes and overreacts to my playful shove. She may be my media handler here with StarOne Racing over the past few years, but she's also like a little sister. Snarky. No bullshit. And will snap back at me if needed.

"I have an idea," I murmur.

"I don't like when you have ideas," she jokes. "Mostly because they're crazy or daredevilish or are bound to get me in trouble."

Or make me more well-known when it goes viral as some of my others have done.

No press is bad press.

"Nothing crazy. Maybe just time for another video."

"You mean another look inside Spencer Riggs's addiction to chasing the adrenaline high?"

"Exactly." I flash a grin that wins most women over and has them undoing their bras without asking.

It doesn't work on her.

I may have tried way back when.

I'm glad it didn't.

"Great. I didn't hear that." She covers both of her ears.

"What? You helped with the last one."

"You mean the video of me frantically trying to talk you out of skydiving? That wasn't me trying to help you go viral. That was me trying to help you stay alive."

I hold my hands out to my sides. "I lived." She rolls her eyes. "Besides, is jumping out of a plane with a parachute strapped to my back any more dangerous than me going two hundred miles per hour?"

She gives me a dubious look. "You do know that at some point your contract is going to be revised to forbidding all death-defying feats unless it's you behind the wheel of their car."

I flash her a grin. "Great. Guess that means I better get them all in before that happens."

She rolls her eyes and groans. "You're annoying."

"Perfect. That's what I was going for." She's so easy to rile up.

"Try to not get yourself killed, okay?"

"Isn't that the goal every day?" I shrug as she just shakes her head.

"I'll see you later, Riggs. Stay out of trouble, will you?"

"You know that's something I can't promise." I give her a mock salute and then head to my trailer but falter when I turn.

Sometimes it takes me a second to process the view before me.

The track and its stadium.

The people—fans, track workers, reporters—still milling about the grandstand.

The crews diligently working in the garages and paddock, disassembling all that they'd contributed to create this little city that only lasts a week at a time.

It takes me back to being a kid. To sitting on my dad's shoulders. To getting to be a part of something so big but being so naïve. I had no clue how big it was.

And now I'm here. Really fucking here.

Well *almost* here.

Where so many would love to be. So close to my dream itself. So near to the next level I can all but taste it.

I can handle the Harlan Flanders of the world so long as I get to the top.

The years in karting. The endless hours of training. Putting my life on hold to chase down this formidable dream. The heartache and heartbreak with each and every step forward and then two steps back. The begging, borrowing, and stealing to find a means to be here. To live up to the name I wear with pride. To be part of this whole entity.

Spencer Riggs. Formula 1 driver. One of only twenty drivers in the world who have that distinction.

That's my dream. To feel the growl of the engine behind me, sense the heat of the ground below me, and hear the roar of a sold-out crowd on a Sunday afternoon as I cross the finish line.

I'll make it there.

I have to.

I'll make you proud, Dad.

It's been a long damn road—a grind—but I'm not stopping until I can make you proud.

CHAPTER THREE

Yes. I'm just praying for a great season, Dr. Bergman.

I didn't mean to hear the conversation. The one between my mom and my dad's doctor.

He's fighting as hard as he can, but the stress gets the better of him lately.

She was just standing there on the side of their house when I walked up to their front door, cell to her ear, voice hushed as she talked.

He has his good days and his bad days. As long as the good outweigh the bad, then that's all I can ask for. I do think a win would do him wonders.

The worry wavering in her voice breaks my heart.

Any kind of success would help his state of mind. The bouts of depression and anxiety are coming more frequently. I just . . . I think a successful season might help all around.

Hearing her words, her concern, her love for him . . . solidified my decision for me right then and there.

It's what I've been fighting. Coming back and facing the demons that remain. That are dredged up when I swear they've been dead and buried.

But this is for my dad. To help him however I can in this fight, even if it's simply to help reduce stress levels. This is for my mom, so that she can have my dad here longer and her job as a caretaker remains easier for now.

If this is the only way my parents will let me take care of them—will let me help—then it's an opportunity I'm taking.

It's not as if what he's offering wasn't once my dream. It was *all* I wanted to do.

But being *all* I wanted to do back then looks a little—okay, a lot—different now. It's leaving a job I love. For ego's sake, I'd love to say I'm irreplaceable. But I'm not. I've built a great team around me who could easily step in and do just as good of a job. That doesn't mean the transition would be effortless though. How do you write down everything that's in your head for someone else when you don't even realize it's in your head?

Then there's the complexity of picking up my life and moving across Europe to the UK. Sure, I could leave my own place behind and keep it for when I go back home—but there are plants to be given away, friends I need to say goodbye to, delivery services I need to cancel. All the little day-to-day things you don't think about need to be thought about and taken care of.

Not to mention packing my belongings.

Being financially fortunate affords me the opportunity to leave my furnishings behind, but I still need to pack up clothes, personal belongings, and the like.

It's an absolute upheaval of my carefully curated world and my sanity. I'm not too thrilled about either . . . but how can I not agree?

It's my dad. The man who has given me the chance to have anything and everything. How can I say no?

Sometimes loving someone means sacrificing yourself for their benefit.

This is one of those times.

With a resigned nod that I'm about to throw my life in a blender and hit the start button, I enter my parents' house without letting my mom know I'm here.

It's extravagant by most standards—big rooms, lots of light, white furniture and natural wood. It looks like it belongs in a house on the beaches of Malibu in my mom's native country of the United States instead of an English countryside—my dad's adopted land after Italy. Everything about it is a reflection of my parents.

Elegant but warm and welcoming. Spacious but homey.

There's no question where my dad will be. His love for cooking has been a constant in my life and a major source of stress relief for him. The scent of garlic and basil tells me I'm more than right.

"Hmm. It smells like heaven," I murmur as I walk up and press a kiss to his cheek. He holds out a spoon for me to taste his homemade marinara sauce—as if I had any doubt it was going to be incredible.

"See?" He lifts his eyebrows. "You should visit more often. Then I could cook for you all the time."

"Does the same stand if I'm more than just visiting? Like say . . . if I'm moving here to take a marketing position with this little, unknown racing team?"

I'll remember the smile that crawls over my dad's lips for as long as I live. His eyes light up. His dimples deepen. His whole body relaxes as he sets his knife down and looks at me with tears in his eyes before he blinks them away. "Really?" he asks.

I nod. "Really. I just need a week or two to head home and button stuff up. Then I'll be back."

He reaches his hand out. "A season."

I shake it. "A season." And then I pull him in for a hug and hold on tight.

If my dad can face his demons, then I can too.

We can both confront them together.

CHAPTER FOUR

Camilla

"SO YOU'RE REALLY HERE TO STAY?" GIA ASKS AS SHE RUNS A hand through her silky black hair and roams her eyes over the patrons at the bar before bringing them back to me.

I shrug and lift my glass of wine to my lips, savoring the rich Italian red on my tongue. It tastes like home with its rolling hills and sunny skies. I know I'm going back in two days to start packing everything up to return here as an employee of Moretti Motorsports, but it feels way too long since I've been there, even though it's just been weeks.

I guess I better get used to it though since it's official that I'm moving here. Wellingshire. A place I've called a second home over the years, but never a first. My parents moved here when my dad took the helm from my nonno, and I moved along with them, but I was a teenager. I was under their wings still. This will be the first time living here as an independent adult and so much has changed since back then,

"I am." I nod and then shake my head, almost as if I'm still trying to make myself believe what I've agreed to. "I'm heading home—back, whatever you want to call it—for a week or two to organize and pack and I don't know . . ." I chuckle in disbelief.

"You're struggling with this, aren't you?" Gia asks.

I nod. "I am, but . . . new beginnings and all that," I say as if trying to convince myself of it. And I have gotten slightly more excited about the change, but that doesn't mean it's not scary as hell too. "I'm dreading the packing and the *sorting*—if that makes sense. It's a lot to wrap my head around in a short amount of time."

"Of course it is, but I have an idea," Isabella says, the only woman I know who can make a pixie cut look downright sexy. Could be that it's complemented by her six-foot height, her razor-sharp cheekbones, and the perfectly pouty lips she displays every time she takes the catwalk in a show, but who's counting? "Why don't you leave all your clothes at your place in Rome? That way I have an excuse to take you on a fabulous tour of every designer shop in London? We can shop until we drop and come out the other side with a total makeover for you."

I purse my lips as I stare at her. Shopping is dreadful. Yes, I'm not normal. "Thanks, but I'd rather watch paint dry than do that. Besides, I have plenty of clothes. I just need to get them here."

Gia and Isabella exchange a look that I don't exactly understand and am not sure that I want to.

"What?" I ask.

"Nothing," Isabella says, but I know her better than that.

But just as I'm about to talk, Gia redirects. "Just think of the excitement you're throwing yourself into. Lots of traveling. Famous people trying to woo you so they can get into the garage during race weekend. Glamorous parties with sponsors. I'm dying for the fashion alone."

I lift a lone eyebrow as if to imply she's missing the reality of it all. "A crap ton of work. Lots of headaches. Never being home."

Gia just waves her hand at me to show she's ignoring me. "Sounds like lots of excuses for me to come join you in all those crazy places. Lots of hot men to be met." She wiggles her shoulders and looks at Isabella. "Right?"

"Definitely. I'm all for it," Isabella murmurs, preoccupied with something on the other side of the bar.

"All for what?" Gia asks, calling her on it.

Isa rolls her eyes. She even makes that look sexy. "Jet-setting. Hot, sweaty men in race suits whose egos are probably bigger than mine." We all snort at that because no one has a bigger ego than Isabella. "I mean, that is *if* I can fit it in my schedule."

Gia looks at me and we both burst out laughing. "Oh, our apologies, your royal highness. We don't mean to interrupt your globe-trotting and self-importance tour."

"Whatever." Isabella waves a dismissive hand our way, completely unaffected by our comments. "You guys know what I mean."

"Yes, dahling." Gia draws the word out. Teasing Isabella is just something we do. We're not even close to being ignorant of how ridiculous we sound. To the rest of the world, we lead a more than privileged life. When it comes to comparing the three of us, there are no qualms that Isabella is most definitely the diva. Even better, she owns it.

"So . . ." Isabella says, turning her attention toward me and getting a look in her eye that worries me.

"I don't like when you start sentences with 'so' and you look at me that way," I say, turning to follow the direction she keeps looking over my shoulder.

There's a group of five men at the far end of the bar—all extremely attractive—and when I look, two of them are looking our way. The way one nudges the others when we both look, says they know they're being checked out. I look back at Isa and lift an eyebrow. "The answer to whatever it is you're scheming in your head is a resounding no. Full stop. Not going to happen."

I know what it looks like when I'm about to be railroaded by my two closest friends.

This is what it looks like.

"So opinionated when you don't even know what I'm going to say." Isabella laughs as she does with everything. She looks back at the men, then at Gia, then to me, her smile widening. "All I was thinking is that if you're going to make this big change in your life, maybe we should help you."

"Help me? I already don't like the sound of this."

Wine. I need more wine. Desperately.

I look toward the bar for our server and mistakenly meet the eyes of one of the guys standing there. He's tall with dark hair and light eyes. That's all I grasp because in the best of times, my eye aversion game is strong. Right now is no different.

"What do you have in mind?" Gia asks Isabella as if I'm not sitting with them.

Isabella studies me, eyes narrowed and lips pursed. "Like I hinted at before. Hair updates. Clothes and style overhauled—"

"There is nothing wrong with my hair or clothes," I assert.

"If you want to remain single and sexless, there's not." Isabella scrunches up her nose. My fashion sense has been a bone of contention of hers since we first started hanging out five years ago. It's been a running joke that she's determined to rectify my wardrobe at some point. "Baggy jeans. Button-up shirts. Air-Jordans. The Camilla Moretti uniform is fine if you're . . . *not you*. Why are you hiding your gorgeousness?"

"Gee. Thanks a lot." I laugh, not offended in the least. My clothes are a choice I consciously made years ago that have become a habit. I look down at them, then back up at her and grin. "They're designer at least."

"It wouldn't be a thing," Gia says, "if we hadn't seen old pictures of you without the Camilla Moretti uniform of today."

"You've got a body, girl. Show. It. Off," Isabella says and takes a long suck on her straw.

"Says the woman who has no problem traipsing around naked." I shake my head. "It's a no-go on the clothes."

"Cami," Gia draws out.

"Look . . . I'll compromise. You can revamp the hair—*not* a pixie—but the clothes stay. This is what I'm comfortable in. I'll even let you up my shoe game if that makes you happy."

Isabella eyes me, lips turning up into a smile and brows raising. "Can they be something without a thick rubber sole? Like something strappy with heels?"

I sigh knowing I can give on this. It's a compromise at least. "Yes. Sure."

"I'll take every little victory I can get. So, hair. Shoes. *For now*. But we are going to revisit this again."

"We'll take what we can get," Gia says, eyeing Isabella again.

"God," I groan. "What else are you guys scheming?"

"Not scheming. Just . . . *helping*." Isabella offers a placating smile.

"More like offering assistance that you don't even know you needed," Gia adds.

Yep. *Definitely being railroaded.*

"Gia and I want to set you up with one of our friends here since, *one*, you don't make any time to do anything for yourself other than work and, *two*, you're in a new place so it's a good idea to meet new people—"

"*One*," I say, mimicking Isabella, "maybe I don't want to date anyone. Men are more trouble than they're worth. *And two*, I meet plenty of people—*when I want to.*"

"Which is never." Gia laughs.

"I'm more than fine with hanging with just you two," I say, ignoring her comment. "Besides, I'll be way too busy for dating or commitment or having to worry about someone's feelings."

"Oh my God, Cami. When did you become so boring?" Gia teases in a whine as she playfully shoves my shoulder.

"I *am not* boring. I have you guys. I have a job that will be all new to me, so I'll have to throw myself into it. In the coming weeks when I relocate here, I'll have a new place to explore in a non-touristy way—grocery stores, coffee shops, that kind of thing."

"The excitement of it has me on the edge of my seat," Isabella says drolly.

I hold my finger up to shush her. "And when I *want* sex—or need a bit of release that can't be found in eating chocolate and drinking copious amounts of wine—I'll find a nice guy and have sex without worrying about strings to get tangled up in." I state the lie with a nonchalant shrug. "See? Your concern over my love life is unfounded."

"And when exactly did that happen last, huh? And I'm talking about the *good sex* part?" Gia asks, arms crossing over her chest and eyebrows lifting. "I mean . . . it's been a *cold* minute."

"That's kind of what happens when you swear off men," I assert to their blatant snickers.

"See? That's where you made the mistake. You were supposed to swear off assholes like Daniel and Blake and . . . whoever was before them who jaded you but you won't talk about. *Not men in general,*" Gia says. "You've simply had bad luck with men. The plus side? Bad luck can be broken."

Or maybe it's me who's broken.

What happened is dead and gone. So what if it's made me indifferent to sex? That it's made me push people away?

"Which is why we're already planning on who to set you up with. The excuse that you live in Rome isn't going to fly anymore when you're living right here in the same town with us." Gia's eyes light up like a kid in a candy store. That look right there says I'm screwed. That steps have already been taken. That plans are already being made.

Lord help me.

"As I've said numerous times, in the many other times we've had this conversation, I can handle my own love life, thank you very much."

Isabella's smile is a slow crawl across her lips. "Love life is different than sex life. One you purport to have—we know differently. The other is nonexistent."

"Which is just how I want it," I lie, willing to die on this hill.

"Great." Gia flashes a grin. "We can help with that. You won't put yourself out there for either option so that's what you have us for."

Why do I feel like I just fell into their trap I didn't see coming?

"I told you. I'll be too busy for sex," I say.

"Nice try, but you're not getting out of this one that easily," Gia says. "Besides, you promised us you were going to put yourself back out there. That was three or four months ago, and I've yet to see you even put your pinky toe in the dating pool . . . so your friends are coming to the rescue."

"I have my reasons." A truckload of them, actually.

"We all have reasons, but I distinctly remember a specific night in Paris," Gia says. "A few bottles of wine. A big heart-to-heart. And you taking a fortifying breath and saying you needed a change. With work. With scenery. With your love life. With being braver in how you face the world."

"It's almost as if the universe listened, Cami, and is giving you the chance for all of that right now," Isabella says, joining the pep talk.

And they're right. We did have that talk. I left that outdoor café a little buzzed and a lot more determined to quit jumping at shadows.

But I'm still jumping, aren't I?

"So grab it by the balls—or whatever man you find"—Gia winks—"and take it for a ride."

"In *all* respects." Isabella laughs.

"Ugh." I close my eyes and scrunch up my nose knowing they're absolutely right. "Fine. Okay. Yes to hair and shoes. To putting myself out there. But can I get settled a bit before we throw me to the dating wolves?" Maybe that will buy me some time. Then I'll be so busy traveling with the team that it won't be a possibility.

You're running again, Cami, and it's only been seconds since you said you were going to stop doing just that. Kind of pathetic.

Gia gives me a dubious look as if she doesn't believe a word I'm saying. She knows me well. And then says, "So updated hair, still working on the clothes, a few blind dates, what else are we missing, Isa?"

"A place to live," Isabella says. "We know a few areas that would be perfect for you."

"I already have that sorted," I say. "I have appointments to look at a few places tomorrow. Pretty sure by the pictures and the proximity to work that I already know which place I want to rent."

"Wow. Impressive. You move fast," Isabella says. "In that respect at least." She winks and I roll my eyes, ignoring the comment.

"Yeah, well, it was either that or listen to my parents tell me over and over how I could live with them. I love them and all, but . . . um, no."

"And living with parents is never good for the booty call scenario," Gia says.

"True," Isabella says. "But I still think you should look at a few I've found in my area."

"I will if I need to," I say simply to appease her, but I don't exactly want to be in the city center where it seems like no one ever sleeps and where horns and voices echo through the neighborhood at all times of night.

"So when will you be back so we can start making plans?" Gia asks, one hundred percent on the Camilla Moretti Glow-Up plan.

"We need to schedule Genovese from The Salon for her," Isabella says. "She's in the know on all fashion, all everything, here. "Then Valentina for skin."

"And I'm thinking the first meet-up will be with Hunter, don't you? He has the same vibe as Cami. Laid-back but uptight," Gia says and laughs, talking like I'm not even here.

"Hunter. Then Archie. Possibly Paddy after. She needs choices. Strong, independent women like choices."

"Where is the wine?" I mutter, glancing again over my shoulder to see where our server is. Our glasses are more empty than full, and I think I'm going to need several rounds to get through tonight.

When I look back, they're both grinning goofily at me. "Why don't you go find out the status of our drinks while Gia and I plan your life overhaul?"

"I feel a headache coming on," I grumble.

"Wine helps with that," Gia says and winks. "This is going to be so much fun."

They high-five me as I rise and head toward the bar.

This was a planned ambush.

No one is going to make me believe any differently.

CHAPTER FIVE

Camilla

"**I**T'LL BE JUST A MINUTE, LOVE," OUR SERVER SAYS TO ME WHEN I REACH the bar. Her hair is pink, a ring is in the side of her lower lip, her clothes are funky, and her accent is cockney. I love everything about her. "We're slammed tonight. I apologize for being slow."

"Not a problem. We're not in any hurry," I say.

"Yeah, but I'm sure you didn't come here to drink water." She laughs and lifts a tray teeming with drinks that looks like it weighs more than she does.

I laugh with her and when I turn to head back to the table, I come close to running into the guy who I locked eyes with earlier. What the distance left to the imagination, doesn't disappoint up close and personal.

He's striking.

Dark hair with a wave to it. Light gray eyes framed by thick lashes. Sharp features. A smile that he clearly uses on the regular by the way he flashes it at me and expects me to react.

I hate to admit that I do.

My return smile is automatic as I take a step back. "Sorry." My laugh sounds edged with nerves as I hold my hands up. "I apologize. That's what I get for not watching where I was going."

He narrows his eyes at me but his smile still plays at the corners of his mouth. "I'm questioning the sincerity of that apology," he teases, angling his head to the side and studying me. "In fact, I think you make it more than a habit of running into devilishly handsome guys—such as myself, of course—"

"Naturally."

"Because I'm getting the feeling that you're too shy to walk right up to them"—he raises one hand—"*me . . . and tell them what you want.*"

I shift on my feet and hold his stare. Normally, this isn't my thing—being approached in a bar. But when the option is talking to him or going back to Operation Glow-Up with Gia and Isabella, I welcome the distraction.

"And you would know this how?" I ask as he shifts his weight and places his drink on the cocktail table beside him.

"Call it a hunch."

"Are your hunches always right?" I ask.

"We'll see." His smile lights up his face even more. "Ask me that again in about ten minutes."

"Ten minutes?" I bark out a laugh. "That's how long you think it's going to take for you to convince me to tell you exactly what I want?"

"Yes."

"You say that with absolute confidence."

He lifts his eyebrows and nods. "And?"

"And nothing." I shrug. "But I'm pretty sure I'm going to prove you wrong."

The pout he gives me is more than adorable and has me wanting to cave. But before I do, he says, "I know how you can make it up to me."

"Make what up to you?" I laugh.

"You not telling me what you want. You not being mesmerized by my confidence." He ticks the items off on his fingers. "The fact that you're not giving me your undivided attention."

"I'm not?"

"Nope."

God, his grin is a mixture of adorable and sexy, and how is that combination even possible?

"Why do you think that?"

"Because you keep looking over my shoulder at your friends wondering if you should let me keep talking to you or if you should give them the sign to come and rescue you."

"The sign?"

"You know, *the sign.*" He nods. "A twirl of your hair. Your fingers crossed at your side. The predetermined thing you agreed on with your friends that tells them you need rescuing."

"Ah. Yes. *That sign.*" I glance over his shoulder to where both Isabella and Gia have noticed us and are staring intently. *Great.* Just what I need.

Then again . . . maybe I can make them think I've hit it off with whoever this guy is—it's not like it's a hardship when he looks like he does—and get them to lay off the forcing me to date their "friends" component of their plan.

"There's no sign. None whatsoever," I say.

"No?"

"No."

"Then why do they keep staring at us?" he asks, flashing them a grin and a salute of a wave before turning back to me and waiting for an answer.

"They're just busy trying to plan my move here, my love life . . . you name it." I roll my eyes.

"You're moving here?" he asks.

"I am," I say with a nod.

"Lucky girl. This is a pretty awesome place to move to."

"Says the native."

"No. Says the person who moved here myself."

"Same difference. Accent is all the same."

"But it's not. You'll soon find that out."

"I'm sure I will." I tilt my head. "Why here though?"

"I'm manifesting something."

"Right now it seems you're manifesting how to get a woman back to your flat."

"Is it working?"

The look I give him in response—shoulders sagging, eyes looking up from beneath my brows, lips pursed in chagrin—tells him all he needs to know. *No.*

He twists his lips and fights his grin. It only serves to make him even cuter as those storm-cloud gray eyes of his light with humor. "And your love life? You said they're over there planning it?" I nod. "Do you want them to be?"

I sigh. "God, no. Who knows where I'll end up, being forced to do some ludicrous, whimsical *something* with a guy named Guy or Rocky or something like that."

"So much to unpack in that statement." He laughs. "*Ludicrous whimsical?* Is that even a thing?"

"It is," I say with a definitive nod to back up my words.

"I'm assuming that's in reference to something one would do on a date—an activity, a place—two straws, one milkshake kind of thing and *not* something else."

"Correct. A date. *Not something else.*" I roll my eyes. Leave it to a guy to infer something sexual.

"You're the one who said it. Not me." He holds his hands up and chuckles. "Besides, what do you have against ludicrous, whimsical dates?"

"Nothing. They have a purpose—just not for me."

"Then what exactly is it that you like to do on dates?"

I lift a lone brow and shrug and then immediately realize how that response will most definitely be interpreted. His grin widens. Yep. Nailed that one on the head.

"Is that so?" he murmurs.

"I didn't mean it like that. I meant—"

"Shh." He leans in so that I'm hit with the crisp, clean scent of his cologne. He smells incredible, but it's his warm breath against my ear that has chills racing over my skin. The visceral reaction surprises me. "Don't say that too loud. You're in a room full of desperate men. For all you know, there might already be a line forming at your back."

"Is there one?" I tease as he takes a step back but remains closer than he was originally. He's tall with broad shoulders and muscles that bunch ever so slightly beneath the fabric of his shirt with each movement.

He makes a show of looking behind me before meeting my eyes. "Not yet. But I assure you it's coming."

"Ah, yes. The ever-constant line of men just waiting for me wherever I go."

"There should be one."

I tap my glass of wine against the neck of his lager. "Thanks for the compliment, but no thanks. Not interested."

"No thanks regarding the line queueing for you or no thanks as in *me?*"

"How about just a general no thanks?" I smile and lift my eyebrows.

He snorts. "No wonder your friends are planning out your love life."

"What's that supposed to mean?" I ask.

"It means you have a man standing before you blatantly flirting with you, and you don't even realize it." His eyes hold mine and heat suddenly rushes to my cheeks.

I'm not good at this. *Who is?*

But I used to be. Isn't that what bugs me more?

"Maybe I assumed you were just a nice guy who needed a break from his friends just like I'm a nice girl who needed the same."

He hisses. "Wow. Is my game that weak?"

I laugh. God, it feels good to laugh. "No. Your game is perfect. You're funny. You're good-looking. You're—"

"Would you look at that. You're finally flirting back."

"No. I'm not. I'm—"

He barks out a laugh, his dimples deepening. "I think I should be offended by that."

"You shouldn't. I'm just . . ." I shake my head and groan at my inability to speak.

"You're just, what?"

It's okay to flirt back, Cami. Isabella's crazy nods over his shoulder say as much.

"It's a long story." I empty the rest of my glass, a refill needed now more than ever.

"Stories always are, aren't they?"

"Mmm."

It's like I gave myself permission to flirt, and now I can't form words.

"I'll tell you what. You're in need of rescuing from your friends and you were right, I'm in a bit of a situation where I need to be saved myself."

"You're in need of saving? I highly doubt it."

"Not so much saved but more *helped* out."

"Helped out?"

"Yep. I'm in a bit of a sticky situation."

"Then unstick yourself."

"The lady has jokes."

"Always." I nod. "So what exactly is it that you need help with?"

"Well, truth be told, it's my fault. I let my ego get the best of me." He nods, head angled to the side and eyes laser focused on me.

"Is that so?"

"Yep. We were all shooting the shit, having some beers, one thing led to another, and I might have bragged that I could get any woman in this pub."

"Any woman?"

He rocks his head from side to side. "That's what I said."

I make a show of looking around the vast warehouse-type pub with its dark lighting and vibrant décor. "There are a lot of people to choose from.

Should I be offended that out of all these women, you looked at me and figured I'd be the sucker who'd fall for a line like that and help?"

"Ouch. I feel the sting of that rebuke."

"You should."

"But." He holds his finger up for me to wait, his smile widening. "What you didn't let me get to is that when I made that statement, my mates one-upped it. They bet me that there was no way in hell I could get the prettiest woman in here to give me the time of day so . . . here I am." He mock bows as his compliment settles in. "Trying to win that bet."

"Ah, look at that, you just found your game. Nice try." I know a line when I'm being fed one.

He laughs but glances over his shoulder to his mates and just like Gia and Isabella are, the four of his friends are all glancing our way.

Maybe it's not a line.

Maybe it's true.

And how does that make you feel, Camilla?

"*Time of day?* That definition seems to be painted with a very broad stroke," I say. "What exactly does that mean?"

He grins. "That remains to be seen, now doesn't it? The bigger the better I'm assuming."

"Always." I'd be lying if I said I didn't like the quick widening of his eyes and flaring of his nostrils.

"And her flirting gets better with each passing minute," he murmurs as his eyes look me up and down. "I think that begs me to stand here all night and see how things turn out."

Our gazes hold as sexual tension charges between us.

I can't help my smile. He's charming in all the right ways. He's definitely good-looking. A woman would be stupid to walk away from this conversation.

But isn't that what I would have done in the past? Let myself become uncomfortable and walk away?

Not this time.

Not when I'm trying to prove to Gia and Isabella that I am being more self-assured. That I'm putting myself out there. That I don't want to be set up.

"This bet of yours," I finally say. "What do you get if you win?"

"My pride kept intact. A few extras thrown in on their part."

"Extras?"

"My bar tab picked up for a month. Bragging rights. Hopefully a phone number I can call at a later time for a date," he says.

"Ah, so that's the *time of day* portion. A phone number as the proof that I've given it to you."

"It could be proof, yes. There might be a scale involved."

"A scale? Like talking to me is the first rung. My phone number the second rung. Something else the next rung up?"

"Yeah. I think beyond that I'd get extra credit."

"Extra credit, huh?" He nods. "And if you lose the bet?" I ask.

"There may have been some kind of dare involved."

"Such as?"

"A precariously and embarrassingly placed tattoo."

"How precarious and how embarrassing?"

He snorts. "We'll just say I would prefer to maintain my dignity."

"I can't help you then."

"Seriously?"

"Yep. I need the details," I tease.

He huffs out a breath and shakes his head. "Tinkerbell on my bicep."

"Wow. I see." I fight a laugh and fail. "And you took that bet, *why?*"

"Because I hate to lose." He shrugs. "I *don't* lose."

"There's a first time for everything." I snicker.

The server steps up and replaces my empty glass with a fresh one. "On the house for the wait," she says.

"That's not necessary," I say.

"I insist, love. You've been more than patient."

"Thank you."

"May I get another when you get a chance?" Bar Boy asks. And as he busies himself placing his order, I look at my phone buzzing in my hand. Of course, Isabella is texting me: **You better act on whatever you have going there or else we're going to come over and tell him just how long it's been since you've had decent sex and proposition him for you ourselves.**

I whip my gaze up and meet her and Gia's challenging lift of their eyebrows and arms crossed over their chests. *Dare us* is written all over their faces, and I don't have to question whether they would do it or not.

They have in the past, and we don't need a repeat of that. Visions of standing on a bar top, a megaphone, and a row of shots flicker through my mind before I tuck them away.

But it's enough of a reminder to know that she's good on her threat.

"Are you getting texts too?" he asks as he looks up from his phone in his hand and its screen that keeps lighting up.

I chuckle. "Yep." I hold my phone out long enough for him to see the text screen but not for him to be able to read it. "They're threatening to come over here and proposition you themselves on my behalf."

He laughs. "Mine are telling me that I'm all talk and no action. That there's no way in hell I'm going to get your phone number. That my time's up and so I need something more than that."

"More than my number, huh?"

"Yep. It's either that or my date with the tattoo needle is coming." He laughs.

"What if you get more than that?" I ask, my mind spinning over how to sell this to both of our friends.

"I'm curious what you have in mind."

"Well, there is a way that you can help get my friends off my back, and I can help you win your little bet."

My idea is to fake it. Swap our numbers. Set up a date over text that we'll never take, but that we can both show our friends as proof. Flirt a little bit more so there is no mistaking we like each other.

Kill two birds with one stone.

But when I look up and see Gia rising from our table so she can get a better view of the two of us, I get the feeling that a fake arrangement to meet up isn't going to fly.

The text from Isabella that buzzes my phone says as much: **Actions speak louder than words, Moretti.**

I walked over here with a personal pep talk that my friends are right. That I need to live more and dwell on the past less. Well, that's not exactly what they said—but they don't know the whole truth about why I am how I am. Only two people do: myself and the one other person I've avoided like the plague.

"You think we can both win our respective fights?" he asks, his smile toying with the corners of his lips.

"I do."

"And how do you figure to do that?"

I don't have time to summon courage like I normally would. Gia and

Isabella bearing down on me is sufficient motivation to push me out of my comfort zone and into the goddamn fire.

"Like this." I step up and press my lips to his.

I think we're both shocked by the action, but it takes a split second for his surprise to wear off and his body to respond.

And oh, how he responds.

His hands slide up my back and one fists in my hair as his lips command mine. As his tongue slips between my lips, tasting slightly of the lager he's drinking, and teases mine. He emits the softest of groans, yet I can hear it at the same time I feel it rumble against my chest.

But one thing outweighs all those things by far—it's the way my body reacts. The sharp but sweet ache that burns bright. The chills that chase over my skin. The way I crave more of his kiss and the feel of his hands on my skin.

A feeling I haven't felt in years.

A feeling I thought I'd never feel again.

A feeling that proves to me I'm not broken.

The kiss lasts but seconds as we're in a roomful of people, and the sole purpose was to prove a point and make our friends wave their white flags.

But when we part, when we step back and our eyes meet, it's obvious he's as staggered by my kissing him as I am over the way the touch of his lips made me feel.

I stare at him.

Astounded.

Dumbfounded.

My lips tingling and body feeling like I'll shock anything I touch.

I can't remember the last time that happened.

I take another step back, unable to process the peculiar look on his face because I'm too busy *feeling*.

"That's one way to convince them," he says as he scrubs a hand over his jaw. His smile widens. There's a sheepish quality to it that softens the arrogance in the best way. "You good? I mean, I know I'm feeling good and all, but *whew*, that was one for the ages."

The cocksure grin.

The pale gray eyes.

The bob of his Adam's apple.

"I'm good. Yeah." I shake my head and try to rid it of the buzzing in my ears. That's when I notice Isabella and Gia standing a few tables down, jaws lax and eyes wide with surprise etched in the lines of their faces. "I, uh . . ." Why are my lips still tingling? "Hope that helps you win."

"That should more than do it." One of his friends shouts something across the bar—I don't quite catch it—but it makes him turn his head and hold a finger up to them. "I, uh—I've got to get going. We have . . . plans. For later."

"Yeah. Right." *Thank God.* I need to find my bearings.

"Thanks for helping me out."

"Same goes for me." We both take a step backward as a sudden awkwardness settles between us now that the shock has worn off. "Oh. Our numbers. We need to—you know—to sell it."

"Right. Yes." He sets his phone down on the table and reaches out to take mine. Within seconds he has sent himself a text from my phone. "That's me," he says, setting my phone next to his on the table. He reaches out to shake my hand. It feels so formal after we were literally just kissing. But I shake it. "Nice doing business with you."

We laugh and there's a moment where we both stare at each other. His eyes darken. His lips part. And then just as surprising as when I kissed him, he cups the back of my neck and brings his mouth down on mine.

His kiss is more commanding this time. More take control. More of everything that mine was, *but better.* The pressure of his hand on my neck. The softness of his lips. The way he angles his head to deepen the kiss. The brush of his thumb over my jawline.

Nope. What I felt the first time definitely wasn't a fluke.

It was real—*is real.* The tingle, the ache, the sweet burn. All three are owning my body for a second time.

And when the kiss ends, when he leans back and stares at me with that cocky, lopsided smirk of his, he gives a nod. "There." He taps the table beside us with his hand. "*Now* we're even."

I chortle as he grabs his cell phone and beer off the table, gives me one more nod, and then heads back to his friends.

There's a whoop of cheers and high fives all around as he sits down with them. It's only when I go to grab my own cell and glass of wine off the table that I notice the business card he left behind.

Or at least that's what I think it is until I turn it over and see the bright blue DARE printed in fancy font across the top in bold letters. And then the following words written beneath: Find the woman least likely to be hit on and get her phone number.

I stand there and stare at the dare card, trying not to be offended by it, but it's only natural that I am. Anybody would feel the same.

Talk about a blow to my ego.

Talk about proving my own words right about men not being worth it.

Dumbfounded and ignoring the pressure in the center of my chest, I look in the direction of his friends and see them laughing and patting him on the back.

Tears threaten and my throat burns. *This is why. Why on earth would I put myself "out there" only to feel like this?*

"Hey. What was *that?*" Isabella asks with a little shimmy and a hand held up for a high five that I don't return.

"You got his number, right?" Gia asks. "Because, damn girl, that was hot and you definitely stepped out of the box."

I nod and palm the stupid card, hoping to hide my mortification. "Yeah. I did. We're going to meet up when I get back. I—uh—I'll be right back. The bathroom."

"Do you want one of us—"

"No, I'm fine." I muster a smile and then try to walk as calmly as possible to the restroom on the other side of the bar.

It's only once I shut the bathroom stall door that I sag against it and let the emotions hit me. Shame. Anger. Disbelief. All three of them run a race through my head as I stare at the stupid card.

I was the butt of their joke. Of *his* joke.

I try to shake the thought off but it doesn't shed completely.

"They bet me that there was no way in hell I could get the prettiest woman in here to give me the time of day so . . . here I am. Trying to win that bet."

Well, he was right about one thing—trying to win a bet. And I was right too—that I was the one who looked the most gullible. The easiest mark picked so he could win his fucking dare.

Leaning against the bathroom stall, I close my eyes and give myself a pep talk that doesn't relieve the demoralizing hurt.

C'mon, Cami. You promised yourself you'd never give another person the power to knock you down. To steal your pride. To take a part of you and ruin it. To make you a victim.

I close my eyes, the card in my hand feeling like lava singeing my skin.

And then I laugh like a loon into the empty bathroom. At myself. At the situation. At what this entire evening has turned into.

An ambush. An accidental meeting. An arousing kiss. An abject disaster.

Isn't it just like me to find the only man who made my body feverish . . . yet I was the butt of his jerkish, testosterone-laced joke?

Screw him.

I think the words while shrugging away the sting with the intent of exiting the bathroom, making an excuse to my friends that I don't feel well, and heading back to the hotel.

But the minute I step back into the bar, his table's laughter hits my ears and eggs me on, my sensible plans now forgotten.

Rather, they've been replaced by the desire to embarrass him in front of his friends. To take a bit of my dignity back. To let him know that *I know.*

So many times I walk away from situations and think of what I *should* have said. Not tonight. Not this time. I'm going to say it now.

With the card in hand, I stalk over to where the jerk is busy basking in his victory.

"Excuse me," I say as I step up to the table. My voice has the five of them whipping their heads up and their voices falling silent. My smile is smarmy at best when I angle it at the nameless jerk. "I think you forgot something."

I slap the card down on the center of the table, the atmosphere turning icily silent as they realize I know their juvenile game.

"Look, love—"

"Save it." I hold up my hand to stop him from speaking. "No need to explain to me why grown men think shit like this is funny, just like there's no need for me to tell all your friends that your game is pitifully weak and your kissing skills are subpar." Shock flashes through his eyes. "But hey, we all can't be good at everything, right?" I say with a shrug and a *fuck you* smile. "Lose my number."

There's a round of nervous chuckles as if they're not sure if they can react or if they should.

"I'd tell you to enjoy the rest of your night, but I'd be lying. Cheers." I turn on my heel and don't make it ten feet from the table before I hear his voice.

"Hey. Wait."

I feel his hand on my bicep.

It takes everything I have not to yank my arm out of his grasp. Instead,

I grit my teeth and calmly turn around with my eyebrows raised and a glance down to where he's touching me.

"Nah. I'm good. You can kindly take your hand off me. Pity fucks aren't my thing."

"Hey, come on now," he says as he glances over his shoulder at his friends and then back to me—almost as if he's afraid of them hearing him. "The card was . . . real—at first—but then I ran into you and—"

"And saw a woman least likely to be hit on. Way to boost your ego while hurting mine. Class fucking act."

"It was a bloody game."

"I know. And that says so much more about you than it ever could say about me." I look at him. The shame turning to astonishment. The hurt morphing into anger. "I don't want your apologies. They're not accepted." I take a step back. "I'd say it was nice knowing you . . . but it wasn't."

"I wouldn't have kissed you a second time if the card were true," he blurts out.

"I wouldn't have kissed you at all if I knew about the card." I retreat another step. "Feel better now? Your guilt absolved? You can go back to feeling like the good guy you aren't."

"Look. I said I was sorry."

"Was that on a dare card too? To apologize to some unsuspecting woman who—"

"I don't even know your name," he says as if I'd tell him.

"Lucky for me." I glance over his shoulder to where his friends are trying to pretend they aren't paying attention. "The rest of your asshole pack are waiting for you. Best not keep them waiting."

This time when I walk away, I don't look back. And if he starts to follow me, I'm none the worse for wear for not knowing.

Good to know what I told my friends earlier was on point. Men aren't fucking worth it.

They're just not.

And the rare times that they are? It seems that's when they can do the most damage.

CHAPTER SIX

Camilla

"Tell me why you agreed to pick up and move."

I stare at my therapist. Her blond hair and soft features look like they belong with the "everything neutral" theme of her office. Her voice is soft and her smile softer. She's been my North Star through all of this. The only person who knows what happened.

What started out as weekly visits turned into monthly ones over time. Then we progressed to every few months.

Now I'm saying goodbye because I'm moving away.

My own smile matches hers because I've thought about this a lot over the past week that I've been home and packing up my life.

"If not now, then when, right? Maybe I want more time with my dad while he's okay. Maybe I don't want to let him down. Maybe I'm intrigued by the challenge. And maybe it's a bit of all three."

She nods in that stoic, *I'm hearing you but not judging* way. "And maybe you're agreeing to be there at the expense of you. In an environment that could possibly trigger you."

"The thought has crossed my mind. More times than it probably should have . . . but truth be told, maybe this is what I need to finally get over that final hurdle. Maybe it's time to get my life back."

"I thought you'd already done that."

I nod. "In a sense. But I'm sick of living life scared. This is my chance not to."

"Scared?" She muses. "I would never say you were living scared. I'd say it was more along the lines of living safely. We've worked on the mental aspect of what happened. You've had boyfriends since then. Taken lovers."

"And we've talked about how that went."

"Baby steps, Camilla. No one is allowed to steal your happiness or to tell you how you should act or how your body should feel."

But what happens when it doesn't feel at all?

"Mechanical. Cold. Numb. Should we continue with all the reasons I've been dumped?"

"And like I said, when the time is right, everything will fall into place, just like you said it did the other night. The guy might have been a jerk, but you said it was the first time someone has touched you that made you and your body feel alive. That's nothing to trivialize. That's huge."

Our kisses live rent-free in my head. The ache that burned between my thighs even more so.

It's been a sensation that only I could create for myself during the past six years. That is until I kissed the asshole from the bar and now, it's front and center in my mind. The whole getting a drop of water in a desert metaphor seems a fitting description for how I've felt since then.

"It's pathetic is what it is," I joke.

"No. It's a good sign if you ask me."

"Not sure if I agree with that theory," I say.

"Why's that?"

"Because I tried to replicate the feeling, the situation . . . the moment, and *nothing*."

"Tell me more."

"Some of my coworkers wanted to send me off in style so they organized a farewell party of sorts at a club. I went out on the dance floor after I'd had a few drinks and my guard was down. There was a guy. He was cute. Nice. We flirted. He kissed me. Looking back, I think I openly wanted the kiss to happen to see if I could summon that feeling again—but nope. *Nothing.*"

"If you weren't physically feeling anything, what were you thinking?"

"Can we get this over with? So, see? I'm still broken." I chuckle because it's easier to do that than to admit how much that burns. To think I wasn't— finally—and to realize I still am.

"You're not broken. There's no such thing. Look at it this way—you don't shy away from the act of sex like many do in your situation. In fact, you've used it as a measuring stick to try to prove to yourself that it's okay. That you're okay."

And it seems to only have proved that I'm not.

"If at first you don't succeed, try, try, and then try again," I joke, but am more than serious in my own mind. Indifferent. That's how I've been, how I've felt toward sex for so long, that I crave something other than indifference.

"Sex has been your litmus test and that's fine. But what you really need to do is quiet your head and just listen to your body. It's okay for something to feel good and to want more of it. To kiss all the men in the room until you find the one that lights your skin on fire and when you do, hold on tight so you can burn together."

"Is that an official prescription? I mean, sleep around? There's a not nice name for that, that I'd prefer not to be called."

"You make jokes when you're nervous, Camilla. Just as you are now. That means whatever that guy made you feel sparked something inside you. Maybe scraped the wound open but offered a salve to tide you over. Who knows what might happen next?"

CHAPTER SEVEN

Riggs

"HE'S OKAY THOUGH, RIGHT?" I WATCH THE REPLAY ON THE monitor for what feels like the tenth time. Tires screeching. The car lifting. Flipping. Cartwheeling. The metal giving. The tires flying. The gravel spraying.

Then comes the fire.

I shake my head and hold my breath momentarily as I fight memories just as terrifying. Memories that have faded in clarity with time but not in the sucker punch to the stomach department.

But regardless of the visceral reaction, I can't seem to tear my eyes away from the screen.

My stomach remains dropped at my feet as I watch each slow-motion replay even though I already know what happens next.

Maxim motionless as the car finally comes to a stop after skidding across the gravel.

His hands moving as they work frantically to unpin the steering wheel trapping him in the car.

His white helmet bobbing its way up through the flames.

His body rising through the halo and then falling, flopping onto the scattered tires that moments before were a safety barricade.

He stumbles. Then falls. Then crawls away from the heat until he collapses . . . seconds before the safety crew rushes to him and drags him away from the ticking time bomb of a car.

It's every racer's worst nightmare.

The wall rushing at you. The car collapsing around you. The fire engulfing you.

Maxim. His lifeless body. The crew doing their best to shield him from the cameras in case he's gravely injured, and it's not caught on camera to become a viral spectacle.

So his family doesn't have to watch him die on camera. Like my mum did. *Like we all did.*

"He's in the hospital," Pierre says stoically.

"What does that mean?" I demand, my feet needing to move and every part of me antsy as fuck.

My days in karting flash through my mind. Hours on end spent hating the bastard for having everything he needed to succeed—the parents, the money, the sponsorships, the equipment—and then learning to love him like a brother once I realized he was just like me. Driven to succeed in a sport that single-handedly robs you of your confidence while becoming your one and only focus.

Maxim and I are competitors. There are days that I like the guy and others that I loathe him. We belong to an elite group of drivers all vying for one of twenty coveted positions on the F1 grid.

He's gotten his spot there with Moretti Motorsports.

I'm still pushing for it.

Am I jealous that he has his? That most of my class who has grown up together in this odd circuit has made it to the penultimate level? Fuck yes. Do I wish harm on him because of it?

Only a fucking arsehole would wish that.

And yeah, I am one on so many levels—but not when it comes to something like that.

But now . . . now? Who the fuck knows if he's okay?

Because if he can be hurt—then we all can be, and that's not a thought any of us want to have. Ever.

A thought I've lived with the reality of my whole life but that I've pushed aside with the justification that technology has advanced miles. The cars are stronger. The safety equipment more protective. The sport safer.

But that justification means shit if Maxim is hurt.

"Have you gotten any word on him? On how he's doing?" I ask, forcing myself to look anywhere but the screen where the accident plays on repeat. My crew is doing the same. They'll explain it away as if they're studying how the car performed—where it gave, how it fell apart, and the like—but I know they're just as horrified by the crash as I am. By the fact that Maxim got out of it. By the unknown of whether he's okay or not.

"Neck brace is always precautionary," he murmurs, lifting his glasses up and rubbing his eyes before shutting the monitor off.

"But they airlifted him out, right? I mean—shit." I go to grab my mobile. "I'll text his brother and see—"

"You need to get in the car, Riggs," Pierre says, stepping in front of me and putting me in my place. The order is more for me to get my head in the right place than anything. It's a means of forcing me to swallow down that inherent fear that lurks just beneath the surface with every fucking limit we push. With every lap we cheat death.

"We're short on track time this week," he says. "We need to make the most of the time we have."

I hesitate when I shouldn't and then get pissed at myself for doing so. Leave it to Maxim to fuck with my head even now despite being in separate circuits.

"Fuck it," I mutter and grab my balaclava and yank it down onto my head.

I don't say another word as I put my helmet on, get my body belted in, put my gloves on, and lock my steering wheel in place.

I visualize the curves of the track I'm about to drive on. Over and over, I trace the map I've etched in my mind. Anything and everything to push the jarring image of Maxim's body flopping onto the ground out of my head.

Everything to fight the memory I see each and every time my engine roars to life—my dad. His lips stained blue from candy floss. His laugh a rumble above the roar of engines that were always sparking to life. A smile he saved just for me.

My engine revs. My radio checks. And I spend the next fifteen laps becoming as one with the car as I can. As much as I fucking hate it on a good day, right now, I like that the car isn't adjusted right. It gives me something to concentrate on. Something to lose my thoughts to.

But the minute I pull into the garage and get out of the car, the first words out of my mouth are, "Any word?"

Pierre glances over to Ricky and then back to me. "Not yet. Unofficially? Something about an induced coma to help with swelling or some shit like that. Brain shit is never good. I'm not a doc so I don't know what the fuck that means other than that."

I know what it means, but he doesn't want to tell me. Coma. Swelling. Brain shit. His injuries aren't just a quick jaunt to the medical tent to be looked over and released.

This is way more serious than that. *Fuck, man.*

I worry my bottom lip between my teeth, fighting the urge to ask the fucked-up question that's on the tip of my tongue. The question that makes me a selfish bastard for simply thinking it, let alone putting a voice to it.

Pierre saves me and answers it for me. "Not that I'm an expert, but his injuries mean he's going to be out for some time."

"That's a rough blow for Moretti. Maxim was starting to kick some arse. That and their reserve driver was picked up for his own ride with Centurion last week," Ricky says. "Who the fuck are they going to get to fill his shoes?"

Pierre meets my eyes for a beat but doesn't say a word.

Do you think it'll be you?

He doesn't have to.

I'm qualified. More than qualified. I have my Super Licence. I take advantage of the connections I have through my father's name to get in the cockpit of an F1 car at least once a month. *Will they consider me?*

"I think we're all thinking that," I say to Ricky and then exit the conversation.

The last thing I want to hear is their speculation about who it should be. Who it should be is me, damn it.

But it won't.

Deep down, I know it.

I've been through this song and dance too many fucking times. The high of soaring hopes. The jump at the phone ringing. The crushing despair and doubt when someone else is called up.

No way in hell am I giving up this dream. But each and every time a situation like this happens, I feel like another tiny piece is chipped off my resolve. Another part of me gone toward a wasted dream many think I never should get the chance to achieve.

I walk out of the garage area and into the paddock. Other F2 drivers are milling about, but there's an unspoken anticipation in the atmosphere. An anticipation that's as exciting in nature as it is sick.

Who'll get his seat?

I'm not the only one hoping my phone rings.

Will the call come down today? Will Moretti treat this like the business it is and prepare a driver to fill Maxim's shoes for the next race?

Because that's the one thing about this fucking sport. It's a passion, but above all else, the empire's bottom line is what matters. It's profoundly rewarding yet fiercely cruel.

We all know it's dangerous. That it's one millisecond, one overcorrection, one tire bump away from utter destruction. From possibly dying.

And yet we get in the car day after day. We push the limits lap after lap. We give our all for our team, for ourselves, for our fans, but know the machine of F1 will move on faster than shit when we can't.

Nothing is ever good enough, ever fast enough . . . we're never satisfied. And the sport either rewards us with a win or punishes us with a crash.

The in-between is just as unsatisfying.

I meet the eyes of a few drivers standing with their crews and words don't have to be spoken to know what they're thinking. *I hope it's me. I hope I'm the one who gets the call. I hope I'm the one who finally gets the chance.*

I'm praying for the same fucking thing too.

We're wishing the best for our fellow driver who's clearly hurt while silently hoping this is our chance. That this will be our call-up.

The difference between Maxim and me? A lucky break? A split-second decision that makes or breaks you?

We all have the skill. It's just the timing that has fucked us over in some way or another. The amount of money we have to spend on equipment that might have made the difference at one point or another. The last name that might mean something in this small but elite circle.

Then again, I have the last name—mine just seems to garner me occasional pity and a wide berth for people to stay away.

"Riggs?"

I look over to Elio, my pit crew chief, who's waving me back into the garage. "Yeah?"

"Let's go over that last adjustment we made," he says, his tattoo-covered forearms bulging against the cuff of his team shirt. His headset hangs loosely around his neck, and a bead of sweat trails down his temple.

"Yeah. Sure. Okay," I say distracted, thinking that I need to go grab my phone—*just in case*—but not wanting to appear more eager than I already am.

And feeling like a prick for wanting my phone.

I keep myself occupied. Elio and I talk about the tweaks and what he aims to accomplish with them. I go over finances with my team manager because fuck if F2 isn't like that weird dichotomy of looking like you have it all while knowing you're single-handedly paying for it out of your own fucking pocket.

To the world, it looks like you're eating caviar when to those in my shoes, we're lucky if we get fucking sardines.

Is Moretti going to pull a reserve driver from another F1 team? Or will they temporarily promote a driver from F2 to fill Maxim's seat until he returns?

Seconds drag into minutes. Minutes slide into hours. None of us drivers want to leave—*just in case.*

But we do. One by one. Little by little. The track empties out as rumors begin to settle in around me.

Haskell rushed out of here with his phone to his ear. Did he get the call?

Diego has shut himself in his driver's room and is on the phone with someone.

My phone rings. I scramble and have it picked up before the second ring only to deflate. "Yeah? What's up, Fontina?"

"Don't sound so thrilled to hear from me." She chuckles sarcastically.

"Sorry. It's just . . . what did you need?"

"That video you did yesterday has gone viral. You keep this shit up, and I'm going to get fired, and you're going to be driving and doing your own social media for the team."

"Of course, it went viral. It's me, isn't it?" I joke, but I had no fucking clue.

I make a video. I post a video. I'm too fucking busy to sit there and watch the likes or views tick up one by one.

I'd much rather live life than watch it pass by on a screen.

And yet, I still post. I still contribute.

"You're such an asshole." She sighs.

"Thank you. That's not anything new, now, is it?" I open my mouth to ask her if she's heard anything but then snap it shut. If she had, she would have told me. She knows how badly I want this. Every driver in my shoes does.

"I mean, how did your comment to Flanders become a meme?"

"Comment?" I made a lot of comments. Some I'm not sure if I voiced or not.

"Yeah, the whole, *if you're trying to make a name for yourself, do it using someone else's back.*" She pauses. "You did know that, right?"

I chuckle. "No. I didn't. I told you I'm not on social media much. But sure. Awesome. I'm all for anything that can keep that prick in his place."

"I second that sentiment, but maybe next time we can work on it together so I can at least take some credit for it with the boss."

"You want to film me getting out of the shower and my towel accidentally falling off? Be my guest."

"Ew. Gross." She overreacts as expected.

"Clearly it's not so gross if millions have seen it, right?" I laugh. The video that I'm assuming went viral was more than just a hint at my body. It was a transition—me with a towel around my waist, the towel dropping, and when I picked it back up, I had my fire suit on and a megawatt grin. If girls can do *Get Ready With Me* segments, why can't guys?

Obviously, it did the trick.

"Millions. Ha. If you haven't seen it, how do you know how many views there are, huh?"

"I don't. Just a guess and by your reaction, it's a correct one."

"If your ego gets any bigger, we're going to need to upsize your helmet."

"Just a warning. Don't check my DMs. It's like the crazies unleashed themselves this week."

"He doesn't watch the videos, but he checks his direct messages. I'm beginning to think you're lying, Riggs."

"I like to keep you guessing. But seriously, don't check them."

"Ugh. Worse than normal?"

"You don't want to know." I'm all for pics being sent in—what guy wouldn't be? But I draw the line at seeing things put in places that shouldn't be there.

There's something to be said for leaving something a bit of a mystery.

"Noted. So very noted." She laughs. "If they knew you, they wouldn't be sending anything," she teases.

"It's not my personality they're after, Fontina."

"Ew. Gross again. Are you trying to make me throw up my lunch?"

"You're so easy to rile up."

"And you're so easy to distract." Her voice falls softer. "I hope it helped."

I scrub a hand over my jaw and give a half laugh, grateful for the call. "It has. Thanks. I appreciate it."

She sighs in exasperation. "Go home, Riggs."

"I'm working on it," I say as I grab my backpack, sling it over one shoulder, and decide to call it a day. If I haven't gotten the call yet, it's not coming.

Another opportunity gone. Another chance being passed up.

But why does this one already hurt so much more?

Because I deserve it more than anyone else here. Sure, they're thinking the same thing, but I've been here longer than most. I'm the only one left of that promising crop of drivers who all entered together that hasn't gotten their shot. I've won the Eurocup, F4 and F3 championships and gained the points to maintain my Super Licence.

It's. My. Time.

No doubt Ari will be in my ear soon. My agent is notorious for calling me with a debrief over all the reasons I've been passed up this time—too flashy, not flashy enough, or I come off like I'm not serious because I have too much fun.

The one I hate the most? I take too many risks, that I'm dangerous like my dad was, and they don't want my blood on their hands.

My favorite is *Riggs is too selfish*.

Well hell, fucking yes, I am. That's a requirement to be a successful, long-running F1 driver. They should want me to be. They should want my sole focus to be the end game and not worrying about hurting people's feelings.

There's a lot of senseless money spent in this sport, and no one is satisfied with finishing off the podium.

I've heard them all. Every single excuse as to why I haven't been pulled up.

No doubt another one's coming tonight. That's why it's best to head home now, to grab whatever my drink of choice will be, and to wallow in solitude.

Or with a woman.

I'll decide which one as the night progresses.

But I'll allow myself one night.

One reprieve of pity.

One night where I hate being Ethan Riggs's son.

One moment where I hate fucking everybody before getting back to the grind and to the grid, tomorrow.

CHAPTER EIGHT

Riggs

THE WALK OFF THE PREMISES IS A LONG ONE.

Down the paddock where everyone is glancing at each other, but no one is talking.

Through the turnstile, with its security guards and those milling just outside of it, waiting for a quick picture or interaction with a driver.

Then out to the almost empty car park.

Just my luck, that's when my mobile buzzes in my hand.

At least there won't be any witnesses to the bad news being delivered.

"Ari Fornierj. What reasons were you given this time?" I ask by way of greeting, the sarcasm dripping from my tone.

"Spencer."

My feet falter at the gravity to his tone. At the use of my first name when no one ever calls me by it. *It's Maxim. Has to be. Christ, it's not good, is it?* I glance around at the car park and then stop altogether. "What is it?"

"It's you."

"What do you mean *it's me?*" I ask.

"They called. It's your turn, Riggs. It's finally your fucking turn."

"Ari . . ." *Fuck.* Emotion swells in my throat and tears burn in the backs of my eyes as I try to find words. "You better not be fucking with me."

"Not on something like this. Never." He pauses and clears his throat, the moment clearly getting to his calloused heart too. *"This is real. Believe it. Your time has finally come."*

"Maxim?" I try to process this. The thrill that rides shotgun next to the guilt that I'm getting a chance because my friend is hurt. The sudden rush of adrenaline that everything as I know it is about to change.

"His injuries aren't grave, but he's going to need some recovery time. By all preliminary reports, he'll be fine."

"Good. That's good." I will myself into believing it to ease my guilt that his crash is my fortune.

"But Moretti has to fill his shoes in the meantime. Luckily, there's time before the next race, but that doesn't mean they aren't already thinking about it. They've strung together a few good outings and don't want to lose momentum."

I know Moretti has had a rough go of it lately. Maxim was their number one. That means their number two, Andrew Erikkson, will shift to one, and I'll come in as the number two driver.

But they've had two good races after a dismal past few years.

It's the perfect place for me to step in and try to make a name for myself—the motorsports icon, which has been mediocre as of late. I couldn't ask for better timing.

There will be expectations but not of miracles. While we use the same tracks in F2, we race on different weekends, so my familiarity with the courses is also a plus.

"Holy shit." It's all I can think to say as I try to align my thoughts and remember what circuit is next for them.

"What a lucky fucker you are to have moved to Wellingshire. Moretti's headquarters is right there."

"It's all that manifesting that you said was bullshit."

He barks out a chuckle. "I never said it was bullshit. Just more like . . . *new age-fandangle shit* that is for wanna-be-hippies."

I laugh, the tension leaving my body with each passing second. "Well, whatever it is, it worked, right? I got the fucking call." I fist-pump the air when what I want to do is shout it from the rooftops.

"You did, Riggs. God, you did."

Reality hits. The chaos that's about to ensue for me over the coming days. Chaos I've witnessed firsthand so I'll be prepared for the whirlwind to come.

"So what's next? Where do I go? When do I need to be wherever I need to be?" The adrenaline starts to ebb. My hands tremble and my voice wavers.

"I've requested the specifics. I'm sure they'll get you some time behind the wheel either here at Silverstone or have you head out early to the next race. It's going to be crazy—seat molding, suit fittings, pressers, photos, meetings with the race engineers on telemetry data."

"I know. I'm . . ." *At a loss for words.*

"Get home. I'd say pack, but I'm not sure if you need to pack yet. So maybe go home and clear your head and manifest or some shit like that."

"You're a regular comedian," I say as I slide behind the wheel of my car.

"Always. They're sending over a contract. Once I look it over and make any necessary changes, I'll get it to you. For now, all I know is it's a temporary spot. Race to race, but if it's determined that Maxim is out for an extended period of time, there's room for revision and adjustments."

"I'll take whatever."

"It's more money. A lot more. More perks. Top-of-the-line travel accommodations—"

"None of that matters, Ari." *The* more *is the opportunity.* "This is the chance I've been waiting for. It's everything."

"It is."

"That's all that matters." Holy shit. This is really real. "Talk to you in a bit."

"Sounds good." I'm just about to end the call when he says, "Hey, Riggs?"

"Yeah?"

"Congrats, man. You deserve this more than anyone."

The call ends. I sit in my car, hands gripping my steering wheel, head against the headrest, and emotions rioting through me faster than I can process them.

I squeeze my eyes shut. The rush of my pulse the only thing I can hear. The thumping of my heart making my body feel like it's jumping with each beat.

This is it, Riggs. This is the chance you've worked toward your whole life.

My shout reverberates around the closed confines of my car. I belt it out until it falls hoarse and morphs into a disbelieving laugh.

Holy shit.

Holy fucking shit.

My cheeks hurt from smiling and my head dizzies with excitement.

This is happening. This is really happening.

Did you hear that, Dad? I did it. I finally made it.

I wipe away the tear as quickly as it falls.

My thoughts race with the things I need to do. With the things that are probably going to happen next. With the possibilities that are finally at my fingertips. With how I'm the only person who can make the most of it.

But there's one thing I need to do more than anything.

"Mum," I say when she answers the phone.

"I knew it. I knew it. I knew it!" she shouts, the phone making all kinds of fuzzy static noises from what I can assume is her jumping around. "Oh God. You're not saying anything. Please tell me I'm right."

I laugh and it feels like a pressure valve releasing steam as I do. "You're right." I almost whisper the words, the gravity of it all hitting me. "All of it finally paid off."

Memories flash through my mind like a slide show.

Kart races where I was the kid who showed up with a kart built by scrap parts, a mum who taught herself how to work on them so she could help her son—so she could be the dad he needed because he didn't have one, and a race suit she sewed herself so I could look like everyone else.

Sure, I was Ethan Riggs's son, but Ethan Riggs's money had been eaten up by a shitty agent demanding more than his fifteen percent, greedy lawyers taking their cut, and the penalties on income taxes that were never paid.

All lessons learned the hard way.

What we were left, my mum held on to tightly.

So we slept in our truck the night before a race to save money since hotels were so expensive. We played silly games to occupy ourselves while we lay in the bed of the truck under the camper shell and waited for the morning to come.

At the time it embarrassed me. A former F1 driver's son trying to step into his father's oversized shoes but not having the money to do it. The comparison I could never live up to.

I hold those times close like a badge of honor. Especially now. I made it without the money. With very few connections. With the grit of my mum and my own fierce goddamn determination.

Then she sucked up every ounce of fear she had when I progressed to cars. I know she was terrified for me to follow in my father's footsteps, but she let me follow the passion that took her husband from her. She let me be who I am and didn't try to cast her fear onto me. Her unwavering support has both kept me grounded but allowed me to soar. She has been a silent pillar of strength when I failed and questioned if all this work was worth it.

She's been my rock—always, forever, and even when I didn't deserve it.

Of course, she'd be the first person I'd call.

"Spence. I don't even know what to say or who to tell or how to even celebrate." She's flustered, and it brings a smile to my face.

"I know. I feel the same way." I pound my fist against my steering wheel because it's the only thing I can think to do.

"So what's next?" she asks and then I hear her muffled voice say to someone at her work, "My baby. He got the ride." Then squealing.

I smile. I can't help it. "I'm waiting for instructions. On where to go. When to be there."

There is a pause. A deep breath. "Let me know where I need to be," she says softly.

I know how hard it is for her to say those words. The sacrifice she is making in doing so.

She vowed to never step foot on an F1 track again after my father's death. She saw me through my karting days but when I started racing cars, especially on circuits where my dad once raced, she couldn't do it.

She tried. Time and again. It didn't matter the track though, the result was still the same—a panic attack of epic proportions.

But still she showed up.

Still, she tried to be there for me as I struggled my way through the emotions of walking in my father's footsteps. And then there was the panic attack that was so violent and powerful that we all thought she was having a heart attack.

That was the last time I allowed her to come to the track.

I'd already lost one parent to racing. I sure as shit wasn't going to lose another.

I'm sure she felt a similar feeling. My dad was her one true love. She watched him die. I'm the only piece of him she has left.

So we came to an understanding. I'd race. She'd watch from home. It's almost as if the notion of being able to change the channel should something bad happen was enough. There was a mutual understanding as to why she couldn't be present during race weekend.

Hell, it's hard enough as it is for me some days.

It must be brutal for her.

"We made a deal, Mum. You're not allowed at the track," I say even though I'd love for her to be there.

"But this is different."

"No, it's not. Let me get a few races under my belt first. That way I don't have to worry about you and can focus on the track. On the car."

"Spencer."

"I'm serious. Why jinx it now? It obviously worked."

She exhales. "I should be there. I want to be there."

"Mum," I say as she tells another person in the background who then whoops.

"Everyone at work is going to be sick of hearing me announce it," she says of the assisted living facility she works in. "But I don't care. My baby finally made it," she sings out loud and then whispers, "I can't wait to see grumpy ol' Maude's face when I tell her. She thinks the only sport worth wasting your time on is cricket. She's going to be pissed when I decorate the activity room with checkered flags every race day."

"Poor Maude," I say.

"Spencer Riggs," she says softly, and I know she means business when she calls me by my full name. "I am so damn proud of you." Pride brims in her voice and tugs at my heart in every way a child wants their parent to love them. "*He would be too.*"

My chest aches in the way a child who yearns for their parent can.

"I hope so."

"I know so." And as if she can feel the need to break the tension herself, she laughs crazily. "This is so exciting. I have to go back to work. I'm sure you have to go too. I mean . . . yahoo!"

"You're crazy."

"You wouldn't want me any other way."

"Very true."

"I love you, son."

"I love you too, Mum."

I end the call, shaking my head and feeling sorry for the earfuls she's about to give everyone. And no doubt, she will.

I start the engine and begin to head home. The track's silhouette is laid out before me, the sky and clouds slowly beginning to turn the colors of the sunset.

But there is one stubborn cloud that hasn't turned colors yet.

One stubborn cloud that looks like a fluff of blue candy floss.

I love you too, Dad.

CHAPTER NINE

Camilla

I STARE AT THE OUTSIDE OF MORETTI MOTORSPORTS.

It's a monolith of glass and stone that stretches for what looks like forever with a huge man-made lake along its front. The lake is framed by rolling green grass with a replica of one of our original F1 cars placed on it.

My nonno was determined to look out of his office and be reminded of where he grew up in Italy. His small house sat near a lake that he'd visit every day with his brothers.

He brought the lake here with him to the town of Wellingshire when he decided to make Moretti's headquarters here in the UK. It's been that way ever since.

I stood here a little over two weeks ago thinking I was just stopping by to have a casual lunch with my dad before heading back home to Rome. I thought he'd give me the usual, *you should move here* spiel. What I didn't expect was for him to ask me to take the helm of the other family business. The Moretti passion project of sorts.

Olive oil made our name a household one. It also gave my grandfather the capital to fund the one thing he loved almost as much as my grandmother—F1 racing.

Fifteen days ago, I left this building confused and unsettled. Twelve days ago, I sat in a pub with Isabella and Gia, rejecting every possibility over this new glow-up plan before heading home to pack up my things to return for my "new adventure."

Now I return, my life in complete upheaval, my new apartment a mecca of unopened boxes and disarray, and my mind determined to make the best of this.

Caution dances with anticipation before melding with the rumbling excitement of starting something new.

But there's something more to it than that as I stare at the symbol of a racing icon that once was the envy of the industry.

There's the list of promises I made to myself. The list I swore I'd work toward and accomplish when my feet stepped over that threshold for the first time as an employee.

Professionally, I'm determined to make a difference here—revamp our image, create a buzz, and somehow contribute to winning a race, or at least take a podium—during my year tenure.

Personally, the list is more profound. Once I step into the building, I have promised to rid myself of all the fear and insecurities I've let own me for too many years. I'm determined to conquer the ghost that I've let hold me back—including the power I unknowingly gave someone else in the process.

New city. New job. New you.

Here goes nothing, Camilla.

I pull open the door and step foot into my new life.

The morning goes by in a blur. I'm taken from department to department and introduced to the staff. I'm far from blind. I see the knowing glances being exchanged. No doubt there are a flurry of texts being sent across the office from cubicle to cubicle with the word nepotism being thrown around like candy.

But I don't let it bug me. Can't. I'd probably feel the same way if I were in their shoes.

Unfortunately—or fortunately for me—Maxim's crash this past weekend and the concern for his recovery as well as how the team should move forward overshadows my arrival.

"Introductions over?" my dad asks when I walk into the conference room where he's arranged to have us work side by side today.

Because that doesn't scream nepotism either.

"They are over. Yes."

"And? Thoughts? First impressions?" His smile is wide and his eyes alive. He looks happy and for now, that's enough for me to make this upheaval worth it.

"Once they realize I know what I'm talking about, they'll come around."

"They will. I'm not worried in the least." He shifts in his chair. "And we need you now more than ever after this weekend."

"How is Maxim doing?"

His drawn-out sigh says it all. "Third-degree burns on his hands. A severe concussion. Brain swelling that they think they have under control but won't know until they wake him up." He shakes his head, concern etched in the lines of his face. "And who knows what he'll struggle to overcome mentally."

"When will they reverse the coma?"

"Not sure. They figure they'll do the debridement of the burns while he's under to save him some of the misery." He puts his chin in his hand. "Fuck, Cam. I thought he was . . . I mean, if it weren't for the HANS . . . I'd hate to think what this conversation would be like."

Every CEO fears having a death or the grave injury of one of their drivers on their watch. My dad is no exception. And he's not wrong about the HANS. Since the introduction of the mandatory head restraint, there have been far fewer head injuries across the board of motorsports.

Technology has most definitely been racing's friend.

"That's better than what you feared forty-eight hours ago, right? So we have to take every positive we can."

"Agreed."

"I hate to sound crass, but what's next? Who's taking over for him in the meantime?" I ask, knowing the machine can't stop.

His sigh says it all. "Not like there's ever a good time for a driver to get hurt, but this is especially a shitty time. We got caught with our pants down. Pashmi was picked up by—"

"Our reserve driver, right?"

He nods. "Yes. Good for him. He was picked up with a full-time contract. Bad for us though since it happened last week, and we hadn't filled the spot yet."

"So you've had to go shopping," I say in terms I can understand.

"Correct."

"In F2 or one from the reserve drivers of other teams?" I ask. Since drivers can switch teams and teams can cancel contracts ad hoc, I'm curious what he's thinking.

"We've called up a driver from F2."

"Oh." That isn't what I was expecting him to say. "Isn't that a huge transition? We don't have that kind of time to wait for some rookie to get his Super Licence. To adjust. To learn the car."

"He knows F1 and has his Licence. Attends Friday practices on the regular with his current team."

Jesus. "So that means he's not even a reserve driver?" If he'd won championships, he'd surely be a reserve driver somewhere.

"I like him for us."

Great. I'm already not liking this decision.

"And how does one just happen upon an F1 car to practice in randomly? Sounds a little desperate if you ask me."

"Or dedicated."

I eye my dad as he goes about his business, typing on his laptop as if this conversation holds zero relevance. "Dad."

"Hmm?"

I wait for him to look up. "This is why we're losing if we're taking the first driver who's available and moderately qualified."

His smile is slow and steady. His voice holds a hint of surprise. "Are we going to butt heads on our first day, Camilla?"

"Isn't this why you asked me here? To learn? To question? To improve what we have?"

"It is. Yes." He nods slowly. "But it's also to sit back and listen. It's hard to learn when you're judging."

Okay, then. This whole working for him thing might be harder than I thought.

"What's his name?" I ask.

"Spencer Riggs. I'm sure you've heard of him."

"Dad, I've barely had time to catch up on the drivers we have on our team in the past week that I've been packing up my life, let alone educate myself on the F2 drivers I never planned on having to know."

"Understood," he says, his grin widening. "I think you're going to like this guy."

"Why's that? Because he's a good driver or because he's charmed you?" He gives me that look that says I need to watch my step. I hold my hands up in surrender. "It's a valid question."

"He has raw talent, Camilla. He has the fastest lap times in F2 this year. Finishes well when his car does what it's meant to. Heard he works well with his team." He toggles his head from side to side as if he's contemplating something. "Besides, I think you're going to love him."

"Uh-huh. Why's that?"

"He doesn't shy away from the camera. Loves attention."

"Well let's hope he doesn't shy away from the podium more."

"Funny," he says, and I grin, the tension between us easing. "I'm serious. The camera loves him and there's a certain charisma I think you're going to like. He's good-looking. Has a large social following that makes him easily marketable—at least that's what Elise says."

Elise. I rack my brain to put a face with the name. My new right-hand. Yes. Elise Coddington.

At least she has opinions she's not afraid to share. I'm all for that.

"Well, that's a plus," I say. "What's his record in F2?"

My dad twists his lips.

"Dad?" I ask, his lack of an answer, answer enough. "This is the part where I tell you I think you're losing your mind. Don't you think that's a major problem?"

"Please. Speak candidly." He chuckles.

"I thought we covered that's why you brought me on board. Fresh eyes. New takes. Blunt opinions."

"Very true." He meets my eyes and pride brims in the air as he smiles. He leans back and laces his fingers behind his head. "Let's see. Spencer Riggs. In the past two years has won the pole five times."

"How many wins?" I ask. Wins are everything in this sport. Wins earn points. And points are vital for money.

But my dad just holds his finger up to quiet me so he can finish. "The guy was born into the sport. Knows every aspect of it like the back of his hand. He has strong engineering knowledge, superior reflexes, and surprising adaptability to different conditions. He's the first to get to the track every weekend and the last to leave. He does sims after a race to study what he did wrong and how he can do better."

"You still haven't answered me," I say, but haven't discounted the attributes my father has listed.

"He's professional on and off the track and knows that team comes first before self."

I clear my throat and lift an eyebrow. "Dad?"

"He won three races last season, Cam."

"Last season? Not this one? And . . . *that's it?*" I ask. Racers who are promoted to F1 dominate their division. They're championship winners. They are known to the F1 crowd. *Do people even know who this Riggs guy is?*

"He's led many races, but things beyond his control have prevented more podiums."

"Like?"

He gives an exasperated sigh. Clearly second-guessing bringing me on board right now. "Engine failures. Cautions at the wrong time. Being hit. He's strong, tenacious—"

"Sounds like bad luck to me."

"It happens. It's racing. But the kid has talent, Cam. Raw talent like I haven't seen in a long, long time. I think this is his time. I think he can be a strong addition to our team."

"Clearly no one else has seen it either or he'd already have a ride, right?" Should I be worried about the decisions he's making now? I mean . . . "Why not pick up one of the reserve drivers of one of the other teams? Find a contract one of the other teams would let you buy out. Wouldn't that be a safer bet?"

He moves steadily to the window so he can look out at the offices beyond his, one hand on his hip. "It would be, yes, but nothing has changed here by taking the safer bet now, has it?" He turns to look at me and I love the mischief in his eyes. "I want to shake things up. I think Riggs might be our guy to do just that."

There is a very thin line between shaking things up and fucking things up. Let's hope the former is what we get.

"*Riggs?*"

"That's what everyone calls him."

Great. Who the hell goes by the name Riggs?

"I'm reserving judgment."

He laughs. "Never one to be a follower."

"Never," I say.

"You're going to like him. I promise."

"Mmm. A cocky driver just promoted, most likely riding high on the perks that come with that move—money, attitude, and women. Can't wait to meet him."

"Sounds like it. You've been around this your whole life. You know how it goes. Some of it's a show—"

"Some of it's not." I chuckle.

"Well, you'll be able to see for yourself because he's on his way in for everyone to meet him."

"Can't wait," I mutter wryly.

"Make sure you act slightly more enthusiastic when you meet him. We want him to actually think we want him here."

"Well, we may want him here, but he's going to have to earn his place, just like I have to."

CHAPTER TEN

Camilla

S EXCITING AS IT IS STARTING NEW SOMEWHERE, IT'S ALSO downright exhausting. The names to remember. The cubicles to map out so you go to the right one. The current marketing plan to review to understand the overall picture of where Moretti is and determine places that it needs to go.

My dad was right. Their marketing is in the dinosaur age. There is so much room for improvement but when something is as aged as this, resistance to change is going to be real. I have a feeling that resistance is going to come from most, not just a few prickly employees. Let the uphill battle begin.

The only way I can think to navigate this—and it's something I pondered while packing—is to use the team drivers to modernize the brand.

They're young. They're handsome—well, Andrew and Maxim are. I don't know about this Riggs guy. Let's hope I have something to work with when it comes to him.

It's an obvious plan—something that is technically already being done. But I plan to tweak that with the Camilla Moretti flourish and innovation.

"So we'll need to get new shots of the drivers. I even have permission to freshen up the company logo before we slap it on everything we visibly can. We need to look at this through the eyes of people even younger than us. We want the early twentysomethings and teenagers who share posts and then reshare to make things go viral. They're going to be who carry the sport on to the next generation."

"I agree. I think this list we've compiled is comprehensive and leaves enough room for interpretation but not enough that we can't act on it." She taps her pen on the desk. "We're off to a strong start."

"And it's only going to get stronger." I nod to Elise, a pleasant surprise to say the least. She's young, knowledgeable, and more than receptive to my ideas. Frustration was her go-to word about Moretti's marketing so at least we're on the same page. "You've had some great input. Thanks for that."

"I'm excited about this. This plan blows everything out of the water that we've done since I've been here. It's fresh and hip and doesn't appeal to old men in their mid- to late fifties like everything else we've done has."

"True." I chuckle and scoot my chair back. "I'm going to go grab a drink," I say.

"I'll be here." She raises her hand over her cubicle wall as a joke.

"Want anything?"

"No. I'm good. I think a fourteenth cup of coffee might be pushing the lining of my stomach too far."

I laugh. "Yeah. Probably. When I get back, I want to go over both Andrew and this new driver, Spencer. Do a deep dive on their socials, on them in general, and see how we can target this new campaign around them specifically."

"You don't waste time, do you?"

I stop and smile at her. "I've got a lot to do and a short window to do it in to prove everyone wrong—that I'm not here due to nepotism. Besides, with Maxim's name in the media right now, it's a good time to capitalize on it. I know that's borderline poor taste, but that's the nature of the beast."

"Agreed. All around."

"You sure you don't want anything?"

"Nah. I'm good."

I take the long way to the break room, letting the nostalgia of being back here take hold.

I thought it would be weird. That just the proximity to this world would have me clamming up and freaking out. But neither have happened thus far and that gives me hope that it will continue to be that way.

Being at a race, in the paddock or garage, however? *That's a whole different ball game.* And something I'll deal with when the time comes.

The break room for the floor is empty when I enter it—which is a miracle in and of itself considering how many employees are in the building at any given time. I welcome the moment of silence.

With its bright sets of tables and chairs, a few couches, a gaming system in the corner, not to mention a wall lined with baskets and shelves that house every snack imaginable for the staff, the space is welcoming.

And holds so many memories.

As a little girl, this used to be my favorite reason to come to work with my dad. Endless snacks and sweets to a kid are like Disneyland.

They're still enticing as an adult.

I'm perusing the selection, my back to the door, when I hear, "Oops, this isn't the conference room."

I turn around and freeze when a pair of gray eyes meet mine. Gray eyes that are part of a very alluring package that I know to be a farce.

"What are you doing here?" we both ask at the same time and then stop as if scripted.

"Oh look, it's Baggy Bar Girl. What are you doing here?"

Baggy Bar Girl?

"Oh look, it's I'm the Asshole or do you prefer Dare Dick? And I could ask the same of you. But hell, I'm surprised you're even acknowledging my presence without needing a dare card in your hand to do so." My smile is as sarcastic as my tone.

He snorts in response and then looks me up and down with a discernable expression. It only serves to piss me off, to remind me of how mortified he made me feel . . . and to make it seem like I can feel each and every goosebump as it forms before they chase across my entire body.

And there it is. *Again.*

I grit my teeth and hate myself for having any reaction other than loathing toward the man standing before me.

I left the whole situation that night in a place of power. I refuse to let him bring me back to anything other than that.

"I'm waiting for an answer," I say.

"Ladies first."

"Oh, look. He does have manners." I tsk. "Too bad I know they're all for show."

"You're entitled to your own opinion. Just like I am mine." He shrugs nonchalantly. "Just my luck you work here, huh? Let me guess, you're in customer service. A nice voice behind a faceless phone."

I take him in. The chinos. The Moretti Motorsports polo shirt. The wide eyes. The parted lips that turn into a slow crawl of a smile when he thinks I'm still checking him out.

I stutter mentally as two things become abundantly clear.

One, there's only one logical reason that he's dressed like this. *And it's not because he's an overzealous fan who's broken in here for a quick thrill.*

Fucking hell.

He's Spencer Riggs. Our new driver. He has to be.

It's the only reasonable explanation, seeing as I've met every damn person in this building—and he wasn't one of them. Plus, he's wearing a driver's polo shirt.

And two . . . he clearly doesn't know who I am. That I'm a Moretti.

"You're staring." His dimple deepens the smugger his smile becomes. "That must mean I'm right about your job or . . . you're still interested in me."

"No. Wait. *What?*"

He chuckles. "You *are* the one who kissed me."

"You *are* the one who kissed me back," I counter and then realize my statement proves nothing more than the fact we have chemistry. Chemistry I'd prefer to deny. "And you are the one who was a prick."

"I already explained it to you. It was a dare. You were there so I acted on it. We shared two intense kisses that we *both* enjoyed. Case closed."

"How do you know I enjoyed it?"

His smirk turns lopsided. "I didn't see you pushing me away when I went in for a second one. Seemed to me by your hands fisting in my shirt you liked it . . . but what do I know?"

He has me there. Has me when I don't want him to in any capacity, and I'm more than ashamed to admit it. I use my confusion and turn it into anger because it's so much easier than to acknowledge how this large space suddenly feels so very small with him in it.

He glances at his watch and curses. "Look, I get that this is the surprise of all surprises, but I have a meeting to get to."

"Yep. Go right ahead," I say.

"Great. Thanks." He nods and takes a few steps back.

"One more question," I say, unable to help myself.

"What's that?" He stops and meets my eyes.

"Why *me* at the bar?"

"I told you. Convenience."

"Bullshit," I say, and the widening of his eyes says as much. "And the reason I know it's bullshit is because you felt guilty when I found out. You chased after me. You showed a stream of conscience when it would appear you don't have one at all."

"What do you want me to say? That you're right?"

"No. I want you to tell me what it is about me that made you single me out."

"Christ." He blows out a breath and looks over his shoulder as if he expects someone else to be standing there before looking back to me. "It was nothing in particular, okay? You're pretty. Beautiful. But that doesn't mean you're my type."

Give this conversation up.

Walk away.

But I don't listen to my own advice. "And what is then?"

"Let's just say I like women who have a little more confidence. Who own their sexuality rather than hide from it." He looks me up and down again—my baggy jeans, my oversized button-up shirt.

Fuck. *Direct hit. Nice work . . . asshole.*

If he only knew how many times I tried to ignore the little voice in my head telling me I was being ridiculous. How many panic attacks were triggered when I tried to prove to myself that I was. *How I hate that I've felt the need to hide for so many goddamn years.*

"And?" I prompt, clearly a glutton for punishment.

"Nah. I think I've said enough." He glances over his shoulder before meeting my eyes.

"Why stop now, right?"

"Look. I'm not sure if you're doing this so you can further bury me in a hole you're digging for me or if you're trying to beat yourself up some more. Neither appeal to me."

"Or maybe I want to see what others think when they look at me. I happen to know for a fact that you have no problem making people feel like shit."

His sigh resonates, and I almost feel bad for putting him on the spot. *Almost.* But now that my request is out there, I want him to answer it.

The problem is he's damned if he does and damned if he doesn't. Reject my request and he's an asshole. Fulfill it and he looks even shallower.

A pained expression pinches his face.

"A guy's opinion is all I'm asking for."

"We barely even know each other. This isn't cool of you to ask me this."

"Just like the dare card wasn't cool. Humor me, will you?" Why do I keep pushing this? Am I trying to punish myself for suddenly *feeling*? For liking the hum that vibrates beneath my skin when he's near?

"Look." He draws in a fortifying breath. "You're gorgeous. Your face. Your features. Your eyes. But it's more than clear by the clothes you're swimming in that you hate your body." My skin heats at his scrutiny. "You may have something against curves, but I assure you, no one else does."

Tears well in my eyes, and I blink them away as quickly as they come. I sniff and nod.

He wrestles with internal emotions I can't name. It's in the depth of his eyes and the pulse in his jaw. Almost as if he just grew a conscience and realized his words hurt.

"You happy? Got your answer? Can I go now?" The words and tone he has differ vastly from the expression on his face.

"You're an absolute prick."

I don't miss the roll of his eyes. He glances at his watch again and swears as I try to comprehend the change from contrite to arrogant. He clearly wants to leave this conversation. So do I. "Look, is this going to be a problem here? The whole bar thing? Because it can't be. I've got too much riding on this to fuck it up." He shoves his hands in his pockets. "What will it take for you to head back to your cubicle and pretend like that night never happened? Money? Signed shit you can auction off? Me giving you a shout out on one of your socials? On my social? Name your price."

There are so many ways I could screw with him right now.

So many ways I could mess with his head.

But I think I know an even better way.

I give a slow shake of my head. "I don't want anything from you. No worries there. I best be getting back to my cubicle now before my boss thinks I quit."

He eyes me warily. "So we're good then?"

I nod. "We're good."

And I just can't wait to see how *good* he feels when we meet next.

CHAPTER ELEVEN

Camilla

G OD, HE'S HOT.

Those three words have fallen out of Elise's mouth more times than I care to count over the past hour. If she's noticed the narrowing of my eyes each time she says it, it hasn't fazed her.

We've continued adding to our list of possible marketing angles. The current focus entails studying the drivers' social media. Andrew's is basic and boring. Riggs's on the other hand? The man knows how to make a splash in marketing himself.

It's one viral video after another. Skydiving on a tropical island. Fresh out of the shower with just a towel around his waist. A silly prank on his team engineer in Formula 2. Sweaty during a workout with his shorts snug and shirt plastered to his chest.

And that smile of his. Each time he flashes it, I think Elise melts even more.

But me on the other hand? Each video we watch only serves to irritate me more. The fact that he is charming and good-looking only adds to it.

"Like, Maxim is a *great* guy," Elise says as she puts her phone down, "but he has the personality of a doormat. No charisma. All racing, all the time. Not that there's anything wrong with that. I didn't mean—"

"You're fine." I laugh. "It's way easier to market someone who gets it. Spencer—I mean, Riggs—*gets it*."

"Have you met him yet?" she whispers almost as if she's not allowed to ask. "I hear he's in the office today for meetings."

I nod. "He is. Pretty sure he already did his uniform fittings and had the custom mold of his backside made for his seat. He's currently meeting the physio guys and going over a game plan for that. Then he'll meet with the nutritionists and eat. Have more meetings to get to know the crew and their jobs."

"All that before he heads to the track later?" Elise asks, eyes wide.

"Yep. He's being thrown into a blender for the next few days until it spits out the newest Moretti team driver."

"Jesus."

"You got that right," I murmur, still confused by the sudden change in his demeanor earlier.

It's not your problem, Cam. After what he did to you? The bar and the comments today? It's most definitely not your problem.

"We'll have to scour his bio to see what we can pull from it or if there are any angles we can play off." I pat the thick manila folder on the table next to me. "That's my next deep dive."

"You haven't looked him up at all yet?" Elise asks me, her expression curious.

"No? Is there something important I should know?"

"Yeah. His dad was—"

"Cami?"

We both look up to my dad's assistant, Halle, standing in the doorway of my office. She's one of those too cute, too bubbly for her own good types of people but she's so damn nice you can't be mad at her for it. You can only wish you had a tenth of her *everything* for yourself.

"Yeah?"

"Your dad asked if you could come up to the conference room."

"I'll be right there," I say as she walks away, and Elise squeals.

"You're going to get to meet him right now, aren't you?" she asks.

The only thing I can do is chuckle because while she may be excited, I may be plotting the perfect way to walk into the room and shock him. No doubt the hour of watching him shirtless and being charmed by his antics have helped fuel the little crush she has for him.

"Most likely."

"I bet he smells good. And that he's even hotter in person." She catches herself and her cheeks heat. "I promise I'm professional." She laughs and then says low and playfully, "Way to make a first impression with my new boss by lusting after our new driver."

"It's actually a good sign. You're the demographic we want to target so if he can elicit that reaction from you, that means we have hope of overhauling our image."

"Really?" she asks.

"Really. I think you're going to be a huge help in getting us there too."

"Awesome." Elise preens with a huge smile and wide eyes. I remember being new at a job and hoping to be noticed. In wishing that my boss would look at me and see potential rather than a younger kid who didn't know what they were doing.

It's only when I'm on my way to the conference room that I realize Elise never got to finish telling me about Riggs's bio. I'm regretting not picking up the folder when I left so I could peruse it on the way up.

Can't blame a girl for wanting to be informed while she shows someone up.

When I arrive, the meeting is already in full swing, so I stand in the doorway and wait to be pulled into the conversation. Spencer's back is to me, his shoulders broad, hands clasped on the table in front of him, and his head nodding as my dad talks.

Is he nervous? Excited? Cautious? Worried about failing again? Probably a mix of all four and then some.

And why do I even care?

Because I have to.

Because my dad is hanging his hopes on this new driver, who I don't want to like, but it seems everyone else does.

My dad laughs and pulls my attention to him where he's perfectly in his element. The CEO part of Moretti is what he does but it's this—talking to the drivers, discussing the sport, being hands-on with the people who make this world happen instead of behind his desk—that he loves more than anything.

And the expression on his face confirms that.

His smile widens when he notices me. "Cami. C'mon in." He holds his hand out to usher me in while my eyes are one hundred percent fixed on Spencer Riggs.

What's his reaction going to be?

"Spencer Riggs, this is my daughter and the woman in charge of marketing, Camilla Moretti."

A slight flare of his nostrils. A quick clench of his jaw. A tensing of the tendons in his neck. I have to give it to Spencer. He hides his shock well. Well enough that I don't get the satisfaction I was hoping for in surprising him.

Damn it.

And the megawatt smile he flashes as he rises from his seat and holds his hand out to me says he knows it too. "So nice to meet you, Camilla. I look forward to working with you."

Our eyes hold as I try to ignore the heat of his hand and the sudden jump of my pulse. "Congratulations on the call up, Spencer—"

"Call me Riggs. Everyone does."

I nod. "Welcome to the team. I'm looking forward to seeing what you can do."

His dimple winks as he lets go of my hand. "I think everybody is."

"This is a different caliber than what you're used to," I say, trying to get a subtle dig in. "Think you're ready for it?"

"No need to worry about me. I always rise to the occasion." A smile toys at the corner of his mouth, and I swear to God, he's flirting with me in front of my dad.

Flirting with me, a woman who *isn't* his type.

I wouldn't have kissed you a second time if the card were true.

"I guess we'll just have to see what *cards* you're dealt, huh?"

He chortles out a laugh and shakes his head. "Guess so."

Our eyes hold for a beat too long before I jerk my gaze away and look at my father. He has the strangest expression on his face—lips barely turned up, eyes narrowed—almost as if he's reading into a situation that isn't there.

"So, Riggs." His smile turns charming. "Camilla here is my marketing guru. And *my daughter*, but you shouldn't hold that against her."

"No, sir." He plays along and chuckles.

"Today is her first, official day with this division of the company, and I have her hitting the ground running. She's responsible for getting your face out to the public. Having people identify you as a Moretti driver. Create the image that you're going to have to back up with your talent."

"Perfect," he says with another glance my way before looking back at my dad. "I'll do my best to give her what she needs."

I all but roll my eyes. The charm and innuendos are as thick as his bullshit.

Men. Not worth the hassle, the complication, or the effort.

He glances over to me and deepens his knowing grin. Why can't he be ugly?

Then maybe my body wouldn't betray me. Maybe my eyes wouldn't be drawn to him, and my lips wouldn't remember how his felt against mine.

Get a grip, Cami. A huge, astronomical grip. The man is clearly immature and spiteful judging by the selfish games he plays on women. *Remembering his kisses should be weighed against those shortcomings. Those . . . red flags.*

The irony. I've spent forever hating that my body doesn't react at all—even to men I thought at the time I genuinely cared about—and now that it does, I don't want it to.

Beggars can't be choosers, Camilla . . . but they can still be picky as hell.

It's asinine that this *sudden awakening* has happened around him. With him.

I study him. His strong hands and corded forearms. His sun-kissed skin and broad shoulders. His gray eyes and dusting of stubble.

And while all of that is attractive in and of itself, the man carries himself in a way that only seems to add to his appeal. Confident. A little arrogant. A lot charismatic.

All the things I like in a man—but that I don't want to like in this one.

He meets my eyes and smiles as if he knows I'm thinking about him. My first inclination is to look away. The man just tried to pay me off downstairs. But I don't. I meet him stare for stare.

It's my job to build Moretti's presence in the F1 and global market. To promote *this* man. Right now, I can't help thinking the latter would be so much easier on my mental state if I hadn't had prior interactions with Spencer Riggs. If I didn't know he could kiss better than any man I've ever known . . . *and wasn't an immature asshole.*

"If you don't need me," I say, starting to move toward the door, but my dad motions for me to stay. Great. Just what I want.

"Glad you're on board. I'm excited to get you on the ground and running. Now, let's talk schedule . . ."

CHAPTER TWELVE

Riggs

SHE'S DISTRACTING.

Her perfume. Her pouty lips. Her no-nonsense quips that she thinks show me how tough she is but in reality, show me she's still interested.

And I think that's going to be a problem.

Because there's nothing worse than a woman fighting against something she actually wants. It makes her irrational. Catty. Determined to win when she's only fighting against herself.

I won't deny she's alluring though. The first moment I saw her in the bar, I was intrigued. Light brown eyes framed by thick lashes. Her dark hair pulled back in a sleek ponytail suggesting she's all business.

My fingers twitch as I'm reminded what it felt like with her hand gripped in it.

I'll give it to her. She's pretty in that sophisticated, classy way. Enough that I'm curious about what's beneath all those baggy clothes. Not that it matters. She's the boss's daughter, and I know boundaries. This opportunity is too important to me to get distracted.

It's a shame though, as she did have the balls to confront me in front of my friends.

I can at least respect her for that and for her sly digs during this conversation. Do I deserve them? Yeah. Probably. But fuck if a guy can't have a little fun at a bar. No doubt she and her friends were looking at guys and guessing how big their dicks were and possibly dismissing them because of their assumptions. So isn't that kind of the same thing?

And if I had known who she was—a bloody Moretti—I probably wouldn't have tried to use her to win the dare.

Fuck that. I'm lying to myself, I would have. She was equal-opportunity bait just when I needed her to be. No qualms about it. Just like there's no lying to myself that the woman most definitely knows how to kiss.

Like top five out of way more than I can count type of kissing. Is it bad that just the memory of it and the sight of her before me has my dick growing hard beneath the table?

"In other words, a recovery without any date as of right now."

I pull my thoughts back to the room. Back to Carlo Moretti and his statements regarding Maxim's injuries. Things I can't think about or dwell on before climbing behind the same wheel my friend just got seriously injured behind. "He's tough as nails. He'll pull through. Hopefully he'll have no lasting effects from it."

"At least we can say we know our cars are as safe as can be. We can't control fire, though."

"Every driver's nightmare."

"Enough about the scary stuff." He claps his hands together and then clasps them. Camilla whips her head up at the sound, her eyes immediately searching over her father. Something about her look strikes me as odd, but I let it go and meet Carlo's kind smile. "So you have everything you need, then?"

"I think I do. Thank you. I'm just . . . taking it all in."

He nods, his smile nostalgic. "It's an easy thing to do in this building that holds so much of our history. Make sure you take a walk around, soak it all in."

"I will. Thank you."

He glances to Camilla, holds her look for a beat. Something exchanges between them I can't quite read before he looks back to me. "As far as I'm concerned, when you step on that grid for the first time as an F1 driver, your slate is wiped clean. A fresh start. We don't look in rearview mirrors at Moretti. We only look forward. If we all had our pasts held over our heads, not a single person would ever get the chance to move forward. Mistakes are made so we can learn from them."

"Yes, sir," I say, emotion so damn thick in my throat it almost hurts to swallow over it. There were a lot of things I expected to happen today, this most definitely wasn't it.

Our gazes hold, the grace he's giving me more than acknowledged and appreciated.

"Good. I'm glad we have that cleared up. So go explore the showroom. Become a witness to our history. The history we want you to be a part of. You only get to have so many firsts in life." Carlo winks. "This is one where you need to step back, pause, and let it sink in . . . because your life is about to get crazy."

I nod, already liking this soft-spoken man whose presence is like a giant in the room. It takes me a second to find any words at all. "Thank you, sir. I will."

"Now if you'll excuse me, Halle keeps waving at me through the window. I think I'm needed elsewhere for something I'm certain someone else can make a decision on." He rises slowly from his seat. "See you at the track. I look forward to watching your testing session."

He makes his way out of the room, and I stand, ready to follow, thinking it's probably better if I leave things with Camilla as is.

The last thing I need is the confusion I felt earlier in the break room to return. Over the need to defend my bullshit friends and our game at the bar. Over giving the justification she demanded knowing why she isn't my type.

Both I felt uncomfortable giving.

It's one thing with a little liquid courage under your belt. It's another when you're standing face-to-face with a woman, and you see the tears welling in her eyes from the words you just hurt her with.

I didn't exactly like that weird feeling in the pit of my stomach I had seeing her again. Even worse was how it twisted when she stood there with a stern expression but devastated eyes.

Wall up.

Defense mode enacted.

Complications averted at any cost.

Now's not the time to have a heart. Now's the time to buckle down and be selfish. To think only about me and the road it's taken to get here.

And to remember I tried to fucking pay off a Moretti.

Jesus Christ.

"A minute please." She's not asking me. She's telling me. *Fucking perfect.*

"Sure. What can I do for you?" I turn to face her, my smile over the top.

She glares at me with her arms crossed over her chest and a sour look on her face. "Funny how that worked out, isn't it? And I didn't even need a *dare card* to do it."

She wants to lock horns. All is not forgotten as I'd hoped.

"Hi, Camilla. Nice to finally meet the *real* you." I'm going the *kill her with kindness* route.

My hunch is it'll irritate her more than anything. She can't be mad at someone being accommodating and over the top, now, can she?

Besides, what driver in their right mind would purposely pick a fight with the boss's daughter? Not me. Not after all the work to get the chance to be here. And I've already started off on shaky fucking ground with Wills and his damn dare cards.

If she wants to play the bitch role, she can. Her last name affords her that. Mine on the other hand, does not.

She scowls at me.

The smile I offer in return is brighter than the sun. "So would you look at that? Huh. We're part of the same team. Teammates. Coworkers. Two people who work together."

Her expression is stoic as she stands across the room studying me.

"The silent treatment it is then. So should I talk for the both of us?" I ask. "Where should we start? How about with, you didn't tell me who you were," I say.

"Same could be said for you." She shrugs.

"There wasn't much room for talking when you were kissing me." *How are you going to handle that one, Moretti?*

A widening of her eyes. The setting of her jaw. "We're here to talk about marketing. You. The company. That kind of thing."

"Oh. I thought you were telling me to stay behind. That you shut the door so we could have some privacy and talk about us." I smile and lean against the windowsill, mirroring her posture.

She doesn't like it so she shifts.

I do the same.

The scowl she gives me is sexy. So damn sexy. "There is no us, Riggs."

"Ah, but there is."

"How so?"

What's going to break through that goddamn armor of hers and make her relax? Ah. Perfect. "You were thinking about how bad you want to kiss me again."

She scoffs. "I do not."

"No?" I ask, loving getting a reaction out of her.

"No."

"So authoritative," I tease. "Not even just a little bit?"

"This conversation is ridiculous." She huffs and moves to a different part of the room.

I make myself the mirror image of her. "How were you wanting this conversation to go? Did you want me to question your abilities? Ask to see your marketing credentials to make sure you know how to handle me?" I wink. "Ask if you're only here because of your name and not your skill set? Is that the argument you wanted?"

Her only response is to cross her arms and purse her lips. If looks could kill, I'd be a goner.

"Or were you hoping for the grovel? I bet you like a good grovel. Particularly from a man. Does it make you feel powerful? In charge? Is that your thing?"

Her expression remains impassive, her body posture stern.

"If it is, what were you thinking? That I'd beg you for forgiveness for the dare card? For the kiss you initiated that we both can admit was pretty damn fantastic? How would that go? Me on my knees? Me showering you with gifts? Ah, I know. Me winning a race and dedicating it to you, right?"

There is a glimmer of a smile. Perfect. It's working.

"You do know you just tried to pay me off downstairs, right?"

"She speaks!" I throw my hands up and flash her a smile. And then I cross my arms seconds after she does. Her sigh is everything. "And of course, I tried to buy you off. Anything for the good of the company, though, right? You need your driver in good standing with everyone. Especially the people who make this whole world go round." I shrug. "And here I am."

She rolls her eyes. "You think this is going to fly? This whole holier-than-thou schtick you've got going for you?"

"Schtick?" I bat my eyes innocently.

"You forget that I have a partial hold on the keys to your success."

"Ohhh. She's playing hardball now. I've got to tell you, Moretti, a strong female is one of those turn-ons for me. Like, I love a woman who can handle herself. So you've been warned."

"Warned?" Another struggle to deny her smile.

I hiss out an exaggerated breath. "Yeah. We're talking googly-eyes and stuttered words. Weak knees and demands to get in my—never mind. I can't say that here." I give a dramatic look around. "That's not politically correct enough."

"I don't really think you care what's politically correct."

"But out of everything, that's what you're the most pissed off about. My attempt to bribe you in the break room?"

"No." Her mouth goes in a straight line but her eyes—God, those gorgeous fucking eyes—light up with humor.

"Oh, you were thinking about how incredibly hard it's going to be to market me. I'm demanding. So fucking demanding. Viral when I need to be viral, but that makes it difficult when I have a fucking clusterfuck of a history with a self-destruct label attached. A *Riggs* in every sense of the word. *Just like his dad.* Then again, let's hope not or you won't have a racer to market, right?"

I'm on such a roll that I don't even think about the words I say, but her lips shock open, telling me she has no clue about my dad. The softening of her eyes even more so.

I don't want pity. I don't fucking need it. What was just fun and games and banter suddenly became so much more.

"*Riggs?*"

"Nope. None of that." I shake my head, immediately rejecting the compassion in her voice. "Because you know exactly how I feel. Two offspring fighting to make their own names and prove the privilege that came with it doesn't factor in. Yours is an attribute. Mine is a detriment."

I clear my throat. I move about the room. I need to shake the sudden swell of emotion from my head.

This was supposed to be funny. Supposed to be a *kill her with kindness* undertaking and now all of a sudden, I'm uncomfortable and want this over with.

"How about this?" she asks, contributing for the first time. "For the record, I think my dad picked the wrong replacement for Maxim."

My feet falter and thoughts skip around. But more than anything I recognize a lifeline when I need one—and she just gave me one. Something to feed off rather than get stuck thinking about my dad.

"Well, shit. Okay." I nod several times and purse my lips. "I'm the wrong guy, huh?"

I glance her way. She has her arms crossed over her chest again and challenge back in those eyes of hers. "Yep."

"Fortunately for me, your opinion isn't the one that matters."

"Don't be so sure about that."

"Why are you trying to turn this lovely little chat into something different? Are we back on the grovel aspect? Should I get on my knees right here?" I point to the floor and pretend I'm lowering myself.

"Don't you dare," she shrieks.

"Then why? It's because you're afraid you're not going to be able to control yourself around me, isn't it? The looks. The body. The sense of humor. I'm fucking irresistible. I'm thinking nice guys finish last in your book, right? So that means you don't want to like me because of that."

I put the words out there, but I'm not thrilled with her dig. Then again, I deserve that and a fuckton more.

"No. It means we need wins. It's imperative."

"And?" I bait her.

"And I don't think you have the experience to get them for us."

"You're an expert on this, I take it? Much like you're an expert on how incredible I kiss, right?"

"This isn't a joke. I'm serious."

"So am I." I lean my arse against the table and once again mimic her posture. "What's it going to take to prove to you I'm worthy of the ride?" My quirk of an eyebrow at the innuendo a mere habit. *Possibly not.*

"Points. A podium. A win."

"All in that order? I mean, that's a pretty fucking hard bargain you drive."

She shrugs. "It's my job to make this place known again. Those three things will get it known."

"I'll get it known."

Her smile is wide and borderline mocking. "I get you have to be confident to drive two hundred miles per hour—"

"Two hundred thirty at times if we're going to be accurate." She hates the correction. Perfect. "And I can deliver on that."

She snorts. "That's a pretty lofty goal for someone who's never raced F1 before."

"Your dad has no qualms about my ability."

"Why are you here? Are you capable?"

"What?" I ask as I move closer to her. Close enough to see the pulse fluttering in her throat and to hear her quick inhale. My eyes flicker down to her lips and her kiss I don't want but still remember, and then back up to her eyes that are a little wide and startled. My voice is low and even when I speak. "I'm here because I've proven myself. Am I capable? You bet your arse, I am. Am I sorry for hurting your feelings earlier in the break room?

Regretful for not telling you that you're gorgeous with or without changing your style? Yes and yes. What else do you have for me, Moretti?"

Our eyes hold as she opens her mouth and then shuts it—then steps back abruptly, a chuckle of disbelief falling from her lips.

"What's so funny?" I ask. "You were just thinking about kissing me again, weren't you? Is it the ChapStick? It makes my lips super soft and kissable. I'd like to think it's more my skill though—"

"Oh my God. Will you stop it? Please?" She holds her hands up and is met with my grin.

"Why? I was just about to tell you about the little hearts you're going to draw all over your calendar."

Her neck startles like whiplash. "What?"

"On the days you get to see me. You'll be so excited that you're going to color in little hearts on the day—fill the whole square full of them—to annotate it."

She shakes her head, clearly at a loss for how to handle me—which was exactly my goal. "This has been . . ."

"Enlightening. Frustrating. Stimulating? Do you need a thesaurus?" I tease.

"Argh!" she says, and I laugh as she moves toward the door. "I have to get back to work."

"I thought this was work." I narrow my eyes and play dumb. "Is it not?"

"No."

"Okay. I hope you have an excellent rest of your day." I grin as she meets my eyes one last time. "Hey, Moretti?" She stops at the doorway but doesn't turn around to face me. "I'll get you to draw dreamy hearts on that calendar yet."

CHAPTER THIRTEEN

Riggs

POWER.

It's beneath me.

Behind me.

All fucking around me.

The difference of three hundred eighty or so horsepower between my F2 car and the Moretti F1 car doesn't sound like much, but it is. There's a major difference between going two hundred miles per hour and going two hundred thirty.

Plus everything about my new car is just . . . smooth. The suspension. The ride. The way it takes corners. The way it flies along the straights.

And complex. The telemetry. The readouts. The amount of information my race engineer has on my car from a few laps around the track. The way he can use it to help me drive better.

And things I need to make adjustments to. My molded seat. How I come in to box—because while the cars are similar, there's still a difference in handling and a difference in personnel. The steering wheel and the car's reactions to it.

It all feels familiar but new at the same time. Exciting and intimidating. Overwhelming but *right*.

"Good lap time, Riggs," my race engineer, Hank, says as I veer toward pit row and the paddock. "I think once you get a better feel for the car, we'll shave more time off."

"It felt good. Fast. Just need to *feel* this car more. Work on my spatial awareness. How quick it responds. What the different tires feel like."

"Hopefully we'll get an array of weather so we can try the different variations and you can test with them."

"Fingers crossed."

"The team is working overtime on your seat. Should have it in the next two days," he says, referring to the seat that is essentially molded to my body. It hugs where it needs to hug and props me up where I need to be propped up since we essentially lay down as we drive.

That and the seat is removable so in case of an emergency and they need to remove a driver from the car without injuring them further, they can take the whole seat out with them.

"Thanks. A lot of people are working hard to help make this happen. I appreciate it."

"Just doing our jobs."

"It's still appreciated."

"We have all week reserved so we'll get you familiar with everything. We'll go over all the readouts in a bit, once the crew finishes up their tasks."

"Thanks, Hank."

I pull up to the pit marker and cut the engine. Crew members mill around the car, but I just sit a minute. I don't unpin the steering wheel. I don't undo my harness. Instead, I sit with my helmet on, my hands on the wheel, and the visor strip dark enough to hide my eyes as I close them and let this sink in.

Every frustrating DNF. Every karting event where I fought my second-rate kart and the expectation and damnation that came with my last name and still crossed the line before everyone else. The wearing doubts. The endless dedication. The podium victories.

I'm finally fucking here. *Part of the ultimate dream.*

Don't get used to it. Isn't that what Ari reminded me? Isn't that what I fucking know firsthand? To not get used to it because it's harder when you know what it's like and it's yanked away than to imagine what it's like but never get a taste of it.

But it's not going to get yanked.

It's not.

This feels too good. Too right. And yes, I have nerves rattling through me and no doubt will puke before the first race, but I'm *finally* living the dream.

Let Maxim get better. Fine. Great. Let him return to his seat here, to his place here, but only after everyone gets a chance to see what I can do.

There are rumors that two drivers might retire at season's end. I want one of those spots. I'm going to fight like hell to get it.

Hands reach in to help unbuckle me. I hold on to my thoughts with a determination as fierce as the one that got me to this point and unfold myself from the car.

Helmet and balaclava off and hand scrubbing through my hair, I wait for the team principal, Omar, to approach. "How'd it feel?"

"Fast and loose and I say that in the best possible way." I have a feeling I'm going to be getting this question nonstop until I hit some unspoken lap time that makes them all feel more secure in their decision to offer me the call-up. "It flies on the straights. I need to get used to the grab of the brakes. I was a little timid in the corners but that's just because I want to get more confident in knowing where it is spatially before I cut closer to the wall."

"That's good feedback. All normal for someone stepping into it." He adjusts his hat on his head as we walk deeper into the garage.

"Another few days and I'll be good to go. You'll see more time shaved off my lap times."

Omar nods and pats me on the back. "That's what I like to hear. Now let's get inside and look at the metrics. You'll see the data will allow us to make the tiniest of adjustments that will make differences."

"I'm eager to learn more."

"You say that now. Just wait till you're falling asleep and all the data keeps running through your head, keeping you up."

"I won't complain," I say as we cross the alleyway from the garage to the paddock. Normally this is where our logistics crew sets up our hospitality suites, but it's not a race weekend so our whole building is no doubt being transported to the next race on the circuit.

"They've let us set up an office back here," Hank says as he pushes open a door where numerous computers sit on desks with headphones at each table. "Let's start reviewing before Anya whisks you away."

"Anya?" There are so many people and names being thrown at me so fast my head is spinning with trying to keep everyone straight.

"Your PR minder. You haven't met her yet? She'll be your right-hand. Recording all your interviews. Overseeing your schedule. Minding where you need to be."

So my new Fontina, but with a much bigger scope.

"I glanced at your schedule. You're quite the busy man. Physio after Anya. A team meeting to review boxing. Sim time to practice the next circuit. You up for it?"

"Been waiting for this chance my whole life."

"Now go get that thing off," he says, referring to my dark blue race suit from my old team. "We only like red around here."

CHAPTER FOURTEEN

Riggs

"TO OUR BROTHER FROM ANOTHER MOTHER. TO OUR FRIEND. To the man who just got the ride of his life. We wanted to take this last opportunity to party with you before you have to be on the straight and narrow for the rest of the season," Micah shouts from where he stands on one of my chairs to the crowd of people filling my flat.

Some I know.

Some I don't know.

Some are . . . who the fuck knows.

"Straight and narrow? Me?" I snort although that's exactly what I'll fucking be.

This is my last hurrah. One last kiss goodbye to partying and drinking for a while. Not like I do it much anyway but in certain instances, I'll let myself cut loose.

And then I'll pay the price because cutting loose doesn't mean I skip cardio and training the next day. It means I do it twice to punish myself for it.

"Your straight and narrow will last three days tops," Junior says.

"Maybe five," Micah chimes in, "but what you'll lose in hangovers, you'll gain in F1 perks."

The F1 perks: more horsepower, more money, rubbing shoulders with the rich and famous, learjets for travel, five-star hotels to stay in, and pussy galore. That was what we'd decided I was gaining with my step up earlier during our preparty party.

"True, but don't worry, we'll drink for you in the meantime. We'll party for you. We'll fuck for you—"

"Whoa! I can still fuck for myself, fuck you very much," I shout out and get a roar of cheers from everyone in the room.

"I volunteer as tribute," a voice yells out toward the back of the room causing another round of laughter to sound off.

"Promise us one thing," Wills says as he empties a lager and sets his glass down.

"I'm not promising you shit. The last time we did that I almost ended up with a tattoo of Tinkerbell on my arm," I say. The damn dare cards.

"But this . . . this is important."

"Lay it on me, mate," I say.

"Your first major success in F1 must be celebrated with us. Here. Another party like this. Right here." The whole place erupts into cheers and hoots and hollers. "It's paramount to celebrate the victories. Even little ones."

"Yeah, yeah," I say. I'm not promising shit to him. Will I allow myself one night to cut loose? Probably. Many of the racers I've looked up to over the years have expressed how important it is to give yourself a release every now and again.

That even elite athletes need a break occasionally.

"In all seriousness," Micah says, raising his shot glass again and changing the topic—which I more than welcome. "We can't wait to watch you fucking kill it at the Spanish Grand Prix." Wills lifts his shot and we all follow suit. "This is our send-off, be safe, win a race, we're proud of you, party for you. Sláinte, mate."

"Sláinte" is called out by the thirty or so people filling my new flat. It's going to be a fucking disaster in the morning, but hell if I don't have the money now to hire someone to clean it up.

The glass goes up. The burn goes down. And my head fucking dizzies as I make my way around the room, wanting to sit. Needing to sit. But getting pulled every which way by so many people.

I'm slipped more numbers than I've ever been before. I'm asked for more favors to get people into races than possible. I lose count of the number of drinks I consume.

It's not many. I just don't drink that much during the season so it hits me a lot harder.

How in the hell am I going to get up in the morning for cardio? At eight a.m. no less?

Fuck me.

Should have thought of that beforehand, Riggs.

I stumble and Micah's laugh barrels through the room. "You look like hell."

"Thanks." I give him the thumbs up. "Bedtime."

"But it's only two thirty," Junior says, slapping a hand against my back.

"Exactly." I take a sip of water in my hand. "You fuckers can keep going. I've got to sleep." I wobble on my feet as the room does some weird Salvador Dali-like thing in my head. "Just make sure everyone's out of here before you pass out."

"Ah, man. What's the fun in that?" Micah slurs through his smile. "We'll take care of it."

"Thanks and . . ." I try to find my words but my head is so fucking fuzzy. "Thank you for this. It was pretty damn cool of you." I fist-bump both of them and stumble into my room.

Shut the door.

Fall into bed.

And then feel a warm and very naked woman slide up behind me.

Jesus fucking Christ.

F1 perks, indeed.

CHAPTER FIFTEEN

Camilla

"I HAVEN'T BEEN HERE LONG ENOUGH TO BEGIN OPERATION GLOW-UP. Can you give me at least a few more weeks?" I beg Gia who has been all over me today with texts and calls.

"You're going to keep saying that. But I'm a tenacious bitch. I'm not going to let this go." Her laugh is rich as it floats across the line.

"I know that. Believe me I know that. But I'm in the middle of so much chaos. Let me get my bearings before you start changing me."

She sighs but I know she's going to cave. "Fine. Whatever. But you know what would get me out of your hair?"

"What?"

"You do your own glow-up. Surprise us. Then we'd be so shocked we might forget about the setting you up part of our plan."

"So bribe you then."

"Whatever it takes. Or you can bribe me with one of your hot racers. I'll gladly take one of them as a consolation prize."

"You're sick."

"I know and I love it."

"Goodbye, Gia."

"Goodbye, love."

I hang up the phone with a smile on my lips. A smile that sticks with me until the afternoon hits and my constant yawns replace it.

"Tired?"

"Exhausted." I look up to Elise as she moves into the conference room where I've set up camp for the time being. Her hands are filled with folders, her laptop, and what seems to be her always-present Starbucks. She has a pencil tucked behind her ear and the myriad of bangles on her wrists clink together with every movement.

She's stylish in the boho-chic way that I once attempted but never looked good in.

"How'd the meeting go?" I ask.

"Good. Great really. We'll see what their proposal is when it comes across."

"Thanks for taking that for me."

"Not a problem." She points to the various things laid out all around me. "Maybe you should call it a day. Get some sleep."

"Too much to do." And there is. I can list ten things off the top of my head right now.

"Considering you're here before I arrive and still at your desk when I leave, I'm thinking maybe your exhaustion has to do with you working too hard." She unceremoniously dumps her files on the table with a thud. "Give it a few more weeks and everyone is going to ignore your last name and know you're here because of what you know and not because your dad's sitting on the top floor."

"That's the hope. Thanks. But today's lethargy is more due to an obnoxious neighbor with no courtesy."

"Ugh. That sucks." She plops down and takes a long sip of her cold brew. "My old flat was like that. Such a nightmare."

"I'm hoping this was a one-time thing."

She holds up her crossed fingers and smiles. "I have good news that might help. New shots of the drivers are in. The camera loves both of them so it's going to make our jobs that much easier."

"That's always a bonus." I stifle another yawn and eye her coffee. I definitely need a caffeine hit myself.

"It is. I already had the team create mock-ups with their photos. Kimberly is picking up the samples and should have them up here in the next thirty minutes. Once you decide and approve, I think we should get them pushed out as soon as possible."

"Agreed. We'll prioritize that first. Then I want to go over a list of possible campaign ideas we can begin with little planning or involvement with outside forces so we can get some attention to this team. Some may work.

Some may not. You know as well as I do that social media is a crapshoot in getting things to take root."

"A definite crapshoot."

We spend the next thirty minutes filling each other in on what we've accomplished. When Kimberly delivers the graphics, we switch gears and turn our focus on them. The pros and cons of new photos of the drivers. Andrew is a good-looking man—the classic looks of his Swedish heritage—with blond hair and blue eyes, but the man looks bland when standing next to his teammate. Riggs looks dark, edgy, and dangerous, but that is contrasted against his vibrant smile and piercing eyes.

"Jesus," Elise murmurs. "The camera loves him."

I nod, my opinions a weird list of contrasts. The kiss in the bar. The dare card and the hurt it caused. The trying to buy me off in the break room. The conversation in this very conference room where he tried to win me over with his wit and humor. The shock of later that day learning who he was— or rather who his dad was—and not knowing how to respond.

Each one of those interactions brought out a different emotion, a different feeling, and I'm struggling with how to prioritize which ones I should feel when I see him next.

Because seeing him is inevitable. I may have purposely been everywhere he's not the past few days, but I can't make that last much longer.

Is he the villain or the hero, Camilla? Or maybe a little of both?

I stare at his image looking back at me and give a resolute nod. "It definitely won't be hard to push these," I say.

Ideas I've been mulling around start to take form. "I think we need—"

A knock on the open door has both Elise and me looking up. And the image in front of us comes to life in the form of Spencer Riggs standing before us.

Elise sucks in a quick breath beside me.

"Ladies. Good morning." He meets my eyes and nods before crossing the room and holding his hand out to Elise. "Spencer Riggs. Nice to meet you."

Elise is frozen in place, eyes wide, smile plastered on. "Hi. Yes. Hello." She reaches out as he takes her hand, and she slowly melts from the touch. Or at least I notice that she does. "Nice to meet you. We were just studying your package."

Riggs's eyes shoot up and he grins. "Well. If that's what the new marketing campaign is—"

"Oh my God. I mean *marketing* package." She points to the pictures as I die of embarrassment for her. "Marketing. Pictures. Not your—you know—*that* package." She buries her head in her hands as her cheeks burn pink. "I think I might be dying a slow, painful death right now."

Riggs reaches out and squeezes her shoulder, unfazed by the fact that she's clearly crushing on him—and wins points with me for the action. "Don't you hate it when your mouth betrays you?" he says and looks at me with a lift of his eyebrows as if to imply ours both have in the short time we've known each other. "You're fine. See? I already forgot what you said."

"I still think death is a better option," she says but peeks up between her fingers and meets his reassuring gaze. "But thank you."

He nods and then points to the image I like the best. "That's the one you should use."

"Oh, are we a marketing expert now?" I ask, needing to put that wedge back between us that his kindness to Elise removed. And as I sit here and stare at him, I'm not sure why.

I lie.

I do know.

Something about Spencer Riggs scares me. And scares me in all the best of ways that I don't understand or am sure I want to. I've been in his presence a handful of times since we first met. While I purposely limited our interaction, it didn't matter because each and every time, I'm left questioning my innate reaction to him and my sanity soon thereafter.

His presence is like a feather skimming over my skin. It creates chills at the same time I want to brush it away. Or a better comparison would be the static electricity in the air before a lightning strike.

It's there. You can't see it, but you can feel it. It makes my entire body take notice, react.

None of the reactions are wanted and yet they happen regardless.

Ignoring my comment, he moves in between Elise and me and braces his hands on the table to take a closer look. "Not a marketing expert, but I know what catches people's eyes and that graphic will do just that."

I shift my chair to give me distance. I don't need to smell his cologne. I don't need to see the dark gray flecks mixed in the light gray of his eyes. I don't need to feel his arm absently brush against mine.

And by the way he looks at me when his eyes meet mine, he knows exactly what he's doing.

"Why?" I'm not sure if I'm referring to his graphics opinion or why he keeps touching me.

A ghost of a smile paints his lips.

He knows *exactly* what he's doing.

"We look like good cop, bad cop. The face they know and the new one who's unproven. It's the contrast people will like. We're a team but we still look like we're willing to battle on the track." He shrugs. "Make me the bad guy. I don't care. It's always more of a splash when the villain triumphs."

"You're new to F1 and you're asking to be the anti-hero?"

He shrugs. "Call it what you will. I'm just letting you know that I'm okay with however you paint me. It's already going to be a battle to win over Maxim's followers through no fault of my own. They're loyal to him and I'm taking his place. Then there's Andrew who never rocks the boat. And now there's me—a new face they're sitting back reserving judgment on. The men will love that I bring their wives and girlfriends into the sport and hate me for it all in the same breath."

"Wow. You do think highly of yourself."

"No, I know how this game works. Besides, I'll prove myself on the track. I've promised you that." He looks at me and nods. "That's where I'll answer all their doubts."

The yawn comes out of nowhere, as they often do, and I unsuccessfully try to stifle it.

Riggs lifts an eyebrow as he stands to full height—of course putting his crotch right in my line of sight.

"Pardon me," I say as I try to focus back on the graphics.

Riggs turns around and rests his ass on the desk, still between us, and meets my eyes. "Am I boring you?"

"No. Sorry." I give a quick shake of my head. "My damn neighbor kept me up all night. Loud music. People knocking on my door accidentally instead of his."

"We both know you don't have a problem confronting people," he says, "so why didn't you march down there and give them a piece of your mind?"

I glance over at Elise who has her brow furrowed, no doubt wondering how Spencer Riggs knows I don't have a problem confronting people.

"I just moved in. The last thing I want to do is piss people off. People who I might need help from, like getting my mail or whatever, since I'll be traveling so much."

"Tell him your dad's a copper. That he drives by often to check on his little girl or some shit like that."

"It might be easy for him to put two and two together who my father is once he learns my last name."

"True." He rocks his head from side to side. "I still vote for telling him off. It seems you're grumpy when you're tired. That, and you need all the beauty sleep you can get."

I see the mischief in his smile and sense the banter that he's searching for. Elise, on the other hand, doesn't. Her eyes are shocked open and her jaw is lax as he makes his way to the doorway.

I snort. "I guess that means you should sleep twenty-four seven."

"That's not what the public thinks." He winks. "Need anything else from me, ladies? My good looks? My witty charm? My unwarranted opinion?"

"How about better driving skills?" I offer to which he hisses in a breath at the dig. Then the rich sound of his laugh fills the conference room as he turns to face us, his grin sinful.

"No worries. I've got those in spades."

"I haven't seen proof of anything yet."

"Bitch. Bitch. Bitch," he singsongs while rolling his eyes playfully. "I can show you my skills firsthand."

Our eyes hold and no matter how impassive I try to keep my features, my smile wins. "I'd say you wish, but we both know you don't."

"What is it they say? One man's dare is another man's pleasure."

"I don't know who *they* are, but I think *they* have the saying wrong."

"*They* are me, and the saying is right."

"You're incorrigible."

"Thank you." He mock bows. "It must be brutally hard staying mad at me."

"Not hard at all."

He quirks an eyebrow, gives a suggestive purse of his lips, and rocks on his heels. I swear to God that smile has a mainline to something in me even I don't understand. A slow, simmering ache that flutters about and makes me shift in my seat to abate it.

He chuckles and heads out of the room with both Elise and me watching his swagger as he does so.

"Was he just flirting with you?" Elise asks, tone awed. "Because I'm pretty sure that was flirting."

"It was bantering. And it's . . . we met by fluke before." I wave a hand in indifference as if it doesn't matter. "It's a long story. Chance encounter where neither of us knew who the other was." Time to redirect. "Where were we? Oh. Right. Graphics. I think we all agree on which ones work best."

"You're deflecting."

"Am I doing a good job of it?"

She snickers and points to the graphic. "He's right about the villain one."

"Let's not give him any credit, shall we?" I joke.

"Okay, but there's something I want to show you. Something I think we can use somehow to the Moretti advantage."

"What's that?"

She shifts her laptop so we can both see the screen, types a few things in the browser until a social media site pops up, and within seconds, Riggs's face is on the screen.

It's clear he's been running. His shirt is draped around his neck and hanging over his pecs. His hair is wet, making it curl. His chest is misted in sweat, and his face is slightly red from exertion.

"Another one that's viral," she murmurs.

I can see why. The man is definitely not a hardship to look at.

Riggs is holding the phone out as he takes the final strides up a steep dirt trail with lush greenery surrounding it.

"Okay, so I was finishing up my run, a bit hungover if truth be told, so I'm trying to concentrate on anything and everything other than throwing up. And I got to thinking about some advice a friend asked for. Something I want your opinion on." He pauses and takes the end of his shirt to wipe the sweat off his face. He looks over his shoulder at someone and then grins at the camera.

Very convenient placement of his bicep flexing, if I say so myself.

"So this friend of mine was at a pub a few weeks ago, kicking back pints with his mates. A dare was made. Get a phone number of a woman. A woman who you thought would be going home alone that night. Why would she be going home alone, you ask? That was up for the friend to decide. To save his ego, the guy took the dare. He won. Charmed the pants off a girl he had no intention of really dating. She made the first move and kissed him. He made the next and kissed her back."

He's talking about us.

Fucking talking about us.

My expression must be a dubious one because Elise pushes pause and says, "Hold on. I'll make my point when the video's over."

She pushes play again.

"Look. The arsehole used her. Plain and simple. Then she found out it was a dare. Obviously, her feelings were hurt. My friend figured he'd never see her again so no harm, no foul." He scrubs a hand over his jaw and the scrape of stubble can be heard right before his sigh. "But he did see her again. Is he the arsehole for not apologizing to her? Or is the victory, a victory, and he should just take it and run? Should he worry about her feelings and offer an apology or does he carry on like nothing happened? Is he the arsehole or not?"

The video ends and begins to start again, but Elise stops it before it can replay. But even with the video stopped, we can see the number of views and likes ticking upwards.

That's not what the public thinks.

So that's what that comment meant.

"The comments are insane. People asking their own AITA questions to him."

"AITA?"

"Am I the asshole."

"Christ. Riggs has become a regular *Dear Abby.*"

"Look at all these people asking for advice. Giving advice." She stops and looks at me. "Wait. Who's Dear Abby?"

I laugh and shake my head. That just made me feel old. Granted *Dear Abby* was in my mother's time, but I still know who she is. "*Dear Abby* was an advice column. People wrote in to a newspaper. She answered and they published it."

"Like online?"

I hang my head for a beat and chuckle. "No. In an actual printed newspaper."

"Wow." Her eyes widen. "So she's *super* old."

"Something like that." I can't with her right now. I glance back to the screen and the static image of Riggs. "Why are you showing me this . . . *oh.*" I draw the sound out as it hits me. "You think we should have Riggs do an advice column. Interact with fans like that."

"Exactly. If he's getting this much attention with one post, could you imagine how people would react if they knew that they could submit a question and possibly get the chance to have Riggs answer it for them?"

I stare at her, my teeth sunk into my bottom lip as I contemplate her concept. "It could work. He definitely has the star power and charm to pull it off." I pause, my mind running with the idea. "I definitely think we can use this to our advantage."

"Perhaps we can request he be shirtless." She winks and then says, "*What?* You know that would only help the video to go viral."

She's right but . . . how unprofessional is that to ask him to do that?

"We need to find a way to tie it to Moretti," I say.

"Exactly. And we do that by having him give his advice while he's shirtless, sweaty from working out or racing, and with say, a Moretti hat or boxer briefs on?"

"We have Moretti boxer briefs?" I ask dumbfounded. *Why? Just why?*

She laughs. "No, but I'm sure we can have some made up quickly if need be."

"Of course, we can." I roll my eyes, hating that I'm picturing him wearing just those. Picturing him and *liking* what I see.

He'd go for it. He's arrogant enough that he'll enjoy the attention, and I'm selfish enough that I want him to do it because I know it'll work.

Shit. When did I go from hating the guy to wanting to use those good looks that first attracted me to him to my company's advantage?

Talk about a shift in gears.

Then again, that shift began that first night we met, didn't it? When he chased after me in the bar because he cared that he hurt my feelings. It doesn't mean I had to forgive him or even believe the words he said—at the time I didn't—but that also shows he has a conscience.

And now the more I get to know him—in person, through things my coworkers have said about their interactions with him, through the various interviews I've watched—is it so bad that I'm starting to believe he's not just the jerk with the dare card? That he's actually goofy, thoughtful, funny . . .

This is not how *this* was supposed to go.

"You're overthinking this," Elise says.

"No, I'm picturing it. A shirtless Riggs in a Moretti hat or in the paddock with the sign behind him . . . something like that works for the visual, but we need to make a reason for people who don't know him to come to his page and participate."

"What are you thinking?"

"I'm thinking something that you can't buy."

"Quit stringing me along. What is it?"

"An all-expenses paid trip to a race with guest privileges in the paddock."

"Shit," she says. "You're not playing around, are you?"

I grin. "Nope. If we're going to make a splash, we might as well make a big one, right?"

"I love it, but uh . . . I'm leaving it to you to get that one signed off by—" She points overhead, presumably to my father's office.

I wink. "Leave it to me."

"See, you do come with benefits," she teases. "I think this is a stellar plan, but you do know what a pain in the ass this is going to be, right? Sorting through a bazillion entries and figuring out which question for Riggs to give advice on?"

"True, but that means a bazillion people are paying attention to us, and that's a crap ton more than we currently have so it's a win."

"You do have a point."

I lean back in my chair and fold my arms over my chest. "It also behooves us to have him keep his adrenaline junkie shit up that he posts. Stuff that doesn't shove Moretti down their throats. So his page will grow organically and then we'll sprinkle in some Moretti branding."

"His social media is a gold mine. Once you start watching it, you can't help but keep scrolling." She twists her lips with lines of concentration etched on her face while she thinks something over as I've learned she's prone to do. "Now we just need to get the Moretti name visible in it somehow—if he's okay with it since it's his personal page."

"He'll be okay with it. He's trying to impress the new boss. Trying to extend this call up to F1 and turn it into a permanent gig somehow. He's hungry to stay here so he'll let us use that eagerness to our advantage."

She snorts. "And even if he weren't, he's an F1 driver. He's all about himself like they all are. Of course, he'll say yes if it means more attention, more adoration on him."

"Very true." That's one thing that hasn't changed in my time away from the sport. The drivers are all the same. Selfish. Competitive. Skilled. Focused. "Let's let him get his first race under his belt. We'll work behind the scenes while he focuses on that. Then we can launch it the week after."

"So no bringing it up to him?"

"Not yet. I'll figure out when it's best to approach him."

"Makes sense. So actionable items are you'll approach him about AITA, and I'll get with our team and see if we can refine this idea with graphics and slogans and how to facilitate it so we can hit the ground running." She clicks away on her keyboard taking notes.

"Sounds good."

"Do we need to pull Andrew into this somehow?" she asks.

"Definitely. He has the same ego, but his is more the dark horse, quiet achiever vibe. The spotlight isn't his thing like it is Riggs's. Or . . . oh, maybe he does an ask a racer a question type thing. Something that's a little *less* . . . if that makes sense, because he doesn't flex as *loudly* on social media."

"Smart. Good idea." She goes to sip her coffee and then makes a sour face. "Shit. I'm empty." She rises from her seat. "Do you want anything? I'm going to get a refill."

"No. I'm good. Thanks though."

Elise moves out of the conference room, and I hit play on the video again. She's right. Riggs's videos are addictive.

I watch a skydiving one. A mountain climbing one. But I'm drawn back to replay the advice video.

I watch him.

I listen to his words.

Is this his way of non-apologizing, apologizing? His olive branch extended to me to smooth over what happened?

The angel and devil war on my shoulder. Wanting to believe the best of him as a person but also knowing how racers are, how guys like him are, more than I'd like to admit.

Isn't that what drew me to Brandon all those years ago?

I glance back at the screen and Riggs frozen in place. Is that why he popped his head in here out of the blue?

To see if I'd seen his post yet?

To see if I forgave him?

I stare at his bright smile and handsome face and know the answer. Yes. I probably already do.

But there's no way in hell I'm letting him know that yet.

Where's the fun in that?

CHAPTER SIXTEEN

Riggs

MY EYES BURN AND HANDS ACHE.

My shoulders are tight, and my neck is stiff.

Is it from all the extra cardio and neck isometric exercises we've been putting in to try and prepare my body for the g-force?

Or is it simply from hours sitting in this simulator, memorizing every curve of the racetrack I'm going to be starting on this week?

Regardless, I need to work on not being so tense in my neck and shoulders. Or it's going to be a long race. I'll get a headache from the tension. It will affect my reaction time. It will add a few hundredths of a second in a sport where that blink of time matters.

Omar comes into my periphery as the screen goes black, and the simulated racetrack in front of me disappears.

"That was impressive. Better than I expected," he says in his deep baritone.

"I'm going to take a break and then get back at it for a few more hours." I extricate myself from the sim. "But I want my helmet and gloves on. A full dress rehearsal so I can replicate the race with the things I can control."

He lifts an eyebrow. "Noted. I'll let the crew know."

"Thanks. I don't mean to keep them here—"

"Yes, you do, and we're all more than okay with it." He smiles for the first time. "No one at Moretti is going to frown upon dedication."

I don't know how to respond to that without sounding like a kiss-arse, so I don't. Rather I go through my stretches to unlock my muscles, one by one, with the routine the physio has written for me.

"Tell me something," he says.

"What's that?" I look up at him from where I'm touching my toes.

"The sim? Why have you spent so much time on the Suzuka course in there?" he asks, referencing the Japanese track.

I struggle with what will appease him.

The truth will scare the shit out of him. Because it's the track on which my dad died. Because if I can master the one place that terrifies me more than any other, then I know I'm ready.

Because being there, as morbid as it sounds, allows me to feel a small piece of him with me.

I didn't realize anyone was watching what I was racing when I stayed here late and worked on my own.

"It's my benchmark course. One of the more technical tracks," I say. "If I can do well there, then I can adjust and adapt and do well anywhere."

He nods but his eyes meet mine and say he knows I'm partially full of shit. "Every driver has their course they have to master. That must be yours."

"It is."

He lets the topic go and moves toward the door. "Dinner's ready for you in the cafeteria."

"Thanks."

"And don't stay too late. We leave for Barcelona in the morning."

"I won't."

I stand and stare at the door he just went through, his question front and center in my mind.

No one at Moretti has come out asked about my dad or talked about his legacy that floats over my head like a lead balloon. Close enough it's noticeable but far enough away I sometimes don't see it because it's trailing behind me.

Even Camilla hasn't. Not even after our hash-it-out session in the conference room.

But I know everyone knows. I'm pretty sure there have probably been some side discussions about it. I know everyone wonders how I'm going to handle Suzuka if I'm contracted with the team when we get to that part of the circuit.

And yet no one flat out addresses it.

Was it something Carlo mandated? Or do the people here have enough decorum to let me prove the person I am rather than attach labels made for another man?

It's food for thought as I head upstairs, eat a quick meal before jumping back in the sim.

But there's one more thing I have to do before my night is complete and I'm ready to head out.

Something that's going to be harder than hell to do, but that I need as a reminder to ground myself in reality.

To pay my respects for this opportunity.

"Riggs?" Dee picks up on the first ring, her voice more than surprised.

"Hi. How are you?" I ask out of courtesy when I already know the truth. She's exhausted. Frazzled. Owned by worry and fear and everything in between.

"You know," she murmurs.

"I can't imagine." The lump in my throat grows to epic proportions. "Any change?"

"His hands are . . . They're hoping that the skin will heal and eventually allow him the same mobility so he can flex his hands and . . . you know." *Hold a steering wheel.*

I can't imagine loving a man who willingly puts himself in danger. And letting him race again, letting him do what he loves, despite already dancing way too close with death.

Isn't that what Mum did with Dad?

Isn't that what she does for me?

Christ. I run a hand through my hair and draw in a deep breath. "I'm sure it will work. And he's still in good spirits?"

"He is."

"The kids?"

"They're better now that they got to see him, and he doesn't look as scary as he did with all of the tubes and bandages."

"That's good." I pause. "He still doesn't want to talk to anyone?"

"No. I'm sorry. But he knows you've been calling and checking in. He just . . . he doesn't want anyone to see him like this. It's ridiculous but it's not a battle I'm willing to fight right now. It's pride mixed with preserving his image so other teams don't look at him as weak. Nonsense in my book, but it's how he feels."

"Okay."

"Thank you," she says, sensing the conversation ending.

"For?"

"For the flowers. For the texts. For not forgetting about him while you're getting your chance."

I pause for a beat and look at the sim laid out before me. At my dream all around me. "Yeah, it kind of fucks with your head." His accident. His injury. The magnitude of all of this. The demons I'll have to face when I get on the track.

"I'm sure it does," she says softly. "But get in the car and have one hell of a race. Maxim would want that for you. Only the best for his Riggs."

"Thanks, Dee."

And when I end the call, I'm one step closer to being ready.

CHAPTER SEVENTEEN

Camilla

"JESUS. HE REALLY DOES HAVE A HARD-ON FOR RIGGS, doesn't he?" I ask as I hold my badge up to the turnstile screen and am granted access to the paddock.

I scroll through the article written by Harlan Flanders. It's normal to question a racer's ability—especially when he's new—but there's clear spite in the article. Obvious dislike. And a tinge of bitterness.

"He does," Elise says as she walks beside me. Normally she doesn't travel with the team, but I cleared it so she could this time around. It's important to see what she's promoting. "If I didn't know better, I'd say he's pissed about something Riggs did and is getting back at him through the press."

"Great. Just what we need." But this ridiculously one-sided, subjective article is the welcome distraction I need.

It gives me an excuse to have my head down and attention diverted to my phone as I walk into a paddock for the first time in six years.

I don't look up. I don't take in the garages to the left of the wide alley or the custom-built hospitality centers each team has shipped here to the right.

Instead, I focus on my phone.

On scrolling with my thumb.

On pretending I'm not taking a huge, monumental step forward that my therapist would give a standing ovation to.

Once I'm inside our "offices" here, I'll feel better. Safer. In a place Brandon wouldn't dare step foot inside.

"Camilla?" Elise asks.

"What? I'm sorry. I was . . . reading." I look up from my phone.

"It's incredible, isn't it?" I look where Elise is looking and take in the paddock.

Everything is bigger and more extravagant than I remember. Than the pictures do it justice. The hospitality offices are three stories and wide with detailed exteriors. Decks on top with Ping-Pong tables, a catered restaurant on one floor, offices on another. And of course, a place for the media to have their time with the team.

"It is," I tell her. *It most definitely is.*

I stand there slack-jawed and overwhelmed.

But more than anything, the fear I expected to feel—the hand trembling, skittish glances over my shoulder, paranoia type of fear—*isn't there.*

There's an undercurrent of excitement. Of anticipation. Of being back here.

It's completely unexpected and one hundred percent welcome.

I'm under no illusion that the fear won't return at any time. That seeing the back of a blond head and broad shoulders ten feet ahead of me in the crowd, won't incite a panic attack at some point.

But I'll take this as a win right now.

A win I can't wait to experience again.

CHAPTER EIGHTEEN

Riggs

I T'S A TECHNICAL COURSE.

My pulse rushing in my ears is the only thing I can hear as I stare at the light tree in front of me from my starting grid of P10.

Sharp turns. Tight corners.

My hands grip the wheel as my dad's voice—or what I imagine it still sounds like after having memorized almost every interview I could get my hands on over the years—runs endless loops through my head.

Long stretches where DRS can be enabled.

My stomach churns with a mixture of excitement and nerves. Both welcome. Both charged.

There is no room for mental errors. None.

Motors rev all around me. Racers I've looked up to for years. Racers I've competed against on the lower circuits. Friends. Enemies. All are now competitors.

One lapse of concentration can put you in the wall.

I love this sport and simultaneously hate it. Each time behind the wheel—in every level I've competed in—is a struggle between doing what I love and fearing it.

Between honoring my dad and the possibility of ending up like him.

Of taking every turn and forgiving myself for wanting to let up as I imagine him hurtling across the track and then hating myself for the same fucking reason.

"Radio check, Riggs."

"Check."

You've got this, Spence. My dad's voice.

Drive fast. Be safe. Cross the finish line for me. My mum's words from our phone call earlier.

Light. Light. Light. Light. Light.

I jump off the line and into the fray of all the other cars vying for a good start.

Be careful of the first turn. Accident probability is high.

I can hear his voice even now that I'm battling off the line for position and use it as a means to calm me if that's possible. Adrenaline surges through my veins like never before.

You got this, son. You'll settle in. Get the first lap under your belt and you'll settle in.

And I do.

It takes longer than one lap though. In fact, it feels like I'm holding my breath through the first four. Because four laps are farther than I've ever gotten in an F1 race before. Now it's only more firsts from here on out. And at ten laps in, when I overtake my first car, another charge is added to my confidence.

"Well done, Riggs," Hank says in my ear.

I push more now. Drive a little harder. With more certainty.

I fight hard but clean. Perhaps more timid than usual, but this is the big leagues and crossing the start/finish line after sixty-six laps is more important than anything to me. Proving I can handle the car and place in the middle to top of the pack is the goal the team has set.

Proving that a Riggs can once again sit in the seat of an F1 car and not kill himself is what I need.

I fight the ghosts of my past at the same time I fight the competition around me. Lap after lap. Turn after turn. Battle after battle for the next position.

Endurance is the key. You drive to survive. You drive with the hope that when you unfold yourself from the car when the race is finished, you'll be in a position better than you started in.

Preferably one in the points.

It's over in a heartbeat.

The checkered flag waves.

"That's P7. P7, Riggs," Hank says in the steady voice he's directed me with all day. "Excellent job for your first race. Goal accomplished. You finished in the points."

You finished in the points.

That is what Carlo Moretti asked of me today. To finish in the points in my first ever F1 race with Moretti.

Or as he said, in my first ever F1 race, because to him, this is my first.

And I did it.

For the first time in two hours my heart dislodges from my throat and lands back in my chest where it belongs.

But that doesn't mean my head doesn't stop spinning or lips don't stop smiling.

Holy shit.

Holy fucking shit.

"Well done, guys. Thank you for all the hard work," I say to the crew listening over the radio as I pull down pit lane and up to my garage. "Great job. Really great job."

What a goddamn rush that was.

Every single second of it.

Every kilometer of every lap.

I cut the engine and climb out of the car with the help of my crew. Hooting and hollering meets me, and I look up to above the pits to the box where all my friends are hanging over the edge cheering me on, traveling all this way to support me even with the knowledge that I won't be able to spend much time with them due to my whirlwind schedule.

I give them a mock salute then a fist pump before drawing in a deep, fortifying breath.

I finished in the points.

Am I fucking dreaming?

Is this for real?

But before I can do or think anything else, an FIA official meets me at my car. He directs me to the scale in a neutral garage area. They note my weight, which will be added to my car's, to make sure our combined total meets the minimum weight requirement.

"Riggs." I head toward the calls of my name when the official FIA business is done and walk into the Moretti garage. My crew greets me with a raucous round of applause. I may have overshot my pit marker by a few centimeters when I came in to box and scared the shit out of them, but they're still here. Still excited that I earned points for the team.

I'm welcomed with pats on the back and praise, but when I make it through the crowd, I come face-to-face with Mr. Moretti himself. Carlo is leaning against the wall, his hands in his pockets and a look of satisfaction on his face.

"Congratulations on your first race in Moretti red," he says, reaching out to shake my hand. "You did us proud."

"Thank you for the opportunity, sir." I nod. "I'll only get better."

He smiles. "I know you will."

I turn to go . . . I have no idea where I'm supposed to be next so I'm more than grateful when I hear, "Excuse me," cutting through the noise. Anya fights her way through the throng. "Congrats. Great first race. That only means more people want to talk to you than the norm."

"Sure. Fine." Adrenaline still races through my veins. I could talk to the whole world right now and I wouldn't be tired.

"You say that now." She chuckles. "The job is only three quarters of the way done. We have a presser. Photos. Then the team debriefing."

I nod, already having been briefed on what to expect. "Sounds good. I . . ." I meet Camilla's eyes from across the chaos of the garage. She's standing there in her typical baggy jeans and oversized Moretti polo shirt. The expression on her face is unreadable.

"Oh," Anya says when she sees who I'm staring at. She glances at Camilla again before looking back toward me and makes an indiscriminate sound of disapproval. "Just a thought. It's probably not the best idea to piss off the boss's daughter."

"I know."

Why would she be mad . . . *oh*. She must have seen it.

That's the only reason she has to be pissed at me. *That I can think of at least.*

And truth be told I completely forgot I'd scheduled the social media post. I did it days ago without thought. The last meeting we had, she'd told the team what she was hoping to implement after this race. I simply was trying to preempt it and give her a taste of what they were asking for.

But I may have gotten so caught up in race week and all that comes with it—that I forgot about the post.

"Do I even want to know what you did? What kind of mess I'm going to have to try and fix for you?"

"Nope." I flash a grin at Camilla before turning back to Anya, the high I'm on bigger than anything I've ever had before. "I can clean up my own messes just fine."

CHAPTER NINETEEN

Camilla

THE TRACK IS DARK.

The city lights in the distance and the full moon overhead provide enough light to make out shapes—the water barriers and their reflective tape, the chain link fences, the red curbs of the chicane—of the racetrack below me.

I don't know why I came back here. The paddock has been or is in the process of being broken down so they can be stored in cargo containers and shipped to the next track alongside the cars themselves. The stands have been cleaned up of the trash the crowd left over the duration of the race. Yet, I found myself sweet-talking the security at the gate to enter the facility and make my way up to the press box.

Was it perspective I needed?

A chance to decompress and pat myself on the back for overcoming my anxiety and being here this week?

Elise can go for me, Dad. I have so much to do, it's not smart for me to leave the office.

Yeah, that didn't fly. And in hindsight, I'm glad it didn't.

The past few days only showed me that I'm stronger than I thought I was.

And that is never a bad revelation to have.

That's not to say I didn't have a few flutter bouts of panic from near run-ins with him. Or that there wasn't a quick retreat to hide in the bathroom stall and remind myself—*fuck him.*

But I did it.

I got through the week with minimal freak-outs.

I did something I didn't think I could and am partially mad at myself for letting the fear own me and not attempting this sooner.

I'm leaving Spain stronger than I was when I walked in here five days ago, and I'll take those baby steps any day of the week.

"You're not supposed to be here."

I jump at the sound of a voice at the door. A voice I've come to know. I turn and let the sigh fall from my mouth. "You're on my shit list, Riggs," I say.

"Perfect. That seems like a pretty comfortable place for me when it comes to you." His smile is broad and his eyes are playful. "What are you mad about this time?" He holds out his cell phone. "Should I take notes? Make a list? We wouldn't want to forget a single thing I'll need to grovel for later."

Most guys become less attractive the more they open their mouth and talk. Riggs, on the other hand, becomes sexier.

I cross my arms over my chest. A useless form of protection when it comes to him. "The advice post you did last night."

His grin is lightning quick and lethal in the handsome department. "What about it? I was only getting a jump-start on what you and Elise were asking of me."

"I believe the caption was: *Should I or should I not sleep with the boss's daughter? Asking for a friend.*"

"Yeah. Your point? People had all kinds of opinions. *And propositions* for me." He shrugs innocently. "I'd show you, but you might get a little jealous of all of those women wanting me."

"Hardly." I snort. "*My point* is what you're implying."

"I'm not implying shit. Just asking a simple question to the adoring public." He bats his eyelashes innocently.

"People are going to think you're talking about me."

"Let them."

I pick up my phone and glance at it. "One point four million people and counting to be exact."

"That many views already? I'd say mission accomplished."

"No. Not mission accomplished. You weren't supposed to pick the questions yourself. We are supposed to do that for you. We're supposed to—"

"I can handle what questions I answer on my own page. I had Moretti gear on. I made sure the branding and visuals were there. The last thing I like, Camilla, is to be controlled."

"Fine. Great." I throw my hands up, pissed that this has interrupted my peace and quiet. "But you're not the one who had to answer to her dad if I was sleeping with a driver."

Because *that* wasn't embarrassing.

"You're a big girl. I'm pretty sure your sex life is none of your dad's damn business. Besides, last I checked, you hated my guts and all you have to do is lie and say that I'm not particularly fond of you. We can stick to that story and all will be good, right?"

I stare at him for a beat. Open my mouth. Shut it.

"Why, Camilla Moretti, are you actually starting to like me?" he asks, his smirk leading the way.

"No." I scoff. "I never said that."

"You didn't have to. You wear your emotions on your sleeve, and I can see yours for me right there"—he points to my bicep—"like a big ol' tattoo."

"You're insane." But I'm laughing and isn't that something that he seems to bring out of me more than anything else?

"Perhaps." He shrugs and winks. "But let's not tell anyone. We're busy pretending we hate each other, remember?"

"That's not going to stop people from assuming we're screwing around. Life's not that simple."

"Of course it is. Why complicate it? Sometimes making people guess or wonder adds to the intrigue. There's a reason in my videos the towel drops every once in a while, but they never get to see what's beneath."

"Oh Jesus. We're full of ourselves, aren't we?"

My comment is met with a grin and that's it. I hold his stare and take him in. His hair is fresh from the shower. He's wearing a black V-neck shirt and a pair of dark blue jeans.

"Why are you up here?" I ask.

"I could ask the same of you," he says. "We probably have the same answers. We're both taking in our first race under our belts in our new positions."

"I thought you'd be out partying on the town with your friends."

He shrugs. "I went out with them. Watched them kick back a few— I'm in training mode. I'm trying to keep my girlish figure." He lifts his shirt up to show off abdominals that look like they were cut from alabaster. "You think it's working?"

The fact that I have to force my eyes up to meet his says his exercising is most definitely working.

"You don't drink during the season?" I ask. Most drivers give themselves a cheat day every now and again. I'm curious what Riggs thinks.

"Not now, no." He purses his lips and toggles his head from side to side. "I did promise my friends that we'll have one night of reprieve, one night of celebration. That'll be my one slip."

"Your friends. *Those* friends, I presume?" The *dare card friends*.

"Yes. The ones you were so nicely mingling with today. Total monsters and arseholes, right?"

I level him a look. Of course, they weren't monsters or assholes. They all seemed to be pretty stand-up guys. But I'll hold my grudge a bit longer.

"You never answered. You're here. Why?"

His expression softens, almost becoming nostalgic. "I don't know, something drew me back here." He sets down the duffel bag he has on his shoulder and steps up to beside me so he can get a full view of the track. "Maybe it was the quiet after such an absolute high. Maybe it was your dad's advice: to soak it all in—each moment as they come. Maybe it was . . ."

"Maybe it was what?" There's a quiet calm to Spencer Riggs right now that I'm experiencing for the first time. I saw it pre-race today and simply thought it was his preparation. But it's here now and there's something about it, a realness, that's endearing in a way I don't want to admit.

"Maybe I'm just saying goodbye to some old ghosts. Or possibly thanking them. Maybe hoping I can stop finally chasing them. I'm not sure which one's better."

The raw honesty in his tone is unexpected and captivating. The sigh he emits soon thereafter says he wishes he could take his confession back. His attempt to change the subject reinforcing it.

"Why are you here, Camilla?"

I fall quiet for a beat and look out over the dark, desolate track and think about earlier today before the race.

In a startled panic I push open the bathroom door and shut it at my back. My heart races and the anxiety feels like fingers clawing their way up my throat. Closing off my airway. Strangling me.

Breathe, Cam. Just breathe.

I can hear my therapist's soft voice repeating the words over and over as I bend over and put my hands on my knees and focus on my breathing.

It was the capped head of blond hair I caught sight of and that distinctive laugh I heard from across the way. I stood there frozen as he looked over at me and grinned. Fucking grinned like what happened never happened.

The panic took hold then. The trembling. The memories replaying through my mind.

I freeze when I hear the distinctive sound of someone throwing up in the stall on the far end of the bathroom. Before I can pull myself together, the door flings open and Riggs is standing there pale as a ghost, sweat dotting his hairline, and the same shakiness I feel exemplified in his exhale.

He looks shocked to see me in here. To be caught in a vulnerable moment. But he narrows his eyes at me and chuckles as he bends over the sink, splashes water on his face, and rinses his mouth out.

"Looks like I'm not the only one who hates race day, huh?"

"No. Yes." I close my eyes momentarily and see the urinals to the right of me and realize I walked into the men's room. "I'm sorry. I didn't mean to—"

"Camilla." His voice stops me and forces me to look up at him.

"It's okay. It's okay." He nods and then walks out and back to his crew.

The man beside me is no doubt facing something like I am. Earlier today I was convinced it was just pre-race nerves, but then later as I watched him call his mom before he got in the car, as I listened to commentator after commentator remark about his father, I came to the realization that he could be struggling with confronting the memory of his father. The man who had a reputation as a wild and reckless driver. The driver who had been warned numerous times, black flagged by a few others, and who had lost his life in the most horrific way. And Riggs had only been nine years old.

Yes, I looked him up. His faults. His accomplishments. The criticisms and the accolades. And the pictures of a grieving widow and a little boy who is his spitting image then and now.

If my assumption is true, the reason I'm up here pales in comparison to the gravity of Riggs's, but if I've learned one thing over the years, it's to acknowledge that everyone battles something. Even if they're not equal in scope, they're still just as poignant.

"Why am I here?" I repeat. "It's been a while since I've been at a race. It was *a lot* for me to be here today. To be in the paddock. The garage. Much like you, I'm just giving myself a moment to let it soak in."

"That's why you were having a panic attack in the bathroom?" He narrows his eyes at me.

"I wasn't. I—"

"Save it, Camilla. I'm highly acquainted with what they look like. I know them firsthand because of my mum. You were having one. No explanation needed." He shrugs. "All I need to know is if you're okay now."

I study him and wonder who this man is. Cocky one minute. Crass the next. Sweet the moment after. Curious constantly.

"Yeah. I am."

He nods. "Good. So why'd you walk away from the family business? The racing side anyway," he asks.

Wow. That was a subject change I didn't see coming. Rather than stutter through an excuse, I go with being vague. "So many reasons."

The silence eats up the space and when I turn to finally look at Riggs, he's taken a step closer, but it's the look in his eyes that arrests me. Curious. Inquisitive. Concerned.

"I think there's one reason in particular, but I won't push you on it."

"Why do you say that?" My back is up instantly.

His shrug is indifferent but the expression on his face is anything but. "Because we all have that one secret we keep close to the vest. The one we think might ruin us but hope it won't. The one we hide in bathrooms having panic attacks over. And then add another layer of hope that maybe one day it'll get better." He sounds like he's speaking from experience and for some odd reason, that makes me feel less isolated.

"Perhaps," I murmur.

He turns to face me, leaning his hip against the desk, and studies me intently. "Does yours have anything to do with the paddock, that every time you enter it you look like you're afraid the boogeyman is going to pop out of somewhere? Is that why you hid in the men's bathroom?"

My heart jumps at his words, but I temper my expression to avoid giving anything away. "I don't think you have any clue what you're talking about."

"Huh. The prized and only child of the Moretti family. The one who was at every race, all the time, like one of the crew. Then she wasn't. Gone like a ghost. Now she's back." He narrows his eyes at me. "A casual observer would think something might have happened to push you away."

Is this not his version of pushing?

"That something being university to make a name for myself?"

"A name for yourself but you came back to work for the family olive oil business?" he asks, expression smug. "You're not the only one who can google search someone, Cami."

"It's Camilla."

He shrugs. "Maybe I like both."

"Maybe I don't want you to like . . . *never mind.*" It's not even worth the argument. And even worse, is it weird that I oddly like the fact that he took the liberty to use my nickname?

"Why'd you come back to the family empire?"

"What does it matter to you?"

"It doesn't. Just call me curious as to why you left and why you're back."

"I left for school. I left because there was a nasty crash at the race when I was last here and I didn't like it. It's one thing to know the sport is dangerous. It's another to be here when it happens." The lie is smooth as if it's been practiced. It hasn't.

And the minute the words are out, I realize how fucking callous I sound to a man who sat and watched his father die in a crash.

"Riggs. I'm sorry. That was—"

He holds his hand up to stop me, and then speaks as if his history is a different one. "So let me get this straight. You left because of an accident. And then you come back the day after a big one takes the number one driver out. Clear as mud."

"You're reaching into things that don't exist, Riggs."

But his eyes search mine in a way that tells me he isn't believing a word I say. Rather than argue with me, he just holds his hands up as if in surrender. "I'll stop reaching." He smiles softly. "I know what we should do."

I look at him leerily. Why is he suddenly giving up so easily? "What?"

"Celebrate." He turns his back and digs something out of his duffel bag. I'm surprised to see that it's a bottle of Dom Pérignon. I start to refute whatever it is he's going to ask, but he shushes me. "Humor me, Moretti. I think you and I both need to do something to commemorate our first race in F1."

"Where did you—ahhh," I shout out as he pops the cork, which flies somewhere in the booth. It pings off the ceiling at the same time the stream of bubbly liquid spills from its tip and splatters onto my shoes.

CHAPTER TWENTY

Riggs

CAMILLA'S LAUGHTER RINGS OUT AS SHE JUMPS OUT OF THE way, and I right the bottle so it stops spilling.

"Here." I hold it out to her.

"What? Right out of the bottle?"

"Yep. We're classy like that. Besides," I say as she takes it. "It's not like our lips haven't touched before, right?"

"Don't remind me," she groans and then takes a super long sip straight from the bottle. She hisses when the bubbles hit her nose, her cough turning into a laugh.

"Hey, I'm not all that bad," I say as she eyes me over the bottle before taking another sip. I search her face and am glad to see whatever darkened it seconds before is gone and has been replaced with annoyance *for me.* "In fact, I'm a damn good kisser."

She looks over at me, cheeks full of bubbly, and snorts as she swallows her mouthful. "You kiss yourself often, then?"

"No."

"Then how would you know that?"

She hands me the bottle, and I shamelessly take a large gulp. One drink isn't going to kill me, right? Besides, the moment feels like it needs it. "I've been told that. Before. By many people."

"Many. *Huh.* Could've fooled me." She holds her hand out for the champagne, and I pull it away.

"You think I'm going to share with you after you insult me?"

She looks at me. "Imagine that. Being insulted about something you can't change. My clothes. Your kiss." She shrugs and despite her words, her smile and tone are playful.

"Touché." I hold on to the champagne. I still think she dresses like a tomboy, but hell if there isn't something about Camilla Moretti that I'm starting to like. Her attitude. Her sass. That slight vulnerability that peeks through every now and again. "And for the record, I *am* a good kisser."

She snorts.

"Just stating facts."

She rolls her eyes and laughs. "I need another drink to simply stand here and stomach this."

"I'm not sharing anything when you're bagging on me."

"Poor baby. Did I hurt your ego?" She pouts out her bottom lip and then when I mimic her by rolling my own eyes, she lunges for the bottle I'm denying her.

I twist my body to prevent her from reaching the bottle. She trips and I stumble, or some cliché movement like that, but we end up chest to chest, our faces mere inches apart.

The laugh that falls from her mouth stutters to a breathy stop.

I can feel the warmth of her panted exhale on my lips.

Can feel the brush of her breasts against my chest with each inhale she takes.

Can see her pulse skittering along the line of her throat.

For the briefest of moments, I forget where we are, who she is, and my reasons for the dare card that night.

All I remember is the taste of her kiss.

The softness of her lips.

That low, strangled moan that she emitted from the back of her throat that tugged on my balls as if it were her fingertips.

Her eyes are startled wide and look much how I feel. Shocked. Discombobulated. *Turned on.*

I reach up and brush a lock of hair that has fallen over her cheek and tuck it behind her ear—something, anything, to keep my hands busy and my mind off her parted lips and wide eyes. It's been one hell of a day and a bit too somber a night. But this? This feels like something I want but know I shouldn't have. *Like something I desperately need, as if I'm drowning and Camilla is the only thing that can revive me.*

"Should we test your theory about my skills?" I murmur.

"Riggs," she whispers in a shaky voice that has me wanting to step into her and kiss that vulnerability away.

My conscience wars.

With what's right.

With what I don't want but suddenly do.

With the fucking fallout—something I normally wouldn't care about—that I don't want to fuck up given my first complete experience of F1 under my belt.

My fingers skim her bare arm as I bring it down and she jumps back as if I've electrocuted her.

"Sorry. I fell. I didn't mean—"

I shove the bottle toward her to stop her from rambling and to prevent myself from stepping forward and doing what I can't get out of my head.

She's nervous. It's the way her hands need something to do. Fix her hair. Touch the desk. Adjust her shirt on her shoulders. Lift the bottle to her lips and then back down.

"Why do you have that? Champagne? The bottle?"

Huh. The woman who never gets rattled is rattled.

Why do I like that I did that to her?

"Another driver gave it to me today as a congrats."

"Oh." She looks at me and then my hands and then back out to the track.

Knock. Knock. Knock.

The sound comes just seconds before a baritone chuckle rumbles through the press box.

Camilla and I jump as if we're two live wires that have touched. Their sparks fading black as we turn to see the security guard standing in the open doorway.

He has broad shoulders and dark curly hair. He eyes the both of us with distrust. "I thought you were just running in here because you forgot something?" he asks Camilla. His gaze sweeps the room, taking in the champagne in my hand and the portion spilled on the floor. "And I didn't let you in here."

My smile is a flash of appeasement. "I was worried about her. She hadn't come back yet so I came in to find her. You weren't at the gates. You—"

"Oh my God," he says. I see the minute he recognizes me. "Spencer. Riggs. Mr. Riggs. Sorry. I didn't mean to—I'm sorry—but I have my job to do."

It does wonders for an ego to be recognized by the general public. "No worries. We were just caught up in how cool the track is when it's empty." I glance to Camilla and then back to the guard. "We'll get out of your hair. Just give us a second to collect our things."

CHAPTER TWENTY-ONE

Camilla

"CAMILLA." *THAT VOICE.*

I'm restless.

Antsy.

Exhausted from the week.

But the heat of Riggs's breath on my lips.

The banter in the press box hours ago that own my mind.

The rumble of his voice in my ears. It's created an ache that burns as I stare at him standing before me, in my hotel room, looking at me as if asking whether I'm sure I want to do this.

I want to say no. Should. He's a guy I don't want to like. That I don't want to want.

But we shared a car back to the team hotel.

We walked down the hallway toward our rooms.

And he followed me inside. I didn't protest.

Should we test your theory about my skills?

"Camilla," he murmurs but doesn't reach out to touch.

I hesitate, but it only lasts a second before I test the theory I've been thinking about in the taxi all the way back here. *If he touched me, if he did more than kiss me, would I freeze up or would it only add to the burn he's created?*

He leaves the first step to me.

He makes me want it. Makes me act on that want. Makes me crave his kiss and his touch and the feeling of our skin sliding against one another's.

All things that I tolerated before. Tolerated to make the person I was dating feel good. Feel like we were okay. Like I was okay.

But right now feels so much different.

I step into him. Our mouths meeting in a brush of lips. Once. Twice. Then another one that he deepens.

Our tongues tease each other's. The taste of champagne and mint. Of desire and lust.

Our hands roam over one another's skin. Mine up his back to hook around his shoulders. His up my front to cup a breast and the other to span my lower back and hold me against him.

Tiny fireworks going off every place we touch. Nerve endings that I thought were dead and gone forever are detonating. One by one. One after another. Each mini explosion working toward what I hope will be a grand finale.

"Camilla," he groans when my fingertips pull up the hem of his shirt, him pulling it the rest of the way off, as I find his firm, warm skin beneath.

And even that is new to me. Touching him and finding pleasure in it. Tracing my fingertips up the grooves and dents fuels the ache it seems only he can create within me.

I pull my own shirt over my head, desperate to feel his fingertips on my skin. To know what it's like to be touched when it feels like forever since I have and have enjoyed it.

Our lips meet again—hungrier this time. More desperate. And we chuckle against each other's lips as we both reach back to unhook my bra at the same time.

I drop my hands. I let him do the honors. And the way he slides his hands from my ass up my bare back—the strength in them comforting and arousing at the same time—before unclasping my bra and casting it aside.

He leans back, his eyes roaming over my bare chest, and hisses in an appreciative breath. "Jesus, Camilla."

My nipples pebble, the ache as poignant there as between my thighs. I didn't know breasts could throb like this.

"Riggs." His name is a plea and a command all at once.

But he stands there and waits for me to act. To initiate. To show him what I need.

I reach out, put my fingers into the waistband of his pants and tug him toward me. He lands against my chest, but this time—our bare skin touching, the warmth of our bodies against each other's—is like lighting the fuse to a stick of dynamite.

I've waited six years to feel something, anything. And now that I do, I don't want to wait another fucking second.

I want to drown in sensations. Be overcome with feeling. I want to burn from the ache.

"Touch me," I murmur. "Kiss me." I kiss him and tug on his bottom lip. "Fuck me, Riggs."

A chuckle falls from his lips as he leans back and looks at me. "You sure you know what you're asking for?"

I quirk a brow. "I'll hold on tight, but that means you better take me for a damn good ride."

His laugh bellows around the room. His eyes meet mine. A chance for me to back out. To save face despite my spoken bravado.

But I do neither.

Instead, with my eyes locked on his, I begin to unbutton my jeans. To pull down the zipper. To let them drop off my hips and pool at my ankles on the floor.

"Fucking hell, woman," he grits out, seeing me without a mountain of baggy clothes on for the first time. "You're . . . breathtaking."

And if there is one thing I'll take away from tonight so far, it's the way I feel hearing those words. Hearing them from him.

I have a visceral reaction to them. My throat swallows. My lips part. My breasts grow heavy. Between my thighs grows wet.

He undoes his top button.

"Stunning."

Pulls down the zipper.

"Sexy."

Pushes them and his boxer briefs down over his hips so his cock springs free with the action.

"Irresistible," he says. Or at least I think he says it because I'm too busy looking at Spencer Riggs in all his gorgeous, naked glory.

The man is a masterpiece and his cock falls right in line with that theory. He's a little above average in size with firm thighs and a sexy-as-hell V on his abdomen that have my mouth going dry.

"I think this is going to be a problem, Cami."

I whip my eyes up to his. They've darkened and his lids are heavy with desire. "Why? What?" God, no. Please let this happen.

"I've wanted you since that first kiss. Since the conference room. And even more now that I'm looking at you naked."

"Why is this a problem?"

"Because I'm going to need to fuck you good and hard—at first. Work out all that pent-up need I've been carrying around for you. Then we'll go for round two."

"Round two?" My smile is incredulous. *Seriously?*

"Mmm." His eyes scrape over my body, and I can practically *feel* his gaze as it does. He stops to stare at my pussy and no doubt my arousal is visible on my thighs, just like the drop of pre-cum is on his cock. "Definitely round two. We'll take our time. We'll see to all your needs. I'll already have come once so I'll be able to last longer." His eyes dart to my lips and then back up to mine. "Then again, you're pretty damn fuckable, so we might even have to go for a round three."

I stand there, naked but not self-conscious, with my jaw lax and eyes blinking, as if that's going to help me comprehend what he's saying.

"It's time to get started. It's going to be a long *fucking* night." He steps forward and cups the side of my face. "Pun intended." His lips meet mine in a taunting kiss. "You ready?"

I offer a cockeyed smirk and then step backward until I find the bed. I sit down, scoot back, and then spread my thighs. "Does it look like I'm ready?" I love the quick intake of breath. The subtle flaring of his nostrils. The jerk of his cock at the visual.

Then his chuckle reverberates off the hotel room walls as he fists his cock and slides his hand up and down over it.

"You're fucking soaking for me."

A step closer. Another pump of his cock. A lick of his bottom lip.

"Pink and glistening."

Another step. A ragged breath. A twisting of his hand over the crest of his cock.

"I bet you're tight, right? So tight you're going to have to stretch for me."

He climbs onto the bed as I lick my own lips. The cool sheets on my skin do nothing to abate the heat his gaze and words have created.

"Let me check."

He pushes three fingers into me, and I cry out, bucking my hips into his hand. Riding his fingers. Needing his fingers and the onslaught of sensations he's creating.

His strangled groan is sex personified. But it's his eyes—how they glaze over as he watches his fingers slide in and out of me. It's his teeth sinking into his bottom lip as he tries to work me over and up to taking his cock. It's the slick sounds of the movements that turn me on even further.

"Camilla," he groans, one hand working his own cock, the other working me. "So fucking gorgeous. Those tits. Those lips. This pussy. Baby, I'm going to need to use all of them tonight. Every fucking one. You think you can do that for me?"

The visual of him between my thighs. The audible—the words he's saying and the way he's saying them in that pained groan. The physical—the sensations he's creating, the nerve endings he's prepping for his cock are so damn electric it's like my body is a current.

"Fuck me, Riggs."

A cocky grin turns up one side of his lips. "Atta girl. Tell me what you want." He lines the head of his cock up at my entrance and then uses it to spread my arousal around.

When his eyes meet mine, I know there's no turning back. And I know I've never ached to be touched, to be filled, to feel pleasure before like I do right now.

It's all I can think about. All I can focus on. All I fucking want.

"Now," I urge as I reach my hand down and part myself so he can get a better view of what he's about to fuck into bliss.

His fingertips dig into one of my thighs as he holds his dick and pushes into me with the other one.

I try to stay still. I try to play it cool. But my body has other ideas as it convulses in pleasure at the invasion. As it stretches to accommodate him filling me to capacity.

His eyes roll back in his head as he seats himself fully within me. I think I have much the same reaction but mine is accompanied with a feral groan that begs and pleads for more.

For so much fucking more.

Our eyes meet. I give the subtlest of nods.

And then Riggs begins the slow and steady ascent into madness. Into the almost violent pleasure of punishing my pussy with his cock.

In.

Grind.

Out.

Repeat.

He leans over, his lips finding my breasts and sending my body into a parallel spiral of sensations I didn't know existed or that I knew I needed but oh, do I need it. Oh, how I want it.

My fingernails score his back as his teeth scrape my nipples.

My pussy clenches around him while he pushes in, and I love the stutter in movement—the growl in reaction.

Nerve endings come to life.

Aches turn to smolders.

Smolders turn into full-blown wildfires.

I welcome the burn.

Every lick of flame with each push in.

Every ember popping as he pulls back out.

It's the bruising grip of his fingers on my thighs. It's the slap of our skin. It's the building of sensations—layer upon layer—so that when this all implodes, I can only imagine how fucking powerful it's going to be.

An orgasm at the hand of a man. Or rather, by the cock of a man. What's that going to be like? What's that going to feel like?

"Riggs," I pant out.

"C'mon, Cami. Come for me. Show me what my cock does to you. Fucking come all over it."

My orgasm is building as if he's lit a match and is holding it close enough that I can feel the burn, but not too close that I actually get burned.

It's waiting.

It's building.

And it strikes with a vengeance. Dynamite detonated. Haze of oblivion pulling me under at the same time a swell of sensation surges me up.

"Riggs." I cry out his name. I beg him to stop and not to stop all at the same time.

A loud noise startles me. I'm jolted to the present—a hotel room in Barcelona, shadows playing against the wall from the open blinds, and my hands between my thighs. Fingers on my clit, thighs soaked, breath labored, and pussy pulsing from the orgasm so strong it tore me from my dreams.

From my dreams.

That's all it was.

A dream.

Not a reality.

I push my blankets off me and stare at the ceiling as my heart pounds and body rides the high of the orgasm.

As I think long and hard about Spencer Riggs.

As I admit to myself, I've long since forgiven him.

Dare I say, I've started to like him.

Talk about creating problems for myself.

Especially when my job requires me to be face-to-face with the man I'm fantasizing about.

CHAPTER TWENTY-TWO

Riggs

"THEY'RE WAITING."

I look over to Anya. "It seems like they're *always* waiting," I say of the one thing that I don't think I understood about the Formula 1 side of the circuit. The sponsors.

The wooing of the sponsors.

The social events with the sponsors.

The constant presence of them during the entire five days of race week.

"Well, they are helping pay the bills, right? So make sure you wear that pretty smile of yours and bring your charm."

"I know. I'm not complaining. It's just hard to get a moment alone. It seems the only day I get is on Saturdays, before race day."

She nods. "Things will calm down after this race. We're selling your ability to them. Your charisma. Your 'it' factor. They need to be reassured since you're new and they had no hand in picking you. It's a lot of money they're putting up. They want to vet you and make sure their money is in good hands."

Don't I know it.

I technically haven't been home in almost two weeks—unless you count the one night I came back from Spain to then turn around and head back out to a private track. A track where I spent hours upon hours learning my car. Days upon days understanding any and every metric and how I can better help my crew help me. Night after night where these sponsors came out for various activities. Some made me feel like a monkey in a gilded cage. I took others around the track in the two-seat race cars provided by our engine manufacturer.

"I know, but it's okay to miss my bed, right?" I tease.

"It is. Are your friends still partying it up in your flat like they own the place?" she asks.

I groan and nod. "Yep. They sent a new round of photos last night. They look like they're having the time of their lives." I act mad but don't really care. Wills, Junior, and Micah are like brothers to me. We've been friends since secondary school. I trust them implicitly.

I would, however, not be angry for the chance to just kick back with them.

It's been a long two weeks.

Home in three days. And I'm looking forward to it.

"Fix your collar and slap on a Spencer Riggs smile for me."

"Who are we trying to impress tonight?" I ask as we approach the entrance of our hospitality building.

"VidShort."

"Oh," I say of the social media giant where I upload most of my videos to. The platform of choice right now for almost all age demographics.

"Yep. They're loving your videos. The attention the app receives when you post. Camilla approached them about a potential sponsorship, and they were more than interested."

"Wow. Okay."

"Turn the charm all the way on. Let's do this."

We enter the room and I spend the next hour or so meeting people. Learning about them. Trying to figure out what answers they want me to give.

And smiling. *A lot.*

What I don't expect is to look up and see Camilla across the room. We haven't really "seen" each other or spent time of any quality since the press box and the champagne.

The few moments we might have been able to steal a quick conversation during the buildup to race day here in Montreal have been interrupted—most of the time by her. So I'm beginning to think she's purposely avoiding me.

I'm not a fan of the feeling.

And I'm even less of a fan of the man who sidles up beside her and slides a hand onto her back. He leans in and whispers something in her ear. She looks up at him and blushes, her eyes alive and lips curved up into a smile.

I don't like it.

I don't like it at fucking all.

And I like it even less when the man turns to face the room and he's none other than Steele Pennington—the latest actor to be cast as James Bond.

They look cozy. Chummy even. With his hand still on her back and her leaning into him every few seconds with that smile.

"Riggs?" Anya calls to me and it pains me to look away.

"Hmm?"

"Over here?" She lifts her eyebrows and looks toward yet another fucking sponsor.

If this room is full of sponsors, what is *he* doing here with *her*?

"Yep. Sure." I move to where Anya stands with several others as Camilla's laugh carries across the room like a cold draft causing goosebumps on my skin.

This is ridiculous.

"Spencer Riggs, this is . . ." Anya goes on and I claim my spot in the dog and pony show like I respectfully need to do.

But the next time I look their way, they're not there. I scour the room just in time to see them leaving out the front. His hand still on her back.

I roll my shoulders as the door shuts.

Jealousy isn't a feeling I'm used to.

Hell, it isn't a feeling I should even be feeling. It's Camilla. She's her and I'm me and there's nothing between us. Nothing but a few kisses and the memory of how I wanted to kiss her the last time I was with her.

And yet . . . I look back toward the door they just walked out of and I still feel it.

I want to walk after her and see what the hell she's doing with him.

I don't want to acknowledge that all these games between us just might be getting to me when I don't want them to get to me.

You have a job to do, Riggs. A huge fucking end game to accomplish. Focus on that.

Not on Camilla Moretti.

CHAPTER TWENTY-THREE

Riggs

"J ESUS. IS MORETTI SO DESPERATE FOR FOLLOWERS THAT they're using your social media now?"

I look over toward Cruz Navarro and his shit-eating grin and raise my middle finger. The fucker and I have known each other as long as I've been karting. He may have been the one who pulled up in a rig full of extra parts and fancy graphics—an F1 legacy's son in every way that I'm not—but he's always been a decent friend to me.

Not the kind where we talk every day but the kind that when we do talk, it's like no time has been lost.

"Not desperate. They just know a good thing when they've got one and want to use every facet of mine to do so," I say.

"Sounds like what I did last night. Used every facet of the chick I had over." Cruz waggles his eyebrows and my middle finger goes up again. "What? Don't give me that. You and I both know you've had every chance possible to do the same since being called up. Hell, I saw you in Montreal. The track bunnies following you around like a new shiny toy, dropping their phone numbers for you like they're wanting to drop their skirts."

"Perhaps." I shrug. My grin says I just might have taken advantage of it. But I didn't.

Isn't that the crux of it?

I fucking didn't, and I can blow smoke up my own arse and say it's because I'm busy concentrating on making my name known, but if I believe that smoke, it might simply be because it's easier than believing the truth.

There's one particular woman who has taken up residence in my mind.

"It's so painful at the top, I think you should volunteer to go back to F2."

"That's where I say fuck you. I love you, but fuck you."

He barks out a laugh and pats me on the back. "I'm glad you're here even if that means I'm going to have more competition in the female department."

"Whatever. I don't think you're hurting in the least."

"Never." He takes a sip of his water. "Shit, man. Look at the two of us, racing against each other like our dads did."

"Crazy, huh?"

"Yeah, except that you're chasing ghosts you want to catch while I'm falling short of the perfection expected of me."

"Lucky us," I murmur as memories of the great Dominic Navarro belittling his only son for not crossing the finish line high enough dash through my mind.

"Lucky fucking us." He gives a shake of his head. "But you're liking Moretti?" he asks and brushes his thick mop of hair off his forehead before setting his Gravitas Racing hat back down onto it.

"Good. Fine. We're still making adjustments to the car—just like it seems we all are. But I think it's getting there. It's quick as shit."

"Not quicker than me." He lifts his eyebrows and smiles.

"Not yet, but there's time, Navarro."

He barks out a laugh. "Keep chasing and I'll keep waiting for you on the podium."

"Fucker," I mutter playfully.

"Yes, I am." He winks. "But seriously? You good?"

"Dude, I'm just happy to finally fucking be here. And Moretti is solid. Their crew. Their technology. Their engineering. They really have taken care of me." *Unlike Camilla Moretti, who I'd love to take care of me.* Because I've come to realize she's hot in *all* the right ways.

"They run a good outfit over there. Courted me a time or two but my contract with Gravitas is rock solid. If it wasn't, I would've considered it."

"I'm still getting to know everyone but so far so good."

He licks his lips and lowers his voice. "Have you talked to Maxim at all?" he asks cautiously.

I avert my eyes and shake my head subtly, embarrassed by my answer. "He's still not taking calls. I've tried."

Silence falls between us and Cruz sighs heavily. "Yeah, man. So have I."

He meets my eyes and throws his hands up. We're probably both thinking the same thing, feeling the same way. Glad he's not taking visitors because then we'd have to see him and see what we could become. And feeling horribly guilty for feeling that too.

It's fucked up all around and we both know it.

Voices come down the hallway and past the door where we're sitting. The interruption welcome. "So F1. What's your biggest challenge being up here?"

"Fuck, man. Can I opt for all the above?" I ask and we laugh.

"Yes, but from what I hear and see you're catching up to speed faster than most."

"Thanks for the vote of confidence. It means a lot."

"It's the same but so very different, right?" Cruz asks.

"Pretty much. The main thing I fear is screwing up. Not knowing the car enough that I end up causing a crash. Hurting people. That kind of shit."

"Hey, my competition is fair game. I'm not." He jokes as he rises from his seat and pats me on the shoulder. "Time to go face the cameras. Let's hope that ugly mug of yours doesn't break any of them."

"Is that all you've got, Navarro?"

"Nah. That was a warm-up. I'm just getting started."

"Great. Fucking great," I say through a laugh as we enter the press room.

"If I don't get a chance to tell you tomorrow, good luck. Finish high but finish behind me." He belts out a laugh as we take a seat and Q&A with the reporters begin.

Most questions are asked to the established guys. How'd they feel last race? What adjustments are being made to their cars if any? How do they feel their chances are this weekend?

Benign questions.

Softballs being tossed up for them.

It's weird sitting up here, with the F1 backdrop and the banners in front of us. Many of my dad's interviews that I memorized were taken with a setting of this sort.

It makes me think of him, smile, and wonder how he felt about pressers. I know how he answered the questions, but did he mind being asked them? Did he roll his eyes at them or was he so focused on the task at hand that they didn't matter?

"What about you, Riggs? Are you ready to put the third race under your belt tomorrow?"

"I am."

"This was a great track for your dad. He had a lot of fortune here. Does that cross your mind at all?"

Every damn time I get in the car.

I have to overcome the fear. The expectation. The history with its invisible strings, the people in this room, and the memories that restrict me.

"How can it not?" I smile and answer as honestly as I can.

"It seems you're fitting in well with Moretti. The fans have taken a liking to you with your advice column posts."

"There's nothing wrong with having a little fun and interacting with the fans. They love this sport as much as all of us on stage do," I say and I can see Anya's smile widening in the back of the room, clearly pleased with my response.

"Are you afraid it's going to distract you and your focus from racing and the safety of the other racers?"

And there it is. The question they've tiptoed around for the last few weeks. And no surprise it's Harlan fucking Flanders.

"Are you asking me if I'm my father?"

Harlan meets my gaze and doesn't blanche. "I'm asking you what I asked you. In F2, you pushed the envelope in situations when others wouldn't. You took risks and those risks can have consequences for every other person on the track."

"Uncool, man," Cruz says under his breath. Only those on the stage can hear it.

"And those risks got me where I am today." My smile is a *fuck you with love* to him. "If you want to make comparisons, make them. But don't hold back my potential because of something my father did. I have enough ghosts to face when I'm on the track that I don't need you adding more to the pile. Look at each race as they happen. Judge me on those, and I won't judge you by the loaded questions you've asked in the past and the smear campaign you continue to wage without just cause."

When I set the microphone down and look over at Anya, the look on her face this time around is puffed cheeks and raised brows.

Guess she'll have to clean that one up.

Or I just place higher than last time and shut them up.

My money's on that.

CHAPTER TWENTY-FOUR

Camilla

"I know. I'm a busy bitch, but I can't," I say as I push the door open and leave the office.

"Can't or won't?" Isabella asks.

How about both?

"Can't. I have a sponsorship event tonight. I have to go impress bigwigs." I adjust my bag on my shoulder and start across the parking lot toward my car.

"You are a bigwig *and* you're bluffing." She tsks. "I know you too well."

"Let's shoot for when I get back from the next race. I'll do drinks with him then," I say with no intention of doing drinks with anybody, let alone a blind date she picks for me.

"No, you won't. But I'll badger you. Then cajole you. Then stalk you from afar to make sure you show up."

"Perfect. I don't expect any less."

"Later, Cam. Love you."

"Love you too."

I breathe out a sigh of relief. Dodged that bullet. Let's hope I can keep dodging it.

And just as I drop my phone in my tote I hear, "Hey, Moretti?"

Footsteps fall heavily behind me as Riggs jogs after me. As much as I want to keep walking, I stop and turn to look at him.

Jesus. The man knows how to wear a pair of jeans.

And when I see the jeans, I think of my dream. Of the perfect V of muscles they're covering. Of his cock springing free.

And *this*—your ridiculous fantasy—is why you've been avoiding him every chance you can.

"Hey," I say and smile. "What's up?"

He slows to a stop in front of me, his grin lighting up his face. "You're everywhere and nowhere. I just wanted to say hi. See how you were doing."

I eye him. What is going on? My cheeks stain pink as my mind goes to crazy places—like there's no way he could know about my dream.

"Good," I say cautiously.

"I have some ideas for the AITA thing."

"Okay. I'll have Elise set something up to go over it with you."

"I want you in on the meeting," he says, brow narrowing.

"Um. Okay." I chuckle. "Why?"

"Because you're avoiding me, and I don't like to be avoided."

Shit. He knows.

"No, I haven't. I've been . . . busy. Kissing up to sponsors. Trying to get these new campaigns everywhere. And a whole lot of other stuff."

"A whole lot of other stuff. Is that a technical term?" he asks.

"Yes. Very technical."

"That's what I thought." He glances over his shoulder.

"You had impressive results last race. How are you feeling with everything?"

"Good. Fine." He tilts his head to the side and studies me. I squirm under his scrutiny. "I saw you with Steele Pennington in Montreal. What's that all about?"

Oh.

Oooh.

Is that jealousy I detect from Spencer Riggs? Jealousy that has no business being there. *And why do I kind of like it?*

But why is he jealous? He doesn't like me. Dare cards and everything with them.

"Camilla." He groans out my name.

I freeze. My name. The tone in which he says it. The odd desperation laced in it. I swear to God it sounds exactly like my dream. My body sparks to life—not like his presence didn't already do that, but it's tenfold now.

"What? What did I do?" I sound as guilty as I feel.

"Why was he there? With you?"

"Steele likes racing. He's an avid follower."

"And he just happened to be what? A guest of yours to the race?"

This is quite amusing. He's fishing and it's adorable.

"Of my father's. They're acquaintances."

"But you left with him. From the event. *Out the door.*"

The way he says *out the door* is hilarious.

My smile deepens. "I did."

Ask me where I went. Prove my theory right.

He rocks on his heels. "Cool. Okay." He hooks a thumb over his shoulder. "I've got sim time scheduled. I should get going."

"Okay. Have a good training session."

He takes a few steps backward. "I will," he says but he doesn't turn to go. He just stands there looking at me. Lips pursed and eyes narrowed. "So where'd you go with him?"

It takes everything I have not to burst out laughing.

A part of me thinks it would serve him right if I just shrugged and walked away—leaving him wondering.

The other part of me is finding this way too amusing and endearing. It's yet another side to Riggs that I never expected.

"Why do you care?" I ask.

"I don't." He shrugs.

"But you asked, so you do care." I fight my smile as he stands there, clearly flustered and by his body language, not totally comfortable with his own questions.

"Yeah. Whatever." This time he does turn on his heel and walks away.

I watch his backside. The strong shoulders. The nice ass. I wait until he gets to the entrance of the building before I yell, "I was taking him over to find his girlfriend. That's where we went."

Riggs pauses. One foot on the pavement, the other on the curb. He hangs his head and his laugh carries to me.

And then he walks inside, leaving me to wonder, what the fuck was that?

CHAPTER TWENTY-FIVE

Camilla

I'M SURPRISED I CAN HEAR THE KNOCK ON MY DOOR OVER THE BASS pumping against my wall. Or the round of cheers that goes up every so often that sounds like a full-blown cheering section.

Party Guy is in full swing again next door and seeing as it's been a non-stop weekend at our home track, Silverstone, I'm tired—mentally and physically. I'm cranky, despite being thrilled with a fourth and a sixth place finish for Moretti. And all I want to do is sleep in my own bed. Bask in my own silence. Maybe eat my takeout order whose delivery man is probably at my door without . . . all *this* extra noise.

Knock. Knock. Knock.

"Coming," I shout but doubt the delivery person can hear me above the noise.

But when I open the door, it's not my food. It's two incredibly gorgeous but clearly drunk women. Their eyes are glassy. Their laughs are too loud. Their expressions take a second to transition from party mode to confusion.

"Hey. Where'd the party go?" the one in the pink, barely-there dress asks. She looks behind me as if I'm hiding what sounds like fifty-plus people.

"Next door."

"Which way?" the one in the black dress asks, her head swiveling back and forth as if she can't tell which direction the commotion is coming from.

I shrug and smile. "How about where the noise is."

They both look at me with furrowed brows and wobbly legs on top of their high heels. Clearly my neighbor doesn't care about intellect when he rolls out the party invites.

"But . . ." Pink Dress sighs and bats her lashes.

"That way." I point down the hallway. The quicker they go, the sooner I can get back to my pretend peace and quiet.

A loud giggle. Boobs almost spilling out as Black Dress bounces up and down. "Thank you so much. We owe you for life."

I just stare after them as they walk down the hall toward the party. *Was I ever like that? God, I hope not.*

Within seconds I hear a rush of noise when the door is opened and a loud cheer followed by their giggly laughter.

No. I most definitely wasn't like that.

And just as I'm about to shut my door, my delivery person rounds the corner with food in hand and shaking their head. "That's one wild party."

"My headache agrees," I say as I fish cash out of my purse to pay him.

"I had a neighbor like that once. Talk about a fucking nightmare." He hands the food over to me.

"What did you do?"

He shrugs. "I tried to be patient, but after a few months and trying to sleep with a pillow over my head, I'd had enough. I stormed down there and told him to either turn the shit down or I was going to tell all his partiers how he liked to sleep in women's lingerie and that he held Bestiality Anonymous meetings at his house so to make sure they kept their pets away from him."

I bark out a laugh. "That's brutal."

"Maybe, but it worked." He looks down the hall and then back to me with a grin. "He thought I was exaggerating at first but then the next time he threw a rager, I joined the crowd, got on a chair, and shouted for everyone to listen up. That got his attention real quick and he held his hands up in surrender. The music was turned down. The drunk people stopped banging on my door. It was heaven."

"Sound advice. Thank you for it."

"There is no telling the lengths one will go when they're exhausted and someone's preventing them from sleeping."

"I can't agree more."

He takes a step back and tips his imaginary hat. "Best of luck to you. And if you want sleep, it's best you lay down the law sooner rather than later."

His advice runs circles in my mind as I eat my lasagna from the only restaurant here that makes it even close to what it tastes like at home. The worst part is that I'm so distracted by the party noise, I accidentally drop some of my food on my brand-new, white sweatshirt.

"Grrr," I say to no one as I strip the damn thing off and spray stain remover on it. But it's right as I finally sit back down to the food that's starting to get cold that another fist pounds on my door.

But when I answer this time, no one is there.

Seriously?

Annoyed beyond reason that now my food is definitely cold, I put it in the microwave to heat it up.

Just as it's done, there's another knock on the door.

Ignore it, Cam. Eat your food. Pick up your book and your glass of wine, and try to enjoy all three.

But that's the thing—there is no peace to enjoy shit, especially when whoever is at the door pounds at it again.

Irritated.

Annoyed.

Angry.

I stalk over to the door and yank it open. "What?"

Doe eyes stare back at me. "Um, is Wills in there?" She looks over my shoulder. Her face falls when she sees my place is empty.

"Wills as in the future King of England?" I look over my shoulder like she did then back to her. "Nope. Sorry to disappoint you. I'm sure he's at the palace somewhere."

She giggles. "No. Wills as in Wills Wentworth. You know who I'm talking about." She waves a hand in indifference and holds her phone out to me so I can see the text on the screen. My flat number is listed right after the address of our building. "See? He sent the group text out to us telling us this was where the party was."

"Of course he did." There isn't an ounce of humor in my tone. "Dare I ask how many people are on that text?"

She bites her bottom lip in concentration as she slides her finger over her phone. "Twenty-ish. I lost count."

"Great. Even better." I glance back at where my microwave has alerted me several times that my food is done reheating and then back at her. "Why don't I show you where the party is?"

"How sweet of you," she coos like I'm a little child.

Maybe it's time for *Operation Bestiality.*

CHAPTER TWENTY-SIX

Camilla

WE'RE DOWN THE HALL AND KNOCKING ON THE DOOR IN seconds. When it swings open, the girl beside me squeals and launches herself into the arms of the man standing there. He staggers backward under the force of her weight but doesn't miss a beat when her lips find his.

But it only takes seconds—and a few tongues stuck down each other's throats no doubt—for him to notice me. He looks familiar but I can't place from where. *Probably because he's your neighbor.*

"Uh. Hi. And you are?" he asks above the noise behind him that's pouring out into the hallway.

"Your neighbor." My smile is quick and sarcastic as I try to place him.

"Oh. Uh." He moves the woman to his side so that he can face me. "Not my place."

"Whose is it then?" I stand on my tiptoes and try to look around, get my bearings, but all I find is wall to wall people who are clearly having a good time.

Wills, I'm guessing, glances over his shoulder. "Um. One sec. I'll try to find—oh, there he is. C'mon."

I follow Wills a short distance. I bump into people every few steps, decline drinks thrust at me, and weird glances slid my way, which I can only assume is because I clearly haven't dressed the part.

"Hey," Wills shouts. I can't see the person he's shouting at but just as the crowd parts, just as I see the back of someone I recognize, he says, "Riggs. Neighbor's here to complain."

"Fuck, man," he says, but then turns around and jolts to a stop when he sees me standing there. I'm pretty sure we both have the same expression on our faces—shock that we live next door to each other.

But my brain processes more than that. It brings me back to the damn dream. To the imagination-induced, hand-helped orgasm that rocked my world following said dream. The same place my mind has gone each and every time I saw him this weekend at the race.

The reason I continue to avoid him.

And this visceral reaction to an imaginary meeting of our bodies—the sound of him groaning as he comes and the feel of his fingers gripping my hips as he pounded into me—is why I had to.

"Hey, you!" Riggs sways on his feet, clearly drunk as drunk can be, and a slow, crooked smile crawls over his lips. "Camilla. Cam. Cami. Cami-cam-cam." He slurs the words out as he steps forward and wraps me in the biggest bear hug ever.

The part of me that goes to push him away falters when my hands hit the hard plane of his chest, and my mind is brought back to all the reasons I've avoided him.

To fingernails scoring his sweat-misted chest. To strong arms holding me against him. To my panted name on his lips.

"I thought you didn't drink during the season."

"This is my *one* exception. 'Member. I told you about it?" He angles his head and studies me.

"How could I forget?" I murmur. *How can he look both adorable and sexy at the same time?*

"Look who's here," he shouts to everybody as he leans back, arm still on my shoulders, and looks at me with eyes that are glassy but so damn adoring. "It's Camilla who doesn't like dare cards, bastards, or James Bond but loves good kisses, drivers, and champagne straight outta the bottle."

"Hello, Camilla," the crowd shouts back followed by a roar of cheers going up. A roar that explains so much about the sound I keep hearing from my apartment. Clearly this is how they greet people.

I shrink at the sound but raise my hand up in greeting.

"C'mon, Gasket," Riggs says.

"Gasket?" I laugh the word out.

He nods emphatically. "You blow a gasket so easily. Get so angry at the drop of a hat—especially when it comes to me . . . so I officially name thee

Gasket." He grins and waves a pretend wand at me, clearly proud of himself for the nickname.

"You're crazy."

"Guilty as charged." He raises his hand. "Did I tell you I liked your hair? Wait. I didn't because you were too busy avoiding me this weekend—"

"I was letting you work. Just like I was working," I lie, but am flattered that in the midst of this weekend's chaos he actually noticed the subtle change in my hair. The color is a little lighter and the face framing a bit more pronounced—thanks to the first step of Isabella and Gia's glow-up plan.

"Bullshit. You were avoiding me because you were so damn busy trying to talk yourself into believing that my kiss is for shit when you know damn well it's the best you've ever had."

"The man has jokes when he's drunk."

"Baby, I got jokes all the time." He takes my hand and holds it casually in his. "Is this the day you finally did it?"

"Did what?" I ask above the crowd.

"Draw the hearts on the calendar for me? I mean, you're here and so very excited to see me . . . I figured it was. Were they pink? Or blue? Oh. Wait. Moretti red, I bet."

"Ignore him," Wills says. "He's an obnoxiously happy drunk." And it's then that he gets a closer look at me and his eyes shock open when he recognizes me from the track. Or the bar. He might be slow on at least one of them. "Holy shit. You're—"

"Mine," Riggs says, shoving him playfully in the chest and stepping in between Wills and me. He lets out a big sigh as his gaze lands on my lips and then grins. "Hi again."

"Hi."

He puts his hand on my waist to move me out of the way of a bunch of people but once they pass, he doesn't move it off. My skin ignites beneath it.

"If I had known you were next door, I would have invited you over."

"If you had invited me over," I say, my heart pounding in my chest, "I probably wouldn't have come."

"That's a shame," he murmurs and by the flare of his nostrils, I swear the *coming* he's talking about refers to more than an innocent party invite. "It's good to let loose every once in a while." He reaches up with his other hand and tucks a loose strand of my hair behind my ear. "It's good for the soul."

"I'll keep that in mind."

"No, you won't." He winks. "You'll keep on the straight and narrow while I venture down an unbeaten path. You should try it sometime. The adrenaline high is like no other."

"I prefer my feet planted firmly on the ground, thank you very much."

"I think it's time I prove you wrong." He throws his head back and laughs, like a switch was flipped, and without warning, hops up on the coffee table beside us, his hand still holding mine.

"What are you—"

"Excuse me. Everybody, can I please have your attention?" he shouts, and when people don't listen, Wills lets off one hell of a whistle that has voices quieting and necks craning. "Thank you."

"Give it to us, Riggs," someone yells from the back.

"You've already met Camilla," he says and then unbeknownst to me tugs on my arm and coaxes me up to stand beside him. "Or as I call her, Gasket."

Not thrilled with this unexpected development, I stand on the table and glare at Riggs instead of staring out at what feels like a sea of people.

"So, she's the one responsible for thinking up this whole Am I the Arsehole advice column I'm doing on my socials." Cheers go up. "But I only think it's fair that I reverse the role tonight. How about I ask you guys the question and you give me advice this time around?"

"Riggs. What are you doing?" I ask under my breath.

"Relax." He winks and tugs at my waist so that I'm against his side.

"Spencer." His name is a two-syllable warning.

"You ready?" he asks to cheers. "Because I'm counting on you to give me the right answer here." He holds up his hand for them to quiet down. "Here goes. Am I the arsehole for wanting to kiss her right now? For wanting to prove to her I'm good at it?"

The entire crowd roars no.

And before I can process that he's serious, he tugs me flush against him and closes his mouth over mine.

For a moment, I panic at the clumsiness of his motions and the fumbling of his hands as they frame my face.

But it's just the alcohol. It's just Riggs.

And once I bury the memory threatening to besiege me, the crowd slips away. My dream reemerges but in living 3D color as I taste the beer on his tongue and lose myself to his kiss.

As I bask in the sensations it seems only he can evoke.

Whistles break through the fog of lust and the staggering sensations his touch has created within.

He leans back, a smile on his lips. "Change your mind yet, because if you need more convincing . . ."

"Yes. Okay." I hold my hands up in surrender. "You're a good kisser."

"Just good?" He scrunches his face up like a little boy waiting to be praised and it's freaking adorable.

I sigh and give the truth. "Better than good."

He throws his hands up and yells, "Victory," as the room explodes in applause around us.

I laugh. How can I not when I have a drunk Riggs in front of me who is completely and utterly endearing?

He jumps off the table amid a raucous round of high fives as I stand there flustered with lips tingling and the apex of my thighs burning sweetly.

I'm breathless and desperate . . . *yes, desperate* for more of him.

But when Riggs turns to help me down, he freezes. His smile falters. He blinks a couple of times . . . as if he's really seeing me for the first time.

Oh shit.

My own odd panic flutters up my throat as I realize that I'm standing here in a tight tank top and leggings—*not* my usual baggy clothes.

Riggs's eyes darken. I expect him to catcall. To make a smart-ass comment.

He does the exact opposite almost as though, despite being drunk, he understands what a big deal this is for me without me having to explain a word.

"Hey, Gasket?" He reaches his hand out to me to help me step down and keeps his eyes solely focused on mine. They don't roam. They don't take me in. For a man who just had his lips on mine and would normally study the whole package of me that he's made comments about me hiding, he doesn't look once. He waits until my feet are firmly on the ground and the party starts to move on around us before talking. "You okay?"

I nod, my heart in my throat.

So many people in this room.

So much alcohol. Gyrating. Clumsy hands. Wandering, greedy hands.

I need out of here.

Now.

"I uh . . . I'm going to get going."

He lowers himself so he's eye level with me. "Cam?"

"I need to." I force a smile and take a step back. "Okay?"

He just nods, returns my smile, and tries to lighten the mood. "I'll be here waiting for Moretti-red-colored hearts to be colored on the calendar over me."

CHAPTER TWENTY-SEVEN

Camilla

I FEEL RIDICULOUS.

Like absolutely and utterly ridiculous for how I reacted. The mini freak-out was completely unwarranted. And the fact that I let the panic win the war over the way Riggs's kiss and hands on my waist makes what I did even more annoying.

Didn't I accept this job and promise myself I had to be braver?

First challenge and I cowered in a corner.

First chance to maybe act on that attraction between us, and I up and bolted like a dog in a thunderstorm.

To add insult to injury, the party continues to rage on the other side of the wall. More cheers go up. More laughter rings. More music thumps.

I ignore the knock on the door.

No doubt it's another partier on Wills's group text string. They'll go away. It doesn't take a rocket scientist to realize the music is coming from down the hall.

There's another knock but this time it's a fist pounding on the door followed by, "It's me, Camilla. Open up. I'm not going away."

There's no way he knows I'm here. For all he knows, I could have gone out for a drive. I'll save myself from more embarrassment.

The noise is what gets me. The loud, unmistakable thump of what sounds like a body hitting the floor.

I run to the door and fling it open, thinking he's passed out. Instead, Riggs is sitting with his back against the door so that when I open it, he falls inward and backward, his head on my feet. He looks up at me with a goofy grin and slurred laugh.

"Howdy, neighbor. What do you know? You *are* home." He chuckles like the drunk man that he is and then lifts his arms up to me. "I'm gonna need some help."

Within seconds, Riggs is upright and swaying a bit more.

"Your flat is moving," he says as he takes it upon himself to walk past me and survey my place. "But it suits you. Orderly. Fashionably conservative. Practical." He turns to face me and chuckles. "I've slept in way worse places so no complaints here."

"I'm sure you have. Wait . . . what do you mean? You're sleeping here?" I ask as he grabs his shirt by the back of the collar—in the way only guys can do—and yanks it over his head. He gives a quick look around, almost as if to ask where to put it before he crumples it up in his hand and tosses it onto one of my chairs. "*Spencer.*"

"Ooooh, I'm in trouble now. She's using my first name," he says to no one in particular. And now I'm faced with the bare torso of a man I've seen online and enjoyed in my dreams.

"You didn't answer my question."

"You have to use my first and last name. That is if you're *mad* at me. If not, Riggs will do just fine." He grins and holds his hands out—which of course sets off a chain reaction of muscles moving and tightening in his chest. "So where do you want me?"

In me.

On me.

Making that dream of mine become a cold, hard reality.

I cough to hide the shock of my own immediate thoughts.

"What do you mean, where do I want you?"

He flashes a grin that could create world peace. "I'm sleeping here."

And right as he says it, as if on cue, a cheer goes up in his flat next door.

"You can't. You have a house full of people."

"And?"

"And you just can't leave them."

He glances over his shoulder to my closed front door and shrugs. "Yeah, I can. Easy." He dusts his hands as if to reinforce what he says. "Besides, my mates throw parties there all the time when I'm gone. They're potty trained *and* they know how to lock up when they're done." His laugh borders on a giggle.

All I can do is shake my head. "But . . ."

"Sounds to me like they're getting along just fine over there. Doesn't seem like I'm needed. Besides, last party like this, I went to bed and a woman was there. *In my bed*," he exclaims, eyes wide like a five-year-old seeing Santa on Christmas morning.

"You poor baby. I'm sure you wanted nothing to do with her."

His chuckle is pure suggestion. "I mean . . . if you bring a horse to water."

I snort. "So that's why you're here? To avoid women in your bed?" I put a hand on my hip and give him *the look* all while hating the thought of anyone in bed with him.

Guess the jealousy thing goes both ways, now, doesn't it?

"Nope." He mimics my posture and straightens his shoulders as if he's mocking me. "I'm here because one"—he holds a finger up—"I'm not interested and two"—another exaggerated motion of two fingers out—"you didn't want to be there and I didn't want you to be alone . . . so?" He shrugs like what he just said is nothing. *He just rocked the world beneath my feet.*

"I don't—I don't understand." I stand there blinking as if that's going to help me comprehend that this arrogant, self-absorbed man left his own party because he was worried about me.

And just about when my heart melts and I'm turned into a pile of goo, he yanks his shorts down—his underwear with them—and gives me an eyeful of a perfectly well-endowed man.

"Oh my God."

"What?" He grins. "Haven't you ever seen a dick before?"

"No. I mean yes. I mean . . ." Not one that looks like *that*. Good lord. *Good freaking lord.* Definitely better than the dream. "Pull your pants up." I startle. Maybe I take a second to do that because I'm busy staring, but I do startle. It's more because I realize what I'm doing and not what he did. I hold my hands up to block any view of his pelvic region.

The one with a very defined V of muscles, sculpted thighs, and happy trail that leads down to his cock.

His laugh rings out, his grin wide. "It's good, huh?" He looks down at himself and purses his lips. "I can't decide if I'm a shower and not a grower or a grower even with all this already showing. There's been much debate about it."

I fight my laugh. The seriousness with which he's contemplating this while standing drunk and naked in my family room is too much to bear.

So is my body's visceral reaction to him.

Yep, the ache is still there.

"You debate this often?" I ask through the laugh.

He puts his hands back on his hips again, eyes still angled downward. "I mean, not often. But sometimes. Hmm." He concentrates. "I'm gonna go with this is what I've got to show but there's definitely more when it grows." He looks up at me and grins. "Do you agree?"

"I—uh—Riggs—uh . . ." I just lift my hands up and shrug, refusing to give an answer or sneak another peek at the male perfection in front of me.

He smacks his hands together. "Now that that's settled, let's get to bed." He turns and stumbles as he hadn't stepped out of his shorts pooled around his ankles. He laughs again.

"You're not sleeping on my couch naked."

"But I always sleep naked."

"Not here you don't."

"Your bed then?" He starts walking down the short hallway, my groan following him. Then I see his ass and back. Is there anything on this man that's not perfect?

Jesus.

He turns to look over his shoulder and catches me ogling. "Relax. I may be drunk, Gasket, but I also know how to joke."

I pick up his boxer briefs and shove them at him. "Underwear. First." I point to the couch. "Then sleep."

He salutes me and the stern face he gives me is adorable. "Yes. Ma'am." But he does as I say and puts his underwear on. "You're no fun."

"I'm lots of fun. All the fun in the world. But I don't want your bare ass on my couch."

His sigh is dramatic as he throws his shorts in the same pile as his shirt. Sure he's dressed now, but I can still picture what that bulge is like beneath the dark blue boxer briefs.

There's another cheer from his flat, no doubt a late arrival. "Wow. You should really tell that guy next door to quiet down. His party is way too loud."

"Funny."

"I know. You forgot the handsome, sexy, and hung part."

"You're going to hate yourself in the morning when you remember everything you've said."

"No, I won't. I mean, yes, about the remembering, but no, about hating myself."

"You are a handful."

He laughs and adjusts his package so I have no excuse to mistake what his next words mean. "I've been told that a time or two."

"You. Couch." I put my hands on his back and push him toward it. "Blanket's right there."

"Don't blame me if I get hot and when you wake up and I'm naked," he slurs.

"Then take the blanket off. Not your shorts."

"Oh. Yeah. Good idea." He unceremoniously plops down on the couch and then makes a funny face the same time I hear the crinkle of my magazine. He pulls it out from beneath him and narrows his eyes at the Cosmopolitan folded in half to save the page I was reading last.

Please make him be drunk enough that he doesn't care.

But his *humph* says he's already noticed.

Fuck.

"How to own one's sexuality." He reads the title of the article out loud and lifts a lone eyebrow as he meets my eyes. My cheeks flush and damn if my nipples don't harden at the look alone. "Will you look at that," he murmurs. "First changing up the clothes tonight. Now this." He holds the magazine up.

"It's just an article."

"It's what the article says that I'm interested in." He tosses it on the table and leans back and studies me. "I can teach you the same thing this article can, but my lessons are free. *And hands-on.*"

Before I can respond, he lies down and pulls the blanket over him. He stares at the ceiling as I move about the room, turning lights off. It's not until the room is bathed in darkness and I'm just about to walk down the hall that he speaks again.

"This is the part where you can thank me, Camilla. Where you can get it off your chest before you fall asleep."

"Thank you for what?" I laugh the question out.

"That no one was none the wiser over what you were wearing—or really, weren't wearing—or commented on it."

"I had a stain on my sweatshirt," I say.

"I told you. Curves are sexy. And yours?" He kisses his fingers. "Are chef's kiss hot." He groans. "Fucking loved having my hands on you."

"Oh . . ." I don't know what to say but by the time I do, Riggs's gentle snoring fills the room.

I stare at him through the darkness. He thinks my curves are sexy? That my body is hot?

Do I want him to think about me that way when I've spent so long not wanting that kind of attention from anybody?

Yes. *I do want that.* Very much so. But . . .

I can teach you the same thing this article can, but my lessons are free. And hands-on.

I know he's drunk but as I drift off to sleep, the offer is as present in my mind as the taste of his kiss and the feel of his lips. Of the dream that I can't shake from my mind.

I want his hands on me. Again.

More than I've wanted anything in a long time.

CHAPTER TWENTY-EIGHT

Riggs

GROAN.

My mouth tastes like the arse of a dead rhinoceros. Jesus.

What kind of poison did Wills give me last night?

Definitely not enough if . . . *wait*. This is *not* my flat.

My eyes are wide open now as I scrub a hand over my face and through my hair. I mean, why does it look like my place?

Did Chip and Joanna Gaines rob me while I slept?

Not robbed, you dumb shit.

Made over.

Why do I even know who that is?

Because this place looks like mine, but it's different. Browns and neutrals and . . . I shift to a seated position, the blanket falling off my legs and onto the floor. I look around, disoriented and discombobulated, but if the status of my cock is any indication—horny as fuck.

Pieces of last night come back to me. Celebrating another strong finish—in the points once again. Secretly happy that I—the number two—finished higher than Andrew, the number one.

The welcome home party—my one cheat night for the month—with shots all around.

Camilla.

Kissing her.

Noticing her—the clothes, the panic, the fucking incredible body wearing both.

And there goes my cock getting even harder.

My cock.

It seems to be a recurring theme here. Front and fucking center.

"Down boy," I mutter.

"What?" Camilla asks as she walks into the family room from the kitchen area. I had no idea she was there, and for my cock's sake, it's probably better that I didn't.

While her sweatshirt might be baggy again, her legs are bare. Like the long, shapely, and tan type of bare that begs me to stare.

"Do you need something?" she asks as she stops in the middle of the room and studies me. "Water? Nurofen?"

"No," I grumble, voice gravelly and fuzzy head slowly clearing. "I said *down boy.*"

Her eyes slide down automatically to my hard-on. It's not like I can hide it. And she swallows forcibly.

Another flashback hits me. *I like to sleep naked.*

My pants off.

Her eyes wide.

Her smile fucking incredible.

My chuckle is a low rumble. She meets my eyes again, her teeth sinking into her bottom lip. She knows I remember what happened. The whole nine yards.

Or should I say the whole ten inches?

"It's not something I can help, you know," I say, looking down at my lap and then back up with an unapologetic smile. "I just wake up and it's there, doing its own thing, like it has a mind of its own."

"I know basic anatomy." She's flustered, and it's freaking adorable.

"And yet you stared last night."

She opens her mouth and closes it, caught in between acknowledging her wandering eyes and ignoring my comment altogether. "When you're standing naked in my living room, I didn't really have a choice."

"You're supposed to say, *it's not like I could miss it.* I mean, the least you could do is give the ego a little stroke."

"I think you've got that handled all on your own." She moves toward the kitchen. "Coffee's on if you want any."

Owning your sexuality. Another flashback.

I look to the table where I tossed the magazine. Gone.

With a grunt, I rise and follow her. The kitchen is the same layout as mine. Hers is just more put together in most aspects.

"You're more than welcome to help yourself," she says motioning to the coffee, the milk, sugar, and mug out on the counter. "I have to get ready for work."

She walks out and as much as I want to follow her, coffee calls my name like a siren.

That first sip is like heaven. The second has my head clearing. The third has me feeling like a new man.

I walk out of the kitchen with thoughts of getting my shorts on but stop when I hear her fingernails clicking on a keyboard. She's to the right of me at a desk of some sort with those long legs crossed beneath it.

"I thought you had to get ready for work." I rest my hip on the edge of the table next to her without asking and pick up what looks like a paperweight. I study it and then set it back down.

"I have to do a couple of things first." She moves the paperweight back to where I picked it up from.

"Like?" I move the pen beside her laptop, click the top a few times so the ink goes in and out, and then set it back down on a different place on her desk.

"Stuff." She picks up the pen and moves it back to where it was.

"So, in other words, you're avoiding me again." I pick up her Post-it notes, fan through the pad, and then set it down behind me.

Are you going to reach around me to get it?

"Not avoiding you." She goes to reach out on instinct and then realizes she's either going to have to touch me or go through me. She huffs and gives a frustrated shake of her head.

"No? Then why won't you look at me?" I move the paperweight again back to where I moved it the first time.

"Will you stop?" she snaps but finally looks at me.

"There she finally is," I murmur above the rim of my mug. "Good morning, Camilla."

What the fuck are you doing, Riggs?

Her face softens. An expression glances through her eyes that I can't quite interpret. "Good morning. You're on my desk, Riggs."

"I am?" I make a show of looking around. "Wow. *Am I the arsehole* or what?" I waggle my eyebrows.

"Witty."

"I know." I grin as she shifts her chair, which turns her to face me, and those legs of hers, one crossed over the other, are front and center. "First, last night and now this morning. All this skin. Should I be worried that you're not feeling well?"

She shrugs but I can see the set of her jaw. Clearly this is a big deal to her for reasons unbeknownst to me. "Maybe you proved something to me last night."

"Like?"

"Like I can trust you."

I don't know why her words cause a funny pressure in my chest, but they do. I never set out to make Camilla Moretti like me, let alone trust me, but the sap in me, who rears his pathetic head like once or twice a year, thinks it feels pretty damn good.

"If a man has to prove why you can't wear what you want, he's not the type of man you should be wasting your time, let alone a thought on."

"Don't you have a flat to go clean up?" she asks, clearly suggesting the discussion is over.

I decide to play along. Grin. Reach out to tug on a piece of her hair. "Are you asking me to do the walk of shame? That's kind of hard to do when nothing happened."

I rise from my perch and am not immune to her darted glance at my package.

"Like you would remember if it did or didn't," she says, leaning back in her chair and meeting my eyes.

I lean down, put my hands on both sides of her chair, and meet her eyes. "I'd remember all right. Especially when it comes to you." I pause. "I have a feeling you're the kind of woman who leaves a mark."

"A mark?" Her eyes narrow and her head tilts. She's having a hard time not letting her eyes wander.

Perfect. Let's help her along with that. I scratch an imaginary itch on my pec. Then another right at the top of my thigh. I may grunt a little too at an itch being satisfied.

And fuck do I have one that needs to be satisfied.

"Yes. *A mark*," I say, catching her eyes as they snap up from my hand on my thigh.

"Is that a good or bad thing?" she whispers.

"I haven't quite figured that out yet." I stand to my full height—my junk so very close to her eye level. Pause. Chuckle. Then collect my shirt and shorts from last night before heading to the door.

Another flashback hits me.

I can teach you the same thing this article can, but my lessons are free. And hands-on.

"Hey, Moretti?"

She looks over the lid of her laptop at me. With the sun streaming in through the window, it looks like there's a halo around her head. Her hair is messy and her face is naked.

Fucking hell. She's something else. *More* than something else. Beauty and brains.

"Hmm?"

"The offer still stands," I say. I walk out the door, without turning back, and head to my flat and the disaster I'm no doubt walking into.

I'd say it was worth it.

CHAPTER TWENTY-NINE

Camilla

"IT'S GOOD."

My mom's warm laughter fills the line. "Good? That's equivalent to *fine*. Have you been butting heads with Dad again?"

"A few times, but nothing serious."

I stare out at the starting grid to the left of me. This particular track has the hospitality suite above the garage, so it affords me a wonderful people-watching vantage point of the pits below.

Crew members talking shit to one another. A possible secret rendezvous between one of our pit crew members and one of Bickman's PR minders, if the little disappearance behind a trailer is to be believed.

And then there's Riggs. Holy hell is there Riggs. He decided rather than just walk the track with Hank the one time, he was going to jog it again for part of his cardio.

Shirtless.

And now he's standing down below me, his sweat-misted skin glistening in the bright sun, his red Moretti track shorts with a dark red stain from his sweat, and his hair in a messy disarray, talking to Ari about who knows what.

But I'm not complaining.

Not in the least.

"What was that, Mom?" I ask, trying to *un-distract* myself.

"I said, between you, me, and the fence post, he comes home every night bragging about how incredible you are. Your ideas. The way you see things. How well you articulate."

"He's my dad, he has to say things like that."

Her laugh floats through the line. "Actually he doesn't. There have been plenty of times over the years that he has griped about you—"

"Hey." I laugh.

"You asked. I answered, but I'm serious. He's so impressed with what you've already brought to the table." She falls silent for a beat, her voice softer when she speaks again. "Thank you, Cam. I knew this was going to make a difference to him, for him . . . but I had no idea how much. In the short time you've been here, I've seen him relax considerably. Just know, I'm so very grateful that you are making this sacrifice for him."

Tears blur my vision of the blue sky, and I swallow over the lump in my throat. "I'm at work. Don't make me cry."

"Sorry." She laughs through what I can tell are her own tears.

"Truth be told, I'm enjoying it more than I thought I would."

And at the exact moment I say that, Riggs looks up to where I'm standing and grins. Yep, that was my uterus tightening up. That was a full-body ache zooming right in on the location between my thighs.

How much longer are we going to play this game?

"Did you just say you're enjoying it?" She sounds surprised.

"I did. I am." *Look away from him. Step back from the balcony. Save your sanity*—and your panties. "I miss home and everything that's there—"

"This has been your home too," she says. And she's right. It has. The Moretti family has always split its time between Italy and the United Kingdom, but after college, I chose Italy. I chose to be as far away from the racing part of our family as possible.

"It has," I say and smile. "But not like this. Not with such a permanence. But I think the change has been good. I didn't think that it would be when he asked me, but it's been good for me."

It's incredible how I've already begun to create a whole new life here in only a few months. Same friends—just added some new ones. Have discovered new places—vintage shops, hole-in-the-wall pubs, quaint but postcard-worthy gardens all about.

And then there's work. I love the challenge of it. Of having to prove myself. Of trying to bring Moretti to the industry's forefront again.

"Speaking of change," she says in that voice that has me taking notice.

"What?" I ask cautiously.

"I have to find out from social media about the new hair? It looks incredible."

I automatically reach up and play with its ends. We didn't do much, but it's amazing how some shape and subtle low lights freshened up my hair. "How did you know?"

"Isabella and Gia are so very proud of their feat. They may have posted several times about it. Dare I ask what they had to bribe you with?"

Of course, they posted about it.

"Nothing. Well, I take that back. It was the lesser of many evils. Hair. Shoes. Wardrobe. Being set up."

She laughs. "Wow. They really hit you with all the things you hate."

"See? I picked the easiest two."

"Hair and shoes?"

I nod and smile. "Hair and shoes."

"Well if the hair looks that good, I can't wait to see what the shoes look like."

"You'll find out soon enough. I've been roped into agreeing to go shopping with them on Monday." I say it like I'm dreading it, but only the shopping part. Not the being with them part.

They add a little spark to the week, and I can't deny I always leave them feeling in a better mood.

"Ohhh, send pics. Or better yet, enough of these quick stop-ins for a hug and to raid my fridge."

"You're never home." I laugh.

"I am too. Just not the hours you frequent." She laughs. "I've been busy, but fingers crossed that all of my cases are coming to a close in the next month," she says of her volunteer position as a child advocate for those in the foster system. It's been her passion project for as long as I can remember. It gives her purpose and helps others at the same time.

"All at once? How'd that happen?"

"I don't know. A stroke of luck? Fate knowing my baby girl would be moving here so I could shower her with all my love instead? Which is the perfect segue for me. We need to go to lunch. You and me. We need to make our own girl time. I promise I won't force you to shop or anything."

I smile. "I'd love that."

"Good. Now make sure you tell the girls they're invited too. I love how much they love you."

"Me too," I murmur, her comment still on my mind long after the call ends.

I love how much they love you.

The same sentiment has been on my mind a lot lately. They check in on me constantly. They send food my way when they deem I'm working too hard. They kidnap me for surprise massages.

Maybe it's time I just tell them why I don't want to change my wardrobe.

Maybe it's time I finally let somebody in.

The question is why though? Why do I feel like that now?

A noise behind me has me turning, has me looking right into the light gray eyes and devastating smile of one sexy Spencer Riggs.

The man who looked at me, protected me . . . and showed me that Brandon LeCroix is the exception, *not* the rule.

And then it clicks.

Oh, the irony.

Because of Riggs, the man I'd thought egotistical and self-centered, I believe I can finally share what I've kept hidden emotionally for years.

Wow. I hadn't expected that.

Now if I can just bring myself to act on that—with both my friends . . . *and with Riggs.*

Baby steps.

"Hi. You're sweaty."

"It's not sweat. It's called sex appeal. And my offer still stands." His grin turns lopsided as he shuts the door behind him and moves into the room.

I was hoping he had forgotten that whole offer bit. I haven't, but I was hoping he had.

"No, it's not," I say and roll my eyes. "It's called sweat."

He shrugs. Smirks. "That's what happens when you get your heart rate up. *Exert yourself.* You should try it sometime."

"I should, huh?"

He looks up and down the length of my body, his eyes lighting with as much suggestion as his tone does. "Yep. There are all kinds of ways one can accomplish an increased heart rate."

"There are?" I play coy when my body's reaction says it knows exactly what he's inferring.

"Oh, Camilla," he murmurs, "there most definitely are."

He reaches to the side of me, his body skimming mine as he does. "What are you doing?" I demand.

I freeze.

My nerve endings are ablaze at his touch.

His face is inches from mine. His lopsided smirk front and center. "Grabbing a bottle of water."

"Oh. Okay." I go to jump out of the way only to realize the table is at my back and he's at my front. I turn to see where he's looking only to bump into him again. "Wait. That's my wa . . . ter," I say as he upends the bottle and gulps the entirety of it.

His arm is up so his bicep is there—in my face. His chest is at eye level, the striations in the muscles clear as day. And then there's the small amount of water that falls from his mouth and slides in a rivulet down his neck and then drops to the floor below.

Kiss him.

Grab him and kiss him, Camilla.

My angel and devil war with my libido shoving both aside and telling me I better act or it's going to riot.

"Riggs." His name is breathy. Strained.

He takes his time setting the empty bottle down and then looking at me with a quirked brow and a ghost of a smile. "Is there something you wanted?" he murmurs.

You.

One hundred percent *you.*

I gulp as my heart beats a punishing staccato in my chest that I swear he can hear.

"Yes," I croak, my fingers itching to touch and my lips desperate to feel his again.

"Speak up," he says moving even closer, his eyes locked on mine. "I couldn't hear you."

"This is getting ridiculous," I whisper.

"What part? You wanting to kiss me or me wanting to do so much more with you?"

And there go the panties.

How about the part where I want to do this—all of this—with you, but am terrified that I'm going to freeze up? That I'm not going to do or be what you need me to be? That I'm not going to feel anything? Again . . .

"I—uh—"

"Camilla?"

Riggs is already three feet away from me when the door is pushed all the way open.

"Yes?"

"Oh, sorry," Heather says. "I didn't mean to inter—"

"You didn't." I force a smile. Please make her believe it. "Riggs was just showing me his latest AITA video."

She smiles. "Everyone is talking about them. Brilliant. Simply brilliant idea."

"Thanks."

"May I have a minute of your time?" she asks.

"Yes. Of course," I say as Riggs moves toward the door.

"I'll catch you later, Camilla. We need to finish this conversation." He looks back and smirks. "My offers don't stay on the table forever."

Both Heather and I watch him walk away, but only one of us is shaking their head.

CHAPTER THIRTY

Riggs

"IT'S PULLING TO THE RIGHT." The whole car vibrates all around me.

I fight the wheel—been fighting it all fucking race. My arms ache and I keep trying to force my hands to relax.

A tighter grip doesn't always mean a quicker reaction.

"We know." That's Hank's equivalent to we fucking know and we're no closer to having a solution. It's race day. It's way past the time where we can make any major adjustments. "Do your best, mate."

"Understood," I say, determined to muscle this thing to the finish line.

And while I might need to loosen my grip on the wheel, I sure as shit don't stop gritting my teeth every time another driver—Rossi, Laurent, Cavanaugh, McElroy, Navarro, what feels like fucking everybody—passes me.

I challenge them when I can, but more than anything, I stay close to Andrew who's sitting at P3. I help fend them off. It's harder to overtake two cars at once than just one.

Because I sure as shit am not going to get a chance at a high finish, but Andrew can. And that's good for Moretti. It's F1 teamwork at its finest.

So I drive my arse off. No doubt pissing fellow drivers off while at the same time, earning their respect.

I've never worked harder for someone else than I do today.

And when Andrew places P3—takes a podium—when the team erupts into a torrent of cheers, I may be jealous as fuck, but I'm also proud and claim a small iota of the accomplishment for myself.

"Tough day out there. You did what you could, Riggs," Hank says.

"Ten-four. Thanks for all your hard work, guys."

For the first time ever, when I pull into the garage, Carlo isn't there waiting to greet me.

It's not because you didn't finish in the points.

It's because you helped someone else do just that and so he's over celebrating with them.

You're not getting your ride yanked.

I reiterate all the reasons he might not be there—over and over—but there's still underlying panic.

Ari greets me though. "Hell of a drive, mate. Not your fault the car wasn't where it should be. But you battled. You drove a race you should be proud of. Congrats."

I shake his hand, still thinking I could have done better, but deep down knowing I couldn't have.

A little humility goes a long way.

I turn to hand my helmet off to someone and am surprised to see Camilla down in the garage. This typically isn't her place. And it most definitely isn't hers when Carlo isn't here.

But what catches my attention isn't so much that Camilla is in the garage—although my ego more than likes that—it's the expression on her face as she looks into the crowd milling on pit row.

The crowd being crew members of various teams and team dignitaries.

Her face is pale, her expression—the only way I can describe the look on her face is *spooked.*

I try to find where she's looking—see what she's seeing—but only see a shit ton of people. And when I look back at her, she catches me watching her and buttons her emotions up quicker than shit.

I narrow my brows at her, curiosity owning me when I should be worried about the points I didn't earn.

She just shakes her head, offers a tight smile, and then before I can think much more of it, Hank pulls me away.

"So describe the car to me. What it felt like. How the pull on the right front felt."

I'm so grateful that it hasn't taken too long for the crew and me to gel. To find our groove and work well together. To communicate in ways we both understand.

"Felt we had some issues with graining on corner number four. Front end isn't gripping hard enough, so it's sliding, burning through my grip. Some understeer."

"Yeah, I'm thinking we went the wrong way with the tires," Hank says. "We should have changed to medium instead of hard."

"All right."

"Good work supporting Andrew out there."

"Thanks, mate." I head across to physio as I wouldn't mind Tori looking at my right shoulder.

I can't get across the paddock and into the Moretti hospitality suite fast enough.

I all but collapse onto the physio table.

"Where's the pain, Riggs?" Tori asks.

"Right shoulder down into my bicep. Think I tweaked something."

"Okay. Let me see what I can do for you. Then you'll need heat and then ice on it."

"You're the boss." My groans and whimpers follow soon thereafter as Tori and her incredible hands work the knots out of my shoulders and neck.

"I could kiss you," I murmur, my face pressed into the donut of the table.

"If I had a dollar for every time I heard that, I'd be rich."

Her hands feel like heaven. Firm but soothing as she kneads and presses and works the muscles in my back.

"Let's throw caution to the wind. Run away with me, Tori. I promise we could have a good life."

Her laugh rings out—no doubt her husband and four kids would disagree with me—and then she falls silent. *Someone else has entered the room.*

"Go away," I mutter and wave a hand in the direction of the door.

A throat clears. Anya. "A few things," she says.

"Buzzkill."

She chuckles. "Your phone?"

Shit. "Yes. Thanks. I didn't think to bring it. Should I worry about the texts you're seeing on there?"

"No. Do you want me to read them to you?" Her feet make noise as she moves farther into the room.

"Only the clean ones," I tease.

"Right. Your mum said 'Great job working for the team. That's how it's supposed to be done.' Wills said, and I quote, 'Sorry about the car. We'll drink in your honor tonight.'"

"Of course he will."

"And Dee texted." She pauses. "She said 'Maxim said to tell you, it wasn't your fault. Shit happens. Not to worry, he'll stay injured longer so you can redeem yourself.'"

I smile. I genuinely fucking smile because that's Maxim. He sounds like he's back. "Awesome."

"Oh, and he said he wants to see you soon."

I lift my head up to look at her. "He did?"

She nods. "He did."

My smile turns into a grimace as Tori hits a particularly sore spot and I put my head back down.

I let my mind drift.

No points today.

But not a DNF. I fought the motherfucking car. I made a good showing with what I had.

I'll take that as a rite of passage. As my own personal win.

CHAPTER THIRTY-ONE

Camilla

"I'M GOING TO TRIP AND BREAK MY ANKLES IN THESE." I LOOK DOWN at the strappy heels on my feet and know I'm going to have one—most likely *several*—of those moments where you lose your balance and look like a five-year-old wearing your mother's heels. Your foot goes one way, your ankle the other, and then you fall face first to the ground.

That will be me.

Just give me a few more minutes.

"Rule number one of being fashionable? Suffering is a must," Isabella says with the wave of her hand.

"Awesome. Please, remind me why I agreed to this again?" I ask, wishing my water was wine, but one of us has to go back to work after our lunch date.

"We can always take the shoes back and go for the clothes makeover instead," Gia says over the rim of her glass of merlot.

I hold my hands up. "No complaints here. None whatsoever." I laugh and look down again at them and the four bags of designer shoes I agreed to purchase on our shopping trip.

Or rather, *their* shopping. My feet to try said shoes on. My credit card to slap down for payment.

I'd never admit it to Isabella or Gia, but there is something to be said about how these shoes make me feel. Feminine. A badass. Strong but delicate.

If you didn't want it, then maybe you shouldn't have tempted me, Milla. That dress? Those tits? Your body? Don't blame me for taking what you were offering.

Even all this time later, I can still hear the condescension in Brandon's tone as he stood over me buttoning his fly.

Did I "ask for it" by flirting with him? Did I invite it by wearing short skirts and tight tops that showcased my body just like every other girl my age did?

No.

I know that now. I knew it then. But it didn't stop the trauma from making me believe differently. From changing how I presented myself to the world.

But these shoes . . . it's like the slightest touch of femininity has made me acknowledge the power it holds.

Who would have thought shoes could do that?

"She does like them. She keeps staring at them," Gia says as I break from my thoughts.

"I'm getting used to them, is what I'm doing." If I tell them my epiphany, they'll have a whole new wardrobe picked out and delivered for me by the time I get home. It's best to let me digest this a bit more before I let them in on it.

And telling them about my experience has been on my mind many times over the past few weeks. If they knew what Brandon did—the assault, how it affected my sense of safety, my self-confidence, let alone how I feel about my body—then maybe they'll understand why I dress how I do.

And with that revelation, no doubt will come massive guilt on their part. For not knowing. For trying to change my clothes when they had no understanding why I wear what I wear. The last thing I want to do is to make them feel guilty.

So one day soon I'll tell them.

Not today though. Today is for fun—and apparently strappy shoes.

"You're right. She does like them." Isabella's grin is bright enough for the three of us. "First shoes, then who knows what else is next."

"I know what else," Gia says, turning her whole body toward me and lifting her eyebrows.

"What?" Oh, shit. Not *that* look.

"I think there's something you're not telling us," Gia says.

"What do you mean?" I ask.

"Do you think we don't follow Moretti and its racers? That at some point we wouldn't recognize that one particular racer is the same man who you conveniently ran into in the bar that night? I mean, great job marketing; his face is everywhere. And bad job covering it up—because his face is fucking everywhere." She laughs and narrows her eyes at me. "You played us, Moretti."

"I didn't. I swear." I hold my hands up. "I promise. It was just as much of a shock to me that he was the new driver as it is to you."

"Uh-huh." Gia does not sound convinced.

"You know the excuse is going to be that he's an employee now so she can't fuck him." Ever subtle Isabella strikes again.

"Yep. She snowed us. Freaking snowed us," Gia says.

"Hello. I'm right here." I wave my hands back and forth to prevent them from carrying on.

"We know you are, but we also know you bullshitted us into thinking you had something going on with that Spencer guy."

"Riggs. He goes by Riggs," I say.

"Of course, he does," Isabella says.

"And we've kissed," I offer.

"We know. We saw you in the bar." Gia rolls her eyes.

"And a couple weeks ago. And almost at the race this weekend."

That got their attention. "Ooohhh?" It's a collective sound made by both of them.

I nod and suddenly want to spill everything to them—the teasing, the panic attacks, how he slept on my couch, the jealousy, the innuendos—but they'll think I'm crazy for not acting on it. It's not necessary to keep the dare card a secret anymore. I'm completely over it . . . and Riggs is definitely not the guy I thought he was the night we met. Time has proven that to me.

So I tell them.

About the dare card.

"Wait," Isabella says, holding her hands up. "Does that have anything to do with the viral post he did about this?"

Don't lie.

They'll know.

I nod. "Yep."

"Okay, so that was top level, I want your attention because I was a prick, but I'm a guy so I don't know how to apologize type of apology." Gia purses her lips. "I'm not convinced. He needs to grovel more."

I tell them about the first race and the bathroom—our mutual panic attacks and his quiet understanding.

"Hold on." Isabella's eyes shock wider. "Didn't he do an AITA—one about kissing the boss's daughter?"

"And that was after you created the segment—so he *knew* you were going to see it." Gia's skeptical tone suddenly turns more cheerful.

I nod. "And I confronted him over it. Which led to an almost kiss and champagne and—" The two of them exchange a look with smug smiles. "What?"

"Someone likes him," Gia singsongs.

My cheeks heat. I shrug. "I do. Especially after the other night."

"What happened the other night?"

I explain about the party. About the kiss. About the naked man standing in my apartment.

I leave out the frequent dreams he stars in. Riggs on his knees between my thighs. His tongue—a treacherous thing to my sanity—that worked me into oblivion in the most sinfully decadent way. Having an orgasm wake me from sleep as it's rippling through me.

And I most definitely omit that part about how Spencer Riggs is the first man to make me physically react and feel things. I save that for another discussion I know we'll have soon.

Isabella raises a finger as she takes a long sip of her drink. Hopefully she dismissed my flushed cheeks as embarrassment rather than getting hot and bothered over the memory. "You've seen the goods, Cami. You like the goods. Go forth and finally fuck the goods." Her last sentence is a shout that has people turning their heads and me ducking in embarrassment.

"Jesus. Will you quiet down?"

"Nope." She grins devilishly. "You like this guy. Like, really like him, despite the rocky start."

"And he works for the company," I say.

"So what?" Gia throws her hands up. "You said he was a contract driver, right? Temporary for race to race? Are you really going to pass up something with a guy who might not be in the Moretti employ for much longer?"

"You guys are making a bigger deal about this than it is," I say.

Another exchanged look before I get the *mom* look from both of them.

"Camilla. Our sweet Camilla." Gia smiles softly. "There hasn't been a guy since I've known you who has made you get the look you have on your face right now. Even guys who you've had lasting relationships with haven't put the fire in your eyes."

"But—"

"The guy left his own party because you didn't want to be there. He slept on your couch. He does social media advice columns about you. Um, hello? He's into you."

Isabella's comment sticks in my mind as I walk into the office—yes, with my heels still on.

Gia and Isabella made sure of it when they took my purchases and my Jordans with them when they dropped me off.

They know me well enough that I'd have changed out of them immediately.

I enter my office and pull up to a stop when I see my dad sitting in one of the chairs opposite my desk.

"Dad." It's a startled word. "What are you doing here?"

He grins. "I do kind of own the place."

"Funny." Did he find out about the kiss? Did someone record it and post it on social media? Are rumors flying about the conference room when Heather walked in? "I mean, to what do I owe the pleasure?" I ask in my sweetest voice possible.

He chuckles. "I saw the girls drop you off, so I figured I'd meet you down here rather than have Halle call you up."

I move around my desk and take a seat facing him. There are no visible tremors today. In fact, there have been very few that I've seen lately.

I know the lack of them doesn't mean his diagnosis has changed. I'm not that naïve. But it is a good sign that having family around and less stress is a good thing for him.

"You look good. Like *really* good."

"I feel good." He nods and looks out my open door to make sure that Elise isn't still there before continuing. "That change they made to my meds has helped a lot. In a month it might be different, but for now, I'm just taking it one day at a time."

I nod and chuckle nervously. "So . . . what's wrong?"

"Why? Do I have reason to be worried about something?"

"No, but I've been here almost three months, and this is the first time you've been in my office, waiting for me with that cryptic look on your face."

"You always were the worrier." He laughs. "Nothing is wrong, Cam. In fact, everything is good. Both cars have finished in the points four out of the last five races. We got a podium. I watched a driver become a team player with that race. The public is loving the duo of Andrew and Riggs. Maxim's making strides to return. He's slowly increasing his mobility. Oh, and merchandise sales have skyrocketed with that whole A-I-T-A thing you're doing."

I bark out a laugh at the way he spells out AITA, like it's a foreign language. "Dad, do you have any idea what AITA means?"

His blank stare tells me he hasn't made the correlation between the posts and the acronym.

"Um, Andrew is the Animal?" He scrunches his nose up. Even he knows that sounds ridiculous.

"No. Definitely not that." I glance out the window of my office where Elise has since returned and see her snickering. "It means *Am I the Asshole.* That's why Riggs says it with every post."

"Oooohhhh." He shakes his head. "Your generation and your YOLOs and FOMOs and FMLs or my personal favorite, WTF."

I'm afraid to ask if he knows what that stands for. "You sound so old."

"I am old." He pauses and smiles. "I just wanted to come down here and tell you that you and your team are doing an excellent job. It's unusual for profits to reflect marketing changes in such a short amount of time and yet it's trending in the right direction."

"Thank you." I can barely get the words out, my throat is so tight. "That means . . ." *Everything.*

"It's me who should do the thanking." He purses his lips. "You've kept pretty tight-lipped on your opinion about Riggs, other than your initial criticism. He has five races under his belt now with Moretti. Have your thoughts changed any?"

Am I walking into a trap?

Am I the asshole for wanting to kiss her right now? For wanting to prove to her that I'm good at it?

I take a moment to think before I answer. "He's still a little rough around the edges, but I think that edge gives him an advantage. He's racing well and shows he has the skill to rightfully be in F1."

"True." He nods and runs his finger and thumb over his chin in thought. "FIA wasn't thrilled with his overtake in Hungary."

"They weren't thrilled with Rossi's either."

He nods in contemplation and then says softly, "Yeah, well, Rossi is . . . *Rossi.* The exception to all the rules." He chuckles and then gets a wistful look in his eyes. "Spencer's dad—Ethan Riggs—was . . . really something special to watch. You couldn't take your eyes off him. Larger than life. Commanded attention on and off the track. Reckless in a way that you were afraid to look away for a second because you might miss something incredible—good or bad. We were close in age, and I remember being slightly jealous that he got the fun job." His smile is bittersweet.

"Do you think the comparison the media is making is fair?'

"I think it's natural. It doesn't help that they're spitting images of each other. It makes the comparison easier to make." He shrugs. "The same will probably happen when you take over for me someday."

"True." I'm not ready to think about that. "But I don't think it's fair. The comparisons I mean."

"Agreed. He seems pretty unflappable though. He bites back when need be."

"I'm sure that thrills Anya."

My dad grins. He always did like a rebel. "It does, but that keeps her on her toes."

"She's hinted as much." I glance over to the small side table where the posters are laid out. Riggs in his Moretti red and that devastating grin look back at me. "I know all drivers say they're fearless, but they have to get scared sometimes. A hard crash. A near miss. Do you think that fear is different because of his dad?"

"Funny you should say that. Omar approached me the other day about something. Maybe that's why I came to talk to you. To get your opinion."

"About?"

"It's been seventeen years since the accident. All the tracks have been updated or the circuit changed to a new location. Every track except for Suzuka, where Riggs's dad died."

"Oh." I think of the Japanese track and picture it in my mind. Such a peaceful setting—as almost all the tracks are—but with the potential to wreak so much devastation.

He nods, his lips twisting. "It's coming up soon. He's never raced there so it'll be a first. Do I let him? Do I talk to him and give him the choice? Do I task the new reserve driver we just signed on with taking the wheel there? I don't fucking know." He scrubs a hand over his face and for the first time I see a tremor. Clearly, he's been agonizing over this.

I stare at my dad, thoughts flying through my head. The bathroom scene during that first race flashes back to me. Riggs vomiting. My panic attack.

Was it nerves in general or was it the fear he'd end up like his father?

Isn't that the same thing I've wondered myself? My dad's illness? Do I carry the same gene mutation that has made him sick?

How would I feel if someone held me back from something because they'd prejudged me as having it?

"What did you tell me when I asked you why you were hiding . . . *everything?*" I ask quietly with a quick glance outside my office. "That it's your choice *if and when* you decide to tell people about your diagnosis. That keeping your dignity is important. I know it's not even in the same realm, but don't you think the sentiment is similar? That Riggs probably feels somewhat the same? That it's his decision?"

"Yeah. I know. I agree . . . I just . . . Maxim's accident wasn't that long ago. The last thing I want is a driver with an unclear head in the car. I don't need, want, or wish upon us another bad accident." He still carries guilt over Maxim's accident. That much is evident in the tone of his voice and the lines etched in his face.

"No one ever wishes that, Dad. It's the sport. It's dangerous. The drivers know that and isn't that part of the draw for them? The thrill?"

"I know, Cam, I know."

CHAPTER THIRTY-TWO

Camilla

IT'S BEEN A LONG, VERY STRANGE DAY. SHOPPING WITH THE GIRLS. THE talk with my dad. Not killing myself in these heels. And now this.

The Cosmopolitan magazine on my floor where it must have been stuffed under my door. The same magazine that Riggs sat on the other night and that I swiftly moved after he fell asleep—mortified that he read it.

You've seen the goods, Cami. You like the goods. Go forth and finally fuck the goods.

My issues have never come from not wanting sex or not being attracted to the person I'm with. That is simple. It's the fact that when it gets to intimacy, the spark you're supposed to feel? That snap of a live wire when the other person touches you? It doesn't happen. Sex for me is like going through the motions for the sake of going through them.

One should never dread intimacy and yet that has been exactly how I've felt since Brandon.

Do I know what an orgasm feels like? *Yes,* and only because I've given myself one by my own hand to prove to myself that I'm not broken and actually do feel.

But has a man ever physically helped me achieve one?

No. Nope. Never.

Well . . . no man except Riggs. Or rather, the dream version of Riggs.

I pick up the magazine and fan through it. Is this magazine here because he thinks he ruined mine or because he's renewing his offer?

Seconds pass as I stare at the bound pages, my nerves building.

What part? The you wanting to kiss me or the me wanting to do so much more with you?

I drop my purse and my tote bag on the floor just inside the door and stride down the hall toward his door.

Each step my confidence wanes and my nerves dance.

A part of me hopes he doesn't answer the door when I knock. The other part wonders what the hell I'm going to say to him if he does.

And as if on cue, he opens the door, shirtless, and in a pair of gray sweatpants.

Of course he's wearing that.

"Well, hello there." He smirks and narrows his eyes, clearly aware that I'm worked up about something.

"Hi. Yes." *Oh shit.* I stride past him and into his flat. I falter for a minute as I take in the rich colors and weathered wood. It looks so very different—emptier—than the last time I was here.

"You were saying?" Riggs asks, prompting me to turn around and meet his amused eyes and arms crossed over his chest that makes every muscle visible. Bulge. I drag my eyes up to meet his and his raised eyebrows.

Breathe, Camilla. Breathe.

"Here's the deal. I have what you want, and you have something I need."

"Here I am, baby," he teases with his arms out, a cocky grin deepening his dimples.

"Exactly."

"What?" If whiplash were a meme, it would be the snapping up of Riggs's head and the shocked opening of his eyes.

I hold a finger up to stop him from talking just as he starts. "You want a full-time F1 ride. Your perks. For me to put in a good word for you with another team when Maxim comes back."

"Yes." He draws the word out, that cocky smirk now fading as his eyes narrow. "I'm not following you. I mean I am, believe me *I am* . . . but make it make sense."

"I'm working through some things."

"You're going to have to give me more than that, Gasket."

I emit an annoyed sigh at the silly nickname, failing at making myself believe that a part of me doesn't find it endearing.

"Cat got your tongue?" he eggs on.

"Sex."

"A three-letter word. Starts with S. Is a noun but personally I think it should be a verb considering there's a lot of action going on when you have it. And clearly something that makes you blush. What am I missing here?"

"I need to have sex."

He coughs over a laugh. "Need or want? Need's a very strong word."

The amusement in his eyes says he's enjoying toying with me—almost as if he knows why I'm here and is going to make me go through a whole *spiel* to get it.

Dying a thousand deaths sounds more appealing right now than finishing this conversation.

"Nope. Don't stop now." He must see me waffling. "The Camilla Moretti I know goes after what she wants. Whether it's a kiss in a bar. A driver she wants to go viral. And this. Whatever *this* is."

"There are some things that . . . I want to have sex. Sex with you." *Fucking hell.* "Is that better?"

He makes me wait for a response. He takes a painstakingly slow time to do so. "So we went from me helping you find your sexuality to you wanting to have sex. I mean . . . that escalated quickly."

"They go hand in hand."

"Um. Okay. Sure. I can see the correlation, but . . ." He hangs his head and chuckles. Normally I'd be offended but, for some reason, Riggs's reaction doesn't make me feel that way. "Care to expand?"

"It's . . ." I sputter. Then groan. Then scrunch my nose up. "There was this thing, which caused this other thing that made me . . . never mind."

"Sounds like there are a lot of *things*."

"It's complicated."

He takes a step closer, his smirk curling up one side of his mouth. "What is? Sex? Sexuality? Owning it? Wanting it?" He shrugs. "Not really."

"I'll pay you." *Fucking hell. Did I just really say that?* Desperation makes people say the stupidest things. Case in point, right here.

"Oh. So you want me as a driver and as a prostitute." He's fighting his smile.

I'm making a disaster of this.

"No. Not like that. I'd pay you for your time. I mean—"

"So an escort, a prostitute, and a driver. Got it."

"Do you know the courage it took to come down here? How hard it is to ask someone this?"

"I can't imagine."

"Stop making this harder than it is."

"*Hard* is what you're asking for, right?"

"Oh my God." He's enjoying this, isn't he? And he's going to put me through the paces.

His Adam's apple bobs and he coughs out a laugh. "Why?"

"Why, what?"

"Why me? Why now? Why—" He motions to his flat as if it's the third person in this conversation. "This?"

"Why are you asking so many questions? What guy wouldn't say yes to sex without strings? To not having to deal with emotions or feelings?" The dare card creeps into my head, but then I push it away. He may have said I wasn't his type that first night, but every day since then he's shown me otherwise. And yet, doubt creeps in. Insecurity. I buckle. "You know what? Never mind. Just let me go crawl in a hole and die."

But as I try to walk past Riggs, he shifts to block my path and the door. His hands move to my biceps and his voice quiets until I finally look up and meet his eyes.

"Just let me go. *Please.*"

He nods slowly, but his eyes never leave mine. "I know most guys' dreams are to deflower a virgin, but not me. That's not what I want to be remembered for. That kind of thing should have strings. Lots of them."

It takes a second for what he's implying to sink in. "No. God. What? I'm not a virgin."

The irony in that entire statement. Sex—that I didn't consent to—is why I'm in this position in the first place. I've got past what was done to me but am still trying to understand how the body I was left with feels about being touched.

"Then what is it?" He looks at me with an intensity that almost makes me want to tell him.

"It's . . . does it matter why?"

He chuckles, and I swear to God it's the sound of a feather tickling over my skin.

His nearness.

His fresh-from-the-shower scent.

The feel of his hands on my arms.

The warmth of his breath on my lips.

"If you're planning on using me as your fuckboy, then yes, Camilla, it does matter."

Nerves own my every move. My every thought. My every reaction.

"I don't even know what to say to that," I whisper.

"I do."

"What?" Tears burn in the backs of my eyes. Why did I do this? Why didn't I lose my nerve and walk into my flat and lock myself in? This was a grave mistake. One I fear I won't live down.

It's such a weird dichotomy. Wanting him to touch me and knowing he's probably laughing at me in his head right now. "Don't tell me you're going to pull a dare card out to put me in my place and scare me off again."

"No. I'm going to tell you that you made a slight miscalculation."

"About?"

"There are two things I want, Cami. The one you mentioned—keeping a ride in F1—but I can do that myself."

"The other?"

My nerves skitter through every part of me. I need to leave. I can't—

"Camilla. Look at me." He waits for my eyes to flutter up to his, and the serious expression in his eyes shocks me. *You*. You're the other thing I want."

CHAPTER THIRTY-THREE

ME? And before I can properly process the thought, Riggs's lips are on mine. One hand skates up my spine and fists in my hair while the other moves to the small of my back and tugs me against him.

You. You're the other thing I want.

The sensations make their appearances. The ache. The sweet burn. The tightened nipples. The wetness pooling between my thighs.

"There are rules," I blurt out, nerves getting the better of me as I push my hands against his chest.

What if I don't feel anything?

What if this doesn't work?

He tugs my head back by my hair so I'm forced to stop thinking, and I have to look up into his darkened eyes and arrogant smirk. "Are you going to break out a PowerPoint for me?"

"When you're with me, there's no one else."

"Stop talking, Camilla. I'm about to fuck you. I want to think about how good your pussy is going to feel when I push into you for the first time. I want to think about what sounds you make when you come. Not rules. Now is for fucking. For screaming my name. After is for whatever crash course in Camilla Rules there are. Got it?"

"Yes." It's a breathless syllable of consent and thank God because, what was I thinking *talking* when all I want to do is get lost in the already overwhelming sensations and we haven't even started yet?

Your turn, Camilla.

Take what you asked for.

I lean into Riggs and meet his lips. The kiss starts off slow, steady, but there's an underlying hunger in it. A telltale vibration hinting at how hard he's holding tight to his control.

It's a heady feeling.

Empowering.

And I want more of everything.

His hands cuff my wrists against his chest so that our sole focus is our kiss. The meeting of our lips. Our tongues. Our smothered moans and swallowed groans.

His lips coax me, brand me, tempt me, with the promise of what is to come. And with the knowledge if this is what just his mouth can make my body feel—then I might combust when we're skin to skin.

Each kiss grows more urgent than the next.

Each tug of my lip or touch of our tongues creates more desperation.

He releases my hands and the pent-up need to touch, to be touched, explodes in an all-out war to see who can touch each other's skin the fastest.

It's calloused fingertips up my rib cage as I pull my shirt over my head.

It's stuttered breaths as I scrape my fingernails over that perfect V of his and then shove his sweats down so his cock can spring free.

It's even more gorgeous than I remember.

It's his hiss when he sees me shirtless. "Christ, woman. You're gorgeous."

We stand like this—inches apart—for a few seconds as anticipation races through my veins.

And then from one beat to the next, we launch ourselves at each other, meeting somewhere in the middle. We're a mass of hands and tongues and commands and haste.

Clothes prevent what we want the most. To touch. To taste. To see. And so we're discarding them as fast as we can, all the while trying to kiss our way through the delayed gratification.

His sweats get kicked off. And his fingers find their way beneath my panties as he pushes my pants down.

"Yes." It's a strangled cry as his fingers part me, play with me, enter me.

"You're fucking gorgeous," he mutters before his mouth slants over mine again. "Stunning." A slide of his tongue down the curve of my neck. "About to get fucked." His chuckle rumbles against the pulse on my throat and reverberates through me.

But I don't need words.

I don't need seduction.

There's just him doing exactly what I asked him to do—make me feel. Overwhelm me with sensations that I never imagined existed before. I'm like a blind woman seeing color for the first time, and now I want to see the whole damn color chart at once.

And I'm pretty sure Riggs understands my mewls and moans because he doesn't relent. He doesn't give up.

He's everywhere at once, hands and teeth and lips and skin, and it's nowhere near enough to my awakened senses.

We shift backward somehow, our feet moving as our hearts race, until I bump into a wall. A nervous giggle falls from my lips but quickly shifts to a groan as he dips and takes my nipple in his mouth.

When he closes his lips around it and sucks, it's like a mainline to every erogenous zone in my body. At the same time he positions his other hand so his thumb can add friction to my clit.

It's a one-two punch that has me bucking into his hand and begging for more.

The sensations are so much and not enough at the same time.

I'm greedy. Needy. Desperate for more.

We stumble backward into the bedroom, our laughs floating through the air. He pushes me back playfully onto the bed as he gets a condom to protect us.

And as soon as that's on, he's stroking his cock and crawling between my thighs. But he stops short of touching me and I suddenly panic.

"What—"

"You are . . . Jesus, you're hot."

And just as soon as I settle into his words, I gasp as he slides his cock up and down the length of my slit.

"Good God, woman." He groans—the sound an aural aphrodisiac—and uses the head of his cock to spread my arousal all around.

And then he pushes his way into me, inch by beautiful inch, until he's sheathed root to tip. Our mutual groan is the only sound in the room, as he lets me adjust and enjoy the feel of him filling me.

It's the sweetest of burns and the most pleasurable of aches. Nerve endings spark to life. I'm so overwhelmed with the onslaught of sensations, but it's the trembling of his hand on my hip that brings me back.

Riggs's rein on his constraint is slipping.

I writhe beneath his touch. Onto his cock. Needing him to move. Trying to cut those reins.

He hisses "fuck" out into the room seconds before he begins to move. And the minute he does, I sink into the pleasure his cock creates and soar in its haze.

Every thrust in and pull back out causes a chain reaction of indescribable sensations I've never felt and know I'll only want to feel from here on out.

"Faster," I moan as my body begs for more. As my pussy tightens around him.

"Yes. The answer is always yes," he groans, his eyes meeting mine, his eyelids heavy with desire. "You're a fucking goddess. All wet for me. So ready for my cock."

He sets a punishing pace, and I can imagine there will be bruising from the way he's grabbing my hips.

This. Feels. Insanely. Amazing.

I close my eyes momentarily and try to let go. To not think. To focus on the action. On the sensations. On the man giving them to me.

Come on, Cam. It's never been like this. Felt like this.

He looks so damn sexy as he rams me higher up the bed. His biceps that flex as he holds my hips. His neck, taut, angry almost. The slap of our skin. The labored breaths.

"C'mon, Cam. Come for me. Come all over my cock."

I want this. I want this so hard.

My breath grows shallow as my body surges with the unexpected current reverberating through me. It's like I've been shocked but there's no release point. No way to ease the pressure that's building like water behind a dam.

Sweat beads on his forehead, and his body is so fucking tense and his cock swells so big from trying to get me there. From trying to make me come.

I cry out when the sensations become too much. When I'm overwhelmed and frustrated and everything in between.

"That's it, just like that," he coos, thinking that I've climaxed seconds before his strangled, ragged cry fills the room. His body jerks and hands tense as he empties himself. As he claims his hard-fought reward.

And as I acknowledge I can definitely feel more now, sadly, I'm still broken.

He leans forward, breathless.

I did that. I did that to him.

The look of awe in his eyes staggers me. "Camilla . . ." *My name is said with reverence.* "We're doing that again. And again. Damn, you turn me on." He slides his free hand up my rib cage to rest just beneath my breast. "And those fuck-hot heels you were wearing?"

"I was wearing them for me."

"Fuck that. You'll be wearing those and nothing else next time when I take you against a wall."

CHAPTER THIRTY-FOUR

Riggs

MY CHEST HEAVES AND MY HEART RACES AS I LIE ON MY BACK, stare at my ceiling, and will my brain to string together coherent thoughts.

Jesus Christ.

I'm not used to wanting and waiting.

I'm used to wanting and taking.

This whole time, existence, whatever this has been with Camilla, has been like one drawn-out foreplay. And while I never put much stock in the act, I'm beginning to look at it in a whole new light.

The woman is . . . *fucking incredible.*

That's not a thought to string together at all.

She laughs breathlessly and it's the sexiest fucking sound ever. "Well, I guess I can check off the box for *just ask* when I have a precarious question."

"Ask. Always ask," I say as I turn on my side, my head on my hand, staring at her profile.

"Noted." She smiles but keeps looking at the ceiling. Her bare chest draws my eyes. Dusty pink nipples. Soft-as-sin skin.

I already want her again.

"Speaking of always asking. Sounds like you got what you were looking for." I chuckle. *Never had any complaints yet.*

There is a stutter in her breathing. A quick tensing of her muscles. If I weren't staring right at her, I never would have noticed, but all of a sudden, my ego is in serious jeopardy. "You did come, right?"

I replay every single thing I can remember about the last thirty minutes, everything up until I virtually blacked out as I came. But it's the scrunching of her nose and covering of her face with her hands that knock me on my arse.

She doesn't have to say a word.

"Wow. Okay." Disbelief mars my words as my ego deflates rapidly. I'm becoming defensive about my sex skills. No one has ever complained before. Or did they fake it like Camilla just did? "Um . . ." I exhale audibly, at a loss of what to say for the first time in a long fucking time.

Camilla must sense my shock because she shifts onto her side and grabs my face in her hands. "It's not you," she says, eyes concerned but cheeks still flushed from the sex I thought she was enjoying. *Thought* being the operative fucking word there. "I promise, Riggs. It's not you."

"It takes two. I assure you, it takes two."

"No. Listen to me. Please," she pleads, suddenly flustered and sounding desperate for me to understand. "It's me. I'm broken. That's why . . . that's why I asked you tonight. For this. For sex."

"Broken? I don't . . . talk to me. Why would you say that? Everything . . ." *Worked just fine.* Or at least I thought it did.

Instead of answering, she shakes her head rapidly and starts to get out of bed.

"No." I grab her hand and tug her back down, immediately shifting to straddle her. I lace kisses up her bare torso until she wiggles from the sensations. Until she is caught up in them so much so that her eyes shock up to meet mine when I stop.

Now I've got her attention.

"Lay it on me Moretti. Time for the truth. Did you have an orgasm?"

Even in the darkened room I can see the emotions war across both her face and her eyes. I think she's going to stonewall me, but she shakes her head again softly. "Riggs." Her voice is barely audible as she averts her eyes before fluttering back to mine. "You made me feel things I've never felt before. Sensations. Aches. Pleasure. Things I'd resigned myself to believing I'd never enjoy and to me, that's more than enough."

I swear to God, tears well in her eyes. I'm so glad when she blinks them away because I'm a man—I don't do well with tears.

"Fuck." The word is a sigh as I scrub a hand through my hair and try to process what she's telling me.

"Sex isn't like riding a bike. You just don't get back on it and everything works."

"It does if you speak up and tell your partner what you want. How to pleasure you. How to—"

She snorts. "I could barely ask you for sex, Riggs. Did you expect suggestions when I don't even know?"

"No, but I thought . . . never mind what I thought." *When I don't even know?* Her words hit my ears and finally process. "Wait. What did you mean by that?"

"Nothing." Her smile is fake, placating. "Forget I said anything."

"Camilla. You're naked beneath me. My cock was just in you. It's resting on your stomach and already wanting to have you again. Are you telling me that a guy has never made you come?"

Her cheeks flush and she suddenly grows shy, but in a way that gives me pause. She has a rocking-hot body but wears baggy clothes. Why?

Why does she seem inexperienced, yet—

Oh fuck.

Did someone hurt her in the past?

"Camilla, did something happen to you? Before? In the past?"

"Riggs. I . . . can't. I just . . . can't."

Who fucking hurt you? I want to demand an answer. Need to. But the look in her eyes . . . makes *me* panic.

So I lean forward and press my lips to hers. I don't know what else to do. I feel helpless and guilty and enraged that anyone could use sex like a weapon. Resting my forehead against hers, I shush her. "It's okay. I shouldn't have asked. You don't have to trust me with that information. You've already trusted me with way more than that."

I feel her chest shudder against mine, and it's as though the tension leaves her body in relief.

So many things make sense now.

Baggy Bar Girl.

Yes, you're the arsehole, Riggs, who called her that.

I'm not good with shit like this.

How can I help her? Is it my place to fucking offer?

She came to you for sex, Riggs.

My lips meet hers again. Briefly. Gently. But my brain won't stop thinking.

What if I could help her orgasm? What if I can make her feel so good? About herself. About sex. *Sexy.* That's what she is, and she should know that. Own that. *Is that what she needs?*

What if I could teach her that sex can make her feel good?

It's not like it's a hardship to fuck her. Not in the fucking least.

I lace open-mouthed kisses down the curve of her neck and the slope of her shoulder. I work my way to her breast, taking the nipple in my mouth and sucking on it. Teasing it with my tongue.

"Riggs. What are—"

"Shh." A kiss to beneath her breast. "I'm a determined man." One pressed to her navel. "If at first I don't succeed." To where her strip of tight curls begins. "Try." I spread her thighs apart with my hands. "Try." I take her in. Inhale her scent. And am immediately hard again. "And try again."

I look up to meet her eyes when I lower my mouth and slide my tongue down the slit of her pussy.

CHAPTER THIRTY-FIVE

Camilla

"LET ME WALK YOU TO YOUR FLAT."

"You're being ridiculous. It's just right"—I point the short distance down the hall—"there."

"You never know what might be lurking on the way." He grins and it makes me feel all sorts of different things. Things I don't even want to question. Things I just want to enjoy.

"True. Very true."

He's standing in his doorway with one hand on the doorjamb. He's wearing a pair of gym shorts and pretty much nothing else other than a rumpled head of hair, no doubt from where my hands gripped it tightly.

Yes, Camilla. This really did happen. Every single second of it.

It's like I started feeling and now I can't stop.

The air is colder against my skin. My pants hit just the right way when I shift, and it's a blatant reminder of what just happened. My lips still tingle from his kisses—*both* sets of them.

Our eyes meet. Hold. And that slow crawl of a smile turns up one corner of his lips.

Jesus. My nipples tighten from the visual alone.

"You do know that this was supposed to be good, lighthearted, grip-the-sheets, laugh-somewhere-in-the-middle-because-we-bonked-heads sex, right? You weren't supposed to . . . take on the burden of—"

"First, I did see some sheet gripping, so uh, if you're trying to hurt my ego again so you can have more sex, I'm not falling for it. *All you have to do is ask.*" He winks. "And second, you, this, tonight *was not* a burden. In fact,

I'm pretty sure I just found my newest outside-of-work hobby. A mission, if you will."

"Riggs . . . a mission? What?"

"Yep. How many orgasms can I give Camilla?"

I bury my head in my hands and laugh, all while riding the high from the first one and trying to imagine having more than one during the night.

"In fact, those little hearts you're supposed to color on the calendar because you're excited to see me have now been officially changed to represent orgasms. The question is, how many hearts can you fit on one of those tiny squares?" He grins, clearly proud of himself for this idea. "I guess we'll find out."

I laugh. The sound bubbles up inside me and there's no way I can stop it. It just feels so damn good. So damn freeing. My cheeks hurt from smiling. "I mean, the last thing I want to do is prevent you from completing your mission."

He steps into me and without preamble, frames my face and kisses me. My body has been awakened to so many sensations in the past few hours, so many ways to feel that I didn't know existed, and yet his lips meeting mine, his tongue touching mine, only serves to awaken even more.

"I'm a competitive fucker, Gasket. I don't like to lose." He pats me on the ass as I take a step back. I smile.

"Good thing I'm a team player."

His chuckle follows me as I saunter down the hallway to my flat.

I can feel his eyes on me as I walk. Each step awakens the slight soreness between my legs. My God, I had no idea it could feel that good. Just thinking about it . . .

The desire heavy in his gaze as he dipped his head down and slid his tongue between my thighs.

The coarseness of his hair grasped in my fingers as my hips bucked and thighs clenched.

Jesus, holy mother of all things. I've given myself orgasms. With a vibrator. With the stream of water in my shower. With my own fingers . . . but how is it even possible that the sensations were more intense, more overwhelming when they came by the hand—or rather the very skillful tongue—of Spencer Riggs?

I thought I'd get the buildup but never reach the point of no return.

I reached it all right.

I reached it and I never want to look back.

I close my door and slump against it, closing my eyes, my grin permanent on my lips.

Fuck.

Riggs looks up at me from between my thighs.

My arousal coats his grin.

My body still pulses—big waves that turn to little waves that morph to ripples. My skin tingles. My inner thighs still feel the scratch of his stubble. My pussy still feels his mouth as he sucks on my clit.

I feel every damn thing. In places I never knew my body could feel.

Even the sheets are almost too much for my new hypersensitivity.

But Riggs, shifting onto his knees where he is between my thighs, cock hardening again, is welcome to touch. To pleasure. To take whatever he wants from me.

And the satisfied grin as he crawls over my body and presses his lips to mine says he knows as much.

He props himself on his elbow and lifts an eyebrow. "Now please, please, please, tell me that wasn't faking it. Because if it was, you deserve a goddamn academy award."

He asks just as another tremor shudders through my body.

I chuckle against his lips, his tongue dipping to tease mine. "I've never been happier to not win an award in my life."

I laugh into my empty flat. The sound echoes in the emptiness but feels so damn fulfilling.

For years and years, I've let Brandon LeCroix's actions bind me.

His touch shackle me to feelings of doubt and insecurity.

His words inhibit my own sexuality. Constrain my body's reception of any other touch.

But not anymore.

I may not be able to fully replace or repair those parts he stole from me, but Spencer Riggs just did a mighty job of showing me I can enjoy another man's touch. Sex. I *can* orgasm.

I feared I'd never feel whole . . . sensual. But now?

The cracks I thought were broken in me just might be filled.

The scars will always be there—faded and beneath the surface.

But after tonight, after what Riggs showed me is possible, I might just finally be free.

CHAPTER THIRTY-SIX

"**A**ND THEY'RE TAKING CARE OF YOU WELL?"

I snort. "Yes, Mum. I have handlers and PR minders and physio trainers and dieticians. I mean, if there's a position you can think of, Moretti has it."

I glance across the paddock and lift a hand to Oliver Rossi. He raises a middle finger in turn. The fucker.

"Well, that's comforting to know. And all that travel isn't getting to you?"

"Mum, nothing has changed travel wise, except the accommodations are way nicer, the food better, and the overall treatment is top-notch. I promise you, I'm not being mistreated."

"It seems all so different now than it was," she murmurs.

"Isn't everything these days?"

"True." She pauses. "You've had better success than the talking heads on television predicted you would. Like I had any doubt."

"I just needed a chance. I'm taking it and running with it."

"And you're doing a magnificent job."

"Did you doubt me, Mum?" I tease.

"No, Spence. I didn't. You know that. You must know that." But there's something in her tone that tells me she's worried.

The silence that follows communicates that her concern has to do with way more than me thinking she was doubting my abilities.

The giant elephant in the room that we've been skirting around since I took this contract makes its presence.

"I plan on being there," she says softly.

And there it is.

The Band-Aid ripped off. The wound sliced open.

She's talking about when we race in Japan. At Suzuka. The track where my father died.

It's not for a few weeks now, and yet it feels like every fucking person is talking about it. It was brought up out of the blue in the presser yesterday. It's been in articles written with no real correlation other than to mention the track in the same sentence as my name.

I sigh. Would I like her there? Of course. Is it a good idea for either of us if she is? No.

"I don't think it's a good idea, Mum," I say softly, knowing how much those words are going to hurt her. "It's going to be hard enough being back there, racing that turn, fighting the memory. I need to have a clear head, and there will be enough ghosts filling it that I won't have any room to worry about you or how you're doing." I sigh. "I know that sounds selfish, but—"

"What if it's something I need to do?"

There's quiet desperation in her voice. A sadness that weighs on the connection. "I'll tell you that I understand why you feel that way, but that it also makes me feel like you need to be there because you fear something is going to happen. I can't acknowledge that in any way, shape, or form, or else I'll start to worry too."

"I understand," she says quietly.

Her quiet eats at me long after she hangs up, and I take a stroll through the massive complex that houses this week's race.

Suzuka.

I've been racing now for years in all levels but have yet to return there in any capacity. Not as a spectator. Not as a driver. And sure as shit not as a son remembering his father.

I have mixed feelings on the place in general. And of course, it's the one track that has remained the same. It'll be the one and only time I'll literally be walking in his footsteps. And while that's powerful to me, those footsteps will also lead me to the place that took his life.

And I'm not sure what I will or should do to confront and then move past it.

I've tried to control the one thing I can in this situation—me and my preparation. I've spent endless hours in the sim, trying to understand the turns and curves of the course. Trying to make it so second nature that I don't think about it. So I don't hesitate when I come to it.

I have a few weeks yet before the race to perfect that indifference I'm striving for. It would be even easier to do so if the media would just leave me the fuck alone about "upcoming" races—with the upcoming meaning the Japanese Grand Prix—and let me focus on the one at hand. The race two days from now that needs my undivided attention.

Yet . . . it's draining. I need a distraction. Something other than dwelling on the reporters' questions thrown at me yesterday. Anya's now laying down the law regarding future interviews with me.

And I find that perfect distraction when I look up as I walk into our hospitality suite.

Camilla.

She's sitting in the far back corner of one of the conference rooms in our portable suites.

I know I shouldn't, but I stop and stare.

I can't help myself.

Sex without strings is an awesome fucking concept. It's not my first setup like this so I know how it's supposed to go: the built-in pussy, a person to laugh with over a quick bite before jumping in the sack, the want that isn't easily sated—but without the fucking complications.

There are no hurt feelings if we have other plans. There is no need to divide time between my mates and my girl without someone getting pissed.

There is sex.

There are a few moments of lying there, panting as our hearts decelerate and our bodies come down from the high of sex, and talking about the most random things.

There is clean up.

Then a kiss goodbye at the door.

And the night left to do our own thing.

But fuck, man, this time around—the Camilla version of sex without strings—is so goddamn different. I'm pretty sure the woman with the furrowed brow looking at her laptop right now is the reason for that.

So far, sex with her has been incredible. No further explanation needed.

We may have only been doing this no-strings shit for eighteen days during the mandatory summer break—yes, I'm counting—but they have been some pretty fucking incredible days at that.

The record so far—the hearts she could fill in on the calendar—is four in a night. *Four.* A vibrator. My tongue. My cock—*twice.*

I might have set the bar too high with that one because the woman is insatiable—and I fucking love it. Even better? Watching her confidence skyrocket over the past few weeks. Hands that were timid to slide down and rub her clit to enhance her pleasure, now go straight there. She parts herself so I can see that sweet fucking pink of her pussy, and then goes to work helping get herself off—with her eyes on me the whole time. Watching me watch what she does to herself. To me. To us.

And with that confidence comes a desire to get better at other things. She wants to learn how to suck cock better? I mean . . . it's a hardship, but sure, she can practice on me. *Not a problem.*

A phone call for a cup of coffee in the morning ended up with her bent over my dining table.

A request for some company on a weekend afternoon jog resulted in us slamming against the closed door just as we got home and having rip-the-clothes-off-each-other sex.

The few evenings we've spent together weren't too fucking shabby either. Where we took our time exploring each other's wants and needs before one of us would head back to our own flats.

And when we part ways, I find myself wondering if she enjoyed it. If I gave her what she needed.

And that has never fucking happened before. It's not like I haven't cared about past lovers' enjoyment or fulfillment, but it's never been such a priority. Yes, I'm an undeniable selfish arsehole.

It's as though I feel a self-determined pressure to ensure Camilla knows that all men are not arseholes.

The irony, given I normally am one.

But not the kind I think she's experienced.

I've had to turn my brain off. I've had to tell myself that each touch of her skin, each grip of her hips and nip at her lips, doesn't take her back to whatever he—presumably—did. If I'm honest, it's been fucking brutal.

But I've been successful at it thus far.

"Knock. Knock."

Camilla looks up from the table where she sits. She has papers and printed graphics sprawled out all around her. Her laptop is open, a pencil is tucked behind her ear, but there's the slightest change about her. It takes me a second to see it. Her typical button-up white shirt is present, but it's unbuttoned a few buttons and there's the hint of a red tank top beneath.

Is it surprising that I stare a bit longer, my mouth watering, my mind jumping back to two nights ago and the hunger she greeted me with when I knocked on her door? A yank of my lapels. A meeting of mouths. And so much more with a lot less clothes soon thereafter.

"You're smiling," she murmurs, those expressive brown eyes meeting mine across the short distance.

"I'm remembering. Reliving." I shrug, happy with myself for leaving her with two damn hearts to color in when I left her flat to go back to mine.

"Well, finish reliving by Saturday because you need a clear head going into qualifying," she says and smiles.

"Thanks, Mum," I tease but then step into the conference room where she's seated. "What is this?"

She leans back in her chair and pride emanates off of her. "We just signed a sponsorship deal with Conmigo," she says, referring to a major tequila brand. "I guess a lot of teams have been chasing after them, but they liked our AITA posts and our use of social media to promote the brand so . . . they signed with us."

My grin is unstoppable, knowing I contributed in some way to this. The more I can give this team, the harder it's going to be to part ways with me. I may be sleeping with Camilla Moretti, but I'm not under any illusion that's going to help me keep my ride.

Nor do I want it to.

"Congratulations. Like . . . that's huge." She sits a little straighter, eyes alive under the praise. "I'm guessing your dad is patting himself on the back right now for bribing you to come work here."

"I don't think my dad pats himself on the back for anything," she says. "He's not a man who's satisfied easily."

She says that, but she doesn't see what I see when I watch them interact. The pride brimming in Carlo's eyes as he watches her work with or lead her staff. The love that exudes off him when she speaks up about something.

It's like a punch in the gut sometimes. A reminder of what I don't have. Another flag waving to add to the one my mum just raised.

I glance over my shoulder and then back at her. "I need a distraction, Gasket."

"A distraction? I'd think going two hundred thirty miles an hour would provide plenty of distraction."

"Hmm. It does. But it also creates a whole lot of unused adrenaline in my body that needs to be released . . . *somehow*." I step farther into the room and shut the door at my back. There's a window in the door, but I'm more worried about what people will hear than see.

I'm just a driver talking to his marketing manager. A discussion about the new endorsement.

Not a lover telling his partner he has needs that he might be desperate for her to meet.

"There's a gym just down the hall. A treadmill. An exercise bike. Hell, there's a whole track just beyond that door that I'm sure you could find your way to jog around." A smile toys at the corners of her mouth that is anything but innocent like her voice hints to be.

"I see how you are. You have demands and I met—*meet*—them regularly." I brace my hands on the table across from her and smirk. "Isn't it about time that I make my demands known?"

She chuckles and leans back in her chair, crosses her arms over her chest, and meets my gaze with a challenge of her own. "Is that so?"

I lift my eyebrows. "If this is a *no one else* situation, then, uh, you're going to have to help me ease that abundance of adrenaline."

She twists her lips but it's only to fight her smile.

How did I think she wasn't my type? Baggy clothes. Some clothes. No clothes. The woman is downright sexy as sin. "Please tell me you're not asking me to fuck you in the paddock?"

"They don't call it *paddock pussy* for nothing." I shrug as her eyes shock wide.

She coughs over her own breath. "Please tell me you're joking."

I shrug and make a noncommittal sound, loving her stunned reaction. "There's a lot of closed doors everywhere for a reason." I glance behind me at the glass door to the conference room. "Too bad there aren't blinds on this door."

"No. Not here. I *cannot* have sex with you here. I'm partially your boss. Your—"

"I know what you are. And for the record, that makes it even more tempting. Even fucking hotter." I groan at the thought.

"You are seriously crazy."

I rest a hip on the table, never taking my eyes off hers. "I'm sure you've had a tough time getting some of the guys on board with listening to a woman. Especially since you seem to be stepping in for your dad every now and again. It might ease your stress if I let you have your way with me. Take control. Grab me by the cock and lead me around by it."

"More like lead it right into my mouth," she murmurs, her cheeks flushing and eyes darkening.

My grin is immediate. My cock hardens. "You think I'd complain about that?"

"What I think is that you're out of your mind."

"You're the one who offered to pay me for sex."

"You're the one who gave it to me for free."

We wage a visual war as the sexual tension virtually combusts in this room. I glance at the table she's seated at and quirk my eyebrows. Definitely a useable surface. "Before the end of my . . . tenure here." I almost choke on the thought of being relegated back to F2. "I'll get you to fuck me somewhere in the paddock."

"I'll be your paddock pussy?" she asks, amused. "You're pretty sure of yourself."

"I'm a racer, Camilla. I live for the danger. I have to be sure of myself. And this? This I'm sure of."

CHAPTER THIRTY-SEVEN

Riggs

"**B**ox. Box. Box," Hank says.

I grit my teeth, my concentration unwavering as I chase after Evans.

One more place.

I want one more spot up the grid.

It'll be the highest one-two finish for Moretti in five years . . . and it's just within my reach.

If I shave off another hundredth of a second, I'll be within DRS range on the next straight. I'll slingshot past Evans, hope for a caution to save the tires, and end the race with the highest finish I've personally had for Moretti thus far.

"Box. Box. Box. We have harder tires ready for you," Hank says.

"These are fine. Let me stay out." My voice vibrates with the higher downforce of the car. I fight against the pressure it exerts.

Evans is right there. Right fucking there to reel in. *C'mon, fucker.*

My arms are tired.

My legs strained.

My eyes are burning.

So goddamn close.

"We need to box."

I'm flying down the last straight, trying to shave off that time, waiting for Hank to tell me DRS is enabled.

Pit row is coming up.

Closer.

Closer.

Fuck. I hit traffic. Costas is there squeezing me out, our cars bumping and pushing me off to the outside as we take the corner.

I grip the wheel, feeling for damage from the contact but not finding any.

We come out the other side of the turn, and I go wheel to wheel with him. My temper gets the best of me. My only focus is passing this fucker and getting back the time he's made me lose on Evans.

I take the outside line, pushing the car to the limits . . . and subsequently miss my exit to pit row.

Subconsciously? I don't fucking know but Hank's radio checking in my ear tells me he's turned it on to say something and then turned it off. No doubt he's keeping the cursing off the radio since it's for public consumption.

"Riggs." It's all he says. All he has to say.

I just disregarded my race engineer's directions. That's not going to go over very well. Not at all.

Later, Riggs.

I pull past Costas and renew my effort to reel Evans back in. To close the gap.

Think about it later.

"You are within DRS range," Hank says, ever the professional, leaving anything else he has to say off race comms.

"Understood," I say and push the button to engage.

Go. Go. Go.

I come around Evans. We're wheel to wheel.

I edge ahead.

He tries to stave off my attack.

I push harder knowing a turn is coming and if I don't get him now, I never will.

The car brings it. Speed and grit. I edge past Evans as we slow to take turn one. Just as I'm about to accelerate out of it, the car shimmies violently.

Fuck. A tire.

No.

Fuck. No.

I grip the wheel and hold on to try and control the car as it pulls and resists. As I struggle with it.

Sparks fly out behind me.

Smoke.

Screeching.

More smoke.

"You okay, Riggs?" I hear through the headset.

"Holding it, but fuck."

"Get across to the gravel trap."

"Yep."

This is on me. All fucking on me.

It's my fuck up. No points. A DNF. A damaged car.

Moretti is going to be pissed.

I limp all around the track to get into pit row then pull into the Moretti garage.

Christ. This one's going to hurt.

I'm unclipped and climb out of the car into a very chilly reception by my crew.

Hank is standing before me in seconds. "Back room. *Now*," he commands, ever cognizant of cameras everywhere.

Fuck.

Fuck. Fuck. Fuck.

I follow him, pulling off my balaclava and unzipping my suit as I go.

The minute the door shuts, he's in my face.

"What the fuck was that, Riggs? You think your last name is Moretti now? That you own this fucking team? You think you know this car better than I do? You've been in F1 for a hot fucking minute. I assure you that you don't. Not even fucking close."

I nod. It's the best course of action as Hank's face turns red and the tendons in his neck grow taut while he paces the room like a caged animal.

I deserve the ration of shit being handed to me. Every goddamn bit.

Self-preservation—the fear of going back to F2—has me wanting to place blame. On Costas for the dirty air. At Hank's call to change the tires. At fucking everything.

"The quickest way to lose a ride is to ignore your engineer, Riggs." He stops pacing and looks at me. "You're talented as fuck as you showed today by moving up to P4 from your P10 start. But that shit? Ignoring your team? It will be your arrogance that will send your ass back down to F2."

"Sorry." One word. And he probably won't even accept that.

"I don't want your fucking sorry. This is your first warning. Make sure it doesn't happen again."

He storms out of the room without another word, leaving me standing there staring at the anger left in his wake.

I hang my head and take a deep breath.

You fucked up, Riggs.

You made a rookie mistake. A huge one. There are no do-overs. No retakes.

You made a mistake on a public race comm that no doubt will be shared on social media like wildfire. It'll look bad. It *is* bad.

And all those teams I want to impress to give me a permanent ride will most likely see it too.

I expect the knock on the door before it even comes. Anya peeks her head in before I can respond.

"You good?" she asks.

I look behind me. "Do I have any arse left?"

She shakes her head and laughs. "If you had pulled that off you would have been hailed as a serious, seasoned F1 driver. But you didn't hear me say that."

"I didn't hear you say a thing," I say, grateful for the vote of confidence but not so ready for the upcoming media questions.

"But you'll need to hear me say this. It was a bullshit move that you'll be questioned about relentlessly. Harlan Flanders? You just gave him the material he's been dying for. The people still doubting you? You just made it that much harder to win them over. When risks pay off in this sport, you're a hero. When they don't, the hole is hard to dig out of. Especially with your pit crew."

"I know."

"No, I don't think you do. I suggest you do this presser and then go on an apology tour in your garage."

"I will." *Fuck.*

"C'mon, let's go."

I follow Anya down the hallway, accepting the baseball hat and sports drink she hands me to replenish my electrolytes. We're just about into the garage when we pass an open door and something catches my eye.

Anya keeps walking, unaware that I've stopped. Through the cracked doorway, I see Camilla standing with Carlo. His hands are on her shoulders but shaking, tremoring, as she holds his waist and tries to what looks like, stabilize him.

For the briefest of seconds, my fuck up is forgotten as I blatantly stare, trying to understand something that clearly isn't my business.

Camilla must sense me there because she looks up over her dad's shoulders and meets my gaze.

There's a quick look of panic that flashes in her eyes and then a subtle shake of her head.

What does that mean?

What is going—

"Riggs?" Anya calls me from the end of the hall. "We have media waiting."

"Yeah. Sure. Right." I force myself to look away, to push aside what I saw.

To not care even though I do.

"You're going to get a firestorm of questions. You need to . . ." She continues directing me on how to respond, while I just keep seeing Carlo and Camilla from moments before.

CHAPTER THIRTY-EIGHT

Camilla

IT'S LATE. The lights are off in most of the cubicles and the whole building is quiet.

And Riggs is standing in the doorway of my office. He has his trademark black V-neck on, blue jeans, and ironically, Jordans. My shoe of choice.

There are so many things that probably need to be said after what he saw after the race this past weekend, but I've been avoiding him so the chance to talk hasn't been there.

Doing other things with him occupy my mind instead. It's so much easier to think about sex. To think about pleasure. To research ways to return the favor for him since I'm not exactly the most experienced lover out there.

"You do know it's not usual for a driver to be this present around headquarters, right? Most live in Monaco and only come in when needed."

He nods. "Yes. I'm more than aware. But seeing as I'm not a full-time contracted driver yet, Monaco seems to be an extravagant bet I can't make just yet. Besides, I figure if I'm around more often than not, you guys won't have cause to fire me. Maybe I'll grow on you. Maybe you'll want to keep me around. Maybe you'll keep me on for next year."

"That's why you're here this late? Hoping I'll want to keep you around?"

He hooks a thumb over his shoulder. "I'm putting some time in on the sim," he says. "My home module is having issues, and I didn't want to skip a day."

"Look at how dedicated you are."

His grin does things to my insides that should be illegal . . . and yet I feel this weird, invisible wall between us.

"You want to get out of here?" he asks.

"What do you mean?" I ask because we don't get out of anywhere together unless it's the bed.

"I'm asking you to get out of the office. To get out of our flats. And after this weekend—you're avoiding me—again. Either because of my fuck up on the track or . . . *other things.*" He shoves his hands in his pockets and shifts on his feet. "We travel the fucking world together, Camilla, but we don't *do* anything. You work and tell me what to post on social media. I drive and meet hundreds of people. But we don't enjoy anything outside of that because we're so focused. So let's go do something. *Anything.*"

I swallow over the lump in my throat. I don't know why this simple request has gotten to me. "People know who you are now," I say, giving a futile excuse I don't really mean. "We can't be seen together."

"Your point?" He points to the window. "It's dark outside. There are plenty of places we can go where we can hide in the shadows. Where we can talk and laugh and just be." He walks over to me where I'm sitting at my desk and holds his hand out to me. "*Please, Gasket?* I'm going fucking stir-crazy."

The expression on his face—earnest, hopeful, playful—sticks with me as we make our way through town after town. The top is down on his convertible, and the warm night air whips around as the stars above grow brighter and brighter.

We stop for some food from a local delicatessen that's just about to close. One look at Riggs and the owner's eyes grow wide, and his hand about to flip the closed sign pauses. We buy some of everything he has left, determined to make his few extra minutes of time worth it. Then we head out to a popular park area that's closed at this time of night.

Riggs takes my hand and leads me to a closed gate.

"Riggs!" I whisper as if someone is close and can hear me. "It says closed. We can't go in there. It's breaking and entering or whatever it's called here."

"It's not breaking and entering." He chuckles and then starts to put in the combination on the lock to open it up, while I look at him slack-jawed.

"What are you—I mean—" I look all around us. Clearly, he knows the combination, but that doesn't mean this is allowed. "Riggs."

He puts his hand on the back of my neck, pulls me against him, and meets his mouth to mine. His kiss has a dizzying effect on me. My head spins and my body tingles.

Does this ever stop?

I mean, it's new for me—like everything has been awakened—but does it fade at some point? Do you just get used to feeling and that high-frequency buzz becomes a low-grade meh?

"It's okay to break a few rules, Gasket. Relax. You're earning your nickname right now."

"But—" His kiss cuts me off again.

"Keep arguing and I'll keep kissing you."

"That's a win-win situation for me, Riggs." I smile against his lips as his chuckle rumbles against my chest. "I just might keep arguing."

He leans back and brushes hair off my forehead, his eyes meeting mine under the moonlit night. "Then you'll miss the best view in a one-hundred-kilometer radius."

"Oh really?"

He nods. "Oh really."

"How do you know the code?" He quirks an eyebrow and glances at my lips in warning. "Just a question."

He picks up the bag of food, the blanket he had in his trunk, and leads me through the gate, locking it at our back. "My mum used to work for the local municipal department here. She'd bring me here when I was a kid. It was our place to go after . . . after everything."

Our hands find one another's as we walk. We lace our fingers like it's the most casual thing, when to me, it isn't.

It's . . . intimate in this setting. The dark night. The stars above. The privacy.

We walk for a while, the night noises filtering around us. The rustle of trees. The songs of insects. The fall of our feet. And when we clear a ridge and Riggs steps aside, I understand why we're here.

The whole of London is laid out before us in the distance. She's beautiful with her twinkling lights and her domed churches, and the chimneys interrupting the skyline.

"Wow." It's all I say as I take it in.

"I know." He lays out the blanket. "I haven't been here in a long time. I forgot how incredible it is."

"Just admit it. This is your go-to spot where you bring women to impress them."

"Huh. Never had to impress a woman until now," he jokes.

Or at least I think he jokes, but the look on his face says otherwise.

"Seriously. You've never brought a girlfriend here before?"

"Nope. Never had a girlfriend to bring here." He takes a seat.

"You're full of shit."

He's never had a girlfriend? With those looks and that charm? *And the skills in the bedroom?*

"Camilla, just come out and ask whatever it is you're asking."

"I'm not asking anything. But if you expect me to believe—"

"Have I dated? Yes. Have I had my time with one-night stands? Yes again. Have I ever had a serious girlfriend? No," he says with a resolute nod. "I'm too busy trying to chase this dream. Too busy focusing on me and all I need to get here and stay here—that it wouldn't be fair to someone to be with them, but to not make them my number one priority. Does that answer your non-asked questions?"

"Um. Yeah. Sure."

"C'mon. Sit." He tugs on my hand. "I'm starving."

I do and we begin to open and sample the varying things we bought. We know what some things are. Others not so much.

"Oh my God. Whatever that is, get it away from me," I squeal and shove a plastic container his way as fast as I can when I see some kind of clear jelly mixed with things I don't want to eat.

He takes the container and looks in it. "Jellied eels." He shivers. "No. Thank. You." And then he starts laughing. "My dad played a prank on my mum once with them. He put them under her pillow so when she slid her hands beneath it to sleep, she—"

"No. Stop." I cover my ears and squeal. "Your poor mom."

His smile is so damn bright and bittersweet. "I forgot about that memory. I thought it was so funny that I pointed them out to her in every store or restaurant we were in."

"I'm sure she loved that." I study his profile as he relives the memory in his mind. "Are you two close?"

He nods. "Very. She lives near Birmingham now, so I don't see her as much as I used to with all the travel, but yes."

"She hasn't been to any races, has she?"

He twists his lips. "No. She doesn't do well with them. Remember I said she has panic attacks?" I nod. "The track is the only place they happen."

"That must be hard for you."

I can't imagine loving a sport that also took something so very vital and meaningful from you.

He shrugs as if it's no big deal but then drops the bomb. "We were there that day. When he had the accident. It makes complete sense why for her."

"There's nothing I can say to even . . ."

"I know." He reaches out and links his fingers with mine. "I know."

We sit in silence for a few moments. There's a siren in the distance. A loud wash of music from a car going by somewhere close by.

All I can think about is watching the one you love die in a fiery crash and feeling absolutely helpless to do anything about it.

And then the irony hits me. How different but how very similar our stories are. I'm doing the same with my dad. A helpless bystander, standing and supporting him, but unable to do anything to prevent the inevitable.

The unexpected realization hits me like a battering ram.

"You've been avoiding me," he finally says, filling the silence with the truth.

I clear my throat. I'm more than grateful when he gives me the time to gather my thoughts. "Belgium was a tough race all around. Andrew ended up in the wall on the last lap. You . . ."

"I fucked up and didn't follow Hank's directive." He nods but doesn't look my way. "But we both know that's not what I'm talking about, is it, Camilla?"

Fuck. What I'd give to be able to share this burden about my dad's diagnosis with someone. To have a shoulder to cry on with the one person I seem to spend more time with than anyone else these days. But I can't betray Dad's confidence. I can't dignify his indignity.

I can't burden Riggs with more things than I already have. Because sex . . . the sex has been phenomenal between us and yet, after the orgasmic haze has lifted, I notice him studying me as if he's afraid he hurt me.

Yet another secret I'm not ready to share.

But that's not what he's talking about.

He's talking about what he saw the other day after the race. The sliver of doorway he looked in. My dad's acute attack where he lost his balance after tremors overtook his body. The episodes are few and far between but are violent when they do hit.

I had walked by, saw him struggling, and rushed in to help, trying to prevent him from falling. My only error was not closing the door all the way.

That and Riggs seeing us.

"You trust me with your body, with the broken you think you are but really aren't, but you won't trust me with your thoughts," he says softly, causing tears to well in my eyes before I blink them away.

"You're one to talk." It's a defense mechanism I learned . . . *after everything*. Deflect. Redirect. Dissociate.

"Me? I thought we just were talking about me. What more do you want to know about me before you'll share some of yourself, Cam?"

"Tell me about your dad."

"You know about him. Everyone knows about him. It's all I hear and it's a blessing and a curse." He shrugs. "I'm glad that his memory is still alive and well, but I'm also more than sick of being compared to his ghost."

"I take it the article bugged you then?" I ask. Moretti just landed a few large spreads in magazines and platforms that reach beyond the racing world. Elise worked her ass off to land them for us. To expand the brand into mainstream. Riggs's AITA notoriety and daredevil antics helped us get those.

The articles were humorous, insightful, and occasionally a bit harsh in their comparisons of where the sometimes revered, sometimes vilified Ethan Riggs was in his career at his time of death compared to where his son is at a similar age.

"I'm sure you know about my father," he says without answering my question.

"I've heard he was funny and charismatic and—"

"Reckless. You forgot to throw that in there. Gotta make that comparison or else you wouldn't be like everyone else."

So it does bug him. How could it not?

"Actually, I wasn't going to say that. Clearly the comments and comparisons bug you, as they should. You're your own man in a sport he might have raced but that has changed exponentially in the years since he was in it."

"Seventeen years. God." The pain in his voice is heartbreaking and such a foreshadowing of my own future that it's hard for me to hear. His sigh is heavy. Resigned. "I try to use the comparison to my advantage, but fuck yes, it bugs me. They use the word reckless like it's a bad thing. Like it's what led to the accident." He looks over and meets my eyes, the grief still there after all these years. "We're all reckless. We must be to be in this sport or we wouldn't be any good, so stop using it as a negative. As a means to try and shame a man who was larger than life in almost every aspect that I can remember. There was so, so much more to him."

His voice cracks and hell if my heart doesn't right along with it—for the man beside me.

I have my dad. He's been my rock my whole life. How lucky am I to get to say that? How incredibly naïve am I to have taken that for granted? How stupid was I to contemplate turning the opportunity down to work with him when someone like Riggs would kill for that chance?

Nine years of memories with your dad isn't enough to last a lifetime. That's all Riggs gets though.

God, I'm fortunate to have the chance to make more with my dad.

"Tell me about him. The *more* people don't know. I want to know him."

His smile is the most genuine I've ever seen. It lights up his face and his eyes and is so hauntingly beautiful. The love he has for a man he most likely barely remembers is clear. That, in and of itself, says volumes about how much his mom kept his dad alive for him.

"Candy floss," he murmurs. "I remember it at races. I'd get the package that had two colors—pink and blue—and eat them in that order. I'd try to measure it perfectly, a bite per lap, so that there was one bite left after he crossed the finish line. When he'd get out of the car, he'd rush over to me and pick me up in the biggest of bear hugs. I'd give him the last bite of candy floss and he'd say *victory is sweet*."

I let him revisit the memory in silence with our fingers linked.

"He traveled all the time for the job, but it always felt like he was there somehow. With what I know now about the sport, I don't know how he did it, but he did. And more than just birthdays. I'm talking silly school events, weird craft fairs that my mum wanted to go to, Monday night movie nights." He smiles. "God, he loved his movies."

"What was his favorite?" I ask to keep him talking. To keep that beautiful, bittersweet smile on his face.

"*Back to the Future*. We could recite all three in the series line for line. Watched them at least once a month. He liked the concept of being able to go back and fix things you'd done wrong. My mum just liked Michael J. Fox." He chuckles and I immediately think of my dad and the illness he and the actor share. Riggs continues, completely oblivious to my connection. "He's the complete opposite of my dad's type so I'm not sure if she really liked him or was just trying to get a little dig in on my dad after he said he wanted to buy a DeLorean."

"That's hilarious."

"The teasing between the two of them every time we watched it was epic."

"Must have been for you to remember it."

"Hmm," he murmurs. "It was. To this day, she donates annually to Michael J. Fox's Parkinson's foundation in my dad's name. A way to keep their joke alive almost two decades later."

I have similar memories of time with my dad. He might have been a busy businessman, but he always made time for me. Now, *I* wonder how he did it.

"He sounds like he was a good dad. A good man," I say.

"He was. Sometimes I worry that I'll get so wrapped up in the noise about him that I'll forget stuff like that, you know? As time and memories fade."

"No one will be able to change your perception of him. You knew him. They didn't."

"Yeah." He falls quiet.

"I'd be remiss if I didn't ask if you're worried about Suzuka? It's coming up."

His whole body stills. His head dips down for a beat as he stares out at the city beyond. "Are you asking as a Moretti or as the woman I'm sitting beside and currently sleeping with?"

"How about I'm whomever you want me to be?"

He smirks, and I welcome the sight of it. "That's an open-ended response that could lead to some serious roleplaying."

"Oh really?"

"Hmm." He leans over and presses a kiss to my lips. It's unexpected, but so very welcome. He rests his forehead on mine for a beat before nodding, almost as if he's fortifying his answer, before sitting back up.

"*The race. The race. The race.*" He groans. "It's all anyone wants to talk about. Or rather not talk about because they'd rather pretend they're not thinking it and just stare at me like they're waiting for . . . I don't know what they're waiting for from me."

"That has to be . . . hard. Intrusive. Annoying. All of the above."

"Yep." He sighs and falls silent for a beat. "Does it cross my mind? Of course it does. How could it not? There's a reason I've worn that track out on the sim. I mean . . . the only way to face this track is head-on. It'll have taken me seventeen years to get there, but it's probably about time."

"That still won't make it any easier or the watchful eyes on you any less curious."

"I know. Believe me, I know. My plan? To be a robot. To block out all emotion. I've been a pro at doing that my whole life, so I guess I've been practicing for this moment. I don't fucking know." He runs a hand through his hair and purses his lips. "It's easy to shut down when the one thing you loved more than anything is taken from you. I mean, I have a few close friends who've breached that wall. I guess, until you." He smiles softly. "I mean, yeah. *You*. I don't talk about this shit with anybody really."

He glances over at me and shakes his head as if he can't believe it himself.

"Well, I'm glad I can be that for you."

CHAPTER THIRTY-NINE

WHY IS IT SO COMFORTABLE TO SIT IN SILENCE WITH HER? Just why?

Why do I find myself telling her shit I don't even talk with my mates about?

Granted I don't fuck my mates either so there's that.

But she switched topics when I asked about her. Turned the focus on me. Asked me about my dad when clearly there are things going on with her dad.

Maybe the rumors are true. Maybe she's here to learn the ropes and eventually take over the company.

But if that's the case, then why not just tell the whole of Moretti Motorsports that?

"This is perfect. The view. The night. The—"

"Company?"

"Yes, the company. Thank you for bringing me here," Camilla murmurs from where she's tucked against my side.

I have so many ways I can respond to her comment, but fuck if it hasn't been a pretty serious conversation for a night where I just wanted to laugh and not think.

Maybe it's time to change course.

"It is." I nod and decide to pull out the cheesy line. "But there's something else I'd much rather look at."

She leans back, her arm still hooked through mine, and snorts. "Ah, it seems that someone is trying to flatter me so he can get some . . ." She narrows her eyes and squints. "What would you call this?"

God. How is she reading my mind? How does she know where my train of thought is and prompt it?

Then again, I am a guy. At any given moment, my mind is one thought away from sex.

"Well, it sure as fuck isn't paddock pussy, so I'm thinking it's . . . *scenic pussy?*" I offer and then bark out a laugh when she nods her head emphatically.

"Exactly. *Scenic pussy.* That has a nice ring to it," she says as she shifts up on her knees and faces me. "Well, *are you?*"

I don't even fight my smile as I stare at her and welcome the devilish gleam in her eye. "Oh, is this where we roleplay? Where you are . . . what are you?"

She bats her lashes and twirls a lock of her hair. "I'm just the lowly secretary trying to get my very important boss's attention on my . . . work."

"Your work?"

"Mm-hmm." She leans forward and licks the seam of my lips. "My assets."

"I'm partial to those assets." I palm the cheeks of her arse and pull her to me. She makes quick work straddling me so that we're face-to-face. I'm not going to complain.

"Oh, Mr. Riggs," she coos breathlessly. "Whatever do you need?"

I'm hard instantly as she wriggles over my jean-confined cock.

"Me bent over the desk? Me on my knees? Me pressed against the window, ass out?" She breaks character and starts laughing.

It's the best fucking sound ever.

In fact, I've come to love hearing it. At headquarters. At the track. Breathless in my bed.

Who knew the woman I initially thought had a stick shoved up her arse would be someone whose banter, sense of humor, and quick wit, I'd look forward to spending time with?

I lean forward and kiss just where her shirt is unbuttoned on her breastbone. "All I know is I'm really liking this new change. The unbuttoned shirt. The tank top. It gives everyone else a hint, but it's a reminder to me what I'm tasting later." I lick a line up the curve of her neck. The heat of her pussy through our clothes is my own personal heaven and hell.

"You never answered my question, Mr. Riggs," she says, falling back into character as she grinds over me.

My chuckle vibrates through the night. "Ride me, Camilla. I want to watch you in the moonlight."

She pauses, her eyebrows lifted and her lips in a perfect fuckable pout. *Yeah, that will be happening later too.*

"Well, Mr. Riggs. I'd love to comply with your demand, but it seems we have way too many clothes on to make that wish a reality."

"How about we make a bet?"

She breaks character and looks at me drolly. "I do believe a bet is the reason we're sitting here right now."

I bark out a laugh. "You've got a point." I press my lips to hers. "I'm still proposing a bet."

"And what would that be, *sir?*" The breathless Moretti is back and fuck if it doesn't make me rock hard.

"Whoever gets undressed the quickest gets oral later."

A slow smile crawls over her lips. "But I have more clothes on. More to undo."

"Then you'll get a head start." We both rise to our feet. "Three. Two. One."

I have to hand it to her. Camilla can undress quicker than shit. It's only seconds before we're both breathless, laughing, and tripping as we step out of our jeans.

"Victory!" she shouts as she raises both arms in the air, her tits bouncing as she does.

I groan at the sight of her in the moonlight. I won. Even with the head start, I still won, but I'm not calling her on it. What man would miss the chance of licking her pussy? Of feeling it tighten around his tongue as she came? Of tasting that sweet tang of her arousal on his tongue?

"Get over here," I growl as I sit down and reach my hand out to her. She climbs onto my lap and straddles my hips so that my cock is right at her entrance.

She leans forward and kisses me. It's laden with a demand for more but a desire to take things slow. To enjoy. To savor. To give. To receive.

My hands are on her breasts, thumbs rubbing her nipples as she slowly lowers herself down onto me.

"Jesus Christ." She swallows the groaned-out words as her body accepts me. As the warm, wet heat of her pussy takes me in and squeezes around me.

Her head falls back from the sensation of me being inside her.

My hands slide down to her waist, to hold her still for a second more so that her arousal seeps out and coats my balls. So I can feel her every-fucking-where I possibly can. I've never wanted to be more marked by anyone in my life than I do right now.

"God, I love your cock," she murmurs seconds before she starts to move. Her hands are on my shoulders as she rocks her hips back and forth over me. As she creates one angle on my cock for the ride down and another angle for the slide back up.

It's a mixture of sensations.

A contrast of pleasure.

And I'll fucking take anything else she throws my way because the woman knows how to own me in moments like this.

Up.

Down.

Grind.

The visual is incredible as I lean back on my elbows and watch Camilla work me over. Ride me. Fuck me.

Her body. Her face to the sky. Hair falling so far down her back that the ends tickle my thighs, adding yet another sensation. Her beautiful nipples pebbled from the night air. The top of her pussy—the tight strip of curls—glistening with moisture as she rides me. Her hands, pressing against my chest and her nails digging in ever so slightly as her desire turns ravenous. The moans falling from her lips turning to pants as her greed becomes need.

"Riggs," she groans.

"I know, baby. It feels so fucking good," I say, unable to take my eyes off her. "Just like that. Fuck my cock like you mean it. Like you want it. Like you live for it."

I live in sensations. The tightening of her thighs on my hips. The slap of her pussy against my pelvis as she picks up her pace. The feel of her arousal dripping off my balls. The sound of the mewl deep in the back of her throat. The scent of her perfume tickling my nose. The feel of her muscles bunching beneath my fingertips with each piston of her hips.

"I'm gonna need you to come for me, Cam," I groan as she slams down harder on me.

"Like that?"

This woman . . .

"You're so goddamn gorgeous riding my cock like that."

She lifts so that just the tip of me is inside her and teases me as she pulses there. "Or like this?"

"Fucking cock tease," I murmur but my smile is dirty and my cock aches it's so hard.

"Tell me what you want, Riggs," she says.

"You." I grip her waist and hold her still so I can piston up into her. "Just fucking you," I grunt out with each thrust.

She gasps and leans forward, hands on my shoulders, tits swaying in my face.

I can't resist. I take one in my mouth. Swirl my tongue around its bud as my orgasm builds and builds and builds.

"Come for me," she coaxes in that throaty voice of hers. "Fill me up. Show me what I do to you."

What you do to me?

Ruin me.

Wreck me.

Own me.

Every part of me is tense. Riding an edge. On the verge of control snapping as I wait for her to come. To call out and jerk her hips over mine.

But I can't do it.

I can't last.

The orgasm hits me like a bolt of lightning. Fast. Fierce. It burns in my body as it ricochets from my toes to my fingertips. I ride the electric current. The white-hot heat it creates has me seeing stars.

I come hard. My body jerking, cock twitching and lungs grasping for air as my heart races and my mind fills with the haze of bliss.

My hands ease on her sides as I come out of the climax coma.

"Don't move," she whispers as her pussy suddenly tightens around me.

Her moan fills the warm night air. Her lips part, her head's thrown back, her hands are cupping her own breasts, and her breath hitches as her body slips into the coma with me.

Jesus, she's a sight to behold.

Camilla Moretti.

There you go owning me again.

And as soon as the thought hits, Camilla says, "Dismount," and playfully falls sideways so that she lands on her back with a thump as her laughter rings out around us.

"What's so funny?" I ask, propping myself up on my elbow amid our tangle of clothes beneath us.

"I can picture it now. This is going to be the next AITA."

"What?" I bark out a laugh.

"This is Spencer Riggs, back with another request for advice." Camilla does her best impression of me.

"I do not sound like that."

But she continues. "Am I the arsehole for fucking a girl on a grassy knoll that we illegally broke into? If the coppers were to come, is it okay if I outrun her so she's left to take the fall?"

"Bullshit," I say and press my lips soundly to hers to stop her laughter. "I'd push you down first, then run."

"Hey!" She swats at me but then grabs the back of my neck and yanks me back down so her lips can find mine again.

"Don't look now, Moretti," I say against her lips. "But this was a beautiful, whimsical something kind of night."

Her lips spread into a smile against mine and then she kisses me again.

What a perfect fucking night.

CHAPTER FORTY

"**S**HOULD WE BE WORRIED THAT YOU INVITED US TO YOUR flat *and* that you cooked for us?" Isabella asks.

It's not like she'll eat anyway. She never does.

Gia looks around, eyes narrowed, as if she's trying to figure out what's different in my place.

"It's all the same since you helped me unpack," I say, figuring I'll help her out. Besides, I'm nervous for some ridiculous reason.

I shouldn't be.

But I am.

"So what's going on, Cam? Please tell us you're not pregnant—"

"Oh my God. No!" I laugh and it eases the tension. "Where in the hell did you get that idea?"

"Let's see," Gia says. "You haven't explained if you have or you haven't slept with Race God but when we ask, you change the subject despite there being a"—she points over to the edge of my couch—"man's shirt sticking out from under your couch."

There is?

Oh. Shit. There is.

Oopsie.

My cheeks heat as I recall exactly what we were doing when that shirt happened to make it to that location.

"We tried to set you up with Archie this weekend but, only after you make every excuse under the sun why you can't go, you invite us over for dinner. So we're thinking pregnant or engaged," Isabella says, leaning back as she crosses her long legs and takes a sip of wine.

My eyes widen, horrified at the thought of either at this point in my life.

They eye each other and smile. "You were right," Gia tells Isa.

"About?" I prompt. Of course they had conversations about me before they came here.

"Just come out with it. You didn't have to invite us over—although we love that you did—to tell us you're falling for Spencer Riggs," Isabella says.

"We already figured that," Gia adds.

"I NEVER said I was falling for him," I assert.

Their laughter rings out. "Uh-huh," they say in unison as they tap their glasses against one another's.

"You two are annoying," I grumble. "Even though you're wrong."

"And we love you madly," Gia says. "Even though we're right."

"No—"

"Save it, Camilla. You're wearing the new shoes *even* when we're not around. You scheduled an appointment to get your hair done again without us prompting you. And you're unbuttoning the top buttons of your shirt and showing a little cleavage with that tank top underneath. I mean, that screams *I've got a man* all over it."

Now or never, Camilla. She just gave you the opening you needed.

"About that," I say and then blow out a long exhale that definitely piques their interest.

"About what? All of it? We're right about Riggs? What?" Isabella asks through a laugh.

"Not about Riggs. About me. About my clothes. I . . ." Nerves rattle inside me, but this is Gia and Isabella. My girls.

Curious eyes study me as I resolve to follow through with the decision I made last night.

The one to finally let Riggs all the way in and tell him what happened. He keeps opening up to me and I keep deflecting.

But he's right. I can share my body with him, but not real parts of me.

Besides, it's time. I've spent six years hiding something that isn't my fault. Like a dirty secret . . . *that I didn't bring on myself.* I want to be open with the man who helped me see that.

But these two women who have stood by my side and held my hands, unknowingly helping me. They deserve to know.

I want them to know.

Gia looks at Isabella, suddenly concerned, and asks, "Sweetie, what? You're scaring us."

This is the new me—Camilla Moretti—strong and in control.

I take a deep breath and then meet their eyes. When I speak, my tone is even and unemotional. "He told me I asked for it because of what I was wearing. That I deserved it."

"Let me at that fucker," Gia says, throwing the pillow on her lap to the floor and starting toward the door. "I'll rearrange Riggs's face in—"

"No. *No. It wasn't him.*" I laugh, the idea ludicrous. The sight of her fuming mad and ready to defend me is the most beautiful definition of our friendship I could ever experience. "But . . . thank you."

"Then who?" Isabella asks as Gia sits back down, her face pulled tight, and eyes alive with anger. "What? *Talk to us.*"

Each of them reaches out to hold one of my hands in silent support.

"I . . . the details don't matter."

Gia squeezes my hand, the three of us at the edges of our chairs, a small circle. "Tell us only what you want. We're here to listen. To support you."

"And to feel fucking horrible for teasing you about your clothes and not considering the fact that there might be a reason behind it," Isabella says with tears swimming in her eyes. "A *real* reason."

"I don't blame you. You didn't know. Couldn't have." I smile. "It was six years ago. Before we met. Like I said, the details are irrelevant at this point, but as you seem to already have worked out, I was in a situation where I didn't give consent. He took what he wanted and insinuated *I'd wanted it,* based on what I was wearing."

"Jesus Christ," Isabella murmurs with tears welling in her eyes.

"We understand why you don't want to talk about it," Gia says, her own eyes glassy. "If you ever do, though, we're here for you."

"You held this in all that time. You're a warrior," Isa says.

But what I feel is stupid. Stupid for not telling my best friends. For thinking they'd judge me for it. For worrying they'd think differently of me.

If only I knew then what I know now . . .

I smile softly and sniff back the tears that threaten. Tears that are happy. That are relieved. That make my soul sigh in the best way.

"I've never told anyone about it. Other than my therapist." I chuckle. "I don't know why I was afraid to tell you," I say.

"That doesn't matter. Not one bit. You did and we're here now and whenever you need us, we'll be here in a split second. We're so honored you've trusted us with this," Gia says as she rests her head on my shoulder.

"I have another confession," I murmur.

"The one where you tell us you're falling for Riggs?" Gia asks.

"Yeah, that part." The words come out smoothly. Almost as if I needed to get one thing off my chest to acknowledge another.

But I appreciate that Gia and Isabella don't gloat about being right. Rather, they both smile.

"Any man who makes you secure enough to be you, who stands quietly beside you to slay whatever silent demons you're facing? Who makes you want things you didn't want before, and who makes you smile as much as you do nowadays? Is most definitely worth falling for," Isabella says.

"Yeah, but if he hurts you, I'm still kicking his ass," Gia adds.

I roll my eyes and laugh. "There's not a doubt in my mind you would."

CHAPTER FORTY-ONE

Camilla

PULL THE RADIO COMM HEADSET OFF MY EARS AND REST IT AROUND MY neck when I look over to see my dad staring at me. He has a curious expression on his face, and I make my way to where he's sitting.

He's made it a point to sit more around the guys now. After the incident that Riggs saw, we decided to take a few more precautions so he doesn't fall again.

He hates it. I know he does, but if it's any indication by the long text chain between my mom and me, we didn't take lightly the decision to broach the subject with him.

"Hi. It's good to see you down here."

He pauses, his eyes searching mine. "I'm always here. You're the one who seems to make it a habit to not be."

"And?" *I like to watch Riggs.*

"And nothing. I just noticed the change is all." He shrugs and sets down his cup of coffee as another team's car flies past on the track outside for qualifying. Our cars are still in our garages, mechanics milling around them, double-checking every little thing with our qualifying coming up soon.

"Then why do I feel like I'm in trouble?" I laugh.

"Not in trouble at all. You're being ridiculous. I just saw you standing there with the headset on and I was hit with déjà vu. You sitting on your nonno's shoulders with an oversized headset on and a sticky something in one hand while your other was reaching down holding his."

My memories may be faint, but I do remember the view from those shoulders. It felt like chaos all around me as he stood in the middle of the garage with the crew moving at a lightning pace.

"I vaguely remember that."

"Your mom has so many pictures of you like that. Books full of them."

"I'm sure she does."

His smile softens. "Now that her child advocacy work is done for the year, she'll be here more. It'll be a real family affair."

"Really?"

"Really." His smile lights up his face, but when he meets my eyes, he lifts his chin in the direction of the garage. "Thoughts on Riggs thus far? You weren't keen on me hiring him. It seems you've changed your mind."

"You already asked me this."

"I know I did. I'm asking you again. It's the job of this position to re-evaluate constantly. Race by race."

"He's consistent. Moretti's placing higher than we did before him. Clearly, he's fitting in and adjusting. Has he erred some? Yeah—the whole stunt of not listening to Hank in Belgium is one example."

"But?"

Where is he going with this? My dad rarely asks the same question twice.

"But I think he's a quick learner. Dedicated to improving. Clean on the track so far. And if we all were judged by our mistakes, then heaven help me." I snicker. My dad just gives me a look like he doesn't want to know the crazy things I may or may not have done.

Maybe he's just rethinking everything with Suzuka coming up soon.

"It seems the two of you are getting close."

Hmm. Maybe that's not where he's going with this.

I fight the urge to look around at the garage. Averting my eyes is a dead giveaway to my dad that something is going on.

"He's our driver."

"So is Andrew," he counters, "but I don't see you as close with him like you are Riggs."

Fuck. What is he getting at?

"Andrew doesn't make himself as readily available as Riggs does. He has his girlfriend and that's where he prefers to spend his time outside of the track. He does what he's told but doesn't care to stick around for the glory. Riggs does. He loves it and the whole campaign we've built around him. The campaign that has taken off and benefited Moretti tenfold. So yes, of course, we've gotten close. That's the only way you can be when you're working with some-one day in and day out. Just like I am with Elise. With the rest of my team."

"That's a whole lot of explaining for a simple answer."

Our eyes meet. Hold. And I fear that he can see right through me.

I'm fortunate at that moment that Omar walks over to have a word with my father. I take the chance to escape.

But his comments stay on my mind well after we've parted ways. I think of all the things I could have countered with but would have only drawn more attention.

"There you are," Elise says as she walks to the upper lounge area in our Moretti paddock space. I'm standing in front of the television, watching Rossi's qualifying lap. He's going to be placed high on the grid judging by his time.

"Yep. I'm here." It's still hard to get used to watching a car on televi-sion and then hearing it outside the building we're in. I walk over to the re-mote control and turn down the commentators' voices. "Just working on the Conmigo stuff with the new campaign for Perfection Oil up next. I want to get it done so I can watch our qualifying runs."

"Where can I step in and help—oohhh," she says, pointing to my shoes. "Very cute. Like *wow*." She looks at the shoes and then back at me. "What's gotten into you? First the hair. Then the slight changes in your outfits. The sexy shoes."

"It's nothing."

"Love looks good on you."

I sputter over the sip of water I just took. "What did you just say?"

She levels me with a look that says *don't fuck with me*. "There's only one reason a woman changes up those things. And it's a man."

"Not in my world." I look out the window of my second-story room, and of course Riggs is walking past down below. In some respects, she's right, but in reverse. I did let one man define what I wore, how I felt about myself. But I did the changing here. I finally had the strength to realize I was letting one insignificant man reign over my psyche.

These changes were for me.

"Elise, a man can tear you down quicker than shit, but only you can put the work in to feel better about yourself."

"Uh-huh. So that extra pep in your step and I don't know, color in your cheeks, had absolutely nothing to do with a man. Got it." She lifts her eyebrows and I give up the fight to hide my smile.

"It's not the reason . . . but it might have helped me feel better about myself. Is that a more suitable reply?"

Her grin is enough of an answer. "Well, whatever and whoever it is, it looks good on you. Now if you can whisper something similar around Riggs, maybe he'll get the subliminal message that I'm the whoever that would look good on him."

This time it takes everything I have to not choke on my own breath.

The garage is buzzing.

Like electricity snapping, excitement ready to explode.

And it does—a raucous roar of cheers goes up—when Riggs and Andrew walk into the garage after qualifying for P3 and P4 starting grids for the race.

The highest one-two punch for a start that we've landed in two years.

And Riggs missed P2 by two hundredths of a second.

They both pull off their helmets. Grins wide. Hair disheveled. Sweat beading on their skin.

But it's only one racer I'm staring at from behind the darkness of my sunglasses.

There's only one person I want to run and hug fiercely.

There's only one man I'm slowly falling for.

And that was *never* supposed to happen.

CHAPTER FORTY-TWO

Riggs

I don't even get a second to process my P4 finish.

Just off the podium, but so damn freaking close that I can all but taste it.

Just off the podium because I defended my teammate's position, so he didn't have to.

I did what a number two driver is supposed to do. Fight for my team's overall success rather than just mine.

For a man who is hell-bent on proving he deserves to stay here, would I have liked the podium for myself? Hell yes.

But will showing how much of a team player I am endear me to other teams for a possible contract next year? Definitely.

It's the long game I'm forced to play in a constricted time frame. Prove I can be successful myself while proving I am a team player. It's a dichotomy that isn't always fun to have to weigh against each other.

What it comes down to is the fact that I contributed to Team Moretti in the way they needed me to. When Hank asked me to defend, I did.

And now we're sitting higher in the overall points standings because of it.

"Brilliant driving, Riggs."

"Another finish in the points, man."

"Way to be a team member, mate."

Comments are called after me as I'm thrown into the washing machine of press quicker than usual for one reason or another. Anya explains the reasoning behind it, but I don't really process it between the pats on the back and the hands being offered to shake.

Seven races in Formula 1 and I've finished in the points in all but one of them.

That's better than some of these drivers with permanent spots have accomplished this year.

Carlo's happy. Omar is happy. Hank is happy.

I can see a future for me here. I don't know what path it'll be on, but I'm starting to see one with the track record I'm laying down.

"Okay. We have you set up right here," Anya says, leading me to a cordoned-off area with the Moretti banner behind it and a half-moon of reporters waiting. She gets her recorder out, because every interview we give is not only noted by the reporter but is recorded by our staff.

It's an attempt to prevent a reporter from misquoting the driver and creating their own narrative for the headlines.

I spend the next ten minutes fielding questions. Some by reporters I like. Some by reporters I don't care for. Some by ones I don't really know.

But I do know when I look up halfway through and spot Camilla across the way, watching me, that I stand a little taller.

"Talk to us about that near miss with Evans at the start of the race."

I explain the situation but am definitely preoccupied.

She's wearing heels. Sexy boot-type heels that I can imagine digging into my arse as her legs wrap around me.

"And how are you feeling having to fend off the field to protect your teammate?"

Like it was bullshit. Like I could have leaped past Andrew and gunned for my first podium.

I swallow down the selfishness and respond with the company line. The one that's expected but that still feels like acid on my tongue.

A glance back over to Camilla has me noticing her outfit. Her jeans are a bit tighter, her shirt different—not the classic button-up she hides behind.

Talk about a welcome distraction.

Fuck. What's Rossi stopping to chat with her for? He's the only driver on the grid I want nowhere near her.

"Riggs?" Anya prompts, pulling me from Rossi and Camilla to the here and now.

I smile at the journalist through gritted teeth as she asks her next question.

"The jump from F2 to F1 has appeared seamless to outsiders. What is your comfort level in the car right now? Do you still feel there is room for improvement?"

"There's always room for improvement. I'm still trying to better my reaction times. My skills. My everything. I'm pretty comfortable in the—" My words falter. Rossi's gone. No complaints there. But even with the distance separating us, it's plain to see something startles her.

Her expression pales. Her face falls—that's the only way I can describe it—as she shakes her head ever so subtly back and forth before rushing in the exact opposite direction of Moretti's position in the paddock.

What the fuck?

I've never seen Camilla with that expression on her face, and I hope I never do again.

"Excuse me but—"

"Riggs has room for one or two more questions, before we head to the multi-driver press briefing," Anya says, cutting me off.

Fuck.

I can't get out of that.

And as I'm directed away, I look over my shoulder, hoping that Camilla's okay.

CHAPTER FORTY-THREE

Riggs

DON'T EXPECT HER TO ANSWER HER HOTEL ROOM DOOR WHEN I KNOCK, but I try it anyway.

My texts haven't been replied to. My calls unanswered.

She wasn't in the paddock when I finished with the media. Then with the team debriefing. Then with Omar over a few quick things.

Meeting after meeting and all I can focus on is where the hell Camilla is and what the hell happened.

Or am I seeing shit and making mountains out of molehills?

But here I am in an empty hotel hallway. The team is out celebrating but I couldn't. I needed to be here. I needed to know what's going on.

My first set of knocks goes without a response.

I want to call out to her to open up. That I'm not going anywhere. But in the off chance that a team member decided to head back to their room, I can't look like a jilted lover trying to gain access.

So I do the next best thing. I take a picture of me standing outside her door, alone, and text: **I'm not going anywhere. Either let me in or the crew will find me sitting against your door. Talk about having to explain.**

Seconds pass.

I think she might not be in there.

And right when I'm about to walk away, I hear the lock on the hotel room door clink, the door pulls open, then her footsteps pad away.

I enter her room. It's exactly the same as mine. No one can claim that Moretti skimps on its accommodations of its drivers and crew. She's sitting in the small seating area. Her bare feet up on the table. Her head is resting against the back of the couch, eyes are closed.

She's a picture of beautiful melancholy. Of quiet strength. Of unspoken despair.

And I'm at a fucking loss of how to approach her.

But I have to try.

I take a seat on the table, beside her feet, and pick them up and move them onto my lap. Needing something to do with my hands, I begin to rub them.

At first, she tenses up, but then she moans softly. Her eyes still closed.

"You want to talk about it?"

"No."

"Well, tough shit." Her eyes flash open, and I nod. "You avoided questions the other night. I talked instead. I let you in. I trusted you. Now it's your turn to do the same, Camilla."

She inhales a shaky breath, and the sound makes my chest ache. To carry something with you so powerful that it hurts to talk about it? That must be brutal.

"Who did you see in the paddock today?" I ask softly, not expecting an answer. "Because I can draw some conclusions for you. Conclusions I made while I was in press conferences and debriefings and who the fuck knows what because I was so worried about you. About the look on your face when you bolted out of the paddock. Do you want me to share my thoughts?"

"Yes." The single syllable is barely audible.

"Remember when I told you that we all have a secret that holds us back? That hurts us? I think yours has to do with why you walked away from F1 years ago. I think it has to do with why you needed to work through 'some things.'"

I feel like an arse even saying that to her. But of course, I've considered and reconsidered that various reasons or events could have caused her insecurities, her . . . inability to trust a man during sex.

I've tried to talk myself out of believing the only conclusion I come to time and again.

But the talking myself out of it doesn't negate the facts that add up the same way no matter how I stack them.

Someone hurt her.

Possibly assaulted her.

And I hate him with every fucking fiber of my being.

I've debated having this conversation with her a hundred times. The timing never seemed right. I don't want to be another person to hurt her. The excuses go on and on.

But after today, after that expression on her face, I hope she'll tell me. I hope she'll trust me enough to let me in.

"And . . . I think the man who hurt you remains a part of this very small community."

Her brown eyes flutter open and well with emotion. But the slightest of nods tells me I'm right.

Fuck how I wish I weren't.

My fists ball. My teeth clench. And every part of me wants to punch a fist through the wall at the thought of someone hurting her.

Who is it?

Whose face can I go rearrange?

Whose body do I need to go bury?

And then the thought hits me. *Is it another racer? One of this band of twenty brothers?*

Jesus fucking Christ.

What. Then?

I swallow down every demand I want to make of her. *Calm down, Riggs. Your anger is the last thing she needs considering she's already upset.*

"Tell me only what you want to tell me." Those are the hardest words in the world to utter because I want to demand she tell me everything. Want to shake answers out of her. But I keep my cool.

She's silent a bit longer. Her breathing even and measured. "You're right."

Which part? About what?

"I was almost nineteen years old." She pauses. "It was my gap year. I was . . . busy being young and wealthy and not having to worry about tomorrow. Sounds ridiculously entitled, but true. I lived at the track. In the paddock during race week. There was a group of us who were friends. I was the youngest by far, but they didn't mind. The guys were old enough to get jobs with various teams and travel the world. We had this weird bubble of a life that no one understood except for us. We grew close. We hung out during downtime. We went out when we were off the clock."

"Is he a driver, Camilla?" I have to ask. I wouldn't be me if I didn't. And

I'm more than fucking proud of myself for keeping the murder out of my voice.

She stares at the ceiling and ignores my question. "We all went out. There was a club. There was drinking. There was fun. *I felt safe.*" She meets my eyes for the first time. "That's what I remember more than anything. Being with my friends and feeling like I was safe."

And then she resumes her position looking back at the ceiling. She can't look at me and tell me, can she?

That guts me.

"We ended up back at one of the team hotels. We're hanging out, having a few more drinks, playing music, just being young and having the time of our lives. There were a lot of us in the room . . . and then there weren't." She shifts on the couch, but I keep rubbing her feet. Needing the connection. Needing her to need it too.

And that's a first for me. I've never felt that with another woman, like I need to be her strength. The one she can confide in.

"Christ," I sigh, knowing what happens next.

"He started kissing me. I was more than buzzed. He was cute, and I was over the moon that he liked me. But then his hands were under my shirt and under my skirt and I tried to push him away. I told him no. I screamed no. To get off me. Sure, I'd messed around with guys before, but—"

"But your past, your experience, doesn't factor into this at all. The only thing that does is that you told him no."

She nods but keeps her eyes on the ceiling. The lone tear falls from the corner of her eye into her hairline. It's fleeting but I see it and I dread hearing the next part.

"He shoved me onto the bed. Pinned me down. Told me that if I didn't want sex, I wouldn't dress like I did." She pauses, and I keep rubbing her feet.

I feel helpless. Gutted. Sick to my stomach.

"I fought him. I tried. I screamed. I said no. The music was too loud? People don't pay attention to screams in hotels? I don't know, but no one came to help like I prayed that they would. He was far from gentle. He was so crass, telling me I was getting exactly what I deserved for dressing like the little slut I was. Mentally, I went somewhere else. Had to—"

I need to move. To walk. To abate my rage. But if I get up, if I let go of her feet, will she think my disgust is with her and not her rapist?

So I remain where I am with a jaw clenched so tight, I'm surprised my teeth don't shatter.

"When it was over, when he was finished, he released my hands and I clawed at his face." Her body tenses from the memory while I silently cheer. "The scratch I scored across his cheek earned me a backhand to mine. Then as he buttoned up his pants, he spit on me and told me what a lousy fuck I was. That I was no better than a *cold-fish cunt*. Then he left, telling me I better be out of his room when he came back and if I went to the cops, he had enough pictures of me all over him all night long. That he'd pull the lovers scorned card and no one would believe me."

"Camilla." Her name is all I can manage.

"I know." She shifts in her seat, so she has no other option than to meet my gaze. "*I know.*" Shame swims in her eyes. "I was young. Dumb. Drunk. Alone in a hotel room with a guy. I knew how it looked."

"It wasn't your fault," I say softly.

"I know that now. I knew it then, but I was scared. My dad was . . ."

"He was what?"

"My dad was going through some health scares. Had just taken over running the business. I . . . the last thing I wanted to do was be a burden to him."

"I see the way he looks at you, Camilla. You're his world."

"Exactly." Her smile is sad. "If he knew . . . how would he have looked at me then? With shame? Embarrassment? Like I should have known better?" Emotion floods her voice.

She didn't go to her parents. Not because they wouldn't believe her, but because she didn't want them to look at her differently. Because she didn't want her father to look at her—his world—and see damage.

Christ.

Fucking Christ.

My skin feels like it's tightened on my frame as I fight the fury coursing through me. As I struggle to keep the defeat out of my voice. As I try to figure out how to be the man she needs right now.

"There's nothing I can say to make it better and as a man, that's a hard pill to swallow. We're supposed to fix things. We're supposed to make them better. I can't do any of those things for you, but I can tell you it wasn't your fault. I can tell you I understand your reasoning, but I disagree with it. And

I can tell you all of that is probably the wrong thing to say, but I don't know what the right thing to say is."

"There's nothing to say. To fix."

"You saw him today, though, right? He's still part of F1? Of this community? I can fix shit real quick." My smile is quick and cruel as she nods and worries her bottom lip between her teeth.

"And you're not going to tell me who he is?"

"It won't do anyone any good. I've moved on. You've helped me move on. Isn't that enough?"

I grunt. That doesn't mean the fucker isn't or hasn't done it to someone else though.

"It was hard enough living with myself most days. Walking away, changing my course . . . you have to understand that."

She sits up, her feet dropping to the floor, and cups the sides of my face, her eyes holding mine. "You're the only person I've ever told the *whole* story to, besides my therapist."

"Thank you for trusting me."

"I never intended for anyone else to know. I refuse to be the victim ever again. Me talking about it makes me that."

"I disagree . . . but I understand." Is that the right thing to say?

She runs her thumb back and forth over my bottom lip. "Thank you for listening."

"Of course. Cami . . . anytime."

She nods and smiles softly again as I shift to sit beside her so she can curl up against my side.

We sit like this for some time, her head on the crook of my arm, and my fingers laced with hers.

We settle into the silence of a new norm that I'm not quite sure I understand yet but know that I like.

This woman walked into my life—a life I've dedicated to racing and myself for so damn long—and made me reconsider that decision to shut everything else out.

She made me look forward to something other than racing—*her*. Sure I've dated people on and off, but there's never been someone I wanted to pick up the phone and call to tell something.

She did and I do.

Fuck, man.

She got to me.

And then she made me care. And now this.

I thought it would be better knowing the truth.

Truth be told, it's almost worse.

Because now I know there's a nameless, faceless fucker out there, who I can't hurt or make pay for what he did to her.

And helpless doesn't look good on any man.

CHAPTER FORTY-FOUR

Camilla

DON'T KNOW WHAT I EXPECTED WHEN RIGGS CAME KNOCKING ON MY door, but his quiet understanding and steady presence was not it.

He listened despite the anger I could feel vibrating off him.

He refrained from telling me what I should have done when I know he probably wanted to.

He didn't make me feel judged.

And now as we sit propped against the headboard in my suite, watching the coverage of today's race, all I feel is comfort and compassion.

A graphic is flashed of the final race standings and it's ridiculous how much I shimmer with pride seeing him so very close to the podium.

"Do you know how rare it is for a rookie to finish in points consecutively like you have? It's pretty incredible. You should be proud of yourself."

"I made fun of your clothes." His words startle me.

Here I am thinking about racing while he's still thinking about me.

It's new to him. Fresh. Of course, he's still thinking about it.

Just like seeing Brandon across the paddock today startled me more than I want to admit. Especially after all this time. Especially because I thought I was so much stronger than today demonstrated.

It's almost as if I made the paddock my safe space, and one glimpse of him turned my world temporarily upside down.

But Riggs righted it in the most unexpected of ways.

"You didn't know," I murmur and mean it.

"I know, but what a shallow prick. I made fun of you because you were covered up like you owed it to me and everyone else to show your body."

"You didn't know," I reiterate.

"But I should have."

"Look. Don't beat yourself up. You've done more for me than you ever could have imagined."

He snorts but presses a kiss to the top of my head.

"It's true. It sounds weird to many people, but after . . . everything, I wasn't shy about having sex again. In fact, I wanted to, to prove I wasn't broken. To prove that—" I almost slip and say the bastard's name. A bastard that Riggs may or may not know. "*He* didn't break me."

"I don't understand what this has to do with me," he says.

"I felt nothing. No sensation, no pleasure, no anything. He'd won. He'd broken me . . . and then there was you. When I kissed you in the bar, it was like somebody had plugged me into an electric socket. I burned where I was supposed to burn. I ached where I was supposed to ache. I felt sensations. It was . . . insane."

He huffs on his knuckles and rubs them on his chest. "Glad to be of service," he teases, and I love the levity he's injecting into a rather serious evening.

"I even tried to go out with someone else after the bar. I kissed him. I . . ." Why am I telling him all of this? He's going to get spooked. I asked for sex to help me get through something. For sex without strings. And now here I am telling him he's the only guy in years to make me feel something.

Abort. Abort. Abort.

Otherwise, he'll do the same on this little agreement we have.

"I . . . *what?* Finish what you were saying or did my mere presence knock out your train of thought?"

"Yes. That's it." I look up at him and smile. "That's exactly it."

"I knew it. I'm a jack of all trades. Race finishes. Kissing. Orgasms. A human headrest. Just ask me. I'll tell you."

"And the ego returns."

"And the ego made you laugh."

CHAPTER FORTY-FIVE

Camilla

THE SMELL OF COFFEE IS AS CONSTANT IN MY SUITE AS IS THE silence that settles in around Riggs and me.

Or rather, almost silence since it seems some of our crew has begun a conversation in the hallway outside of my room.

Riggs and I have never slept together. Like sleep, sleep. In the same bed. We meet up. We hook up. We talk some. We part ways.

It's just how this whole thing has panned out over the past few months.

But last night we must have fallen asleep watching television because I woke up with Riggs's arms wrapped around me and my face nestled in the underside of his jaw.

I froze.

Like full on froze.

And it wasn't because I didn't want to be there. It was because I did. It was because I woke up with strong arms around me and a sense of safety I haven't felt . . . ever, I don't think. Other than the unconditional safety I feel with my family.

Clearly those were crazy thoughts.

Still are.

I allowed myself the grace to breathe Riggs in for a few moments. To feel the steady, even beat of his heart beneath my hand. To sink into the feel of his body against mine. To just be without thinking or wondering or . . . anything.

Then just as I was about to try and slip out of his arms to prevent awkwardness, Riggs hooked his arm around my waist and murmured, "Stop thinking. We're just sleeping. It's not a big deal."

It's not a big deal.

His words replay in my head as I watch him make coffee in my hotel room.

Then why did it feel like a big deal?

Because you're catching feelings for a guy who doesn't catch feelings back.

Because you feared that once he knew the truth about what happened, he wouldn't want to touch you again. Instead, he pulled you in even closer.

And he keeps glancing at me over the rim of his steaming mug and not saying anything.

"Can you talk about something and stop staring at me?" I ask.

"Someone's not a morning person," he says.

"No. It's more like you keep staring at me like I've grown a third head rather than actually talking to me."

"You snore in your sleep. It's cute."

"What? I do not."

He just smiles and takes another sip of his coffee, eyes remaining on me. "Everybody does. And you haven't grown a third head. Not that I can see. But you are kind of adorable with bedhead and your grumpiness."

"Are you trying to piss me off, Riggs?"

"Nope. I'm thinking about the gala."

"Wait. What? You just went from bedhead to the charity event in Champagne?"

He nods in regards to the event in France. "You going?"

"Nope. I don't like galas. I don't dress up for galas. I don't do galas."

"I have to go."

"Great. Good for you. I'm sure you'll look ridiculously handsome in your tuxedo charming everyone in attendance."

"Come with me. Keep me company."

I level him with a look. "We both know that can't happen."

"What can't? A Moretti going with their driver? Pretty sure that's allowed."

"Trying to bind me out of obligation, are you?"

"Bind? I mean . . . I didn't think we'd progressed that far in this—whatever this is here—but we can always experiment with that if you want."

It takes me a second to hear what he says and its intention. "Okay. It's time for you to go now." I laugh and point to the door.

"What?" He feigns innocence and that sheepish grin has my heart twisting in my chest. "You brought it up." He holds a hand up. "I'm just here. At your service. At your leisure. At your—"

"About to get kicked out of my room is what you're about to be so you can get ready for your—"

"Hey. Omar."

We both startle at the voices in the hallway then fall quiet as a few more voices ring out.

We freeze then move toward the door to listen.

What we thought was our crew just passing through turns quickly into a powwow in the hallway.

"Um," I whisper and laugh. "This poses a problem. You can't just walk out of here now."

"You're going to have to tell Anya I'm running late for the interview then."

All I can do is chuckle as I text Anya and try to move quietly around the suite.

Minutes pass.

And more minutes.

Riggs is standing across from me. We're both mirroring each other's posture as he leans on the back of the couch and I lean on the edge of the table, our arms crossed, amused but disbelieving smiles as they talk and talk and talk.

"Clearly they have a lot to say to each other," I murmur.

"A lot."

"I wonder what we could do to occupy our time," I say innocently enough but my body most definitely knows the answer.

"No clue."

I make a show of walking over to the bed and pressing on it as if I'm testing the mattress.

He lifts his eyebrows but hesitates. I can see it and then realize the comparison he's probably making in his head. A suite. Alone. An F1 person. Me.

That's the last thing I want him to be thinking of.

"Riggs," I whisper.

"Hmm." He doesn't take his eyes off me.

His eyes darken and his fingers twitch as if he's itching to touch.

But he waits for me to make the first move. He waits for me to show him I want this.

And there's power in that for me.

I turn to face him and shed my clothes in record time so that I'm standing before him naked with our crew outside the door, oblivious.

He stands to his full height and his Adam's apple bobs.

"Occupy my time, Riggs."

"Oh."

"O is exactly right." I smile. "I need some hearts on my calendar for today."

He moves toward me, his eyes devouring every single inch of me as he goes. When he steps into me, he leans down and brushes a kiss over my lips. "Your wish is my command. But you'll need to be silent, Gasket. None of that screaming my name."

He winks and then I laugh as he dives between my legs.

CHAPTER FORTY-SIX

Riggs

Andrew's losing ground.

He's sitting P4 and he's losing pace. Is it his tires? His engine? What the fuck is it?

I grip the wheel and sit just behind his right rear, ready to fend off attackers. The bane of my existence.

My car is dialed. It's quick and responsive and, "C'mon," I shout.

"I understand your frustration, but we're holding," Hank says.

"Why?" I snap back. The podium is within reach. I know I'm faster than the driver at P3. My sector times prove it. "Are we free to fight?" I ask, hoping they'll let me race my own teammate and try for the podium. "Let me fight."

Silence eats the connection.

It's my answer.

It's my rejection.

"Hold, Riggs." But by the time Hank finishes those words, I'm already overtaking Andrew and flying past him with the help of the slipstream.

There is noise in my comms but I don't pay attention. I know Hank won't say much as every fan and every network can hear him.

So I tune him out.

I focus on the car in front of me. On reeling him in. On having the drive of my fucking life here at Monza.

I'm sure he's cussing me out. That Omar is standing with his hands gripping his headset so hard his knuckles are white.

But Andrew's car is competing while mine is dialed in. It's either me protecting a slowing teammate and finishing farther down the grid or me trusting my skills, my car, and my team, and giving them a podium.

The radio is silent for a stretch, but it doesn't last long when Hank realizes that I'm on pace to catch and overtake Halloran.

"Five tenths of a second back," he finally says, his voice clipped.

"Understood."

We pull in to a sharp corner and Halloran gives a sharp fake to the right before closing in tight to the chicane.

But I know this move of his.

I've gone against it when we karted against each other. He got me with it once. He won't get me with it again. Not when it matters even more.

He fakes right and I drive straight for his fake so that by the time he's correcting himself, I'm already half a car length into him.

And then I'm past.

I don't touch him.

We don't connect.

But he overcorrects and, in a quick glance in my mirror, I see him spin out into the gravel.

"Yes, Riggs. Yes," Hank shouts, excitement in his voice. "You're currently P3."

And P3 I finish.

A podium.

My first fucking podium in F1.

My head spins with elation.

I pull up to the marker and my chest aches from holding back the elation.

I'm out of the car.

I'm jumping into the arms of my crew.

And then it's all a blur. The trophy. The champagne spraying. The sting of it in my eyes. The ache of the smile on my cheeks.

The whole fucking experience.

I soak it in. Every damn bit.

But as the adrenaline subsides.

As the euphoria fades.

I realize that my actions in the moment may have been justified—in my head anyway—but they sure as hell weren't sanctioned.

And when the cameras leave, when the press moves on to the next driver, I'm walking into a garage and a loaded situation.

Fuck.

CHAPTER FORTY-SEVEN

Camilla

"YOU KNOW WHAT TO DO FOR ME."

I look at my dad and hate the churning in my gut. I know what he's asking of me and it's so cruel in nature, but only because of who he's asking me to do it to.

I nod, wanting to ask him again if he's sure he's not feeling up to doing it, but know how that will look.

Weak.

Showing favoritism.

Obvious.

"I do."

"Hank already gave him the first warning. Moretti protocol is upper management gives the next."

Of course, it is. And *of course*, today is a day where my father's illness is more present than not.

"And you need to go down and address him in front of the crew. *Right now*. They need to know that we, the management, make the calls. That we stand up for them when their driver ignores their requests. That we notice it wasn't their error in judgment."

"But . . . he took a podium. It's not like he went against Hank's direct order. Hell, he never even gave him an answer—"

"Exactly." My dad's voice is like thunder in the quiet room. "Riggs didn't wait for instruction. Last I checked, I own this team. Omar's the principal. And Hank gives the instruction."

"But Dad—"

"This is a team, Camilla. Plain and simple. And as a member of it, you're to follow the goddam rules—even when you don't want to. Rules like, don't ignore your engineer. Like, just because you have an opportunity to beat your teammate, that doesn't mean you can take it without Hank's approval—*especially* when you're the number two driver." His tone reminds me of when I was a teenager and would question him. It says *there is no room for discussion on this.* "Or like how *you* need to go down and confront said driver for being in the wrong. Understood?"

I don't understand why he's pushing this so hard. "Understood."

He raises his eyebrows and glances toward the door as if he's waiting for me to do it.

Every step down to the garage is painful. Riggs just took a podium. Something some of the other nineteen drivers in the field have yet to do, even though they've been at this level way longer.

And now I have to go rain on his parade.

Was he wrong not to wait for Hank's response? Yes.

Was he wrong to take matters into his own hands? *Yes.*

But did his gamble pay off and turn out in his favor? In the team's favor? Also yes.

Couldn't we just let this slide and as a team, celebrate a new driver and his incredible success?

Of course not.

I swallow down the discord and walk into the garage with my shoulders square and my spine ramrod straight.

"Riggs," I say loudly, causing the circle of crew around him to quiet as the whole of them turn to face me.

Riggs's brow furrows as he takes me in and the look on my face. "Yeah?"

"First, let me congratulate you on your podium."

"Thanks." The concern in his expression fades when his smile turns up the corners of his mouth.

He thinks I'm here to congratulate him. The pride in his eyes says as much and makes what I have to do next that much harder.

"For the record, just because you've had a few good results in the time you've been with Moretti, doesn't mean you run this team and get to call the shots. He's your race engineer," I say, shoving my finger in Hank's direction. "You're the driver. Your whole team works hard to protect and guide you on the track. Hank directs you according to their input. That's your job. The quickest way to see your way out of a ride is to not listen to your race engineer's direction. That's your second warning, Riggs. And as you know from your contract, there are only three warnings before the contract is terminated and you're out of this team. Are we clear?"

The garage is so damn silent you could hear a pin drop, and that's saying something considering we're at a racetrack with nine other teams still working about.

"*Crystal*," Riggs says, the muscle in his jaw pulsing and anger burning in his eyes.

Not only was he just berated in front of his team, but it was done by a female. I know Riggs is an equal opportunity type of guy but being emasculated in front of his team has to be brutal. But he signed the contract. He knows the rules, and they're in place for a reason. It's not a new code to Moretti.

But still . . . I hate this.

Every part of me tries to tell him with my eyes that I'm sorry, that this wasn't my doing, but I'm met with a stone face and steel in his eyes.

"Are we done?" he asks, everyone still silent, unmoving, and by the furtive looks being darted around, clearly uncomfortable.

I look around at our crew. Some seem like they understand why I just did what I did. Others are clearly pissed at me. I meet his eyes again and nod. "Yes."

I turn on my heel and head back to where I came from. My chest aches and tears burn in the backs of my eyes. The lump in my throat feels like it's a boulder.

I go into my office in the hospitality suite, needing a moment of reprieve. Even a second where I can text Riggs and explain.

But I startle when I look up from my phone and find my dad sitting behind my desk. His head is angled to the side and his eyes are locked on me.

"Yes?" I ask cautiously.

He doesn't speak right away, and I despise the sinking feeling in my stomach that comes with his silence. "It's hard having to deal with employees when they've become friends, isn't it?"

I stare at him, blinking, as if the action is going to make me comprehend what he said that much quicker. "You set me up." Disbelief and hurt mars my tone.

"No. I thought it was important for you to understand that this is a business. First and foremost. It puts food on people's tables. It creates jobs.

It creates an escape from the daily grind for so many others. I learned this lesson the hard way. I lost a lot of friends because they couldn't separate work and personal."

"So, what? You think Riggs and I are friends and so that was going to put him in his place and stop our friendship?"

"No," he says the word slowly. "I think you needed to be reminded that you are a Moretti first and foremost. You needed to show everyone that *you* knew that. It was a hard thing to do, but no doubt you just earned the respect of every single person in that garage."

"Every person except for Riggs."

He twists his lips and meets the challenge in my glare. "He's a big boy. He's been chastised by worse. He's good, Cam. He's cocky and skilled and one hell of a fucking driver, but he's also selfish—"

"As we expect all drivers will be."

"Don't look now, Camilla, but your friendship is apparent."

I grit my teeth to prevent myself from saying anything more.

He made his point.

And there's no way he's going to even entertain mine.

He rises from my chair, all tremors from earlier absent. He sees that I notice. He realizes that I know he just played me.

"Good job." It's all he says as he nods and heads out of my office.

I stare at his back until I can't see him anymore before sinking into my chair and having a pity party of my own.

My duties drag on way longer than I want them to. It doesn't help that every time I check my phone, Riggs hasn't responded to a single text of mine.

At the first available opportunity, I head back to the team hotel and go straight for his room.

But housekeeping is in there when I get there.

He'd already checked out.

He left without letting me say a word.

CHAPTER FORTY-EIGHT

Riggs

D ID I CHANGE MY FLIGHT AND HEAD HOME WITHOUT THE TEAM or the accommodations it booked?

Yep. Sure did.

Have I ignored every text and phone call and smoke signal that Camilla has tried to send my way?

Again, yes.

Is there a reason I've headed to my flat through the back entrance for the past two days so I don't have to pass hers and accidentally run into her?

Fuck, yes.

Yeah, I did the proverbial crime, but my crime gave Moretti enough points to at least keep them in contention for a higher finish in the Constructors Championship than they've had in five years.

Fucking ridiculous.

No doubt Wills, Junior, and Micah are sick of hearing me bitch about it. The fact they stopped answering my texts today—when they always answer them—says as much.

But fuck, man. It still irks me forty-eight hours later. Still eats at me. Still leaves a bad taste in my mouth.

"The quickest way to see your way out of a ride is to not listen to your race engineer's direction. That's your second warning, Riggs. And as you know from your contract, there are only three warnings before the contract is terminated and you're out of this team. Are we clear?"

Are we fucking clear? Yes. I know the contract. I know the rules. I acted on impulse.

Something you know all too well about, right, Camilla? Isn't that how the two of us got ourselves into this mess? On your impulse to kiss me?

Christ.

She hurt me.

Fucking hurt me when that's something I don't allow to happen. It's something that can't happen because I never let anybody in.

But I let her in. Obviously. And now I feel more fucked than anything, and I'm not quite sure what to do about it.

I turn the corner to head to my front door and Camilla is sitting there. She hastily stands the minute she sees me. My feet falter momentarily but fuck it, right? It's my door. My flat.

I stride up to it and the thought crosses my mind to pick her up and physically move her out of the way, but I don't. My glare says enough for me.

She doesn't back down.

And damn it to hell. I may be angry but she's fresh-faced with no makeup, hair pulled up in a pile on top of her head, and a tank top on when she doesn't wear tank tops in public . . . and I hesitate.

"Do you want to do this out here in the hall?" she asks, shoving her hands on her hips and taking a battle stance. "Fine by me. Let's go."

I growl. It's the best I can do. People in our building know who I am now, and no doubt would enjoy selling something juicy to pay for their next years' worth of rent.

She moves just enough that I can unlock my door before storming in behind me and slamming it at her back.

I pace to the far end of my place. My bags from the last race are still in a pile on the floor because yes, I'm acting like a spoiled, rotten brat.

And I don't fucking care that I am.

She hurt me.

And now I wish I hadn't let her in.

"Riggs." My name is a plea. A question. And pretty much every fucking thing in between that I don't want to acknowledge.

"What?" I turn to face her. Arms out. Anger front and center.

"I had to. I was doing my job."

"A marketing manager giving a driver a warning? Berating him in front of the entire fucking crew? Last I checked, that wasn't in your job description."

She has nothing to say for that and that means she's not telling me the whole truth about something. Should I care? Should it bug me? Fuck if I know.

"Cat got your tongue, Moretti?"

"I did what I had to do." Her voice is quiet. Resolute.

"Really?" I scoff. "You called me out in front of every fucking person in that garage like I was an errand boy who fucked up instead of a driver who just kept you in the game."

"You're goddamn right I did," she shouts.

Her bark back surprises me. "Why?" I ask.

"Why?"

"Did I fucking stutter?" The expression on her face—pain, hurt, apology—almost gets to me. *Almost.* "Or do I need to repeat the question?"

I'm being a dick. I don't care. She was a dick to me. Turnabout's fair play.

"My boss asked me to deliver the warning," she says.

"You mean your *daddy?*" I hold my hands up in mock apology and chuckle like the prick I am. "Oh. My bad."

"Don't be that way."

"What way? Trying to understand why my—" girlfriend. *Girlfriend?* What the fuck, Riggs. "You acted that way."

"What? Professional? Impartial? Putting a driver in his place for basically saying *fuck you* to management? You were in the wrong, Riggs. You were the one who fucked up."

"And you're the one who made it personal."

"No, I didn't. I did my job, as you should have done yours. And I couldn't be soft on you."

"And why's that? So you could prove you were the big man on campus? Congrats. Mission accomplished. Half the crew are pissed at you and half the crew think you're a bitch. Looks like a win-win to me from where I stand."

"Fuck you," she grits out.

"Yep. Sure. *Fuck me.*" I move. My hands. My feet. Needing to abate the anger and the thoughts in my head. The ones that tell me I'm so pissed because she means something to me. Because I want her to. "But you still haven't answered my question."

"Which one is that?"

"Why, Camilla? Fucking why?"

"Because if I hadn't, then every fucking person in that garage would have looked at me and seen right through me. They would know that . . . You know what? Never mind."

She goes to turn around, but I have my hand on her bicep and her body spun around to face me. "Know what, Camilla? That we're fucking? Yeah? So?" I shake my head, trying to think straight when I want to kiss her. When

I want to fuck away the hurt that I put in her eyes. "I fucking finished on the podium, and it wasn't because I did what was right, so what makes you think it's right or wrong when it comes to being with you?"

She stares at me, chest heaving, jaw clenched, shoulders rising and falling—hurt radiating. She opens her mouth to talk and then shuts it.

And then from one beat to the next, my lips are on hers. I pour every ounce of hurt and anger over her dress-down into the kiss. Every iota of confusion over this sudden realization that I'm falling for a woman where there weren't supposed to be strings.

There's a stunned shock at first.

Then the floodgates open and we're a mix of hands gripping and teeth nipping. Of clothes being discarded and hushed commands.

"Hurry."

"Quick."

"I need you in me."

"I need to fuck you."

There is no foreplay. Not testing to see if she's ready for me. The week has been painful enough. The only salve to the hurt is being buried inside her. Is feeling her give for me. Is knowing she needs this as much as I need her.

I need her.

To taste her.

To feel her.

To fuck her.

We fall backward on my bed, her breast a pillow of bliss as she falls on top of my chest. "Riggs." It's breathless. Desperate. Just like I am.

"On your knees," I say, this sudden need to put myself back in control of this relationship. To right our boundaries. To let her know I control her fucking pleasure, not her controlling me.

"What? I don't—"

"On your fucking knees. Crawl up here. Sit on my face." Her eyes startle wider. *Yeah. You heard me right.* My hands go to her hips and guide her over my shoulders. "I'm going to fuck your pussy with my tongue. And then I'm going to fuck you good and hard with my cock."

"I . . . what if you can't brea—*oohhhh*," she calls out as I bury my face between her thighs, my nose and lips and chin coated instantly with her arousal.

Fucking heaven.

"Don't worry about me," I say when I feel her tense and try to sit higher up. I use my hands on her waist to hold her down onto me. "I'll come up for air when I'm goddamn good and ready. But right now, fucking drown me."

She emits a half sigh, half yelp as I dive back in for more of her sweet velvet. She bucks on my tongue with my nose hitting her clit and my chin hitting her arse. It's fucking glorious.

Every goddamn lick. Each fucking suck.

I work her over until she's drenching my face. Her pussy swells and grows wetter.

Her body becomes tenser.

And when she cries out my name, her fingers are gripping my hair and yanking on it, and her orgasm's gripping my tongue and drowning me in the best fucking way possible.

It's her hiccupped sighs that do me in. Almost as if she isn't sure how to take pleasure like that. To own it.

She gasps when I guide her hips down one more time for one last taste. But I can't last another goddamn second. My cock is so fucking hard, my balls ache fiercely.

Within seconds I have her flipped over; her gasp turns into a laugh—but both are eclipsed by the growl I emit when I bury myself in her with one swift push.

I see stars. Immediately. Without question.

They fucking align so goddamn fast that I don't think. Can't. All I focus on is how good she feels, how her tits jiggle with each slam into her. How her pussy is so fucking slick and tight. How our bodies fit together.

And how, with those sex-drugged eyes, she looks at me with way more than lust.

But it's too much to think about right now when all I care about is this ache building at the base of my spine and the pressure in my lower belly.

I pick up the pace. Over and over. Again and again. Her eyes stay on mine the entire time. Owning me.

Urging me.

Pushing me over the goddamn edge just like her body is.

And when I come, I've never had an orgasm hit me harder.

Or with more impact than I've ever felt before.

One thing's for sure, whatever this is between us, we sure as shit know how to kiss and make up.

At least there's that.

CHAPTER FORTY-NINE

Camilla

MY HEART DOESN'T STOP RACING AND FOR SO MANY MORE reasons than just the physical.

I stare at the ceiling and try to process the past thirty minutes.

Hell, the past few days.

The incredible highs. The stomach-churning lows.

And then the way I felt when I finally saw Riggs. The all-encompassing need to make things right again. To apologize, even though he was in the wrong. To clear the hurt and anger and something else I couldn't quite place from his eyes.

His hand finds mine and he laces our fingers together. It's the simplest of actions but the quiet reassurance—that *we're okay*—relieves the pressure remaining in my chest that the sex didn't ease.

"My dad," I say and then hesitate.

"Those are definitely two words no man wants to hear after having sex." He chuckles and presses a kiss to my shoulder.

He shifts in the bed, his head on his hand, but the silence only exacerbates the weight of his stare on me.

"Talk to me, Moretti," he murmurs, his lips still pressed on my skin.

I struggle with the start to my confession and the words that normally would follow.

I can't break my promise to my dad. I can't be the one to tell his secret. But at the same time, Riggs means enough to me that I need to make him understand. I need him to see that what happened in the garage wasn't a power play on my part.

That there was a reason behind it.

In the same breath, the last thing I want to do is lie. I opt for a partial truth. Enough to try and mend this fence but not enough to tear the one down that's protected me my whole life.

"My dad had a health scare," I say. "It was enough that he realized he needed to start thinking about Moretti Motorsports beyond him."

"And so he called you back home," he says quietly.

"In so many words. Marketing is my focus, but he's also determined to teach me every aspect of the business."

"As in reprimanding drivers."

"As in he wanted to teach me a lesson."

"What lesson would that be?"

"That sometimes it's hard to be friends with employees. That there are a whole lot of people depending on their paychecks."

Riggs flops on his back, his sigh emanating through the entire room. His silence eats up the space but there's also resignation that I'm not sure I understand.

"I was faster. My sector times. My overall lap times. Erikkson was fading. I could see Halloran in the distance, and he was within my realm to reel in." He pauses. "I've had to prove myself my whole life. Prove that I am Ethan Riggs's son, that I drive like him, but that I'm not him. It's a constant balancing act. I know it wasn't right in terms of Team Moretti, but I saw a lane to prove this and I took it. Did I fuck up? Yeah. Reprimand made, but point made on my end too. Moretti wants their crew to know the team backs them, but I deserve the same."

I don't speak. I don't approve or condemn his reasons for what he did.

Personally, I understand them, but this is the part where I listen without action. Being a driver on an F1 team means you listen to your engineer. Period. They know what they're doing. They see the bigger picture. They know the cars inside out. But I suspect I don't need to tell him this. Hopefully, he'll see past the reprimand, past the podium, and see the bigger picture. *That* will take him from being a great driver to being an exceptional F1 driver.

"I got word from my agent before the race that Maxim is looking better than expected. That . . . my time might be limited."

"I'm aware. I found out just before the race too," I say, not wanting him to think I was hiding it from him—although I do have every right in my position to do so.

"I don't know, Cam. Maybe what I did was a desperate attempt to prove to everyone that I deserve to be at this level."

I squeeze his hand and shift so that my head is on his shoulder, my hand on the steady beat of his heart, and my leg hooked over his. A silent show of support without betraying the lines in the sand my last name has drawn for me.

We settle into a comfortable silence, our confessions our apologies.

"Is he going to be okay?" Riggs finally asks.

I close my eyes a beat and then shift suddenly so that I'm straddling him. He laughs as I dip my mouth down and meet his.

"I think we've done enough talking," I murmur against his lips.

"Is that so?"

I crawl my way down his torso, my lips kissing their way as I go. My eyes never leaving his.

"Are you complaining?" I ask as I take his tip to my lips and kiss it.

"No. God, fucking no."

CHAPTER FIFTY

Camilla

RIGGS'S HANDSOME FACE FILLS THE SCREEN, HIS SMILE FRONT and center. "Hi there." He gives a salute. "Back for another round of Am I the Arsehole. I know we took a break last week and posted a race Q&A, but your complaints were heard. Loud and clear. So . . . back to our regularly scheduled program." He shifts the phone some. "This AITA comes from someone with the last name Gasket. Love the name, dude." He gives a thumbs-up while I eye my phone screen warily. If this isn't a post directed at me, I don't know what is. "Gasket's question is as follows: Hey, Riggs. Am I the arsehole for lying to my mates about having to go to a work function when all I want to do is hang with the girl I've been seeing?"

And when he grins and looks into the camera.

I swear he's looking straight at me and the goofy grin I have on my lips.

CHAPTER FIFTY-ONE

Riggs

"**W**hat's your feel on things?" I ask Ari as I lift a hand to thank the flight attendant for my drink.

Singapore Grand Prix, here we come.

The private jet that Moretti provides its racers for travel is top of the line in all aspects—including *service* according to Andrew. The same Andrew who is currently smirking at me from across the aisle because apparently, he's taken advantage of said service.

I guess his service came with the first name of Savannah. Guess he's no longer with his girlfriend. Or maybe he is. Who the fuck knows?

"You can't talk, can you?"

"No."

"People in front of you?"

"Yep. You guessed it," I say, trying not to make it obvious that we're talking about shit that's private.

"So Maxim has a week or two. Maybe three. His goal is to get back by next month. Either Qatar or Austin. The gist I'm getting is that he's feeling a little threatened by your success and sees the need to get back and prove himself back into his ride before you steal it."

My chest constricts—from pride, from dread, from the unknown, and a healthy dose of panic.

"And?"

"You're asking where that leaves you?"

"Correct."

"I'm not sure to be honest. There are a few scenarios. Moretti cuts you, you don't find another ride, and you go back to StarOne Racing to wait for the season to end and hopefully get picked back up. Moretti cuts you and another team picks you up. There are two drivers who are underperforming, and their positions might be up for grabs. Or . . . Moretti keeps you. Either as their number two, because they're not one hundred percent convinced Maxim's ready, or they keep you as a reserve driver."

"The first option needs to be taken off the table."

"We need to be reasonable—"

"I am. My work stands for itself." Andrew glances up at me and his nod says he agrees with what I'm saying.

There's an unspoken code between drivers. We don't talk shit about one another. We may not like each other, we definitely have heated moments, but we keep our dirt clean to the public. Infighting looks bad for the sport. Talking ill of fellow drivers even more so. And if you do, you risk losing any secondary support from that driver's fan base.

"It does," Ari says, drawing me back into the conversation. "But there are twenty seats at the start of every season. It's rare for teams to cut drivers mid-season . . . but it has happened."

I'm not going back.

I deserve to be here.

I've earned the right to be here.

"Noted." It's all I can say.

"I'm fighting. Just know I'm fighting for you like always."

"Thanks."

"And don't be surprised if you see me at an upcoming race."

"You?" I bark out a laugh. "Mr. Busy and Important?"

"That should tell you where you land on my list of priorities, Riggs. *High.*"

"Thanks, mate."

"We're going to do everything we can to keep you here."

I end the call and rest my head back, close my eyes, and sigh.

Two warnings.

Two fucking warnings.

What if I fuck something else and get a third? What if—

"Teams like you, man," Andrew says and waits for me to meet his eyes before continuing. "There's talk going around. Teams like your grit and skill. It'll come around, Riggs. It'll come around."

"Thanks. I appreciate the vote of confidence."

"You've earned it. Hands down. And I'm not the only one who sees it."

Let's hope so.

Let's fucking hope so.

CHAPTER FIFTY-TWO

NERVES RATTLE THROUGH ME.

Nerves I never anticipated I'd feel when I was sitting at the last race in Singapore and the idea for tonight's adventure came to me.

An idea that was so out of the blue but that felt so perfectly right. There will always be another gala, but there will never be another chance to distract Riggs, to give him the time and grace to have a quick reprieve from all the pressure surrounding the upcoming Suzuka race.

So here I am with a plan in place, nerves present, and excitement bubbling up.

It's ridiculous, really. The man has seen me naked from every angle imaginable.

So why when I'm dressed to the nines am I nervous for him to see me like this?

Because he never has.

After looking both ways down the hall, I draw in a fortifying breath, and then knock on the door of his room.

He opens the door swiftly and the moment he sees me says, "You're not my driver . . ." But it's the widening of his eyes and the quick, audible intake of air he emits when he sees me that has me preening ridiculously.

"Hi," I say, suddenly shy.

"Hi? You can't just stand there and say hi when you knock on my door dressed like that and expect me to be able to speak. I mean, Camilla . . ." He twirls his finger to prompt me to turn around, and I do. The low whistle that follows has a smile turning up the corners of my lips. "Holy fucking shit. I'm speechless. I mean, other than saying holy fucking shit, I'm speechless."

I know I look good. Is that conceited to think?

After six years of my public Camilla Moretti uniform, I think I deserve the right to think that. And by Riggs's reaction, he thinks the same way.

My dress is a deep red. It's formfitting with spaghetti straps, a sexy but not too revealing neckline, and falls just above my knees. My heels are nude, my hair is up, and my makeup is there but a muted natural.

I debated doing this. The dress. The surprise I have in store for him. But I figured if there is any time to get his mind off the day-to-day and what's coming up this weekend, it's right now.

Plus, the look on his face is too priceless to have not seen.

"You like?" I ask coyly as I take in everything about him in his classic black tuxedo. The tailored fabric. The broad shoulders filling it out. The way the collar hugs his neck. How goddamn devastating he is in it.

"Baby, I more than like. If I wasn't waiting for my driver to come take me to the gala right now, I'd pull you in here, lock the door, and show you just how much I like."

I grin. Why does his praise feel so good to hear? It's ridiculous, but it does.

"Well, about that. Your driver isn't coming."

"What do you mean he's not coming?"

"Something came up and as far as everyone knows, you have a sudden, undeniable stomach bug."

He eyes me. "I do?"

"You do."

"What's going on here?"

"You're coming with me." I take his hand and try to lead him down the hall, but he hesitates.

"Gasket?"

"No one is here. The others staying here for the even have already left for the gala. I might have a lookout." I wink. "It's just you. It's just me. And a car waiting to take us somewhere."

"Camilla—"

I put my finger to his lips. "Shh. Trust me."

He gives me one more long, disbelieving stare, but he follows me when I start walking again.

An hour and one helicopter ride later, Riggs stares at me as the aircraft flies off into the sunset and leaves us atop a hill in the outskirts of Champagne.

The winery is stunning. It sits above a valley that has ripples of smaller hills below, some bathed in the golden glow of long grass. Others lined with the unmistakable hanging trellises of grapes and their vines.

The actual building is small in stature but rich in architecture. Its exterior is carved stone arches with rich green vines crawling across its façade and beds of colorful flowers at its base. The wood inside is dark, the marble floor shiny, and the chandeliers above cast a soft yellow glow over everything.

"Camilla," Riggs says for what feels like the hundredth time.

I link my fingers with his and start walking toward the structure. "It's ours for the night. The chef has left food. The sommelier has left the proper wines to go with it. And the suite has the bed pulled down."

He tugs on my hand and when I turn back to look at him with the sunset at his back and his storm-cloud gray eyes staring at me, I know I've fallen for this man. I'm in love with him.

And fuck if that's not the heaviest of thoughts to have in a moment like this.

"Why?"

It's the simplest of questions and often the hardest one to answer.

I step into him and press a tender kiss to his lips. "Because you deserve it." Another kiss. "Because sometimes you need a minute away from the chaos to enjoy this life we live. Because . . . because I wanted to do something special for you."

It's his turn to kiss me. It's a slow simmer of a kiss. One that's not rushed by time constraints or the fear of someone seeing us. It's dreamy in nature and laden with a promise of so much more.

When it ends, he brushes the strands of hair off my face and just looks at me for a moment. "You look stunning, Cam. With clothes. Without clothes. With the Camilla uniform. Without it. The clothes don't define you or your beauty, this does." He taps on my chest just above my heart and every part of me grows weak from his words.

"You made me see that," I whisper.

"No." He shakes his head with the ghost of a smile. "You made yourself see it. You may have put your trust in me, but you did the work to make yourself feel comfortable to wear this tonight. You did this."

"You're the one who made me feel safe enough." My voice wavers and his smile widens.

"That's the nicest thing anyone has ever said to me."

My emotions clog my throat and rather than try to control them, I step into him, against him, and kiss him with all the words I can't say but want to.

"I think dinner and wine might have to wait. I want my dessert first," he says and then I yelp when he picks me up—one arm under my legs, the other under my back—and carries me into the villa.

I'm most definitely not going to complain about that.

CHAPTER FIFTY-THREE

Riggs

WE MOVE IN THE SOFT GLOW OF CANDLELIGHT. Slow and sensual kisses accented with the rich tang of wine on our tongues.

There is no rush.

No urgency.

It's just in an empty villa atop a desolate hill with the moon up above and the most gorgeous thing in a ten-kilometer radius beneath me.

Her smile is desire drugged when I slip into her. A soft gasp that shifts into a sensual moan.

Chills chase over her skin. I see them ripple across her flesh.

Her nipples pucker. Her stomach muscles bunch. Her thighs clench.

"Kiss me," she murmurs and who am I to tell her no?

We kiss. Our tongues dancing, slipping in and out of each other's parted lips as I enjoy every slow, deliriously intoxicating grind of my hips into her.

"So good," she murmurs against my lips. "Feels so damn good."

I cup the back of her neck with one hand with my other on the globe of her arse as we move together.

Her action is my reaction.

My exhale is her next inhale.

We don't need words. We don't need to direct. We know each other's bodies now. We know each other's minds.

And I know that every time I touch her, she only thinks of me now.

That I've erased his touch. That I've shown her how good this can feel when it's right.

And fuck is it right between us.

My forehead is against hers, and it moves ever so slightly with each thrust. This—us taking sex slowly—is so different. We're usually a frantic mess. Enjoying the high. Chasing the orgasm—the end game.

But this time? This is enjoyment. This is reveling.

This is fucking perfection.

This is . . . *love?*

Fuck. Is that what this is? Have I fallen for Camilla Moretti?

My breath hitches as I lean up on my elbow and look at her. Her eyes meet mine and I'm fucking sucker-punched with what I see in them.

Trust.

Love.

Desire.

Her. *Just fucking her.*

"What?" she murmurs, her smile soft.

"Nothing," I say and slant my lips over hers.

We lace our fingers together, just like our bodies are—and apparently my fucking heart is—and I get lost in her.

Isn't that the one thing I haven't had to question in all this? How easy it is to get lost in her? To be with her? To want her?

"Come for me, baby," I murmur. "Just for me."

And this time when I come, it's powerful but poignant. Instead of the sharp crescendo that hits and dissipates with my decelerating heartbeat, it feels like it burns through me, marking my veins with its heat. Marking me in a way I don't think I'll ever forget.

Her lips meet mine one more time. A smile spreading wide when we part.

Thank you.

She gave me this night when I needed it the most—to forget about what I'm about to face.

And unknowingly gave me so much more.

A "more" I'm not one hundred percent sure what to do with.

CHAPTER FIFTY-FOUR

MY HEART IS A STEADY STACCATO IN MY EARS. A CONSTANT thump as the sound of my breathing fills the interior of the helmet and the car around me vibrates my entire body.

It feels good to be back in the cockpit.

To have my apologies about what happened during Monza and my mediocre finish in Singapore be heard by my crew.

To have Hank's confidence in me restored.

To have that slow, even nod and, "All right," from Carlo Moretti after I faced him and admitted fault.

None of them made it easy for me. Stone faces were the norm with doubt present in their eyes.

But I busted my arse to prove to them that I meant what I said. That I knew I was wrong, and that the whole of the team comes before the individual ego.

And I needed that before I could face this race. Before I could walk in the footsteps of the only giant I've ever wanted to be like at the only track I ever could get the chance to—Suzuka.

Dad. Please protect me. Please direct me. Please make me be okay.

I glance up at the sky. At the puffs of white clouds just beyond the light tree. At the stretch of racetrack that leads to the turn that changed my family and my fate forever. At the Sharpie on the dash with his initials.

And then I let it all go.

All thoughts.

All fears.

All need to prove everyone wrong or right or in between.

All comparisons to the man whose name I bear.

And for the first time in my life, I may be racing for Team Moretti, but I race for me and me only.

I race for Spencer Riggs.

For my future.

Not to outrun ghosts I can't outrun.

CHAPTER FIFTY-FIVE

SHE LOOKS NOTHING LIKE HIM.

She's petite with blond hair and blue eyes.

She's quiet and pensive with a soft voice and a quiet smile.

She's worried—noticeably—by the tight grip on my hand. We stand side by side and watch the man we love battle lap after lap to finish a race on a track that is an emotional powder keg for this family.

She must be terrified and proud of her incredible son.

We don't speak more than anything basic. Hell, Riggs doesn't even know she's here, but we hold on to each other for emotional support in the private suite I had set up for her.

Each lap down her grip lessens slightly.

Just like with each lap down, I take another bite of my candy floss knowing I'm going to finish the game Riggs never got to finish with his dad and is seventeen years in the making.

There were a few close calls that had me on the edge of my seat. A challenge from Grimladi on lap nineteen when they went two wide into a turn, but Riggs was able to fend him off.

A near miss of a flying tire when Bustos and Finnegan connected and spun off into the gravel.

But he finishes strong. With grit and determination and a little luck, the crowd roars as Spencer Riggs crosses the finish line in P2.

Clara Riggs yelps in relief and wipes tears off her cheeks.

And I smile because I have one piece of blue zucchero filato—or as Riggs calls it, candy floss—left.

Chaos ensues upon the finish. The media is clamoring over the story of the son finishing the final race his father never could. The stands breathe a collective sigh.

I want to run to him and hug him like his mom does, but I stand back. I shake his hand like an owner would a driver. I act like a proud parent rather than a woman in love with a man.

But the waiting is so worth it when Riggs finds me in a side alley of the paddock. My grin is wide and my heart is so full—of love and relief—that I fear it might burst.

What I want is to jump into his arms and kiss him senseless. What I do instead is hold the remaining piece of blue cotton candy out for him.

Time slows.

It's just him.

It's just me.

Despite the noise around us, everything seems to simply hush.

It's like the world around us has faded away.

His eyes shock open and then well with tears. He tries to sniff them away, but one slips over as he takes the piece I hold out for him. He stares at it with the most bittersweet of smiles and then whispers, "Victory is sweet."

My own tear slips over, the moment so poignant, so powerful. The love I feel for him prompting me to reach out, frame his face, and wipe his tear off with my thumb.

He's just about to put the candy floss in his mouth when the snort at the end of the alley has us both jumping.

I freeze when I notice Brandon standing there.

"She's all yours, man. I mean, if cold-fish cunts are your thing."

CHAPTER FIFTY-SIX

Riggs

I SEE RED.

Murderous red.

The candy floss is disregarded.

Camilla's gesture is forgotten.

All I can see is the bastard who hurt her.

All I can feel is a rage so intense I never knew existed.

And all I focus on is making him pay for what he did to her.

I'm on him in a second. My fists flying, his face crunching against them.

Then I'm straddling him. Each punch a little piece of redemption for Camilla.

For hurting her.

For assaulting her.

For making her doubt the woman she is and the choices she made.

With thoughts of this man—*this gutless wanker*—hurting Camilla. Assaulting her.

I don't hear the shouts.

I buck the hands off me that are trying to pull me off.

I see him hurting her.

I hear her crying for him to stop.

I see him spitting on her.

I hear him telling her she's a cunt.

I'm hauled off him at some point. There's blood. Everywhere. On my hands. On his face. On the asphalt. On my race suit.

And cameras.

They're fucking everywhere right along with the spectators in the stands who have stopped to watch the show.

I don't care. I can't see through the rage. I can't see through anything.

Cold-fish cunt repeats in my head.

All I see is the smug fucking smirk on the prat's lips.

All I feel is the crunch of his cheek beneath my knuckles.

Satisfying.

Necessary.

When I look up from *everything,* I see Camilla standing there. Tears are streaming down her face. Her body is pulled within itself. Her arms are crossed over her chest as if she's protecting herself from him.

It has to be from him, right?

Not from me?

She knows I wouldn't hurt her, doesn't she?

I try to meet her eyes. I try to tell her I'm sorry. I'm yanked backward by two crew members before I can relay any of it.

So I do the only thing I can. I mouth to her, *"He can't hurt you again,"* seconds before I'm pushed into the garage by my team.

And right into the waiting office of Carlo Moretti.

He glares at me with a rage I feel but that he can't understand.

"What the hell was that, Riggs? Are you fucking kidding me?" He paces the small space, almost stumbles at one point he's so focused on me, but rights himself. "Care to explain?"

I stare at him. I can't fucking tell him why. I can't betray Camilla's trust. I can't explain a thing.

"He had it coming to him." It's all I say.

"What? Your ride in F1 wasn't enough that you decided to risk it with some juvenile bullshit from some old grudge?"

"I've got nothing." Each word is like a dagger to my heart because I already know what's coming next.

But she is more important than this.

I don't know when that happened, but it did.

"That's your third and final warning. Grab your shit and get out. You're no longer a driver for Moretti Motorsports. You've just embarrassed this team, this sport, and me as an owner. Do you have anything to say for yourself? Anything to explain why you just beat another team's crewman within an inch of his life?"

I clench my jaw so hard it might break.

I can't explain. It's not my story to tell. I can't hurt her any more than she already has been.

I look at a man I admire and know if I had the chance again, knowing the consequences, I'd do it all over again.

In a heartbeat.

"Being in a relationship has a lot of parallels with being a good F1 driver. Always maintain your integrity, always show respect for yourself and your wife, and always win for the team. It's all about the team."

My dad's voice fills my head. One of his many interviews that I memorized comes back to me, right now when I need to remember it the most.

Almost as if he's somewhere watching. Almost as if he knows right now, I need to hear the advice he never had the chance to give me.

Those words—that interview—never really made sense to me until now.

Until this moment. Because right now, as I hear his words, I realize that is what Camilla and I have become—*a team.*

And I know which team I must choose.

So I look him in the eye, I nod, and I whisper, "Thank you for the opportunity."

And when I leave the room to go and gather my things, I leave my hopes and dreams there with him.

CHAPTER FIFTY-SEVEN

Camilla

"Where is he?" I ask the minute I see my dad standing in the room with his back to me, his hands on his hips, and his shoulders set.

"Where's who?" he asks without turning to look at me, but there's a bite to his tone, showing me I've made a grave mistake. I just showed my cards, and he knows. "Where's who?" he repeats but this time he turns to look at me with a scrutiny that makes my breath catch.

Carlo Moretti is a kind man. A forgiving man. But fuck with him or lie to him and he is anything but.

"He's off the team and frankly, it's for the better. *All around.*"

He's not good enough for you.

That's what his tone says. That's how his gaze reads.

"Dad. You can't. *You can't.*"

"And why's that?"

"Because . . ." My voice is a desperate waver as I struggle with the adrenaline running through me. *I need to get to Riggs.* I need to see if he's okay. All that blood. *His anger.*

And my dad? His tremors? I refuse to load him with more stress right now by telling him something that happened six years ago.

Later. I'll tell him later. When more is resolved.

"Dad. You have to listen. He had his reasons. He . . . you can't do this."

"I can and I fucking will," he thunders as he moves about the small space, his body slow and his tremors enhanced by the stress.

"No. *Please.* He was trying to protect—"

"He just disgraced this entire team over some school boy stunt for who knows what. I have more than just your boyfriend to think about."

"My boy—"

"You think I don't know every fucking thing that goes on with my team? I do, Camilla. I do and I'm hurt that you kept this from me."

Oh God. He knows. I hate disappointing my father.

But I need to speak out here. Act now on this and then we'll revisit this discussion later.

"You're wrong for so many reasons. Riggs was defending—"

"So now you're going to lie for him to defend him? Now you're going to ruin your reputation—"

"DAD," I shout but he just walks out and slams the door behind him.

Fuck. I can't explain now. He's too worked up. His Italian temper too triggered. Later. It will have to be later.

I need to find Riggs.

Thankfully, he's in his driver's room. He's slamming shit around as he shoves it in a bag. "Riggs."

"Not now." His back is to me, his hands braced on the table in front of him, and his head hung low.

Defeated. He's the personification of it.

"C'mon. Talk to me. Please. How are you? Are you okay?" Nervous about the unknown, about how to fix this, I ramble. "I didn't mean for you to—"

"I'm fine. Fucking fine," he says evenly. "I just . . . I need a minute."

Desperation rattles its way through me. "I'll get him to hire you back. I'll make it right. I'll make it—"

"How?" He turns to look at me and my heart breaks. There is blood on his knuckles. I can see it now. His own cheek has a red blemish from where Brandon must have landed one in defense. I want to reach out—touch him, comfort him—but the expression on his face tells me now is not the time. "The whole world just saw me bash the fucker's face in. You wanted viral? You just got it with the ten cameras that happened to be filming. Congrats. I'm sure it's good for the Moretti brand."

"We can make everyone understand. We can—"

"How? Do you actually think I'm going to make you share with the world what happened? Why I reacted? Do you think so little of me that I'm going to throw you under the bus to save me?" He steps into me.

"I don't know what to think."

"You know me better than that." His smile is reticent and so sad. "You're okay, right?"

I nod.

"I needed to see that for myself. I did. Now . . . I don't know what the fuck I need."

His words are a quiet roar that weave into my soul and stick a dagger in my heart.

"*Please*, Riggs." I go to reach out and he yanks his arm away.

"Just." He holds his hands up. "Just don't."

"I'll get your ride back. I'll—"

"Don't worry about it." He heaves his bag over his shoulder, gives me one last look—one I'll never forget—and moves past me to the door.

I turn to watch him. He stops and hangs his head, his back to me. "I'd do it again in a heartbeat. Even knowing the consequences. Just—don't follow me. Respect that I need . . . to figure my own shit out. But just know, Cam, *I'd do it again.*" His last words are barely a whisper that rip my heart out and coddle it simultaneously.

And as he leaves the suite, I stare after him until I can't see him anymore, one thing abundantly clear.

I'm in love with Spencer Riggs . . . *and I think I just lost him too.*

CHAPTER FIFTY-EIGHT

Riggs

SEE THE NODS SENT MY WAY AS I MAKE MY WAY THROUGH THE GARAGE and out into the paddock.

Moretti wants me to go?

I'll fucking go.

But I'm not going to slink away in the back alley. I'm going to do it here, where the cameras are present. Where it's obvious I'm not hiding.

Yeah, I did something wrong. But it's the reason I did it that has me holding my head high.

I stride out into the main area and keep going.

"Riggs."

I ignore the voice calling my name.

Fuck Carlo if he thinks he's going to chase after me and make a scene right now. If he wants to show everyone what a piece of shit I am.

The only thing I'm guilty of is not killing that fucking guy.

That's it.

"Riggs," he commands, his voice closer. I don't stop. "I watched the tape."

I falter but keep moving.

"I saw what you said to her."

My feet stop.

I turn to face Carlo Moretti as he rushes after me, the goddamn fucking camera crews close behind.

There's a buzz around him, the press moving in to watch the fireworks of Carlo Moretti firing the new driver.

Too bad they don't already know that's happened.

He closes the distance, his eyes on mine. His chest heaving. When he stops, he seems a little shaky on his feet.

"I said, I saw what you said to her," he says quietly, motioning for the cameras to back the fuck off.

They do, but they're still there, a little farther away, but still so very present.

"So?"

"It's not my business, but it doesn't take a genius to draw conclusions. To put the two and two together I've questioned for more years than I care to count. To be ashamed that you were able to defend my daughter when I didn't even know she needed it."

"Sir? I don't know what you're talking about," I say, still unable to betray her confidence, but I make sure my eyes tell a different story.

He nods. "I know you don't. And I respect you for that more than I think you'll ever know."

"Again, thank you for the opportunity." Those are the hardest fucking words I've ever had to say before giving him one last look and turning to leave.

"Spencer." I look over my shoulder, and Carlo holds his hand out to me to shake it.

The tremor catches me by surprise. It's violent and obvious and, before the concern finishes flashing through Carlo's eyes, I step toward him, using my body to block the view of the cameras. I take his hand in mine to shake, but don't let go. Why is his hand fucking shaking? Why does he look like he's . . . vibrating? He's stressed, I get that, but—

My dad was going through some health scares.

That's when I started flipping through the evidence.

Camilla helping him in the conference room that day. His tendency to have his hands in his pockets to steady him. The cane he occasionally uses. The tremors that were slight but that I shrugged off.

How did I not string the signs together?

Just like my dad's favorite actor and my mum's Hollywood crush, Michael J. Fox, Carlo Moretti has Parkinson's.

He meets my eyes—surprise and gratitude heavy in them—as I hold on, waiting for it to subside. "You good?" I murmur.

He shakes his head, his eyes darting to the crowd around us.

I keep my hand in his and cuff him on the shoulder to prolong the connection. To help him camouflage what he's been trying to hide.

Another moment passes.

"Thank you," he whispers.

I release his hand and we stand face-to-face. Man-to-man. A dad and his daughter's lover. A gentleman and a fighter.

As two men who love the same woman but in completely different ways.

"We'll figure it out, Riggs. We'll make it right. God fucking knows how considering the FIA will be down our throats with fines. LeCroix's probably going to press charges."

"I'll pay the fines, sir. This is all on me."

"My ass you will. I take care of my family. God knows I clearly didn't in this case."

"Sir?"

"Head out. Let me fix shit. We'll talk later. If you think I'm letting you off this team now, you're fucking crazy. Yes?"

My eyes well with tears I don't want to shed, and I blink them back. "Yes, sir."

CHAPTER FIFTY-NINE

"I TOLD HIM."

"What?" Riggs stares at me with disbelief in his eyes as he stands in my doorway mid knock.

I may have been stalking him and waiting for him to get home. But when I heard his footsteps clomping down the hall and threw my door open, he was standing there, fist raised to knock.

And now standing there with shock on his face.

"I mean, I told him. I couldn't . . . I couldn't make you take the fall. I couldn't let you walk away from a dream you've worked so hard for, that you'd achieved because I was too chickenshit to face fear over—"

His lips are on mine in an instant. Hands in my hair, body pressed against mine, his lips unrelenting with hunger.

A kiss that wars are fought for and conquers all.

And when he ends it, when our bodies are on fire and our lips numb, he leans back, hands on my cheeks and knees bent so we're eye to eye.

"Let's stop playing this game, Gasket."

"What game?"

"The no-strings one. I'm in love with you. Can't you see that? Baggy clothes. No clothes. A Mount Everest of clothes, I don't fucking care. You're it for me, Camilla. The kind of it I never expected, I never wanted. I thought love was for weak men and saps. I'll be the first to admit I was wrong. Hands down. Head over heels wrong. You drive me crazy but fuck if that madness doesn't make me love you more. You challenge me. You make me the kind of man who would give up his dream because it's the right thing to do. And that's fucking saying a lot. Because I would. I did. And I'd do it a million times over if that's what you needed, because I'm in fucking love with you."

I stare at him as my heart swells so much it hurts. Tears well and speech escapes me.

Love isn't supposed to hurt.

Isn't he the one who taught me that?

It's supposed to heal. It's supposed to fulfill. It's supposed to make you whole.

"It's the nickname, isn't it, Gasket?" he asks. "You hate it so much that you can't love me back."

I cough over my sob and wipe away the tears on my cheeks. "No. It's perfect. Just like you are."

The tension in my chest eases for the first time, and the ache is filled by a love so poignant it's almost hard to believe.

But isn't it funny how when you start believing, that you realize it's actually real. That you know it can be real.

"We're a fucked-up pair, but my broken makes you whole. Your broken has made me whole. Now it's time to let those breaks heal. For the scars to fade like nothing ever was."

I launch myself at him and kiss him again. I pour myself into it. I can't get enough of it, of him, of this feeling, of this possibility.

I frame his face with my hands and know that my grin *must* look as goofy as his does. "When did you know?" I ask.

"Know what?" He plays dumb.

"That you love me."

"It was my drunk night in your flat. When you thought I had passed out but you came back to peek under the blanket and check out my cock."

"I did not!" I slap at his chest and he just wraps his hands around my wrists and kisses the inside of my palm.

"No, but you were thinking about it." He chuckles. "Seriously? I can't pinpoint one specific event. It's like one minute you were kissing me in a bar and the next minute you were everywhere. And I *liked* that you were. You won me over. Heart by colored heart on the calendar."

"I think I'm going to have to buy a new calendar."

"A lifetime supply coming right up," he teases, and I laugh as I brush my lips to his.

"I'll gladly take it."

"Good." He nods resolutely. "There's one more thing I have for you."

"What's that?"

He pulls a bag of cotton candy out of his backpack. "I never got to enjoy the last bite. That's one moment that's been waiting seventeen years to come full circle. I don't want to miss the chance to share it with you."

And there goes my heart tumbling to my feet, *again*.

He holds out the bag and we both take a chunk of the blue. We hold it up, eyes locked on each other and put it in our mouths at the same time.

"Victory is sweet," he whispers, emotion thick in his voice.

"It is. I love you Riggs. It's as simple and as complicated as that."

He chuckles and the sound makes my heart swell. "It is. Good thing we have all the time in the world to figure it out." He presses another kiss to my lips, the taste of sugar on his tongue. "Victory is most definitely sweet."

EPILOGUE

"I DON'T UNDERSTAND WHY THEY'RE DEMANDING THAT I COME HERE to see the ad spot," I gripe to Elise. "Can't I see it just as easily from my desk? On my computer?"

"Someone pissed in your Cheerios this morning, didn't they?"

I slide a glare her way. She's in bright pink today. The color suits her. Her bubbly personality that comes with it a bit too much for me today.

To say I love her is an understatement, but she's been buzzing around like a bee all day, hovering.

"No. I'm just tired. With Riggs in the States, I'm not getting much sleep because we're up talking with the time difference."

"Oh, to be in love," she says. "I'm still blaming you for stealing my future husband away, but I'll let it slide this time."

"Just this once." I smile.

"Did you just smile? Holy shit, everyone," she says to the empty grand-stand at Silverstone. "Camilla Moretti just smiled."

"Funny."

"Thank you."

We walk a bit more and I can't help but smile as I think back to how different my life was a year ago when I was last here.

And how it's changed for the better.

Moving in with Riggs. Riggs getting a ride for the entire season with Moretti—now a full-blown F1 driver just like he's always dreamt of. I'm still learning the ropes from my dad, but if there's one thing being with Riggs has taught me, it's to enjoy every second I have with my father. My mom is back with a full case of kids to advocate for. And Gia and Isabella have found F1 to have much more eye candy than they thought. They're now frequent guests of the Moretti Motorsports hospitality suite.

"Man," I murmur.

"What?"

"Just thinking about what a difference a year can make."

She rubs her barely showing belly. "Don't I know it," she beams. "Oh, look." She points to the Jumbotron screen that the grandstands look out at. It flickers to life.

"This better be damn good for driving me all this way out here."

"Is this thing on?" booms from the speakers followed by a tapping sound like on a microphone.

But it's the voice that's talking that has me sitting straighter.

Riggs's face flashes on the screen, in much the same fashion as his AITA series we still do, but more sporadically now.

"What the . . ." I look over to Elise, but she's nowhere to be found.

Something is most definitely going on.

"So, in our normal fashion, I have a very special edition of Am I the Arsehole today. I had a very good friend write in and ask a question I'm going to need your help with." Riggs pulls the camera closer to his face and widens his eyes. "You ready?"

Is it silly I have tears in my eyes? Happy tears. Tears, because it's been two weeks since I've seen him, and I miss him desperately.

"Okay. You're ready. So here goes. Am I the Arsehole for falling in love with this incredibly intelligent, beautiful, kind woman and for planning our engagement party before I even ask her to marry me because I'm that desperate for her to be my wife?"

What?

Oh my God.

This can't be—

"Riggs?" I call out, but the screen goes black.

I whip around to find Elise to ask her what the hell he's talking about, but when I do, Riggs is standing there. A smile on his handsome face as he lowers himself to one knee.

"You're supposed to be in Austin," I whisper, afraid to believe what I'm seeing.

"No, I'm right where I'm supposed to be. Here. With you."

I take a few steps forward, my eyes blurring with tears as I try to process what's happening.

"Yes. This is really happening," he says, reading my mind. "I'm really here, on my knee, asking the woman I love to marry me. I'm really here, telling her that life hasn't been the same since my massive fuck up at a bar where I almost lost her before I even knew I wanted her. I'm really here, asking her to take the dare card this time. To marry me. To do this life together with me. To break into private parks for picnics and have a ludicrous, whimsical life together where we never know what comes next but are excited for it because we'll face it together. Marry me, Gasket. Please."

"Ludicrous whimsical, huh?"

"Not my term." He laughs. "It's my wife's."

Wife.

Chills dance over my skin at the term.

And at the love in his eyes.

"Yes. Of course, yes."

He rises and presses his lips to mine, before throwing his head back and shouting, "She said yes!"

A cheer goes up.

I spin around to see everyone precious to me. *How did he manage that?* My mom. My dad with his cane. Gia and Isabella. Riggs's mom, someone I've grown so close to over the last twelve months. Micah, Wills, and Junior. Elise.

Everyone that matters.

Everyone I love.

Everyone who I want to make more memories with.

Victory is indeed sweet.

Let the ludicrous, whimsical adventures begin.

THE END

Did you love Camilla and Riggs's story in Off the Grid? Do you want to meet the rest of the drivers in the Full Throttle series?

Be ready for another lap around the circuit in these upcoming books, available for preorder now.

On The Edge—The playboy of Formula 1, Cruz Navarro, is coming January 2024

Over The Limit—The grumpy sunshine of Formula 1, Lachlan Evans, is coming June 2024

Out of Control—The bad boy of Formula 1, Oliver Rossi, is coming August 2024

Looking for another sexy racecar driver to read until my next one comes out? Have you met Colton Donavan yet in The Driven Series? He's a reckless, bad boy with a good guy heart buried underneath. You can meet him in this completed series.

ABOUT THE AUTHOR

New York Times Bestselling author K. Bromberg writes contemporary romance novels that contain a mixture of sweet, emotional, a whole lot of sexy, and a little bit of real. She likes to write strong heroines and damaged heroes, who we love to hate but can't help but love.

Since publishing her first book on a whim in 2013, Kristy has sold over two million copies of her books across twenty different countries and has landed on the New York Times, USA Today, and Wall Street Journal Bestsellers lists over thirty times. (She still wakes up and asks herself how she got so lucky for all this to happen.)

A mom of three, Kristy finds the only thing harder than finishing the book she's writing is navigating parenthood during the teenage years (send more wine!). She loves dogs, sports, a good book, and is an expert procrastinator. She lives in Southern California with her family and their three dogs.

You can find out more about Kristy, her books, or just chat with her on any of her social media accounts. The easiest way to stay up to date on new releases and upcoming novels is to sign up for her newsletter or follow her on Bookbub.